FORTUNATE SON

THOMAS TIBOR

This is a work of fiction. Unless otherwise indicated, all the names, characters, businesses, places, events and incidents in this book are either the product of the author's imagination or used in a fictitious manner. Any resemblance to actual persons, living or dead, or actual events is purely coincidental.

First paperback edition March 2022

Cover design by Vanessa Maynard and Rhett Stansbury
Interior design and formatting by KUHN Design Group

ISBN 978-1-7358564-0-7 (paperback)
ISBN 978-1-7358564-1-4 (ebook)

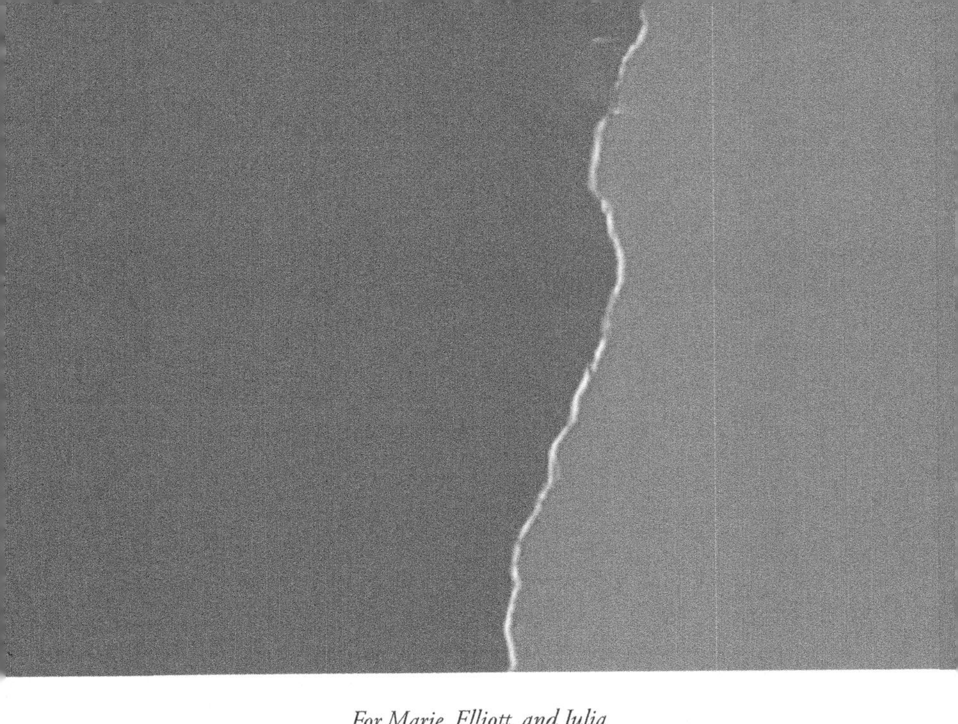

For Marie, Elliott, and Julia

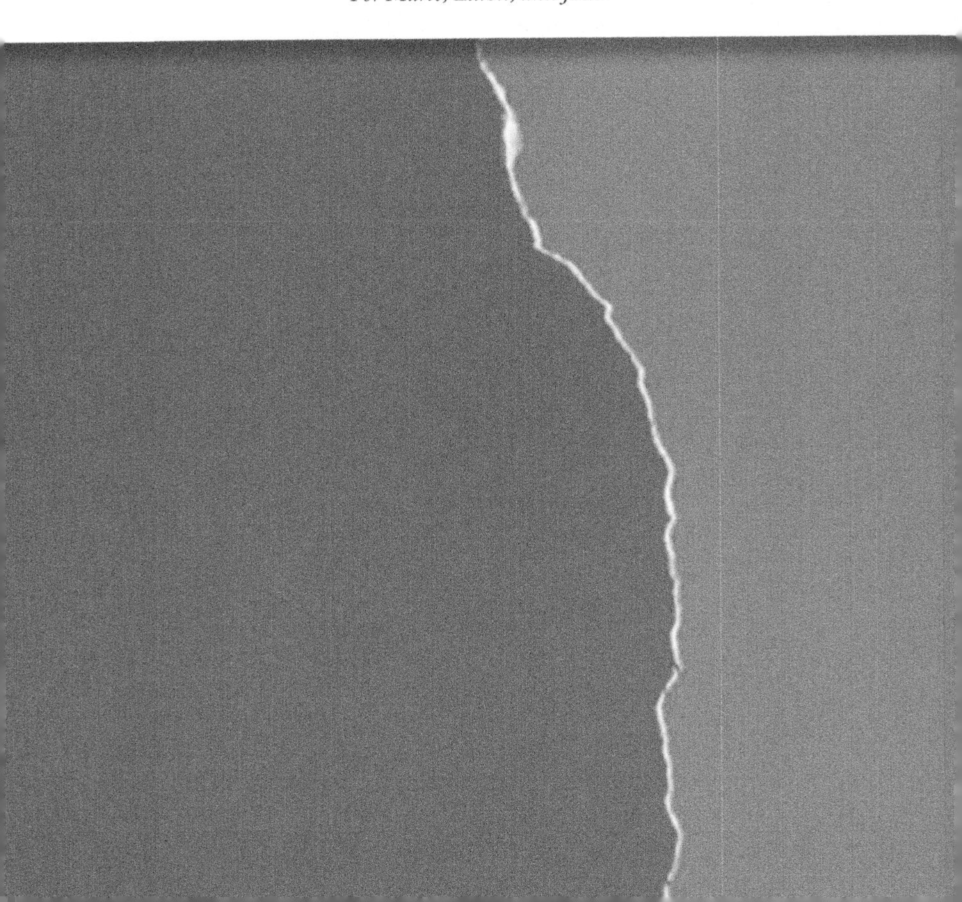

SATURDAY, MAY 16, 1970

On the night Annabel decided to drown herself, Reed Lawson was drunk. Not falling-down, but close enough. He stumbled out of the packed Rathskeller Bar well past nine o'clock. The smell of stale beer and cigarettes and the pounding of the Rolling Stones' "Midnight Rambler" bled into the warm Florida night. The bar had advertised LSD—Large Size Drafts—for twenty-five cents, a clever hook to lure in more business.

Reed checked his watch—the same model worn by his father, Commander Frank Lawson, U.S. Navy. *Dumbass.* An hour late for his shift, which never happened. On time for Reed always meant fifteen minutes early.

He shuffled through the crowded parking lot searching for his car, past students and locals drinking beer, slouching against fenders, passing joints amid the shadows. Then he remembered he'd parked around the corner.

Ten minutes later the Mustang rumbled to the curb in front of a brick bungalow, and Reed stumbled out. Twenty years old, he had a lean, muscled frame that suggested rigid self-discipline. But tonight his swarthy, olive complexion was pale, black hair unkempt, deep-set brown eyes glazed over, Levi's wrinkled and T-shirt slept in.

Waves of nausea washed over him. Gagging, he was sure he'd vomit. Should've eaten something to soak up the beer.

Down the street, the branches of live oaks arched over the sidewalk. A quick gust drove clumps of Spanish moss across the pavement. The university's iconic Gothic buildings loomed a block ahead—the Florida Polytechnic Institute and State University, better known as Florida Tech.

Reed trudged through patches of weeds that passed for a lawn and onto a porch cluttered with a threadbare sofa, metal chairs, and overflowing ashtrays. A single yellow bulb illuminated a hand-painted sign on the door: *Lifelines.*

Just what he needed—another Saturday night shift, always the craziest of the week. No way out, though. Maybe two cups of their caffeinated mud would sober him up. With any luck, the call volume would be light.

Reed stepped inside. The hotline phones occupied the bungalow's largest bedroom, with two desks, two chairs, and a bulletin board papered with warnings about drug side effects, emergency phone numbers, and guidance for handling calls.

Meg was on duty, earnest and professional as usual in sensible shoes, ironed slacks, and a buttoned-up blouse. Her robin's-egg-blue eyes widened in shock at his drunken, disheveled appearance.

Reed collapsed into the empty chair and mumbled, "Sorry I'm late."

Meg flicked auburn bangs from a freckled forehead. "Called your dorm earlier. You just missed Annabel."

His stomach knotted with dread. "What did she want?"

"I tried to find out, but she would only talk to you. Seemed super freaked out. After she split, I called her mom. Turns out Annabel left the house after lunch and hasn't been back since. Also, her mom found joints and Quaaludes in her room."

Shit. Annabel's favorite drug cocktail.

"Sorry," Meg said. "I begged her to stick around."

"Not your fault. Any coffee left?"

"Got a fresh pot brewing."

In the kitchen, every cup was coffee stained. Reed scrubbed and filled one. He listened to the murmur of conversation from the adjacent bedroom—a volunteer talking somebody down from a bad trip. He was way too wiped to deal with anything tonight. Not Annabel, not a tidal wave of callers.

Stepping back into the hotline room, he asked, "Sure she said nothing else?"

"Well, I followed her outside to stall her, but she was in a big hurry. Said something about the river."

"The river? That's it?" Annabel must have meant the Black River, where they'd spent so much time together. Reed slammed the coffee mug on the desk, scalding his wrist with the overflow, and raced outside.

—

Moments later the Mustang roared to life, and Reed barreled onto Broad Street—the city's main east-west artery—and weaved through stop-and-go traffic. He barely noticed the crowd waiting for a table at Rossetti's Pizza, the gaggle of students watching dryers spin inside Groomers Laundromat, or the usual stoners lingering outside the Second Genesis head shop.

At the first red light, his left hand trembled on the steering wheel as his right massaged the gearshift. A sobering breeze swept in. He rolled the window farther down to invite more cool air, then smacked the wheel. Should have seen it coming. The signs were there, clear as day. When she'd most needed a friend, he'd let her down, pushed her away to wallow in his own despair.

The light was taking forever to change. Screw it. Reed stomped on the gas and roared through the intersection. Horns blared. Oncoming traffic skidded to avoid a collision. He blew through two more red lights before swerving onto the highway that led out of town.

More alert now and pushing the eager V-8 to ninety miles an hour, Reed peered into the rearview mirror every few seconds, expecting to see flashing red lights. Cookie-cutter suburban houses soon gave way to open farmland. The road narrowed to two lanes lined by a thick forest of southern pines.

On a curve, driving as fast as he dared, Reed roared past a truck, then cut off two denim-and-leather-clad bikers astride chopped Harleys. One lifted a middle finger in salute.

After five more miles that felt to Reed like fifty, the Mustang skidded into a dirt parking lot at the river. He pulled alongside a dusty green Chevy, jumped out, and ran to the shore. Familiar bell-bottoms and sandals lay strewn on a thin strip of sand.

"Annabel!"

He scanned the fast-moving current, illuminated only by pale flecks of moonlight slicing through heavy cloud cover. Gnarled branches of cypress and mangrove dangled over the river. Darkened by tannins from decaying vegetation, the tea-colored water gave the Black River its name. If she'd gone in, it would have been here.

"Annabel!"

A cacophony of tree frogs and crickets answered him. What if she already lay at the bottom or had drifted downstream? Heart pounding, he spotted a glimmer of movement in the middle of the river. Annabel? Driftwood? Or just a ripple on the surface?

Ripping off his sneakers, he waded into the inky river, the muddy bottom sucking at his feet. Though a confident pool swimmer, Reed was nervous in water where he couldn't see the bottom. Shaky, he labored with clumsy strokes to the middle before pausing to tread water.

"Annabel!"

A crane screeched. A stiff breeze quickened the current. Reed imagined water moccasins stirring beneath him, gators paddling in from the riverbank.

"Annabel!"

A memory surfaced from high school English class—beautiful but forsaken Ophelia from Shakespeare's *Hamlet* plunging from a willow tree to her watery death. If he was too late and her slender body lay somewhere beneath the surface—skin ivory, lips blue, raven hair fanned out—he had only himself to blame.

PART ONE: HONOR

THREE MONTHS EARLIER

CHAPTER ONE

MONDAY, FEBRUARY 16

Winter sunshine splashed onto the university's Reserve Officers Training Corps building. Two royal palms flanked the oak door, their fronds scraping the red brick. Dozens of students packed the sidewalk, crowding the entrance, hoisting handmade signs:

If the Government Won't Stop the War, We'll Stop the Government!
There Is No Way to Peace; Peace Is the Way!
This Is an Antiwar University!
U.S. Imperialists Out of Southeast Asia!
ROTC Off Campus Now!

They chanted in unison: "Down with ROTC!" "Killers off campus!" "One, two, three, four, we don't want your fucking war!"

University police in white helmets and short-sleeved shirts stood guard. Billy clubs and revolvers dangled from their leather belts. They looked bored. The demonstrations had become a daily routine.

At 10:05 a.m., the oak door burst open to release a stream of Navy cadets. Wearing starched tan uniforms, faces clean-shaven and hair cropped, they waded through the protesters.

On cue, the chanting grew more strident. A passing car slowed; its driver yelled, "Fuck Rot-cee! Shove the war up your asses!"

Another driver shouted from a pickup truck: "Fuck you, commies! Go, Navy! Go, Nixon!"

Reed Lawson was the last cadet to emerge. All squared away with a fresh crewcut, smooth shave, starched uniform, and spit-shined shoes, he strode with purpose, as if eager to confront and vanquish all obstacles.

He scowled at the protesters and muttered to a fellow cadet, "Great. Ho Chi Minh's foot soldiers, hard at work again."

"We're easy targets," the cadet said. "It's nothing but street theater, man. Like they're waiting for the TV cameras to show up."

"Yeah, well, I'm getting sick and tired of it," Reed snapped. Commie sympathizers had targeted ROTC all year. Sometimes a few, sometimes enough to fill the sidewalk and spill onto the lawn. More had shown up since October 15 last year, when hundreds of thousands nationwide had demonstrated against the war in Vietnam.

In November, Reed's older sister, Sandy—a senior at George Washington University—had joined half a million protesters gathered in Washington, DC. As usual, Sandy had lectured Reed during Christmas break. "This will spread everywhere until we stop the war. Count on it."

"Fat chance," Reed would have replied, but they'd given up arguing about the war by then.

A sign blocked Reed's path. *Bombers Are Killers, Not Heroes!*

What the hell? The rest of their stupid slogans meant nothing, but this one struck home.

Reed glared at the girl holding the sign. Tangled, sun-bleached blond hair fell to her shoulders. A red-and-black armband emblazoned with the number *644,000* encircled her left biceps. She wore faded, ripped jeans. Pert breasts swelled beneath a snug T-shirt that proclaimed *Sisterhood Is Powerful.*

The girl lowered the sign and squinted at Reed.

"What are you staring at? Fucking warmonger!"

Disgusted, Reed stalked to his Mustang. It wasn't a run-of-the-mill factory stock model but a 1966 Shelby GT350. Royal-blue paint and white racing stripes gleamed from three coats of wax and hours of elbow grease.

The personalized license plate read DASH-*1*.

Reed climbed in, let the V-8 rumble, and switched on the radio.

"According to official military sources," the newscaster reported, "the number of Americans killed in Vietnam this month passed the forty thousand mark."

The war had staggered into its seventh year with no end in sight. The thousands of American soldiers shipped home in body bags, not to mention news of battles with vague, shifting objectives and few decisive victories, had eventually eroded public support. Demands had increased, especially from the antiwar left, for an unconditional end to U.S. involvement. But Reed was among those Americans who still hoped for a decisive victory.

The Nixon administration's latest strategy to win the war, known as Vietnamization, aimed to transfer combat responsibilities to South Vietnam and withdraw American troops. This policy, the newscaster acknowledged, was also facing criticism.

Unable to focus on the news, Reed glared at the blond bitch waving the *Bombers Are Killers, Not Heroes!* sign.

His father was a bomber.

Commander Frank Joseph Lawson flew A-4 Skyhawks from carriers stationed off North Vietnam's coast in the South China Sea—or he had until he'd been shot down three years ago and classified as missing in action. Since then, Reed's family had received zero information about his fate.

Reed guessed the blond protester was about his age. She was beautiful enough to audition for Miss Florida Tech…if she gave a rat's ass about fake-waving from a homecoming float.

Okay, so she knew nothing about his father. Didn't matter. The seething resentment Reed harbored for antiwar protesters threatened to boil over. His right fist clenched, then opened and closed, opened and closed. Like a boxer eager to punch somebody. Anybody.

Reed checked his watch—an Abercrombie & Fitch Shipmate, a gift from his father for his sixteenth birthday. Plenty of time before Thermodynamics and Quantum Mechanics class.

He turned off the engine, climbed out, and marched toward the girl holding the sign. She was chatting with a tall, skinny chick. The tall girl nudged the blond, who turned.

Contemptuous gray-blue eyes bored into Reed's. "Yeah? What do you want now?"

Reed froze, tongue-tied. "Listen up," he managed. "I am *not* a warmonger."

"No kidding. Is that a fact?"

"You heard me. I am not. A fucking. Warmonger."

"Then how come you're in Rot-cee?"

That Reed could answer, just as he had whenever his uniform drew hostile attention. "Maybe to defend your constitutional right to wave that stupid sign around?"

"Give me a break." Her eyes narrowed with scorn. "How can you possibly support this immoral war?"

"Well, among other reasons, to save South Vietnam from communism."

"How about bombing the shit out of a defenseless Third World country?"

"How about sticking that sign where the sun don't shine?"

The girl smirked. "Sure, go ahead. Drop your pants and bend over."

Amid laughter erupting from surrounding protesters, their eyes locked—a standoff that lasted seconds but felt longer and oddly intimate.

Reed looked away first. "Screw this shit."

"And screw you too."

"Fascist asshole," the tall girl added.

Seething with humiliation, Reed stomped away. Sensing eyes on his back, he spun to find the blond chick still staring at him, her scorn tinged with the slightest spark of curiosity…or perhaps he had imagined it.

He was unable to concentrate in class that afternoon. Replaying their interchange, Reed considered returning to the ROTC building, just in case she might be there, and explaining why the sign had rattled him. How agonizing it was to live with the unknown, year after year. To every day confront the question ricocheting through the crevices of his mind: *Is my father dead or alive?*

—

On Tuesday morning, Reed headed across campus toward the library, dressed in his civilian "uniform"—starched polo shirt, crisp Levi's, pristine white running shoes. He was still thinking about the blond protester, anger and lust dancing like dueling scorpions in his head. No question the chick was a major fox, but the university teemed with stunning girls. So why couldn't he shake this one from his mind? She hated everything he stood for.

Yet beneath their hostile exchange, he'd sensed a spark…of something. He chuckled at the image her insult conjured—him with his pants down, buttocks spread, ready to receive the offending sign. Okay, she'd gotten in the last punch. Score one for her.

He weaved among the throng of students crossing the Quad. This year the grassy expanse of shade beneath live oaks, sabal palms, and magnolias attracted anyone with a gripe.

Reed frowned at a creep waving a mock FBI wanted poster:

President Richard Milhous Nixon
Age: 57
Height: 5'11"
Weight: 160 lbs
WANTED for Genocide, Homicide, Conspiracy

Funny. Except had Reed been old enough in 1968, he would've voted for Nixon.

He glared at the jerk tacking a sign onto a tree trunk:

Why is the White Man Sending
the Black Man to Kill the Yellow Man?

Clever. But plenty of white men's blood also soaked the soil of Vietnam.

A blond crossed Reed's path. Same faded, patched jeans, same women's-lib T-shirt.

"Hey," he said.

The girl responded with a pleasant *Do I know you?* look.

"Sorry. Thought you were someone else."

Moving on, he spotted more blond hair among a circle of students seated on the grass, meditating. Nope. It was some other hippie chick, sitting with her legs crossed, hands resting palms up on her knees, chanting "om" in unison with the others. Like the weirdo Hare Krishnas, except these kids didn't sport the usual shaved heads, pigtails, and peach-colored robes.

Adam—Reed's roommate—practiced transcendental meditation, inspired by the Beatles, who'd been tutored by Maharishi Mahesh Yogi in India. For Reed, sitting around chanting mantras and focusing on his breath amounted to a navel-gazing waste of time.

On Wednesday morning, he scanned the students passing by outside his physics class. No sign of the blond.

"Excuse me, Mr. Lawson?" Professor Carnell hovered. He wore a short-sleeved white button-down shirt with a green bow tie and plastic pocket protector. Sandy would label Carnell "a hopeless square from the Eisenhower administration." He handed Reed his graded quiz—a perfect one hundred. "As usual, top-notch work."

In the dining hall at lunch, Reed scanned the entrance for arrivals as he put away a cheeseburger, fries, and Coke.

After class, walking across campus, he checked out students tossing Frisbees on the shaded lawn next to his dorm.

At the pull-up bars near the ball fields, he strained to do twenty-one while searching among the girls playing intramural softball nearby.

No sign of her.

Reed searched for the blond again on Thursday morning along the cross-country course that meandered around campus and the university's research farms. He preferred to run at dawn before the crisp February air thickened with humidity, and routinely completed the five-mile course in thirty-five minutes. The protester, however, was not among the few girls who'd taken up jogging for fitness.

Behind the dorm that evening, Reed adjusted the Mustang's carburetor and screwed in new spark plugs.

A cute blond stopped to watch. "Cool car."

Reed smiled. "Thanks." Definitely not the same girl—this chick was far too friendly.

In ROTC class Friday morning, the instructor droned on about Navy war-fighting doctrine, something about "forward projection of military forces worldwide" and "protecting commercial shipping lanes."

Reed copied the words from the blackboard—*Navy Core Values: Honor, Courage, Commitment. A foundation of trust and leadership upon which strength is based and victory is achieved.* During the class, he often glanced outside at the empty sidewalk; the antiwar bozos had probably slept late.

That afternoon, Reed circled back to the ROTC building and spotted the sign *Bombers Are Killers, Not Heroes!* Now it was hoisted by a long-haired guy wearing an olive-green Army jacket. Civilians who wore military clothing offended Reed—you had to earn the right to wear America's uniforms.

Some guy shoved a petition into his hands: *Cancel All Biological and Chemical Research Contracts with the Department of Defense! Dissolve ROTC Courses! Get ROTC Off Campus! Money for the Earth, Not for Destruction!*

What total horseshit. Reed crumpled and tossed the paper.

—

He stepped inside the library's reading room, his favorite place to study. Late-afternoon sun streaming through the room's tall windows glowed on dark wood paneling and stone. With its vaulted ceiling and graceful wooden arches, the library's Gothic Revival architecture would have looked more at home in a dour British university than it did in semitropical Florida.

Every day for three years, Reed had scoured the local and national papers for news about soldiers classified as Missing in Action (MIA) or confirmed as Prisoners of War (POWs). Though his efforts had yielded scant information, diligent reading was better than doing nothing and feeling helpless.

Reed removed the latest issues of the *Miami Herald, Washington*

Post, and *New York Times* from the wooden racks and carried them to a long table.

By the glow of an emerald-shaded banker's lamp, he spotted a story about antiwar sabotage at the University of Miami. Someone had firebombed an Army truck parked on campus. Protesters had also tossed a Molotov cocktail into a security building. It all added up to over a hundred campus bombings in the past year alone. How did the antiwar fanatics expect to stop the war by killing American citizens at home?

Another headline seized his attention: THREE MIAs ON LIST MIGHT BE POWs. The commies had released a new list of sixty-four prisoners. However, this represented a fraction of the hundreds they'd captured—Hanoi had always refused to issue a complete list of POWs.

Worse still, in Reed's view, the list of sixty-four had been released directly to an American antiwar group instead of the U.S. government. Obviously, the commies' propaganda strategy was to communicate only with antiwar organizations to embarrass America. Reed had read that these left-wing groups often reported information they received from the commies to the media, bypassing the government and, even worse, the families of those missing or imprisoned.

Damn. The article didn't include the identities of the three suspected POWs. His heart sank, but he clung to the sliver of hope this information offered. Someone—either the antiwar assholes or the government—must have those three names, and one of them could be his father.

The week before, he'd read an article about the agony of military wives with missing husbands. It described a woman whose husband had disappeared five years ago. Recently she'd received a letter from him—the first evidence she or the U.S. government had received that he was alive.

If it could happen to that lady, Reed figured, the same could happen to *his* family.

He slid the latest article into the folder where he kept media clippings and a news magazine photo he'd cut out. In the photo, two smiling, well-fed POWs were exercising in a Hanoi prison yard. *More bullshit propaganda.* The "happy" POWs had been forced to pose for gullible Americans. Still, Reed couldn't help wondering whether those POWs knew anything about Commander Frank Lawson, MIA.

Heading back to the dorm, he ruminated. Three years to the day had passed since Navy officers had arrived at his home—the day that divided his life into "before" and "after."

CHAPTER TWO

The "before" ended on February 16, 1967. After school that day, Reed had been making out with his girlfriend, Susan, in the Lawsons' 1958 Ford Fairlane sedan, concealed by a grove of pine trees in a city park. Reed's fingertips slid beneath Susan's panties toward the silky, moist cleft between her legs. She arched against the turquoise-and-white vinyl upholstery and moaned.

He would later learn that a black government sedan arrived at the Lawsons' home in Jacksonville at that exact moment. A Navy casualty assistance calls officer and a chaplain climbed out, adjusted their uniforms, and knocked on the front door.

Reed dropped off Susan after arranging another date for Saturday night, then headed home. Eager visions of going "all the way" vanished as he passed the official car leaving his house. Heart pounding, Reed strained to stay calm. Black government sedans rarely augured good news.

Moments later he stood immobile in the kitchen, listening to his mother. Still dressed in the gray skirt and pale-blue blouse she'd worn for her job as a legal secretary, Carol slumped against the counter. She haltingly relayed what the sympathetic but nervous officers had told her.

A letter they'd left behind lay open on the counter. Reed picked it up and skimmed its contents:

On a mission to attack a heavily defended bridge, antiaircraft fire struck Commander Lawson's A-4E Skyhawk. His wingman reported seeing an explosion on the starboard side of Lawson's plane. It then spun downward in flames, through heavy cloud cover, until it crashed into a mountainous area of dense jungle. No ejection or parachute was observed. No emergency communications were received. Continued overcast weather and heavy antiaircraft fire prevented the Navy from immediately initiating a rescue operation.

His mother's red-rimmed hazel eyes gazed out over the slate patio and backyard. "It's odd, you know...when I woke up this morning, I felt so strange...like something terrible had happened. I was sure of it."

Her fatalism irked Reed; how could she know that? But his stomach churned with the fear he fought to suppress. Fear was the enemy. It signaled weakness, which invited despair, which guaranteed defeat.

His father *had* to be alive.

"Mom, he got out." His voice rose in panic. "He's okay. They're gonna find him. Don't worry, those guys don't have a clue what the hell they're talking about!"

Wincing from his tone, Carol spilled the coffee grounds she was attempting to pour into the percolator. "I don't know. I hope so."

His mother had experienced premonitions of doom before, always claiming to sense her husband's emotions, even from thousands of miles away. Years ago, she'd fallen ill one afternoon and insisted something horrible had happened. That very day, Frank had made an emergency landing on a test flight in Nevada, narrowly avoiding a crash.

Reed yanked the fridge door open. No. She was wrong this time. She had to be.

"Where are the Cokes?" Why'd she always remember the milk and her precious fresh-squeezed Florida orange juice but forget the damn Cokes?

"We have to call your sister," Carol said. "She'll be out of class by now."

Reed shut the fridge door and straightened, suddenly dizzy. The grandfather clock in the living room ticked insistently.

Carol reached to embrace him. "Sweetheart."

He twisted from her outstretched arms and escaped down the hall, sensing only later how hurt she must have felt.

In his room, he collapsed on the bed. He felt like smashing something, punching his fist through the wall. Instead, he grabbed shorts and running shoes.

Racing outside, he sprinted up the middle of the road, swerving around passing cars, heading east toward the St. Johns River. Pushing his legs hard, gasping for air, he hoped physical pain would numb the dread in his gut.

After eight long blocks, the road dead-ended at the river. Reed crossed the narrow, grassy embankment to the water's edge and surveyed its mile-wide expanse, waiting for his heartbeat to settle down.

The dire fate implied by the Navy's unbearably brief letter was bullshit. Of course Dad had escaped from his burning A-4 Skyhawk. He was alive, and the Navy would rescue him soon.

End of story.

—

The "after" times began early the following morning. Reed jerked awake, head throbbing, straining to recall the dream that had left him bathed in sweat.

He and his father are flying not an A-4 Skyhawk but a two-seat bomber, an F-8 Crusader.

Reed sits in the pilot's seat, Frank behind him, navigating.

Dropping in altitude, Reed searches in vain for the target amid clouds of black smoke rising from antiaircraft fire.

He checks the fuel gauge—empty—and panics, then sits frozen in fear with no clue what to do.

Behind him Frank yells, "Don't be a dumbass shithead or we're gonna lose it!"

In their path, amid the haze and the smoke and the clouds, looms a forested mountain slope.

Reed yanks the stick to gain altitude, but too late—

A massive tree shears off a wing.

The plane plummets and heads straight for the rocky face of the mountain.

And explodes on impact...

Too drained to crawl out of bed, Reed surveyed his bedroom. On the walls were posters of Navy fighter jets and Ford Mustangs, along with several photographs.

Midshipman Frank Lawson winning the Naval Academy middleweight boxing championship in 1946.

Lieutenant Frank Lawson looking cocky next to an F9F Panther fighter jet during the Korean War.

Lieutenant Commander Frank Lawson with his arm around Reed's grandfather—Admiral John "Black Jack" Lawson of World War II fame.

And Reed and Frank posing beside the new Mustang Shelby GT350.

A bookcase held a complete set of *Encyclopedia Britannica*, every Hardy Boys mystery ever published, and a few favorite novels—*The Call of the Wild*, *The Catcher in the Rye*, and *The Last of the Mohicans.*

What had the dream meant beyond the dirty, stinking lie that Dad was dead? And why had *Reed* commandeered the plane when he didn't know how to fly? He swung his legs out of bed. Dreams were meaningless bullshit. Time to get his ass in gear.

Over the next few days, Reed scoured the letter for signs of hope in the dry, terse bureaucratic language: *Deeply regret to confirm on behalf of the Navy...additional information will be furnished as promptly as it is received...my hopes and prayers for his safety join yours... Vice Admiral Stanton, Chief of Naval Personnel.*

A week later, the Lawsons received an update. An extensive search-and-rescue operation had found no trace of Commander Frank Lawson. He'd vanished into the unknown, and that unknown would become Reed's greatest enemy.

—

As Reed stepped into his dorm lobby, three guys brushed past him, leaving a trail of Old Spice and Brylcreem in their wake. He trudged upstairs to the second floor and shoved hard to open his door. A rolled-up towel crammed beneath it kept the stink of pot from seeping out and alerting the resident adviser. *Son of a bitch.* Hadn't he told Adam to dump the damn weed? Especially since, weeks earlier, university officials had announced possible drug raids on campus.

Crosby, Stills & Nash's "Long Time Gone" was playing as Reed stepped inside to find Adam Gold lying in bed. He was smoking a joint and reading *The Teachings of Don Juan* by Carlos Castaneda. Shaggy haired and pudgy, Adam favored long-sleeved flannel shirts and faded jeans. Inked along the soles of his worn Converse Chuck Taylors were the words *Peace Now.*

"I thought you promised not to smoke that crap in here."

"Uh, yeah, sorry," Adam muttered.

"Because you know if I get busted, my Rot-cee ass is grass."

"Don't worry, we're not gonna get busted," Adam drawled as he rose. He put out the joint, slid the remaining half into his desk drawer, then flopped back onto his bed to resume reading.

Each side of the cramped room featured a single bed, bookcase, desk, and small closet. Adam's side was a disaster area. Although a pre-med biology major, Adam loved his only elective—philosophy—far more than organic chemistry and left half-read books strewn across the floor. Tonight's collection included Thoreau's *Walden*, Epictetus's *Enchiridion*, and Kant's *Critique of Pure Reason.*

A battered black Underwood typewriter, various stacks of paper, a glass bong, rolling papers, roach clips, and a Zippo lighter cluttered his desk. Dirty clothes littered the floor. Reed was getting sick and tired of the stench and vowed to dump Adam's clothes into his own basket and haul it to the laundromat.

Reed's side resembled a military barracks ready for inspection. Ironed clothes hung at attention in the closet. Textbooks, shelved alphabetically, stood on a small bookcase. His bed was made tight enough to bounce a coin off. A topographical map of Vietnam had been taped to the wall. Circled in pencil was the area where his father's A-4 had crashed.

Reed fanned the air—still reeking and thick with pot smoke—and cranked open the window to inhale the crisp night. Tennis rackets thwacked against balls on nearby courts.

His original roommate—a jock who assumed he could negotiate college by missing every class and never cracking a textbook—had flunked out fall semester. From the start, Adam's left-wing politics, dope smoking, and sloppiness had annoyed Reed. Adam, in turn, was irritated by Reed's fervent dedication to ROTC and "anal-retentive" habits.

"By the way," Adam said, "if you ever wanna try some of this batch, it's some righteous weed, man."

"Hell no."

"Might take the edge off for once."

"Yeah, well, maybe I need my edge." Dad had always preached the importance of preparation and loved to quote baseball player Satchel Paige: *Don't look back. Something might be gaining on you.*

Reed stripped off his sweaty T-shirt and removed a clean one from a shelf in the closet.

Beneath the tightly curled black hair that Adam referred to as his "Jewfro," his dark, piercing eyes studied Reed. "Anything new in the papers?"

"Nothing relevant."

"Sorry, man. You wanna talk about it?"

"Talk about what?"

Adam looked hurt. "Never mind."

Reed considered mentioning the articles he'd just read but wanted to avoid Adam's probing. In high school, the kids had labeled him "that guy with the MIA dad," and it had felt awkward—no way did he need anyone feeling sorry for him. So when he'd started college, he'd told no one about his father.

Only grudgingly had he surrendered to Adam's pestering, rewarding him with the barest essentials. Not enough for his analytical roommate.

What did Reed think and feel? How had he coped for three years? What about his mother and sister?

Reed had stonewalled all of that. What was the point? Talking couldn't change anything, especially events happening nine thousand miles away.

When he was a high school senior and his father had been MIA for a year, Reed's school counselor had recommended a psychiatrist. "Just to talk about your feelings. It's not a good idea to keep everything locked inside." At his mother's insistence, Reed consented to one session. Right away, the shrink bugged him—his tweed jacket with those suede elbow patches, the stink of his cherry pipe tobacco.

After endless nodding and mysterious note taking, the shrink delivered his earth-shattering conclusion. "You're suffering from covert depression—the type more commonly seen in older men, often masked by anger."

No shit, Dr. Freud. If your father was MIA, you'd be pissed too. Reed had refused to go back. Shrinks were for crazies, and depressed people were losers who whined about their problems while doing nothing to solve them.

Reed pointed to Adam's Castaneda book, aware he'd been rude and his roommate hadn't deserved it. "Okay, what's that one about?"

"It's deep, man." Adam brightened and flipped to a page. "Here's a quote for you. *To truly become a warrior and a man of knowledge is to look at every path closely and deliberately. Then ask yourself: does this path have heart? If it does, the path is good; if it doesn't, it is of no use.*"

Reed frowned. The path to becoming a warrior went through your heart? The only route *he* knew was guided by Navy values. Ensure your character is above reproach. Don't lie, steal, or cheat. Keep your word. Never shirk your duties or transfer blame. Always accept the consequences of your actions. Clear-cut black-and-white standards.

The heart was unreliable. The heart was a mystery.

"So how do you figure out which path has heart?"

"Not sure," Adam said. "I gotta stop thinking too much. Like Kierkegaard says, *life is not a problem to be solved, but a reality to be experienced.*"

"Interesting." Yawning, Reed opened his Naval Engineering textbook. Reality for him at the moment was a chapter on nuclear propulsion. Looked tough, but no worse than the physics and math classes he was effortlessly acing. So why study on a weekend?

Adam must have read his mind. "By the way, there's a party tomorrow night. Some commune off Route 24 called the Pig Farm. Wanna go?"

"A commune? I dunno, man. Not my scene." Reed pictured hippie families with questionable hygiene, naked babies roaming unattended, freaks floating on acid trips, and rusting school buses painted psychedelic colors.

"Come on," Adam said, "even Superman needs a break from outrunning speeding bullets."

"Yeah? Well, maybe I'm too busy leaping tall buildings in a single bound."

"Yup, fighting a never-ending battle for truth, justice, and the American way must be tiring. But hey, I'm worried about you, man. All work and no play, you dig? Besides, that blond protester you've been drooling over might be there."

Reed remembered the girl's powerful presence, the contempt in those gray-blue eyes, their bizarrely intoxicating exchange. Who knew, she might show up. If so, he'd mount a charm offensive powerful enough to soften her disdain. He imagined them writhing naked in the back seat of one of those hippie buses.

Besides, he hadn't dated much lately. Susan had been his steady in high school. Before his father was shot down, Reed had invited her to an officers' ball at the base—the last evening the Lawson family had spent together. Tacked on the corkboard above Reed's desk was a photo from that night:

Frank's toothy, cocky grin and snow-white dress uniform set off dark eyes and a swarthy complexion, courtesy of his Black Irish roots.

His mother's smile was hesitant, reserved. With honey-colored hair and pale skin, Carol stood poised and elegant in a yellow dress and pearls.

Hippie sister Sandy—a fair-haired, freckled version of her mother—was sullen, "imprisoned in the bowels of the military-industrial complex, surrounded by right-wing fascists."

Reed and Susan beamed, excited just to be dressed up as adults.

Susan had enrolled at the University of Georgia last year. They'd kept up a long-distance relationship during their freshman year. However, after Thanksgiving break the previous fall, she'd mailed him a Dear John letter. On impulse, he removed it from his desk drawer and skipped to the part he hated most:

> *I know it's hard with your father missing for so long. But when we're together, it's like you're always somewhere else. I never know what you're feeling or thinking. About us, about anything. And you never talk about it. Let's face it. I want more than you're willing to give.*

How *had* he felt about Susan? She was pretty, sweet, seldom argued. Although she was intelligent, he'd eventually tired of her vacuous chatter about sorority gossip, clothes, summer vacation plans in Martha's Vineyard, the minutiae of her latest tennis matches.

So I think it's best we start seeing other people, she'd concluded.

"Seeing other people" had meant getting laid, no strings attached. Enter Candy, a petite, chatty, willing brunette Reed met at a frat party. On their second date, Candy wanted to see the sun rise over the Atlantic. Reed drove her seventy miles east to Crescent Beach, straight onto the hard-packed sand.

They arrived before dawn, carrying a blanket and a bottle of Boone's Farm strawberry wine. Candy loved the sea breeze and the roar of the surf. Fine sand from the dunes blew over their naked bodies as they made love.

But that was weeks ago. Since then, no action, except the night a waitress at Rossetti's picked him up. She must have been at least thirty. By the time Reed stumbled out of her apartment, he'd forgotten her name.

Reed crumpled Susan's letter into a ball. "Where'd you say that party was?"

"Praise the Lord and pass the hash."

CHAPTER THREE

The Pig Farm wasn't a commune. No naked babies, no psychedelic buses.

It was a dilapidated farmhouse a few miles out of town, on five acres of untended pasture that included an abandoned pigsty. A young family had purchased the property with no intention of growing anything except pot. They'd stayed for a few years, then rented the place to four students who officially lived there, along with dozens who used it as a crash pad.

Among the dusty beaters, Reed's pristine Mustang stood out. Frayed T-shirts and peasant dresses flapped on a laundry line. Iron Butterfly's "In-A-Gadda-Da-Vida" blasted from open windows.

In the living room, Reed drained his fourth beer and scanned the newcomers for anyone he recognized. Kids roamed the house, danced, or sprawled on beat-up couches, drinking beer or spiked punch and smoking pot. Roach clips, rolling papers, and overflowing ashtrays littered the coffee tables.

A sign taped on a wall declared *No hope without dope.* A girl with streaks of paint on her face skipped around, blowing bubbles, her T-shirt tied under braless breasts, revealing a midriff on which she'd drawn a peace sign with lipstick.

Reed wore running shoes and Levi's but had ditched his usual polo for a favorite Navy T-shirt. It might attract hostility, but he didn't care—if anyone had a problem with the U.S. Navy, they could kiss his ass.

Over the past hour, he'd refused several joints. Back in high school, he'd surrendered to Sandy's incessant nagging and tried some pot. He'd suffered some weird reactions—loss of self-awareness, dread over losing control of his mind.

Unlike his rebellious sister, Reed had always toed the line his father had drawn. Frank had nothing but contempt for drugs and hippies. Quick to judge, he branded people he disdained as "scumbags" or "maggots."

When Sandy had praised Timothy Leary's invitation to "turn on, tune in, drop out," Frank had scoffed, "How about wake up, grow up, and get a real job?"

His father's standards were uncompromising. Long hair signaled poor discipline—Reed kept his short. Physical weakness implied deficient character—Reed ran track, played football, boxed, and pumped iron. Slouching conveyed feeble command presence—Reed religiously checked his posture to ensure his five-foot, ten-inch frame remained ramrod straight.

Spotting Adam lecturing some freaks huddled on the living room floor, Reed strolled over to listen. Pot, as always, had made Adam's tongue even looser than usual. Tonight he was pontificating about alienation.

"Modern industrial life resembles a western movie set," Adam intoned. "A facade behind which lies only emptiness. Alienation is baked into capitalism. We're turning into a vast corporate state that produces nothing more than sterile, suburban conformity. Plastic food, plastic suburbs, plastic people."

His comments elicited a stream of "Right on," "Dig it," and "Heavy" responses from his acolytes, who nodded along like bobbleheads. Reed coughed to cover a laugh.

"It's not about freaks or squares—not whether you smoke grass or drink beer. We're all alienated from nature and from each other. If you ask me, the basic issue is human consciousness itself, which hasn't evolved enough to address our collective problems. The only way for humanity to avoid total self-annihilation is mind expansion. If we can change our heads, we can change our hearts, the culture, and ultimately, the political system itself."

Reed turned away. *Yeah, what about changing your dirty sheets first?* Dad would label Adam a "yakety-yak." Frank hated reflection, overthinking—too much talk, not enough action.

Starving, Reed wandered into the dining room, well-stacked with munchies. In ten minutes he managed to down three brownies with a fifth beer. No sign of the blond protester yet. Maybe she didn't go to Florida Tech. She could be what Reed's commie-hating friend Webb would label "an outside agitator"—a sleeper agent sent by the Kremlin to an unsuspecting campus to pit Americans against each other and weaken the nation's moral fiber.

As Reed chewed his fourth brownie—which had a musty flavor—a girl appeared and grabbed the last one. She wore a headband, a fringed suede vest, patched jeans, and moccasins. Kind of costume-like. Cute. Medium height, slender. Straight dark hair parted in the middle, striking emerald eyes. A cup of red punch in hand, she eyed Reed's brownie.

"Careful. Those are super strong. KGB."

Reed paused midbite. "Huh?"

"Killer Green Bud. Hash."

Reed swallowed and set the rest aside. He felt dizzy, unsteady on his feet, and now suspected why.

The girl giggled. "Jeez. How many have you had?"

"Four?"

"Ouch."

He extended his hand. "I'm Reed."

Her grip was firm for a girl. "Summer. Pleased to meet you."

"As in the season?" She nodded. "You go to school here?"

"Uh-huh. Freshman."

Suddenly, nausea swamped him. The room pitched like a boat, cresting a wave and plummeting.

"Hey, you okay? Look pretty hammered."

"I'm fine."

"Nonsense." Summer grabbed his forearm. "It's stuffy in here. Let's get you some air."

—

The party had overflowed onto the porch and cascaded across the dirt driveway. The Doors' "Break on Through" thundered as Summer led Reed down a grassy slope toward a dock perched over a small pond.

Images of parked cars sparkled. Jumbled conversations floated past, their words crawling into his ears seconds late, like a film with words and images out of sync.

"Lie on down," Summer instructed. "You'll feel better."

They lay on the dock's rough, weathered planks and gazed at a clear sky studded with constellations. The full moon—like a hypnotist's pocket watch—lulled Reed into visions of speed and power. As a race car driver, screaming past the checkered flag at Sebring in the winning Ford GT40. As an A-4 Skyhawk pilot, streaking high above the Atlantic on a training flight. As a champion surfer, riding the barrel of a twenty-foot wave, pounding the beach at Oahu's north shore.

Summer slid closer; their shoulders and hips brushed. Her hair smelled oddly of coconuts, reminding Reed of those that had fallen from trees onto his driveway as a kid. A vision of himself came to mind—scrawny, eleven years old, pounding a screwdriver through the shell to insert a straw and sip the sweet, watery milk.

"The only constellation I ever see is Orion," she whispered. "See those four stars in a rectangle, and the three stars of his belt?"

"Yeah. I always look for the North Star." Reed pointed. "Follow the outer edge of the Big Dipper's bowl with your finger. See? There?"

"Cool."

Reed levitated into the sky, up into the infinite cosmic void, then blinked and fell back to earth.

"When I look up," Summer said, "I feel so small...they say we're nothing but stardust, right?"

Reed's high school physics clicked into gear. Almost every element on earth originated in the aftermath of the Big Bang. Infinitesimal particles binding to create hydrogen and helium. Clouds of gas and dust giving birth to young stars, their cores heating to ten million degrees until they exploded in death and scattered stardust to form planets.

"Uh, basically, yeah."

Summer's smile faded. "When I die, I don't wanna be buried in a box under six feet of dirt with maggots and worms chewing on me. That's so gross."

"But when you're dead, you won't know you're in a box."

"I'd rather turn into stardust. Then you can stick me in a rocket, fly me into space, and spread me around."

The drugs in Reed's system unearthed fevered visions long since buried—Dad's corpse rotting in a rice paddy, veiled by elephant grass, crows plucking out his eyeballs, rats feasting on his decrepit flesh.

Wrong. Dying happened to *old* people, *sick* people, *unlucky* people. *Other* people. Not to Commander Frank Joseph Lawson, United States Navy.

Summer seized his hand. "Come on. I wanna show you something."

Reed swayed when he stood. Wind swept across the pond, and silver dollars of moonlight danced across its surface.

—

Summer led him inside, where the party had swelled to a fever pitch. From huge speakers, Deep Purple commanded everyone to "Hush."

Reed followed her upstairs, then along a hallway. They passed a bedroom where two guys were scooping one-ounce portions of marijuana from an enormous garbage bag into small sandwich bags.

Summer ushered him into another bedroom, furnished only with two seedy mattresses and several frayed blankets. Dust coated the scarred wood floor. Paint flaked from moldy walls. She padded across the room and stepped into the closet, every inch of which had been painted black. A single mattress covered the floor.

"In here. Just lie down."

Reed gaped at the ceiling. Hundreds of stars, meticulously drawn in white ink, twinkled in the glow of a black light bulb.

Summer rested her head on Reed's chest. "Incredible, isn't it?"

"Far out."

CHAPTER FOUR

Reed lurched outside, dizzy and disoriented. The party had thinned out. Flower child Summer had disappeared, and so had Adam.

Figuring it was around midnight, he peered at his watch. Two in the morning? What the hell? He could have sworn they'd crawled inside that psychedelic closet no later than ten. He'd either fallen asleep or blacked out.

As Reed fumbled for his keys, some guy bumped into him.

"Hey!" Beer breath and body odor spewed into Reed's face. Bleary eyes locked onto his Navy shirt. "Fucking cock-sucking Navy!"

"Excuse me, do I know you?"

The jerk flicked greasy blond hair away from his face and shoved a paper under Reed's nose. "Read this bullshit."

The effort compounded the sledgehammer now slamming against the inside of his skull. Reed squinted at the document, a U.S. Selective Service notice—"Order to Report for Armed Forces Physical Examination, April 29, 1970"—addressed to Darryl Warren.

"Not gonna eat for the next two months," Darryl declared. "If I weigh a hundred and ten, they can't take me…right?"

"Sure, sounds like a good idea." Reed feared he would vomit on the creep. "Look, I gotta split."

Darryl yanked Reed's T-shirt sleeve. "The draft, man!"

Anger rising, Reed twisted away. "What the fuck is wrong with you?"

"I got number ninety. What'd you get?"

"Three-oh-six. So what?"

"So what? I'm a *senior*! They're gonna send my ass to Viet-fucking-nam! Don't you give a shit about anybody else?"

"Not now, man."

The jerk grabbed his shirt. Reed shoved him. Hard.

"Hey!" The guy stumbled backward. His head collided with the side mirror of a truck. Knees buckling, he collapsed in the dirt.

Reed froze as partygoers gathered.

A guy Reed recognized from his physics class collared him. "You're a Rot-cee asshole, Lawson."

—

Head still throbbing, Reed guided the Mustang along a narrow country road back toward campus. Turned out the guy he'd knocked down, Darryl Warren, was known around the Pig Farm as Lude. He'd seemed okay when Reed left—only a bump on the head, no blood. Thankfully, for obvious reasons, no one had dared call the police.

For years, Reed had read about draft dodgers like Lude. Some claimed conscientious objector status or persuaded family doctors to manipulate records to show they were unfit to serve. Others feigned insanity, took drugs to flunk the urine test, starved themselves, or pretended to be homosexuals. Thousands fled north to Canada.

Although Reed had paid no attention to the draft, he recognized that many Americans considered the system biased and unfair. Adam had once observed, "Let's face it, white college kids like us are lucky to get deferments, while Black people and poor people get the shaft."

In response to the furor over the draft, the government had set up a system of lotteries and had conducted the first one last December on live TV. Blue plastic capsules containing slips of paper—each with a birth date—were chosen randomly. The first birth date drawn was assigned the lowest number, 001. The last birth date drawn was assigned the highest number, 366. The lower the number assigned, the higher the likelihood of being drafted.

At Florida Tech, groups of students had huddled anxiously around TVs in the student union to watch. Reed had nothing at stake, since he planned to stay in ROTC and join the Navy. He sat surrounded by nervous guys trying to cope by trading lame jokes and drinking lots of beer.

Adam had been quietly jubilant when he drew 260—no chance he'd get called up after graduation in '72. Reed's 306 was irrelevant.

Hands clenching the steering wheel, Reed peered into the darkness. Damn. Where were the lights of the city? He tried to forget about Lude. The guy should just show up for his Army physical and deal with the consequences like a man. Besides, thanks to the latest troop withdrawals, he might get lucky and avoid getting sent into battle.

Crap. He was driving in the wrong direction—away from the city's lights—along a dark road bordered by thick pine forest. His vision had gone haywire. The white lane divider was a slithering snake. The headlights of oncoming cars stabbed his eyeballs.

A shape materialized on the road's edge several hundred yards ahead.

Reed squinted. *A dog? A fox?*

No, a man limping onto the asphalt.

Reed stamped the brakes. The car skidded to a halt fifty yards from the figure.

Holy shit.

Navy Commander Frank Lawson stood there, frozen, in boots and a torn olive-green flight suit as he blinked at Reed like a deer in headlights. Blood trickled down his forehead; black smudges of exhaustion framed sunken eyes. He stumbled across the road, then darted into the woods.

Reed swerved onto the shoulder, jumped out, and ran after him. "Dad!" No response. He scrambled into the dark pines, waded through low brush, shoved sharp branches from his face. "Dad!"

Then he tripped on a tree root and fell face-first onto dank leaves, prickly pine needles, and mud. Blood trickled from a scrape on his elbow. *Son of a bitch!* He managed to rise and stagger a few yards farther, yelling until his throat burned.

Nothing.

Turning back to where he figured the road was, he trudged toward it but found himself even deeper in the gloom, half expecting Dad to appear and lead him to safety. A truck's horn bellowed, its lights painting the trees. Reed changed course and finally found the highway.

What the hell had just happened? *Obvious.* He'd been hallucinating from the toxic stew of hash brownies, beer, and drug-tainted punch. Yet something similar had happened before.

—

July 20, 1969. Two and a half years after his father was shot down. Armed with his mom's Jim Beam, which he'd siphoned into an empty Coke bottle, Reed had taken the Mustang for a drive. He'd been craving fresh night air following a grueling day at his summer job—nailing asphalt shingles onto the roofs of new homes in ninety-five-degree heat.

Past midnight, he'd pulled into a new shopping mall anchored at each end by department stores—Burdine's and Jordan Marsh. Drinking with one hand and steering with the other, he carved aimless figure eights in the parking lot and listened to the radio replaying Neil Armstrong's scratchy voice: "That's one small step for man, one giant leap for mankind."

Reed hoisted his whiskey. "Giant leap! Go, Neil!"

A flash of movement caught his attention, a shape emerging from the oaks bordering the mall.

His father?

Bruised and battered in his flight suit, Frank was limping along, dragging his billowing parachute behind him.

Reed slammed on the brakes and yelled, "Dad!" By the time he'd scrambled out of the car, his father had vanished. Sickened by alcohol and shock, he bent over and retched until his insides ached.

—

Lingering in his car, Reed stared at the dorm's redbrick walls. The discordant strains of Jimi Hendrix's "Star-Spangled Banner" thundered from the building. Students in adjacent rooms had positioned speakers in their windows, facing outside, so they could play the same song in unison and ramp up the volume.

What the heck was wrong with him? Was it the alien chemicals in his system, or was he going flat-out psycho?

—

In the ROTC commander's office on Monday, Reed stood at rigid attention, eyes fixed on the wall above Captain Jim Harwood, who sat behind a big mahogany desk. In his late forties, Harwood had a ruddy complexion. Deep wrinkles lined his forehead, and crow's feet framed weary eyes. He carried an air of perpetual fatigue, the result of brutal wars fought both on and off the battlefield.

"It's not enough that these protesters are trying to shut us down," Harwood growled. "Now I gotta deal with cadets assaulting civilians?"

The asshole from physics class must have ratted him out. "Sir, it was an accident, sir."

"More like conduct unbecoming—"

"Sir, I didn't mean to—"

"Cadet, no one gives a rat's ass what you meant to do."

"Sir, yes, sir!"

A long pause followed. "You can look at me now."

Reed's eyes drifted down to meet Harwood's.

The captain regarded him pensively. "Any news about your father?"

The question surprised Reed. To avoid unwanted attention or special treatment, he'd told no one in ROTC about his father's status.

"Don't look so surprised, Cadet. The Navy takes care of its own."

"Uh. No news, sir."

"After so long, you think he may still be alive?"

"Yes, I do, sir!"

"Well, we can only pray that's the case." Harwood opened a manila folder and frowned. "I notice you've logged no volunteer work yet. Why not?"

Reed searched for an answer more acceptable than claiming he'd been too busy. Volunteering in the community wasn't required but strongly encouraged. "I've been meaning to, sir."

"Cadet, you don't seem to care much about the world around you."

"Sir, with all due respect, that's not true. Sir."

"Because there's more to leadership than memorizing slogans or reading about famous admirals in a textbook—even when they include your grandfather's exploits during the Battle of Midway."

"Yes, sir!"

"Come to think of it, since you've shown such a keen interest in the drug culture, I have the perfect opportunity for you."

Although Reed had no clue what "opportunity" Harwood referred to, he snapped to attention.

"Sir, yes, sir!"

—

After class on Tuesday, he drove to a neighborhood of older rental bungalows and cheap student apartments. He passed a 7-Eleven and a bicycle store named Psycle Shop with the tagline *Because Biking Is Good for Your Head.*

Reed parked in front of a one-story faded yellow bungalow. The branches of a live oak spread over its roof, and palmetto bushes dotted a patchy lawn. A tattered couch, folding chairs, and filthy ashtrays cluttered the porch. A shirtless guy with long hair in a ponytail sat picking aimless guitar chords. Tacked on the door was a makeshift sign—*Lifelines.*

What a dump. Reed had expected some kind of medical clinic. According to Captain Harwood, Lifelines had opened two months ago to help students with drug problems.

Harwood was among a group of university and city officials who'd advocated for the facility. "It wouldn't hurt our image to develop better relations with the community," the captain had said.

In the years before Frank was shot down, Reed and Sandy had sparred over drugs. At seventeen, she'd started smoking pot and tripping on LSD.

"That shit's gonna screw you up," he'd told her.

"With all your hang-ups, how would *you* know? Besides, you're already spending half your allowance paying older guys to buy you beer. That's way worse than grass."

Bullshit. So what if he drank a few beers under the bleachers after football games? "Alcohol's legal," he argued. "Everybody drinks. What about all that acid you're dropping?"

"That's mind expanding, not addictive. It helps me stop ego-tripping, makes me more socially aware. Besides, it's just like you to criticize what you don't—or can't—understand."

Frank drew no distinctions between drugs. All were signs of defective character and poor life choices. "With enough willpower, anyone can kick these poisons."

Stepping out of the Mustang, Reed glanced at a yellow Volkswagen Beetle convertible with Texas plates parked in the driveway. He had assumed community service meant teaching poor kids how to throw a football, fixing up dilapidated houses, or picking up trash. Adam had even mentioned an "environmental teach-in" planned for April to protest air and water pollution.

Was there a way out of this? Nope. Time to suck it up. Dutifully, he marched inside.

The front room was furnished with a battered sofa, two mismatched chairs, and a faded oriental rug. Posters covered a wall: *Women's Liberation*; *Women Unite Against the War*. What did bra burning have to do with drugs?

Reed followed the sound of muffled conversation down a narrow hallway and into a bedroom furnished with two scarred wooden desks—a phone on each.

He froze when he recognized the girl talking on the phone.

The blond from the ROTC protest.

Whose gray-blue eyes had harbored such contempt for him.

To whom he was a warmonger, and his father a killer.

CHAPTER FIVE

The girl's T-shirt read *Women Belong in the House...and the Senate.* She wore tight, hacked-off faded denim shorts, leather sandals, and a silver Navajo bracelet on her wrist. A thin scar, about two inches long, traced a path around her right eye. Somehow the flaw intensified rather than diminished her natural beauty.

She leaned forward as she spoke into the phone, radiating suppressed energy, thighs twitching as if poised to catapult her from the chair.

"Those diet pills are amphetamines. Speed. That's why you can't sleep." She tapped a pencil against the desk. "I know your doctor prescribed them, but it's a big scam. Most diet advice is crap, especially when it comes from men. Honestly, you might oughta flush them and eat something healthy. Not just grapefruit or cabbage soup."

She glanced up and smirked at Reed's white polo shirt with the alligator logo, spotless Levi's, and white Adidas running shoes. "Come on in," she continued to the caller, "and we can rap about real health, not fashion propaganda...yup, thanks for calling."

The blond girl hung up, eyed Reed, and raised her hands in mock surrender. "Okay, I get it. You're *not* a warmonger. So what do you want? We're swamped."

"I'm here to volunteer." He extended his hand. "Reed. Reed Lawson."

She ignored it. "C'mon, you're not serious, are you?"

"Saw a flyer at the student union. *New Crisis Hotline. Volunteers wanted.*"

Her disbelieving gaze locked on his, penetrating to the back of his brain. Flustered, he looked away first.

"Suit yourself." She shrugged, rose, and mumbled, "I'm Jordan."

"Pleased to meet you." He followed her to a rickety card table shoved against the wall, admiring her athletic legs.

As if sensing his eyes on her, she scowled and handed him a thick three-ring binder. "Study this until you come in for training."

Reed scanned the title—*Lifelines: A Manual for Social Change.* What did "social change" have to do with helping drug addicts?

Another volunteer appeared. It was the skinny chick with frizzy black hair from the protest—the one who'd called him a fascist asshole. At least six feet tall, she rounded her shoulders as if to minimize her height. She wore granny glasses, farmer's overalls, and a baggy flannel shirt. Her angular face regarded Reed with thinly veiled scorn.

He stuck out his hand. "Hi. I'm Reed."

"Olivia," she muttered and brushed past.

Why the cold shoulder? No doubt because he represented the evil ROTC. Yet Captain Harwood had emphasized Lifelines' urgent need for help. But hey, if they didn't want him, screw 'em.

Reed stepped closer to Jordan, who'd opened another thick binder on the desk. She wore no makeup and smelled of patchouli and musk, which he recognized—Sandy sometimes wore the same scents.

"This is the call log," Jordan said, turning to a detailed form with spaces for entering the caller's name, date, sex, race, age, their problem, actions taken, referrals made, and "Notes."

He leaned in for a better look. Too close because she edged away, oozing annoyance.

"It's a lot of information, but we want to collect what we can. Some psych professors are analyzing the data to figure out trends in drug use and stuff."

Jordan led him into the adjacent bedroom. A standing lamp dimly lit a single bed, nightstand, and chair. Closed wooden blinds covered the only window.

"This is the quiet room, where we rap with people—about anything, really. Although lately we've been talking a lot of people down from bad trips." She shot Reed a patronizing look. "You know, like, from acid."

"I know what LSD is," he snapped, louder than intended.

"Well, good for you. Anyway…coming down here is better than in a hospital. Doctors will shoot people up with drugs like chlorpromazine, which can cause flashbacks."

Next stop was the garage in the backyard. Although its concrete block exterior was stained with dirt and mold, the inside was clean, with bare walls freshly painted white. Folding chairs, beanbags, and a sofa arranged on a faded blue rug hid the oil-stained concrete floor. An easel with poster-sized paper stood in a corner.

"Anyone can hang out here, just rap, or play music," Jordan explained. "Kids who won't talk to teachers or doctors will open up to other kids going through the same shit. Once a week we do Aquarius Night. It's kind of like an encounter group, where people can let down their defenses and deal with their hang-ups."

Fat chance he was gonna sit around and "encounter" anybody. But he nodded to feign interest. Why give her more ammo to use against him?

As if reading his mind, she smirked. "*Most* volunteers dig it."

Her spiel done, she introduced him to Lifelines' director, Dr. Greta Carlson, then disappeared into the hotline room.

Dr. Carlson appeared to be a few years older than Reed's mother, with kind eyes and dark hair streaked with gray. Unlike Jordan and Olivia, she offered Reed a welcoming smile.

"Glad to have you aboard, Reed." She led him to the assignment calendar pinned to a corkboard in the hallway. "Which shifts would you prefer? Two per week would be wonderful, but one's fine if your schedule's too tight."

Reed spotted *Jordan Ellis* marked down for the Wednesday and Saturday late shifts. The Wednesday shift ran from eight p.m. till two a.m. The Saturday shift was worse still, ten p.m. to four a.m.

Ouch. Twelve hours added to his schedule. A morning person, Reed rarely stayed up past eleven and woke early for dawn runs, ROTC drills, and classes. He really should pick earlier shifts. But Jordan wouldn't be there. Then again, she reeked of hostility. So what was the point? Yet…

"I'll take Wednesday and Saturday, late shifts if that's okay."

"Perfect. Those are the hardest to fill. Hopefully you don't have morning classes on Thursdays."

"No, ma'am." Only Differential Equations and Naval Engineering.

He also had to sign up for training—a four-hour Saturday course, a few shifts shadowing an experienced volunteer, and one or two evening lectures on various topics given by doctors and psychiatrists from the hospital. Oh, well. In for a dime, in for a dollar.

—

When Reed walked outside, Jordan was climbing into the VW Beetle convertible. Dust and mud coated its yellow paint. Duct tape covered tears in the vinyl roof.

The starter ground uselessly, and Reed smiled, back in his comfort zone—neglected machines in need of fixing. He strode over and peered inside, where textbooks, spiral notebooks, and empty Tab bottles littered the back seat. Sandy sometimes drank that crap, which tasted like carbonated cough syrup.

"Hey," he said, adding a *Just here to help* smile. "Can I take a look?"

"No need." Curt, dismissive.

"It's probably something simple. These engines sometimes have electrical issues."

She rolled her eyes. "It always starts. Sooner or later."

When the engine reluctantly sputtered to life, she shot him a smug *I told you so* glance.

Reed watched her back out. What could explain his attraction—beyond the obvious—to this standoffish, prickly chick?

He headed toward his Mustang. A stringy-haired freak was leaning against the hood—torn jean jacket, commie Che Guevara T-shirt, the whole deal.

Reed brandished his key and coughed. "If you don't mind..."

The guy eased away from the car. "Sorry, man." His eyes darted everywhere except at Reed. He scratched the side of his head and picked at his eyebrows—like he had lice or something. "Hey, wanna score some grass? Pure Acapulco Gold."

"No, thanks."

The guy grinned, revealing mossy, grayish teeth. "What about crystal meth? Uppers, downers, whatever you need, brother."

"What I need is for you to take a hike."

"Shit. What's *your* bag, man?"

After the creep shuffled off, Reed wiped his greasy handprints from the hood.

—

Adam was hungry for barbecue that night, but since he didn't own a car, Reed agreed to drive to Sonny Boy's, a local hangout at the edge of town. Their pulled pork and ribs platters were a welcome relief from Florida Tech's bland dining hall food.

"Best-tasting *treif* I've ever had." Adam licked sauce from his fingers.

Reed had spent scant time around Jewish people, much less roomed with one. Adam's penchant for pork represented a protest against his parents' strict kosher regime. He often joked about his uncle Jacob, who lived in Savannah, Georgia. Jacob was an avid fisherman who caught "only kosher shrimp."

"Where'd you end up Saturday night?" Adam asked. "Saw your car but couldn't find you. Had to bum a ride with some drunks. They nearly ran off the road."

"Fell asleep in a closet. By the time I woke up, you'd split."

"Weird. So...uh, what about that hippie chick?" Adam winked.

"What hippie chick?"

"The cute flower child you were hanging around with. Long hair. Headband."

Reed looked off. No point telling Adam about getting high with Summer, knocking Lude down, or stumbling in the woods searching for his father. He'd just ask a million questions, then conclude Reed was bat-shit crazy.

"I wasn't hanging around with anyone, man. Sorry, but that party sucked."

On their way back to campus, Adam grabbed the Lifelines manual from the back seat. "What's this all about?"

"I gotta do some volunteering for ROTC. I ended up at this weird place, but guess who I met there?"

"Pray enlighten me."

"That bitchy blond chick from the protest."

"Lucky you." Adam opened the manual and read, "*Lifelines is a place where people can look for ways to live without drugs and reduce the loneliness, alienation, and dehumanization of life—not only on the university campus but in our broader industrialized society. Only when we, as Americans, recapture our lost humanity will we ultimately solve our drug problem.* Pretty cool."

Reed shrugged. "Ditching drugs is a no-brainer. The rest sounds like left-wing bullshit."

"Why label everything you disagree with 'left-wing bullshit'? What about all the right-wing bullshit this country's drowning in?" Reed didn't bother to reply. "Besides, if you don't dig what they're doing, why not volunteer someplace else?"

Reed grinned. "Maybe I wanna help society 'recapture its lost humanity.'"

"Or maybe you wanna get it on with that blond."

Reed inhaled deeply, summoning Jordan's formidable presence—her musky smell, her figure that reminded him of Wonder Woman from the comics. "So what if I do?"

"Forget about it. To her, you're a lackey in the military-industrial complex. A mindless cog in the imperialist war machine. A baby killer in training—"

"Enough already!" But he couldn't help chuckling as he pulled into the dorm lot. If nothing else, Adam could sure sling a bunch of five-dollar words. "She'll come around," he said, then added a touch of Scottish burr. "The lass just needs a wee taste of that old-fashioned Lawson charm."

"Sure. Scottish charm. *That* will really wow her." Adam caressed the white Hurst gearshift knob. "Just once, I'd love to drive this baby."

Frank's first commandment—absolutely no one but Reed was permitted to drive the precious Mustang. *Ever.*

"Dream on."

CHAPTER SIX

Reed passed the football stadium en route to the gym the next day. The team was nicknamed the Blue Wave, and its stadium was dubbed the Lagoon. Fans fervently assaulted opposing teams with the war cry "We will drown you!"

Near the gym's free-weight area were a boxing ring and several heavy punching bags. Encouraged by his father, Reed had joined a boxing club for a few months in high school. Although hitting people was fun, he lacked his father's discipline to excel at the sport. Instead, Reed had focused on football. Despite being the smallest linebacker, he'd gained a reputation for agility, speed, and vicious tackling.

Reed stepped up to one of the bags. Starting slowly, he settled into a steady rhythm: jab–cross, jab–jab–cross, jab–cross–left hook.

For the past three years, he'd channeled frustration about his father's unknown fate into the heavy bag. Often he thought about Dad's favorite poem, "Invictus." Especially the verse *Out of the night that covers me, / Black as the pit from pole to pole, / I thank whatever gods may be / for my unconquerable soul.*

While hitting the bag, he'd daydream about Dad being trapped—either in an actual pit dug into the ground or in a primitive bamboo cage somewhere in North Vietnam. From that darkness, Reed would rescue him…

It's February 16, 1967. The aircraft carrier USS Thomas Adams plows through the Gulf of Tonkin in the South China

Sea off the coast of North Vietnam—an area the enemy has labeled Yankee Station.

The deck churns with activity as pilots scramble into planes and crewmen wearing bulbous headsets and color-coded jerseys prepare the jets for launch.

Navy Commander Frank "Dash" Lawson emerges from a hatch into a steamy, overcast day. Swaggering bowlegged in his G suit and harness, Frank exudes confidence. Like a gunfighter eager to take on the bad guys, he strides toward a row of A-4 Skyhawks.

Moments later, the A-4 accelerates from 0 to 170 miles per hour as the catapult flings it from the carrier deck up into the pale, humid sky.

Leading an Alpha strike force, Frank's A-4 thunders over North Vietnam, heading for Hanoi. Soon he spots his target—a bridge—and descends to five thousand feet. Huge black clouds of smoke and dust rise from the ground as the enemy launches a barrage of surface-to-air missiles.

One of them hits Frank's A-4. Emergency lights flash, smoke billows, and the plane spirals down.

Frank reaches up to yank the ejection handle. The ejection seat rockets out, followed in seconds by a billowing parachute.

Meanwhile, on the ground, an Alpha team of U.S. Army Green Berets stalks along a trail, cradling M-16s. Faces grease painted, they scan the jungle for the enemy.

Their commanding officer is a shockingly young First Lieutenant Reed Lawson. A lean, mean fighting machine. Reed spots his father's descending parachute and leads his men toward it.

Frank Lawson staggers into a clearing, bleeding profusely from a head wound and dragging a broken leg. Reed and his fellow Green Berets rush to his aid.

Also advancing on the clearing is a team of North Vietnamese soldiers carrying AK-47 assault rifles. They wear dirty khaki uniforms and caps adorned with red stars.

Moments later, an arm draped around his father, Reed scrambles out of the clearing with his team and starts back down the trail.

"Come on, Dad. It's not far," Reed urges.

From deep jungle cover, the enemy bursts into view, but they're instantly slaughtered by a furious hail of American bullets...

It was always at this moment—amid the shrieking of the wounded and dying—that reality reared its unwelcome head.

The first time Reed had fantasized about the rescue, the intrusion of reality had been accompanied by music—something about surfing in the USA—and a booming voice.

"Hey, Lawson, get a hustle on! What the hell's wrong with you, boy?"

It was Reed's track coach, urging him to get his ass in gear. The song blared not from a North Vietnamese jungle but from a transistor radio in the bleachers. Reed wasn't a soldier in Asia wearing combat fatigues but a high school senior in gym shorts and sneakers standing disoriented on a cinder track.

And, like a record needle trapped in a scratch, he replayed the fantasy for years.

In the garage, tuning up the family Ford.

At Jacksonville Beach, bobbing on a surfboard, waiting for the perfect wave.

In high school algebra, his mind wandering from the blackboard...

Or in the college gym, where he now punished the bag with metronomic ferocity until his lungs gasped for air.

A beefy guy in a blue-and-white football jersey who'd been watching him gave a thumbs-up. "Dude. Remind me never to piss you off!"

—

Reed hadn't even cracked the Lifelines manual before arriving for the training session on Saturday morning. Though he'd aced every course so far, the impenetrability of quantum mechanics had finally taxed his brain, demanding extra hours to decipher.

He bumped into Jordan and flashed a grin charming enough—he hoped—to splinter her hostile facade. "Morning!"

"Guess we didn't scare you off yet."

"Not a chance."

"Well, good luck then." She darted into the hotline room.

Reed joined about a dozen people in the front room who were sitting on folding chairs facing a portable blackboard. Mostly the shaggy flower-power crowd he'd expected. More girls than guys. He sat next to a girl about his age—redhead, petite.

She smiled shyly. "Hi. I'm Meg Howard."

"Reed Lawson. Nice to meet you."

Reed learned that Meg was a premed major and planned to become a psychiatrist. She'd been volunteering since Lifelines had opened the previous December. "But I like to sit in on training to help new volunteers."

She wore conservative khaki slacks, a white blouse, and a perfume Reed recognized—White Shoulders, a brand he'd once bought for his mother's birthday.

Dr. Carlson started the training by describing the drug problem on and off campus. University officials were aware that students used drugs in dorms, in fraternity and sorority houses, and elsewhere.

"The basic policy is treatment-but-no-punishment for anyone who goes to the university clinic. Too many won't, though, because they view the staff as judgmental and unsympathetic."

Reed half listened to Dr. Carlson explain Lifelines' mission, organization, and philosophy. He checked his watch often, distracted by the aroma of fresh Krispy Kremes laid out on a table.

Meanwhile, Meg took notes with the elegant penmanship Reed had given up trying to perfect in third grade. Sometimes she brushed stray hair from her freckled forehead.

"To wrap up, we're not about morality trips or put-downs," Dr. Carlson said. "Everyone who calls or walks in here is welcome. Everyone is accepted. We're here to help, not to judge." She finished by mentioning a plan to launch a free medical clinic next month, pitching it as a new volunteer opportunity.

Reed yawned. No chance he'd sign up for that.

Another psychiatrist spoke next, getting more into the weeds about crisis intervention. How to identify the side effects of drugs, when and how to call for medical help in case of overdoses, simple emergency first-aid techniques.

Fine, Reed thought. Stuff you could fix—problems with straightforward, black-and-white solutions.

Then the shrink drifted into touchy-feely stuff. The elements of a "helping relationship." How to practice "active and reflective listening." How to "put yourself in another person's shoes to understand them better." How to talk to depressed and even suicidal callers. He described a twenty-year-old student who'd set himself on fire the previous fall, leaving behind a suicide note claiming drugs had destroyed his mind.

Reed couldn't imagine talking to a crazy—much less suicidal—person. He grew nervous; his right hand repeatedly opened and clenched into a fist. His knee bobbed. Had he ever known—or even heard of—anyone who'd offed themselves? During a Christmas party last year, he'd overheard hushed comments about a Navy officer who'd died of a "gun accident." Could that have been suicide?

Several other speakers followed the shrink—a nurse, a police officer, and a pharmacist. Most volunteers had questions. Eager to leave, Reed asked none.

Jordan wandered in sporadically and leaned against the wall to observe, arms folded beneath her breasts. Once Reed caught her sizing him up before glancing away. Worried she'd see through his boredom, Reed pretended to scribble copious notes.

Afterward, Meg invited him to stick around. "We're still new at this, so the training is kind of basic. We could use a lot more, so feel free to ask me questions—now or anytime."

"Got it. Thanks." He smiled, then wandered into the hotline room.

"So…did you learn anything?" Jordan asked, her voice dripping with condescension.

"Yup. A lot, actually."

"Good." She smirked. "Cause you sure took a lot of notes."

Reed managed an self-conscious smile—score another point for her. "Well, I'll see you next Saturday night."

"Reckon I can hardly wait."

—

Reed caught up with Webb Patterson outside the gym that afternoon. Webb was combing his fingers through the mop of sun-bleached, surfer-blond hair that fell to his shoulders. He wore his usual wrinkled madras shirt, khakis, and scuffed Weejuns with no socks—like a delinquent jock who'd been exiled from a country club.

"Sorry I'm late." Reed had met Webb last fall in the weight room.

"It's cool, man. Just need to get it done before the social." Webb's fraternity, Sigma Alpha Nu, invited sororities over for Saturday night mixers.

In the weight room, Webb struggled to squat 250 pounds. Reed knew he could lift over 300. Well over six feet tall, Webb carried 30 pounds more than the 190 he'd weighed as the star quarterback of his South Carolina high school football team. As a senior, Webb had led his teammates to the 1967 state championship, where he'd engineered a tense march down the field during the final minute, which culminated in a surgically thrown forty-yard, game-winning touchdown pass. Over pitchers of beer at the Rathskeller, Webb had replayed every detail of the game as if the victory was—and might always remain—the highlight of his life.

Disgusted, Webb racked the barbell. "If I wasn't such a fat-ass piece of shit, I could maybe lift some actual weight. Let's bench. You first."

Reed lay on the bench, Webb standing behind him, spotting. At Webb's urging, Reed described Jordan Ellis as he warmed up with 135 pounds.

"Name doesn't ring a bell. But the chick sounds like your typical ballbuster."

"Maybe," Reed said. "Let's go two twenty-five."

"Now you're talking." Webb slid more weight onto the barbell, and his fingers hovered below it as Reed lowered the barbell to his chest and pushed up. After four more reps, Reed's arms trembled on the last two. "Enough."

"No way. One more! Come on, man, imagine this chick Jordan kneeling between your legs..." Reed strained against the bar with all his might. "She's yanking it out of your shorts! Opening her mouth wide...Get it up! Get it up!"

Reed burst into laughter, and 225 pounds sank toward his chest—until Webb seized the bar just in time.

Webb chuckled. "Relax, my man. Always remember—I've got your back. Or, like your dad would say, 'I've got your six.'"

—

Reed picked at his apple pie, topped with a slice of half-melted Velveeta. The dining hall favored quantity over quality—bland combinations like roast beef and rice, southern fried chicken and mashed potatoes, meat loaf and french fries. The string beans were dependably overcooked, the iceberg lettuce reliably wilted.

He glanced at Adam, who was flipping through Kant's *Critique of Pure Reason*. "Aren't you way behind in organic chemistry?"

"Don't worry, I'll catch up."

"Why don't you just break down and tell your parents you wanna change majors to philosophy?"

"Dad would kill me. I have to be a doctor, lawyer, or dentist." Adam raised his hands, palms in, gesturing like the actor Zero Mostel as Tevye in *Fiddler on the Roof* and mimicking his father's New York accent.

"Don't be a rag merchant like me, son. Sure, it's no shame selling clothes, but it's no great honor either. Be a doctor! Cure cancer! Forget about philosophy! Nothing but useless theories, meaningless words. And what did Socrates get for all his trouble? A cup of hemlock, that's what! What a *meshuggeneh*!"

"Not bad," Reed chuckled. "You should switch majors to theater. But seriously, what's the worst that could happen if you told him?"

"Does the word *disown* mean anything to you?"

Adam shoved his book aside and paged to the school newspaper's opinion section, whose tagline read *Advice and Dissent – Apathy Is the Enemy of Democracy.*

"Crap. The editor promised he'd run my letter this week."

Reed had read Adam's rant against American consumerism and conformity. "Face it. Maybe no one gives a rip about plastic people or frozen TV dinners."

Suddenly, a memory flooded back. Sitting with Dad in the living room behind TV trays, peeling back the tinfoil from a Swanson turkey dinner. He must have been ten or eleven. They loved to watch *The Rifleman*, a western about rancher Lucas McCain and his son, Mark. Reed had been captivated by McCain's rapid-fire Winchester rifle.

Thinking about it now, he felt miserable.

"What's wrong?"

"Huh?" Reed was staring at the melted cheese on his pie. "Sorry." He shoved the pie aside. There was something about the TV relationship between father and son that irritated him, but he couldn't pinpoint why.

"How was training this morning?" Adam interjected, sensing it was time to switch gears.

"Way too much to learn. Not enough time to learn it." Not only was he behind in schoolwork, but to keep from screwing up at Lifelines, he'd need to study as if triple majoring in psychology, pharmacology, and sociology.

"I guess fixing people is harder than changing the spark plugs in your Mustang."

CHAPTER SEVEN

Every other Sunday, Reed drove ninety miles home to help his mother with chores around the house. This Sunday was the start of spring break week for Sandy and him. Instead of the faster Route 301 to Jacksonville, he preferred the smaller country roads he'd driven with his father on the rare occasions they'd spent time together.

The Mustang rumbled past the Dixieland RV Park and its sagging mobile homes, their discolored aluminum sidings covered with mold. Past straight rows of green cabbage stretching toward the horizon, then neat lines of trees planted for the pulpwood industry and an auto graveyard where cars rusted amid knee-high grass.

He drove through small towns. Past Eric's Rib Shack (*Smokin' Good!*), the Calvary Baptist Church (*Jesus Saves*), a community center (*Bingo Tonight!*), a pawnshop (*We Buy Guns*).

Signs dotted the landscape—an oversized American flag (*These Colors Won't Run)*, proclamations outside a VFW hall (*Patriotism Equals Freedom* and *Veterans Love You)*, humor chalked on a blackboard outside a bar (*Where the Beer Is as Cold as Your Ex-Wife's Heart*).

He rolled into a neighborhood near the St. Johns River and pulled into the driveway of a one-story home with white stucco walls, a red-tile roof, and black shutters. An enormous live oak commanded the front yard. Its lower branches drooped within six feet of the ground. Perfect for pull-ups.

In front of the two-car garage was an unfamiliar white pickup with

Walker Design and Build printed on the driver's side. Moments later, his mother introduced him to Sam Walker.

About his father's age, Walker wore work boots, weathered jeans, and a polo shirt. A web of wrinkles framed blue eyes, and gray-flecked brown hair fell to his collar. Trying to be hip, Reed figured. Instinctively, he disliked the guy.

His mother wore a navy-blue dress and a straw hat to protect her fair skin. Elegant as always. Throughout his childhood, Reed sensed, she'd played the role of dutiful Navy wife, always polite and gracious, but mostly just going through the motions—even before Dad disappeared.

The thing was, Dad loved parties. Loved to tell stories and off-color jokes, grill steaks, and make everyone vodka tonics. Not Mom. The moment the last guest left, she'd retreat to the bedroom with a novel and a pot of peppermint tea. She preferred analyzing themes in *Huckleberry Finn* to swapping recipes at coffee klatches or organizing the next squadron luncheon. Determined to teach college-level English literature, she was studying for a master's degree at the University of Jacksonville.

"Sweetheart," she was saying, "Mr. Walker's just looking at the bigger jobs we need to get done."

What bigger jobs? "I can take care of anything," Reed said.

"Not replacing a tile roof."

What the heck was wrong with the roof? "Mom, all I did last summer was work on roofs. I can do that."

"Nonsense. You already work way too hard."

Before Frank left for Vietnam, he'd declared Reed "the man of the house" and assigned him a long list of chores that Reed had been methodically completing for the past three years.

"I can handle it."

Sensing the tension, Walker glanced at his watch. "Excuse me, but I've got an eleven o'clock in Saint Augustine." He extended a hand. "Nice to meet you, Reed." Reed shook it reluctantly.

After Walker left, Reed's mother marched to her car without a word, clearly annoyed. He felt vaguely guilty, knowing she was a stickler for manners and couldn't abide the slightest hint of rudeness. But Walker's presence irritated him.

While his mother ran errands, Reed mowed the front and back yards and watered her precious pink azaleas, white camellias, and red hibiscuses. He oiled the squeaky kitchen door and changed two burned-out bulbs. Afterward, he hung every tool on its assigned hook on the pegboard he'd helped Dad build. A place for every tool, every tool in its place.

Reed had never forgotten the day he'd left a wrench in the family Ford's engine compartment—which was discovered only when it rattled as Dad backed out of the driveway. That lapse had earned him one of Frank's milder punishments—getting rapped on the skull with his knuckles. "How dumb can you get?" *Knock.* "Moron!" *Knock, knock.* "Put it back where it belongs or never use it again." *Knock, knock, knock.*

—

As the sun slid behind the sabal palms in the backyard, they sat at the patio table and ate a simple meal of baked chicken, peas, and instant mashed potatoes. Carol drank white wine, and Reed had a beer.

Unlike the other military wives, his mother avoided cooking unless pressured to prepare one of the dinners required of a commander's wife. Her culinary ambivalence showed. Growing up, Reed would occasionally grab a burger at McDonald's before arriving home for dinner and pretending to like his mom's cooking.

Besides, she ate mostly rabbit food—endless plates of lettuce topped with scoops of tuna fish or egg salad. If her five-foot, five-inch frame drifted an ounce over 120 pounds, she'd try another weird diet. One month her diet featured grapefruit, the next cottage cheese.

In the weeks after Dad was shot down, all food made his mother sick. Too anxious to leave the house—in case the phone rang with news from the Navy—she lost fifteen pounds in six weeks. Always cold, she often wore a sweater, even in the heat.

Reed and Sandy, along with Mom's friends, had eventually convinced her to see a doctor, who diagnosed her with a "nervous breakdown" and prescribed a bunch of pills. Mom hated the drugs, which made her drowsy and confused. It had taken her a year to regain the weight she'd lost.

After supper, Reed slid the Sunday paper across the table. "Mom, look at this."

The article described a Chicago businessman who'd just returned from the Paris peace talks and had met with North Vietnam's chief negotiator. The businessman was confident that Hanoi would soon release a complete list of POWs and allow families to communicate with their loved ones.

Carol scanned it and sighed. "We've read this sort of thing so many times before."

"Well, what about this one?" Reed showed her the article he'd copied about wives who'd received letters for the first time confirming that their husbands were alive but missing in action. Some had arrived through the regular mail, bearing Hanoi postmarks. Others had been carried back to the U.S. by antiwar group leaders who'd received the letters from the North Vietnamese.

In 1967, the year Frank had been shot down, the North Vietnamese had finally agreed to accept mail and occasional packages sent by American families to soldiers assumed to be POWs. Letters were limited to one per month and to a mere six lines written on a designated form. Only good news was allowed, nothing about the war. Praying Frank was alive and would receive the letters, his family had written him every month for three years.

None had been answered. None had ever been returned.

"It says eight hundred airmen are missing," Reed said, "but the government has only confirmed one hundred and seventy."

Carol's hazel eyes regarded Reed with a mix of sympathy and resignation. "Sweetheart…it's been three years, and we still don't have a shred of evidence. If your father were alive, wouldn't we have heard something by now?"

He jabbed at the newsprint. "It's right here, in damn black and white. More than six hundred may be alive. Remember that lady in your law office? Her husband was MIA for four years, then turned up as a prisoner."

Carol shook her head. "I'm sorry, but I can't be one of those women who looks at blurry pictures of pilots and tries to convince themselves it's their husband. I…I just can't do that kind of thing any longer."

Reed was familiar with the picture she referred to—a downed pilot escorted by North Vietnamese soldiers. Although the image was almost unrecognizable, hundreds of desperate women around the country had insisted he was their missing husband.

Carol rose and stepped to the edge of the patio. "Week after week, month after month of not knowing. Until it takes over your entire life. Until we *have* no other life."

She had a point. The dark cloud hovering over Reed had infused everything with a leaden tint. Yet even if the Navy was 90 percent sure Dad was dead, that left a 10 percent chance they were wrong. And that was enough to fuel hope.

Why wasn't it enough for her?

Carol sat down, fingered her wineglass, and drew a deep breath. "Sweetheart, there's something I wanted to tell you earlier. For a long time…for a while now, at least…I've been thinking about selling the house."

Huh? It took a moment to register. "What do you mean? *This* house? *Our* house?"

"I don't need all this space. You're in college, and Sandy's going to stay in Washington for law school next fall."

"Mom, I can come home every week. I can fix anything."

"No doubt, but that's not the point. I'd like to live closer to the beach."

What the hell? If she wanted to sit on a freaking beach, it was thirty minutes away. "I don't get it. What's Dad going to say?"

Her shoulders slumped. "We can't keep having this conversation about your father. We just can't."

Reed stomped inside and grabbed another beer. To imagine the house gone was to be exiled to an alien planet. Jacksonville was their hometown, where Dad intended to settle after retiring from the Navy.

Like other military families, they'd moved often. First it was base housing, shuttling between Pensacola, Florida, and Norfolk, Virginia, when Reed was a little kid. Then more base housing in Texas before Dad bought the Jacksonville house. He rented it out when they moved to San Diego. Next came a transfer to Washington, DC. They'd moved back to Jacksonville in 1964 when Reed turned fourteen.

This was the house that felt most like home—where they'd hosted barbecues, tossed the football around, worked on cars. Where he'd made out with girls while his parents were out. Where he'd helped Dad lay new tile on the kitchen floor.

Reed trudged back outside, collapsed in his chair, and set down his second beer. His mother regarded the bottle with reproach. She'd been on his case about his drinking, insisting that it had gotten worse over the past three years.

Bullshit. Dad drank all the time—aviators worked hard, played hard, and drank harder. A few beers were no big deal.

"Sweetheart, we all want closure, but we may never get it."

"You're wrong. Dad's alive, I'm sure."

"The thing is…I'm not a military wife, not a widow. So what am I? Who am I?" Her voice cracked. "I'm just this person stuck on a treadmill, going nowhere. When is the rest of my life going to start?"

Reed was taken aback. Mom had never spoken so openly about herself. Around neighbors and friends, she would murmur the expected platitudes: "We will continue to believe until we learn otherwise." "We will keep praying." "We have no choice but to trust our government."

"Mom, we just have to hang tough, keep hoping."

Carol took a steadying breath as if she'd been rehearsing the words. "The thing is, for me, hope…hope feels like a prison."

Reed sensed a rigid finality in her voice—an internal decision already settled. They sat in awkward silence until the front door slammed. Must be Sandy, home from the beach. She'd arrived the day before from Washington, DC.

—

When he stepped into the kitchen, Sandy was standing at the counter, picking meat off leftover chicken. Her long T-shirt covered a pink bikini, a rubber band held her honey-colored hair in a careless ponytail, and sand she hadn't bothered to brush off caked her flip-flops. *As usual.*

"What's wrong?" she asked.

"Nothing. Why?"

"Mom looks upset. What did you say to her?"

"What do you mean, what did I say to her? *I'm* not the one planning to sell this house."

"Oh…that."

Reed stormed past her on his way to the garage. "Yeah, that!"

—

Sandy was eighteen months older than Reed, though two grades ahead in school. With broad, powerful shoulders, she used to swim competitively. She'd been the popular straight-A student other girls admired. Growing up, Reed had depended on his rock-steady sister to keep him out of trouble.

Then came flower power, hippies, psychedelic music, and—overshadowing all of it—the war. Well before their father was shot down, Sandy had swapped her Villager skirts, collared blouses, and Weejuns penny loafers for patched bell-bottoms, halter tops, and sandals. Even worse, she'd jettisoned the Lawsons' conservative politics to veer far left.

From the moment the evening TV news came on, Reed and Sandy would argue.

Unlike previous wars, shown only in sanitized movie newsreels, the Vietnam War was televised. Vivid images of battle spilled into American living rooms. Soldiers stalking through elephant grass and wading through waist-high, leech-infested rivers. The juddering *thump-thump-thump* of helicopter rotors and automatic gunfire. Fiery storms of napalm. And row upon row of body bags stacked for the long flight home.

Week after week, casualty counts rose, and popular support for the war waned as the enemy—Ho Chi Minh's North Vietnamese Army and its Vietcong allies in the South—proved resilient and determined.

The grim tableaus wrenched families from their meat loaf and potatoes, weary fathers from their evening newspapers, bewildered kids from their homework. After Dad disappeared, Reed had become mesmerized by the TV news, obsessively scanning the images, half expecting his father to stumble, miraculously unscathed, from a bamboo thicket.

In April 1967, Sandy marched in the largest-ever antiwar protest in America. More than a hundred thousand demonstrators converged on the Pentagon.

Afterward, brother-and-sister arguments hardened into familiar patterns—battle lines drawn, trenches dug, positions heavily defended.

"All protesters are doing is helping the enemy and hurting Dad," Reed argued.

"Total garbage," Sandy countered. "We're trying to save American lives."

"By waving commie flags? That's treason—giving aid and comfort to the enemy!"

"Dissent is the highest form of patriotism."

"Bullshit! You're quitting on Dad."

"Isn't ending the war the best way to bring him home—if he's even alive?"

"He's alive, all right! And once we kick the shit out of the commies, they'll let him go."

"Don't you get it by now? This war is unwinnable!"

Sandy also opposed the Navy's policy of quiet diplomacy. From the start of the conflict, the government had warned the bereaved wives of MIA/POW husbands to avoid all contact with the media—no statements to the press, no TV interviews. Speaking out, officials claimed, would only endanger their husbands' lives.

At first, Carol had willingly complied. But by the spring of 1969, Frank had been missing for two years, and even Reed could tell his mother had grown tired of enforced silence, tired of isolation from other POW/MIA wives. She joined a new organization, the National League of Families of American Prisoners and Missing in Southeast Asia.

After Nixon became president, the policy of silence changed. To turn world opinion against Hanoi, government officials now encouraged families to speak out on behalf of the POW/MIAs—so long as they continued to support the administration's war policies.

Carol went to meetings, wrote to members of Congress, submitted letters to newspapers. Unlike other more vocal wives, she resisted the limelight by avoiding radio or TV interviews.

Reed approved of his mother's work but scorned his sister's involvement in antiwar groups like the Student Mobilization Committee and Women Strike for Peace.

"You can't ignore the fact that groups like ours are the only ones facilitating communication between Hanoi and POW/MIA families," Sandy insisted.

"All you're doing is sabotaging the government," Reed said.

Carol had agreed with him—the antiwar left was dividing America and strengthening the communists' resolve to avoid negotiating. "Why do people like Jane Fonda believe North Vietnamese propaganda but not a word from our own government?" Mom had asked.

"Easy," Sandy scoffed. "Because the government no longer tells the truth."

"If we can't trust the government, whom can we trust?"

"Mom, how can you possibly be so naive?"

In frustration, Carol would lash out at both of them. "I'm sick and tired of you two at each other's throats. We're a family, and we'll never survive this nightmare unless we support each other."

—

After dinner, Sandy cornered Reed in the garage, where he was working on the family's Ford station wagon.

"She's alone and lonely. You get that, don't you?"

Instead of responding, Reed revved the engine.

"Must you make that noise when I'm trying to have a conversation? It's so rude."

Reed stepped around to the driver's side and shut off the engine. "She has friends and the people she works with, doesn't she?"

"It's not about friends and jobs. It's this house. It's got bad vibes. Mom walks into the bathroom and smells his Old Spice. She opens the closet door and sees his clothes."

"So 'bad vibes' is a reason to sell the place?"

"Don't put words in her mouth—she's just *thinking* about it. Besides, selling the house isn't the point. Living her life is the point. Do you realize how hard it is for her to even *dream* about doing something for herself?"

Sandy stalked off before Reed could reply.

Furious, he tossed the tools aside. They were ganging up on him. Did anybody care about what *he* wanted?

Needing to get the hell away, he drove out of the neighborhood and onto the highway. When he pumped the gas, the soothing growl of the V-8 reminded him of his father and drew him back to the day he'd first driven the car.

—

April 1966. He'd just turned sixteen, had a new driver's license in his wallet, and dreamed about driving Dad's pristine Mustang. After pestering his father for weeks, Frank had relented. If Reed finished all his chores on Saturday—cleaning the garage, mowing and raking the lawn, washing and waxing the station wagon—*then* he'd get to drive the car early Sunday morning.

Reed had been giddy about the prospect, since he was usually granted minimal time with his busy father, especially after Frank had been promoted to commanding officer of his A-4 squadron. When not absorbed in work, Dad would fly off for two weeks at a time on training missions to bases in Nevada, Arizona, and even Puerto Rico.

Carving out time for auto races was a rare exception to Frank's workaholic schedule. Starting when Reed was twelve, they'd drive down to the Sebring Raceway for the annual twelve-hour road race.

Reed loved sleeping in motels along Lake Jackson, swimming in the pool at the end of the day, eating greasy burgers in roadside diners, and basking in the rare warmth of his father's attention. On those precious weekends, a father-son relationship that usually resembled a drill sergeant barking orders gave way to that of two guys just hanging out.

At the racetrack, they reveled in the snarling of highly tuned cars and the oddly sweet smell of racing fuel. The owners of Corvettes,

Mustangs, and Porsches parked in reserved lots called corrals to show off their machines and admire others'.

The last time they'd gone to the races—in March 1966—they'd roamed the Mustang lot. That was when Dad had fallen in love with the Shelby GT350 model and ordered a royal-blue one for himself, which appeared in the driveway two weeks later.

On that Sunday morning in April, after Reed had worked his ass off finishing his chores, Frank banged on his door at five thirty. "Rise and shine. Time to get your butt in gear and blow this pop stand."

Moments later, after hurriedly dressing, Reed eagerly stepped into the garage and ran his palm over the gleaming hood of the Mustang. He slid gently into the black vinyl driver's seat, adjusted the mirrors, fingered the walnut steering wheel, and inhaled the new-car smell. After his father climbed in, Reed cautiously backed out of the driveway.

"Remember, the brakes are heavy. So's the steering," Frank said. "It's a man's car. You need to show it who's boss."

"I know, Dad. I know," Reed replied, irritated by advice he didn't need. He steered the car toward country roads that wound among the creeks, lakes, and meadowlands of northeastern Florida.

Frank slouched in the passenger seat, holding a thermos of coffee and dressed in his weekend uniform: worn polo shirt, faded khaki chinos, and sneakers with no socks.

Not someone who suffered fools lightly, Frank Lawson was usually preoccupied and impatient whenever he wasn't piloting a fighter jet. After working long days, he'd often arrive home from the base irritable and moody but never mention why. He'd wolf down dinner without pleasure—food was fuel—and then grill Reed.

"Did you ace that geometry quiz?" "How fast did you run the mile today?" "Did you remember to pick up plugs and points for the station wagon?"

Most nights after dinner, Dad would retreat to his wood-paneled office. For hours he'd review officer performance reports, scan newspapers, or tackle yet another massive book. He'd graduated with honors from the Naval Academy before earning a master's degree in history and international relations.

Although Dad guarded his privacy, the office wasn't off-limits. Reed would sometimes wander in and scan the crowded shelves: Sun-Tzu's *The Art of War*, Carl von Clausewitz's *On War*, Marcus Aurelius's *Meditations*, Mahan's *The Influence of Sea Power upon History.*

On that April morning, however, Frank relaxed. A glimmer of a smile softened his square jaw. As the Mustang rumbled along, well below the speed limit, he leaned back to inhale the fresh air and admire the sun rising above the oaks and pines.

"Son, it doesn't get any better than this." He pointed to the open road ahead. "Open her up. Let's see what she's got."

Reed mashed the accelerator and was soon racing over the speed limit. United with his dad via their shared lawlessness, Reed grinned. And so did Frank.

He pulled onto English Church Road, named after the hulk of a nineteenth-century church that sat crumbling in a silent grove of ancient oaks. Overhanging branches formed a mile-long tunnel through which sunshine dappled the road.

Frank pointed ahead. "Careful at the end of this straightaway. Too fast and you'll kiss a tree's ass."

Emerging from the tunnel, the road hooked sharply left. A massive live oak guarded the right shoulder, its thick trunk crowding the pavement. Going too fast, Reed slammed on the brakes, churning rocks, skidding within inches of the tree.

"What did I tell you?" Frank's familiar scolding tarnished the morning's magic.

—

After his father was shot down a year later, Reed kept the Mustang tuned and drove it a few miles each week. Otherwise, it sat in the garage awaiting its owner's return. That changed one Saturday evening in the spring of 1969.

Reed was washing the car in the driveway while his mother watched from the front porch, sipping her favorite orange blossom cocktail. She walked over and surprised him by suggesting he consider it his.

"I don't need the car. Besides, I can't even put the darn thing in gear."

Instead of responding, Reed ran a towel over the hood.

"He would want you to use it," Carol insisted, hinting at resignation.

"It's *his*, not mine. I'll take care of it, so *when* he comes back, it'll be in perfect shape." He waited, daring her to argue.

For a moment she looked like she might, then her face fell and she irritably brushed hair from her face before walking away.

—

On Friday of spring break week, Carol watched him toss his laundry bag into the Mustang. "It's been great having you home for a week."

Actually, he'd been kind of bored. The three of them had gone to the beach twice. They'd seen *Butch Cassidy and the Sundance Kid* and agreed it was great. Reed had surfed with a fellow Navy brat at Daytona Beach and struggled to decipher his assigned Political Philosophy reading from Locke's *Second Treatise of Government.*

"Yeah, it's been fine."

"And I hope you're not still mad at me for thinking about selling the house."

Reed lied. "No."

Despite her disbelief, she sighed and drew him into a hug. "Love you."

Stiffening at her touch, he mumbled, "Me too," before pulling away, but not before noticing a flicker of dejection.

Driving off, Reed realized he'd hurt her feelings. But what about *his* feelings? Paying scant attention to the road, he ruminated about the week. Face it—his mother and sister had given up on Dad, which meant his faith couldn't waver. To lose hope would be the ultimate betrayal.

CHAPTER EIGHT

Even during spring break, Lifelines operated twenty-four seven. Reed was scheduled to shadow Meg Howard, who welcomed him that night with an ever-ready smile. She'd gathered her auburn hair up into a ponytail held in place by a green ribbon.

"Busy?" he asked, pulling up a chair in the hotline room.

"Nothing too heavy. A girl lost her prescription for Valium. The pharmacy was closed, and she wanted more."

"What'd you tell her?"

"Life is hard." Noticing his quizzical expression, she chuckled. "Just joking. I wanted to know why she needed the Valium in the first place. Turns out she's anxious all the time. Afraid to go to class, wakes up nauseous every morning. The Valium's been helping her take the edge off. I'm guessing it's because she's from a small town—only three hundred kids in her high school. Like a lot of freshmen, she feels lost in a college this big. Last year, I did too."

"Guess I was lucky," Reed said. "My high school had three thousand kids."

He shadowed her for several hours, listening silently to her calls from the phone on the other desk. Besides recording information in the call log, she made detailed notes—what the callers discussed, her responses, what she'd learned. When not on a call or talking to him, she studied her psych textbook.

One guy called about his roommate, who'd ingested both Stelazine (an antipsychotic) and Thorazine (a mood stabilizer) at the same time. "Is he going to be okay?" the guy said.

Meg wasted little time explaining the dangers of the situation and convinced the caller to drive his roommate to the hospital right away.

But to Reed's surprise, most conversations weren't about drugs. Callers complained of relationship problems—with parents, friends, roommates. Or about getting used to college—eager to escape parental control but scared to be on their own.

Others were simply lonely and craved a sympathetic voice. One girl—who refused to give her name—offered only a whispered "Hello." Wouldn't answer questions, yet didn't hang up. Meg sat waiting silently for ten minutes, twice assuring her, "When you're ready, we're here to listen."

Eventually, the girl whispered, "Okay, thanks," and hung up.

Meg explained that she'd called Lifelines several times before, saying nothing after "Hello." So tonight, "Okay, thanks" represented progress.

"The hardest part of the job is getting off the phone, saying goodbye to a client, and not knowing what might happen afterward. Some things you'll hear are really eye-opening. In the past two months I've been here, I've learned what an incredibly sheltered, suburban life I've lived."

Later, a volunteer named Hunter walked in carrying a small square of aluminum foil he'd found outside the garage. It contained what appeared to be dried car oil and a primitive pipe, also made of foil.

"Look at this shit," Hunter said. "Freaking black tar heroin."

"You see any drug dealers around?" Meg asked. "Like that guy Eric?"

"No, but I'll keep an eye out."

"Thanks." Meg turned to Reed. "Eric's a speed freak and heroin addict. We've been trying for weeks to get him to come in so we can refer him to this new methadone clinic downtown." When she described Eric, Reed recognized him as the guy who'd been leaning against his Mustang the day Reed had signed up to volunteer.

Reed had assumed junkies were all filthy, emaciated losers shooting up in big-city alleys, not wasted kids hanging around an idyllic college campus. He felt vaguely bad about telling Eric to get lost.

Meg explained that drug dealers—whether students, townies, or street people—hung around the Lifelines neighborhood looking for business.

"But if the police discover drug use or dealing anywhere near us, we'll get shut down right away. As it is, some neighbors already aren't happy we're here."

—

Even on weekends, Reed was typically in bed by eleven and up at six—no alarm needed. So he was already yawning on Saturday night when he arrived for his first ten-to-four shift.

Waiting for his first call, he flipped through the thick call log on the desk. Next to it lay a copy of the PDR—the *Physicians' Desk Reference*—a thick volume of detailed information on thousands of drugs. He scanned a list of referral phone numbers, fact sheets ("Most Commonly Abused Drugs"), and reminders ("Suicide Risk Warning Signs") tacked on the corkboard facing him.

Jordan sat at the other desk, reading a sociology textbook. She wore a rust-colored University of Texas T-shirt, its sleeves hacked off to reveal firm biceps. Reed imagined stepping into the ring with her and sparring.

Like the shivering-cold showers he'd endured as a kid at camp, his first few calls at Lifelines forced him awake. It was one thing to read the manual or shadow Meg but entirely another to answer the phone and somehow know what to say.

His first caller yelled over Jimi Hendrix's "Purple Haze" in the background to describe a pill someone had given her. "It's supposed to be meth, I think."

"What does it look like?"

"It's orange and says *33* on it. My boyfriend said two could help me pull an all-nighter."

Reed flipped frantically through the PDR. "Orange, labeled 33. Just a minute. Hold on for a second."

Jordan's finger pointed to the fact sheet of commonly abused drugs tacked on the corkboard, complete with pictures of the pills and their street names (goofers, downers, red devils, yellow jackets, bennies, dexies). "It's Obetrol—speed," she hissed. "Two twenty-milligrams are way too much. Keep her talking."

Keep her talking? How? About what? To the caller, Reed replied, "It's called Obetrol. You...you probably shouldn't take that much, though."

"Okay, thanks." The girl hung up.

Shit.

Jordan shook her head. "Telling people what they should or shouldn't do isn't going to work."

His next caller got right to the point. "Some asshole dumped twenty-five tabs of acid in the milk, didn't tell us. We poured it over our Frosted Flakes."

"What the fuck!" Reed blurted out.

"No shit, man. What should we do?"

Reed urged the caller to stay on the line and turned to Jordan. "Sorry, can you talk to this guy?"

Noticing her disapproving frown, he felt humiliated. Jordan punched the lit button and lifted her receiver. She advised the caller to stay with everyone who'd ingested the acid and keep them safe and comfortable.

"Thanks," Reed mumbled after Jordan hung up, grateful yet mortified.

"Once you accept the fact there are more irresponsible fools out there than you can shake a stick at, you won't be surprised by anything you hear."

After a precious ten-minute break, his next caller was a woman who sounded much older than a college student.

"It's my boyfriend," she complained. "Since he got back from Nam, he just sits around drinking. Punched a hole in the wall and screamed all kinds of crap. Then went and locked hisself in the garage. I just...I just don't know what all to do."

Reed's mind went blank, his stomach churned, his right knee bobbed furiously.

"Yes, ma'am. I'm sorry, can you hold on a minute? Someone will be right with you." He shot Jordan a pleading look, and she took over.

"Thanks for calling," Jordan said. "I understand how frightening this must feel. Can I ask you—does your boyfriend have any weapons in the garage? Okay, a shotgun. Has he ever talked about hurting you before?"

Reed listened on Jordan's line for a few minutes, then hurried to the bathroom. Olivia passed him in the hall and nodded. Still curt, dismissive.

Heart hammering, he leaned over the sink. What the heck had he gotten himself into? Only three calls in and he was ready to quit. Maybe he could beg Captain Harwood for another assignment. After taking several deep breaths, he washed his hands and returned to the hotline room, steeling himself for more excruciating displays of incompetence.

Although he did slightly better during the next hour, his gut seized with anxiety every time the phone jangled. Fear of the unknown, the unexpected. Dread he'd say the wrong thing, fail the callers, disappoint Jordan, humiliate himself.

—

At one in the morning, Olivia took over his line, and Reed stepped into the kitchen. Empty pizza boxes lay piled on a filthy black-and-white linoleum floor next to an overflowing garbage can. Dishes caked with dried food filled the sink. Stained coffee mugs cluttered the counter.

He scrubbed a mug, filled it with fresh coffee, and headed outside. The guy with the ponytail sat on the porch strumming a guitar, singing James Taylor's "Fire and Rain" off-key.

Reed scanned the front page of a newspaper tossed on the metal folding chair. This week forty American B-52s had pounded North Vietnamese supply lines in eastern Laos, dropping one thousand tons of bombs. The goal had been to halt the supplies Hanoi was sending down the Ho Chi Minh Trail for North Vietnamese and Vietcong troops fighting in neighboring South Vietnam.

Made perfect sense, no matter what the whining left-wingers said about it.

Moments later, the screen door banged open. Jordan burst outside, a small doctor's satchel in hand.

"Rot-cee! C'mon!" she yelled, racing to her VW Beetle.

Reed followed. "Wh-where we going?"

Without answering, Jordan repeatedly cranked the Beetle's engine, to no avail. "Fuck!" She jumped out and jogged to Reed's Mustang. "Gimme your keys! Hurry!"

"Hold on, hold on, I'll drive," he said, reaching for his keys.

Jordan ripped them out of his hand. "We don't have time!" She jumped into the driver's seat. Reed barely fell into the passenger side before Jordan jammed in the clutch. Muscled the shifter into first. Revved too high. Released the clutch too fast, the engine promptly stalling.

"Shit!"

Reed cringed. "We're wasting time! Lemme drive!"

Defiant, she restarted the engine, managed to shove the gear shifter into first, and rumbled onto Broad Street, then braked to a rough stop at a red light.

Jordan glanced left, then right. "Fuck it." She mashed the accelerator and roared through the intersection.

Horns blared, traffic skidded, and Reed envisioned a horrific collision. "What the hell?"

As Jordan raced through downtown, weaving in and out of traffic, grinding the gears—his father's precious machine getting horribly mangled in the process—Reed's foot slammed against an imaginary brake pedal.

"Are you going to tell me where we're going?" he ventured.

"When we get outa town."

By the time downtown traffic had given way to open country, Jordan had better command of the car. Reed relaxed a bit and watched her drive, no longer panicked Dad would return home to a crumpled wreck. He glanced at her powerful thighs working the heavy brake and clutch pedals. Her fingers on the walnut steering wheel were strong, nails trimmed, no polish. Like she worked at some kind of manual labor.

"Nice car," she said, with a hint of disdain. "*Daddy* buy it for you?"

Reed stared into at a pool of light spilling from an Esso station, considered telling her to fuck off, then replied with a flat, "No."

Jordan glanced at him curiously, waiting for more. When it wasn't forthcoming, she explained what they were doing.

"A kid just called, worried because a girl had passed out at a party. Could be nothing, could be an overdose. If he calls the cops or an ambulance, everybody might get busted. So he called us instead. We've done this a few times—we check vitals, respiration, but we can't and won't play doctor."

The highway narrowed. They passed flat farmland and dark stands of southern pine. Jordan slowed to peer into the darkness. "It's here, somewhere."

Up ahead, a dirt road loomed. Damn. Reed recognized where they were and instinctively chose not to tell her.

"This is it." Jordan swerved off the pavement and onto rough gravel, scarcely slowing. He winced as pebbles rattled against the finish he'd waxed to perfection. "They call this dump the Pig Farm. Except the only thing they grow is pot."

The car skidded to a halt in the front yard. Jordan leaped out, and Reed raced to keep up. By the time he'd burst into the living room, she was taking the stairs two at a time. Reed caught up as Jordan dashed into a bedroom—the one he knew would be bare except for mattresses on the floor…and one in the closet.

Beneath the dim light of a bare bulb lay an unconscious girl sprawled across a mattress.

The flower child from the party two weeks ago.

The girl who yearned to become stardust when she died.

Summer.

CHAPTER NINE

Summer's eyes were shut—from either sleep or lack of consciousness—and her mouth hung open. What looked like dried vomit stained the sheet. She wore only panties and a leather headband. Her skin was colorless in the moonlight, drained of blood, made starker by fingernails and toenails painted black. Jeans and a work shirt stenciled with the word *Kastle* had been tossed aside.

All this Reed registered in a few seconds of paralyzing fear.

Jordan knelt and pressed her fingers against Summer's wrist. A kid from downstairs hovered in the doorway behind them.

"What'd she take?" Jordan demanded.

"Dunno. Ludes, prob'ly."

"How many!"

"Three or four, I think."

"Shit! What else?"

"Tequila. We were doing shots."

Jordan motioned to Reed. "No time to call anybody. Let's get her outa here. Hurry!"

Relieved to have something to do, Reed wrapped Summer in a blanket and cradled her in his arms. Jordan grabbed her clothes.

Reed carried Summer carefully downstairs and out to the Mustang. She reeked of alcohol, vomit, and the same coconut oil shampoo he remembered from the party.

When Reed laid her into the cramped back seat, she moaned once or twice, eyelids fluttering but never quite opening. Reed jumped into the driver's seat while Jordan squeezed in back. He roared back up the dirt road in a cloud of dust.

"... six...seven...eight..." Jordan counted from the back seat, hovering over Summer. "Shit, she's hardly breathing! Speed up!"

Hands shaking, imagining Summer dying, Reed stomped on the accelerator. He'd never seen a dead body except when Grandpa Jack died of a sudden heart attack the year Reed turned eleven. He'd found the old man sprawled unconscious in the brown La-Z-Boy chair, thinking at first Grandpa was just napping. And because Grandpa smelled of his usual mix of Old Spice and cigar smoke, Reed had refused to believe he was dead.

In the back seat, Jordan compressed Summer's chest, pinched her nostrils, forced air into her mouth. Reed ran three red lights on the way to the hospital, amazed that no police appeared to chase him.

—

Ninety minutes later, in the emergency waiting room, Reed and Jordan listened to the doctor talk to Summer's mother, Louise. Her husband stood beside her.

Except her name wasn't Summer, it was Annabel Taylor, and she was lucky to be alive. As a precaution, the doctor had placed her under an oxygen tent.

The doctor glanced at his watch impatiently. "Well, if you don't have other questions, I've got patients waiting."

Louise was about the same age as Reed's mother, but more worry lines creased her forehead and framed her eyes, emerald like her daughter's. She wore a housedress of the sort Reed's mother would never wear in public. Tangled brown hair fell to her shoulders.

Bewildered, Louise turned to Jordan. "What on earth was she doing at that horrible place? My God, she turns sixteen next week!"

Reed flinched, sensing Annabel's father eyeing him suspiciously. He looked rangy and tough in jeans and scuffed work boots. His blue work shirt was embroidered with *Decker Motors* in yellow above the pocket and *Ross* stenciled below.

"Ma'am, we don't know," Jordan replied. "I'm so sorry." She handed Louise a business card. "Here's our phone number. Please call anytime. We can refer you to a doctor or psychiatrist."

Louise nodded and took the card. "Thank you."

Her husband grasped her arm. "Don't need no goddamn shrink. Come on, let's siddown. Got a long night ahead."

—

Jordan and Reed stepped into the fresh night air. Thinking about the Quaaludes Annabel had ingested, he remembered his mother had used the same drug for insomnia, especially during that awful first year after Dad went missing. Reed had also struggled to sleep, but he'd coped by chasing his mother's Jim Beam with several beers.

"What's with the Quaaludes she took? They're sleeping pills, aren't they?"

"Yeah, and we've been getting more calls about them lately," Jordan said. "Sopors, vitamin Qs—kids are getting pretty buzzed on them. But they're depressants, and mixing them with alcohol is nuts. If you ask me, ludes are a garbage drug."

Jordan explained that combining Quaaludes and alcohol could cause memory blackouts and respiratory arrest. Annabel's breathing had dropped to only eight breaths per minute.

As they drifted past a long row of parked cars in the hospital's lot, his mind jumped back to the Pig Farm party. Besides the hash brownies and spiked punch, had Annabel also popped Quaaludes?

Reed halted. Maybe he should tell Jordan about that night.

"What's wrong?" she asked.

Where the heck had he parked? Scanning the lot, he spotted the Mustang in the next row. "I've been to that farm before. At a party two weeks ago."

"Funny, I wouldn't have figured it was your scene." She halted. "Wait. Do you know that girl Annabel?"

"No. But I'm trying to remember whether I saw her there."

Her eyes bored into his, puzzled. "Well, we've gotten a lot of calls from that dump. It's a drug bust waiting to happen."

As Reed pulled onto the street, Jordan asked, "By the way, did you get a look at her wrists?"

"No, what about them?"

"Scars. Like from a razor. Healed now. But not too long ago, she may have tried to kill herself."

At a traffic signal, Reed stared at a spinning barbershop pole across the street. His stomach felt queasy, like he'd swallowed sour milk. Had he noticed any scars on Annabel's wrists the night of the party? The light turned green. He sat frozen.

"What's the matter?"

An impatient driver behind him honked. "Nothing."

Back at Lifelines, engine idling, Reed asked, "How often does this kind of thing happen?"

"This *kind* of thing? What do you mean?"

What had he said now? "I'm talking about overdoses. Emergencies, like tonight."

Her eyes flashed instant judgment. "You think you're above all this, don't you?"

"What are you talking about?"

"Because some volunteers are into ego trips, not actually helping people."

"Well, that's not me."

"I hope not, because you can always quit and go back to marching around the drill field in your spiffy uniform."

"I'm no quitter."

Wary, unsure what to make of him, she shoved stray hair behind her ear. "We've only had two emergencies like that. There was this guy last month over at Pineview Apartments. Dead as a doornail when we got there."

Reed shuddered. "Jeez. Guess I got a lot to learn."

Jordan opened the car door. "I reckon you do."

As she walked away, he replayed the night. The frantic race to the hospital, running red lights. His terror that Summer—Annabel—might be dead. Nurses wheeling the gurney down a hallway lit by flickering fluorescent lights.

Returning to the Pig Farm had awakened buried memories from that night in the psychedelic closet. Stars reeling in the glow of a black light. Annabel peeling her clothes off. Straddling him, the dark nipples of her pert breasts stiffening as she guided him inside—her breathing growing ragged, her silken hair draping his face like a tent…

Reed slammed his forehead against the steering wheel.

Lawson, you dumbass shithead.

PART TWO: COURAGE

CHAPTER TEN

Reed drifted off to sleep at five in the morning, awakened only by Adam's chanting at noon.

"Om…shanti…om…shanti, shanti."

Adam sat on the floor, meditating, wrists resting on crossed knees, fingers curled with thumbs and forefingers touching, eyes closed.

He'd explained that *om* referred to the "cosmic intelligent vibration" and *shanti* was Sanskrit for "peace" but also translated to "calm" or "bliss." "This cosmic vibration even created the universe," Adam had claimed. "The vibration exists everywhere around and inside us. Chanting gets you closer to oneness with it."

Adam opened his eyes, placed his palms together, and murmured, "Namaste. What's wrong? You never sleep this late."

Reed rubbed his eyes. "Christ, I need caffeine…big-time."

"How was your shift?"

"Intense."

Adam waited for more.

"I wouldn't even know where to start."

—

Webb slid weights onto the gym's squat rack and joked, "Fifty-six in-and-outs before I came."

As usual, he'd been bragging about his latest sexual conquest. At the start of each semester, Webb would set a goal—sex with fifteen different girls, an average of one new conquest each week. Still preoccupied with Annabel, Reed wasn't in the mood to listen to Webb's boasting and just wanted to get the workout over.

"What's wrong with you, man?" Webb said. "You on the rag or something?"

"No, I must have missed my period this month. Hey listen, ever heard of a place called the Pig Farm?"

Webb leaned against the rack. "Yeah. Been there to score a lid or two. A lot of horny hippie chicks hang out there."

"Yeah, and some of them are high school kids," Reed muttered.

"Really? I didn't know that," Webb said, poker-faced.

Sure he was lying, Reed stepped up to the rack. "Forget it. Let's just squat."

—

Before dinner, Reed washed the Mustang behind the dorm. The filth coating the car sparked another recurring daydream…

After three years in limbo, the Lawsons discover Frank is alive.

A POW in a North Vietnamese prison.

Heroically, Frank survives and is released.

A C-141 plane ferries Frank and fellow POWs home.

It settles onto a sunny tarmac.

Wan and gaunt but still commanding in uniform, Frank gingerly steps off the plane.

Carol, Reed, and Sandy wait—scrubbed clean, dressed as if for church.

After tear-filled hugs and kisses, Reed directs his father to the pristine Mustang.

For once, Frank is duly impressed: "Proud of you, son. Good as new…"

Hardly. Dismayed, Reed examined the gravel nicks marring the car's finish. Repairing it would take hours of sanding and touch-up painting. Leaning into the back seat to wipe off dirt left by Jordan's sandals, he spotted something shoved beneath the passenger seat.

Annabel's Kastle work shirt.

He fished it out and tossed it in a nearby trash can. The burger joint could issue her a new one. Forget about it.

—

Back in his room, though, he couldn't focus on homework. An unwelcome stew of images and emotions boiled up: How featherlight Annabel's body had felt as they rushed away from the Pig Farm. The heels of Jordan's sandals stabbing the back of the driver's seat as she labored to revive the semiconscious girl. The mother's disbelief and shock at the hospital. The father's hostility.

But what did her problems have to do with him? Cutting her wrists was nuts. Her mom should take her to a shrink. But what about their night together? Wasn't he responsible for that? Sure, he'd been high on hash and alcohol. But...screwing a fifteen-year-old?

Dishonorable. Conduct unbecoming an officer and a gentleman.

No excuses. Guilty as charged.

Then again, she'd claimed to be in college and looked plenty old enough. Guys like Webb couldn't care less whether girls were underage. Even if he'd screwed up, though, why get involved now? What would be the point?

For the next hour, Reed ordered his brain to concentrate on quantum mechanics, but it wouldn't obey.

He gave up and walked outside to the trash bin. Shoving greasy pizza boxes aside, he grabbed Annabel's work shirt, brushed off bits of crust, and folded it.

—

There was a Kastle restaurant near campus, famous for small burgers known as sliders. Reed typically ate five per meal.

While waiting for the manager, he scanned the packed dining room. This Kastle, which stayed open late, attracted a varied crowd. Noisy frat guys in Greek jerseys. Quiet stoners satisfying munchies attacks. Janitors—mostly Black people—coming off their shifts at the university. Bikers in sleeveless denim jackets with patches on the back that read *Outlaws Florida*. Everyone kept to themselves, eating in uneasy coexistence.

"Nobody named Annabel works here," the manager told Reed.

Same with the second Kastle next to the interstate.

At the third one, a few blocks from downtown, the manager nodded and scowled. "She's been out sick or something. If she figures to keep this job, she'd better get her butt over here on Tuesday."

—

Tuesday morning after ROTC drill, Reed dove into the frosty water of the pool, which had recently opened for the spring. Still feeling guilty about Annabel, he rehearsed what he might say: *Just checking on you. Hope you're okay. Please call Lifelines. People there can help.*

It all sounded so damn trite. Reed contemplated scrapping the idea. She'd probably think he was some kind of pervert.

After forty laps, he climbed out of the water and passed a deeply tanned girl in a pink bikini lying on the deck. Although a human anatomy textbook shielded her face from the sun, Reed still recognized Candy—his Crescent Beach lay. He hurried away before she noticed him and asked why he hadn't called lately.

—

Arriving before closing time, he parked facing the Kastle employee exit. Five minutes after ten, the door flew open and Annabel burst outside, lugging a school bag. Her black hair was drawn into a ponytail, and a long-sleeved T-shirt peeked out from beneath her baggy work shirt. She looked like a sullen, harried teenager, not the carefree flower child he'd met at the Pig Farm.

Reed stepped into her path. "Excuse me."

Annabel shot him a blank look. "Huh?"

"I'm Reed. Remember?" He handed over the Kastle shirt. "This is yours."

"Wait a minute...where'd you find this?"

"Are you sure you don't remember? Two weeks ago? The Pig Farm?"

"No, but thanks." She grabbed her shirt and rushed toward the nearby bus stop. "The assholes were about to dock my pay."

Reed caught up. "Hold on. Don't you remember us taking you to the hospital?"

She frowned. "I remember waking up and Mom freaking out."

"What about the party? Talking about stardust on the dock? The closet you showed me. You know..."

She studied him as if he were a stranger. "Guess I blacked out. Must have been a bad trip."

Great. All this angst to end up a figment of a teenager's hallucination. "Just wanted to make sure you were all right."

"I'm fine." She edged away. "So, listen, I'm gonna, like, miss the bus."

"Hold on, it's pretty late. How about I give you a ride?"

Misinterpreting his intention, Annabel's expression turned sly—Summer's knowing assurance resurfacing. She eyed his blue button-down oxford shirt and gleaming car. "Well...okay, why not? The late bus smells like puke anyway."

After riding in silence for a few minutes, Reed glanced at her. "You realize those Quaaludes are bad news, don't you? You could have died."

"Can't sleep without 'em."

"And it's worse when you mix them with alcohol."

"Thanks, *Dad.*" She smirked.

"You're welcome."

She removed a crumpled pack of Camels from her backpack. "Mind if I smoke?"

Yes, he very much *did* mind. Once smoke seeped into the upholstery, you could never get it out, no matter how many of those tacky perfumed trees you hung from the rearview.

"If you have to," he muttered.

"Want one?"

"Cancer sticks? No way."

She fished out a Zippo lighter. "You're smart. I should've never started."

He rolled his window down to clear the smoke. "Why did you lie about being in college? Or even your real name?"

"Because high school sucks. And Annabel's a stupid name. My dad got it from a freaking poem."

"'Annabel Lee'?" Seeing her surprised look, he added, "My mom read it to me when I was a kid."

Leaning back, she closed her eyes and recited, "*For the moon never beams, without bringing me dreams / Of the beautiful Annabel Lee; / And the stars never rise, but I feel the bright eyes / Of the beautiful Annabel Lee.*"

Reed continued, "*And so, all the night-tide, I lie down by the side / Of my darling—my darling—my life and my bride, / In her sepulcher there by the sea— / In her tomb by the sounding sea.*"

Annabel exhaled smoke. "To tell you the truth, Poe really creeps me out." Peering into the mirror, she rubbed her forehead. "Jeezus, the stupid grease from the fry machine. It's like you can never wash it off."

She directed Reed into a neighborhood where he'd never been—older working-class homes. "It's the one on the corner. Don't laugh. Mom's crazy about pink."

It was hard not to. Well maintained compared to its shabby neighbors, the one-story stucco ranch was painted a vomit-inducing shade of bubblegum pink. In the yard, three matching pink flamingos stood guard. Their black eyes appeared somehow menacing in the glow of the Mustang's headlights.

"Great. Asshole's out getting loaded again."

"Your dad?"

"Fuck no! Mom's loser boyfriend, Ross."

As Reed climbed out, a dusty white Ford pickup rumbled into the driveway. Two double-barreled shotguns in racks, an *America—Love It or Leave It* bumper sticker.

Ross, the man Reed had assumed was Annabel's father, jumped out. Beneath his scowl, his jaws punished a thick wad of gum. When Ross came closer, Reed smelled Beemans. It was his father's favorite, mainly because famous test pilot Chuck Yeager had chewed that brand for good luck.

Reed extended his hand. "Reed Lawson, sir. From the hospital."

Ross ignored him and glared at Annabel. "What the hell's going on here?"

"Nothing. He gave me a ride, that's all."

"Since when do college kids give you rides?"

"Since when's it your business?"

"I came by at nine to pick you up," he said.

"You know I got late cleanup on Tuesdays."

"Which is why you're supposed to call me."

"Yeah, sure. At which bar?"

She turned toward the front door as Reed looked off, embarrassed. Back talk like that would have earned him a dozen lashes from the heavy leather belt his father wore. When he was about twelve, he'd first talked back to his mother. Moments later he was leaning over the dining room table, pants lowered to his ankles, flinching in pain as Frank punctuated each stroke with a grunt and the fragment of a reprimand. "You'd better...not talk back...to your mother again...understand? *(Yes!)* Yes, what? *(Yes, sir!)*."

Afterward, Reed couldn't sit in a chair for a week, but the physical pain never hurt as much as the humiliation.

The pink front door banged open, and Louise appeared. Wearing a businesslike skirt, cream-colored blouse, and makeup, she looked younger than Reed remembered from the emergency room. But the worry lines carved on her face remained.

"Honey, is everything okay?"

"Yeah, Mom. This is Reed. From the hospital, remember?"

Louise's smile was tense, distracted. "Of course. Thank you again for all your help."

"Yes, ma'am."

Smile vanishing, Louise glared at Annabel. "As for you, we need to talk. Now!"

Annabel rolled her eyes. Before stepping inside, she turned to flash Reed a flirtatious smile and waved. "Thanks again for the ride...Reed."

Aware he'd gotten her in trouble, he was eager to leave. But damn it, Ross was stalking the Mustang.

"So," Ross said, his anger morphing into curiosity, "you got the high-riser manifold and four-barrel Holley carbs in this thing?"

Reed relaxed, easing his hands—which had been primed to either salute or punch—into his pockets. "Yup. Pumps out three hundred and six horses."

"Sweet. Daddy buy you this sucker?" he sneered.

Here we go again. "No. I worked construction to keep it running for my dad."

"That a fact?" Ross inspected Reed's sturdy build. "Well, sure enough, that's hot work around these parts. So who tunes this bad boy for ya?"

"Usually I do, but last time I took it over to this place, Revolution Repairs—"

"Commie hippies! They know jack shit about fixing cars. A bunch of damn spoiled rich kids stealin' money from folks tryin' to make an honest living!"

Reed knew that some college kids ran Revolution Repairs as a co-op. Their rates were low, and for lower-income customers, they offered free service.

"Forget them know-nothings. If you want this thing to run right, haul it down to my shop. On Main, two blocks south of downtown."

"Okay, I will. Thanks."

Ross cocked his head toward the house, anger creeping back into his voice. "As for Annabel, you can go and stay gone. We're *done* here. You get what I'm saying?"

"Yes, sir."

—

Reed wasted no time driving away. Distracted, he couldn't remember the route back to campus and meandered into the Black part of town. Despite the civil rights advances of the past decade, the city remained strictly segregated. In the white neighborhoods on the western side, planning and zoning had created subdivisions with pretentious-sounding names like Windy Hills, The Briarwood, and Sabal Palm Estates.

Here on the east side, though, he saw only poverty and neglect.

Wood-framed homes with sagging porches and roofs laden with moss. A cheap diner named Soul Shack, garishly painted yellow and purple. A used-car lot cluttered with junk heaps—*Cheap Wheels. No Credit Needed.*

Reed had always felt comfortable enough around Black people, although he'd never had a Black friend or acquaintance. But at a traffic signal, idling next to a packed bar, he felt uneasy. "I Can't Get Next to You" by the Temptations spilled from the bar's open front door. Black bikers leaned against chopped Harley-Davidsons, bare-chested beneath sleeveless denim jackets, wearing dark sunglasses even at night. As Reed waited for the green light, several eyed him with hints of suspicion, even menace. He raised a hand in greeting, which was ignored.

More by accident than intention, he found Broad Street and headed back to campus.

He'd given Annabel her Kastle shirt back. Warned her about the dangers of Quaaludes. Told her about Lifelines. She seemed okay. Her family drama wasn't his problem. Nothing more he could do.

CHAPTER ELEVEN

Carrying coffee and a newspaper, Reed emerged from the 7-Eleven early Wednesday morning. He spread the paper on the Mustang's hood and read an article about three hundred antiwar protesters in Cincinnati who'd removed a large American flag from an official building and replaced it with a Vietcong flag. *Commie sympathizers.* Meanwhile, at the University of Colorado, some assholes had lit gasoline and ripped apart the ROTC office.

A third story questioned U.S. involvement in Laos. It reported that nearly four hundred U.S. planes and one hundred U.S. airmen had been shot down in Laos over the past year. Critics pointed to the recent B-52 bombings and claimed the U.S. was secretly escalating the war. Nixon countered that he had no plans to send in combat forces and instead intended to bring seventy thousand more American troops home soon.

Reed's pulse quickened when he came across an article about POWs. The North Vietnamese had submitted a list of fourteen additional American POWs to the Swedish government. This was the first time the communists had released the names of captured American pilots through a neutral government—and the first official confirmation that these pilots were alive.

The previous December, an antiwar group had returned from Hanoi with a list of what they claimed were American pilots who were "Known Dead." Because it wasn't an official document, the deaths could neither be confirmed nor denied by the U.S. government. The Lawsons hadn't known whom or what to believe.

Reed skipped to the end of the article, his stomach hollow, hands trembling, coffee dripping onto the newsprint. The fourteen names did not include Commander Frank Lawson. But if fourteen pilots could turn up out of the blue, so could Dad.

New hope fueled a five-mile run in thirty minutes, 21 pull-ups, and 120 sit-ups.

—

Hours before his Lifelines shift, he headed to his favorite outdoor study spot, Burnham Pond. About a hundred feet wide, it was ringed with benches and picnic tables set beneath the shade of live oaks and a massive magnolia. Guys got tossed in on party nights or when they pledged fraternities, even though swimming was prohibited. On rainy days, kids in bathing suits slid down the slippery grass into the water.

For three years Reed's life had run on a single, focused track. Like a photograph with a shallow depth of field, the mystery surrounding his father had dominated the foreground, while all other relationships had receded into the distant background.

Until now.

Since the night they'd rescued Annabel, his thoughts had continuously drifted to Jordan. So unlike demure, ladylike Susan or pliable, willing Candy. For the first time, a girl to whom Reed was drawn was utterly unimpressed with him. Although patient and sympathetic with everyone else, she was distant, curt, and judgmental toward him. If only he could get her away from Lifelines for a cup of coffee and real conversation.

Last night at dinner, Adam had asked him, "Any progress with that Jordan girl?"

He'd glanced outside at a tennis ball rolling across the brightly lit court. "It's like she's always testing me, and I'm not measuring up."

"Is she really worth the hassle?"

"Yeah...but I can't explain why. She's just so different from any girl I've ever met."

"Maybe if she knew about your father," Adam had suggested, "she'd cut you some slack."

"No, thanks," he'd said. "I don't need anybody feeling sorry for me."

Reed sat at one of the picnic tables overlooking the pond. Possibly, he could impress Jordan by following one of his father's favorite dictums: "When all else fails, try hard work."

He opened the Lifelines manual and poured through it, page by page. Dosage amounts, chemical compositions, side effects, and overdose symptoms of commonly abused drugs—legal and illegal. Life-threatening signs of overdoses and what to do until medical help arrived.

There was also guidance for talking to suicidal callers. Avoid useless platitudes ("You have so much to live for." "Things can't be all that bad."). Focus on specific risks ("You say you've taken some pills. What kind and how many?" "You have a gun. Is it loaded?"). Suggest concrete actions ("I'd like for you to put the gun down." "Will you flush the pills down the toilet right now?"). Get commitment and encourage follow-up ("If at any time in the next twenty-four hours you feel like hurting yourself, would you call us right away?").

Jeezus, he'd actually have to talk to people like that? He tried to recall the scars Jordan had seen on Annabel's wrists and guessed she'd worn that long-sleeved T-shirt to hide them.

He took notes and highlighted critical information as if the volunteer duty was just another exercise in rote memorization.

—

Jordan didn't bother to say hi when Reed arrived at Lifelines that night.

"Take line two. It's busy for a Wednesday."

A guy called with a question about some mushrooms he and his buddies had picked in a cow pasture. Were they psilocybin?

Reading from a fact sheet, Reed described *Psilocybe cubensis*—usually white and slender with a pale-brown center on its cap. Underneath the cap was a black band.

"But if you guess wrong, you could get poisoned. If you can bring them in, we can identify them."

He talked to a guy who took uppers (Dexedrine) to wake up for early classes and downers (Quaalude) to sleep. But sometimes the uppers kept him up too long and the downers made him sleep late. Would other drugs work better?

Reed told the guy that Lifelines didn't make medical recommendations and asked him a few questions. Where was he from? What was his major?

"This is bullshit," the guy grumbled and hung up.

"Okay..." Reed muttered.

As the shift wore on, he fumbled all but the most straightforward calls. Jordan's eyes drifted toward him often—judging, measuring. Kind of like his father, always on his case, willing him to be tougher, hit harder, get smarter, run faster. Why was she singling him out for special treatment? Sure, he was the "ROTC warmonger." But Meg had listened in on his calls for an hour and said he was doing fine.

After midnight, a frantic mother of a teenage girl called. Before she gave her name as Shirley, Reed feared she might be Louise Taylor, calling about Annabel.

"She won't talk to me, her brother, or anybody," Shirley complained. She had the hoarse voice of a heavy smoker. "Just saying lots of crazy shit. I think she's on that acid stuff, but I ain't at all sure."

Reed wished Jordan were there to listen in and maybe take over, but she was in the quiet room, talking someone down.

"Ma'am, you sound very scared. Can I ask, what's your daughter's name, and how old is she?"

"Angie. Just turned fifteen."

"Thank you. Are you with Angie now?"

"Locked me out of her room, then turned that awful music up so damn loud."

"Ma'am, do you know if Angie is acting violent in any way?"

"Don't think so, but she's bawling something awful."

Reed softened his voice. "I understand how upsetting that must be. She could be having a bad trip." He explained what that was. "If you can, try to sit quietly with her."

He gave her more suggestions—comfort and reassure Angie, avoid being judgmental. Shirley listened politely but remained reluctant to directly engage her daughter. Reed got her contact information and encouraged her to call back with an update.

"Hallelujah," he mumbled after hanging up. A call he hadn't totally screwed up!

"Why don't you take a break," Meg said and offered to cover his line.

He stepped into the bathroom, which was like the kitchen—barely presentable—with an unused, discolored tub and cracked tile floor. Lifting the toilet seat revealed dried urine around the rim. He unrolled some toilet paper and cleaned the seat before using it.

Back in the hallway, Reed checked out the bulletin board.

There was a reminder about upcoming cardiopulmonary resuscitation training, which would be held at the university's hospital. Damn, another hit to his already slammed schedule.

A notice for "Aquarius Night" listed suggested activities, including candle making and yoga. Contorting himself into a human pretzel? Thanks, but no thanks.

A flyer advertised a new restaurant—*Mother Earth Café: Organic Food for the Revolution.* What did "organic food" have to do with a revolution? Revolution against what? Swanson TV dinners?

—

In the quiet room later, Reed sat with a girl whose quivering fingers could barely grasp a coffee mug.

"Do you remember what you drank?"

Beads of perspiration dotted her pallid face. "Some kind of grape Kool-Aid…I think."

Laced with grain alcohol, he suspected. Like Webb's frat house parties, where the "punch" contained enough grain alcohol to topple an angry bull.

"I don't really remember. Pretty sure I blacked out," she said. "I'm sorry, but can I talk to a girl?"

"Of course."

She tried to stand, but her legs were unsteady. "Jeez, I don't feel too good."

Then she vomited on Reed's white polo shirt.

Jordan talked to the girl for an hour, then walked into the kitchen where Reed was making fresh coffee, his shirt still damp from cleaning off the vomit.

Her jaw tightened with suppressed rage; the fingers holding her coffee mug trembled. "I'm sure those assholes spiked the grape Kool-Aid with this new drug—GHB."

"Gamma-hydroxybutyric acid," Reed recited. "Also known as sodium oxybate. Central nervous system depressant, sometimes used in anesthesia."

At her look of surprise, he added, "It's easy for me to memorize stuff."

"Hmm...anyway, guys are using it to knock girls out and rape them. I'm guessing that's what happened to this girl—and probably to that girl from the Pig Farm, Annabel or whatever her name is."

Reed clenched his mug. Had the red punch at the Pig Farm party been spiked with GHB? Or even LSD? Had he been tripping that night? Could that explain the vision of his father stumbling across the highway?

"What's wrong?" Jordan asked.

"Nothing."

"Come to think of it, I wish that girl would call or come in. I got bad vibes from her parents. Especially the redneck husband."

Reed wasn't about to tell her that Ross was the boyfriend, not the husband. During the rest of the shift, his thoughts drifted back to Annabel. How was she doing? Had she sneaked back to the Pig Farm to ingest GHB-spiked punch or pop Quaaludes? Maybe the least he could do—despite having been warned to stay away—was encourage her to come in and talk.

—

"Where are you from in Texas?" Reed said. He'd lingered near Jordan's dusty VW after their shift. Even at that late hour, he'd considered grabbing a rag and hose and washing it.

"I grew up in Houston. But I spend summers and breaks with my aunt in Pensacola."

Reed was curious to learn more, but she climbed in and cranked the starter, which ground uselessly again.

"Sure I can't take a quick look?"

"Can you *please* ditch the macho mechanic thing?"

"Okay, okay. I just don't want you breaking down in the middle of nowhere."

"But if I did," she smirked, "you could ride in on your big white horse and rescue me, right?"

"Never mind. Forget about it."

The VW's engine finally wheezed to life. She sighed. "Sorry. Rough night." Then those challenging eyes pierced his.

"By the way, the free clinic starts next week. We could use another volunteer. That is, *if* you're interested."

Reed knew Jordan rented a house with Olivia, who was a senior pre-med major. During the free clinic, Olivia, Jordan, and Meg planned to assist the volunteer doctors.

He hesitated. Three nights a week, with little time for homework? Potential disaster. But it was obvious she expected him to refuse.

"I'll be there."

"Good…and that call with Shirley? Heard part of it. You weren't half bad."

An actual compliment! This must be how a starving dog felt when thrown a bone.

—

He drove away, buoyed. For once he wasn't compelled to run to the point of exhaustion—which sometimes helped him sleep—or drink enough alcohol to quiet the thoughts flitting like hummingbirds in his brain, constantly alighting on his father's fate. Dead or alive? If dead, when and how? If alive and imprisoned, then where and in what condition?

Reed sped onto the interstate and pointed the car north, no particular destination in mind. He inserted a Creedence Clearwater Revival 8-track into his player. John Fogerty's raspy rendition of "Born on the Bayou" thrust the Mustang past slower traffic.

The interstate had opened a few years ago. Motels, fast-food joints, and gas stations mushroomed at each exit, sprouting garish oases in the rural countryside. His mother hated the trend, predicting the country's regional charms would be bulldozed in a few decades to make way for chain stores and restaurants that peddled the same brand of blandness in every state.

She had a point. At the next exit, he turned off and rumbled into the countryside.

Here America was a thin strip of highway winding among fields of cabbage and corn, past weathered farmhouses with sagging barns. The seams in the concrete road—probably built by chain gangs during the Depression—clicked metronomically beneath his tires.

Here America was warm light spilling from kitchens, the sharp scent of pine and wildflowers and brackish ponds. Diners beckoned the hungry to *EAT*. Signs advertised boiled peanuts, peaches, fireworks, and sweet silver corn.

He rolled past a biker bar, walls adorned with psychedelic images of motorcycles, including the Captain America Harley-Davidson that Peter Fonda had ridden in the movie *Easy Rider*.

Gazing up at a clear sky crowded with stars, he felt a kinship with all who'd traveled before him on thousands of miles of highway, which had replaced dirt roads, which covered trails hacked from raw wilderness. Generations of restless Americans, forever on the move. Pushing west, pushing south, yearning to go anywhere that promised to be better than where they'd come from.

During a break earlier that evening, Reed had joined Jordan and Olivia on the porch. In the sultry air, Jordan's face shone with perspiration. Olivia had ditched her farmer's overalls for shorts. Her thin legs were unshaven, as were her underarms—something he'd never seen on a woman.

Olivia relished her soapbox. In her view, the past decade had been "a shit show." Scarcely a year after an assassin gunned down President Kennedy, an undeclared war had erupted in a tiny Asian nation that few knew of or cared about—a spark that ignited a raging fire, relentlessly sucking in over a half million American soldiers.

"But '68 was when the bottom fell out," Olivia said. She talked about King getting gunned down in Memphis, followed by rioting in over a hundred cities that left dozens dead and thousands injured. Black people carrying guns, threatening violence—abandoning King's philosophy of nonviolent resistance. Robert F. Kennedy murdered in a California hotel kitchen in June. "Days of Rage" protests that marred the Democratic National Convention in Chicago.

According to Olivia, the following year—1969—wasn't much better. While bombings erupted on campuses every few weeks, Nixon's "Silent Majority" simmered with resentment. "We spend millions going to the moon while ignoring all the problems here on earth."

"Can't we do both?" Reed argued. "We can't afford to let the Russians get ahead in space."

"Cold War propaganda," Olivia scoffed and plowed ahead.

As the new decade began, America was degenerating into armed camps: white against Black, rich against poor, young against old, men against women. For Olivia, the only positive signs were limited progress on civil rights and the rise of the women's movement.

"But elections won't make much difference. That's just chipping away at the rot. Unless a real revolution starts soon, we can kiss this country goodbye."

Steering back toward the interstate, Reed concluded Olivia's perspective was far too gloomy. He wasn't sure why, but he believed in America, however imperfect it might be. Perhaps the hope he nurtured for his father's survival colored his vision of the country. Or maybe it was the raw energy of the nation he felt pulsing beyond his headlights' cone of light, or the relentless, comforting drone of the V-8 engine itself.

As if power, speed, and restless movement could stem the tide of mistrust, paranoia, and violence.

CHAPTER TWELVE

At the Mother Earth Café on Saturday, Annabel poked at small cubes of white tofu on a plate of brown rice and steamed vegetables.

"What's this white junk?"

"Tofu," Reed replied, although he hadn't tried it yet. "It's made from soybeans."

He'd chosen the restaurant on Meg's recommendation. It was in a strip mall near downtown, wedged between a Winn-Dixie grocery store and a ladies' hair salon.

"You mean that crap they feed to pigs?"

Reed smiled. "Something like that."

"Could sure use some ketchup." Her pack of Camels sat on the table, but smoking wasn't allowed. Reed wished other restaurants would follow suit.

After learning Annabel worked on Tuesdays and Thursdays, Reed had driven to the Kastle and invited her to grab lunch sometime just to talk.

Warily, she'd replied, "What for?"

"To see how you're doing."

"I'm doing fine. But thanks for asking."

"Okay, it's just that I was kind of worried about you."

She'd scrutinized him then, as if probing his intentions. "Okay. Mom and Ross work all day Saturday, so I can sneak out."

Reed looked up from his food and scanned the dining room. On the wall behind Annabel, signs instructed farmers to *Grow Food for People, Not for Profit*, encouraged diners to *Go Vegetarian and Save Animals*, and directed the poor to *The People's Food Co-op—Because the Hungry Deserve to Eat.*

Annabel must have misinterpreted his roaming eyes. "Don't worry. Asshole's out of town. On Saturdays, he drives up to Jacksonville."

Asshole clearly referred to Ross Decker.

"Said he's buying parts, but most likely he's getting loaded with his hunting buddies. He's only been dating Mom for months. Feels like forever."

Taken aback by her venom and unsure of what to say, Reed swallowed a bite of tofu. Strange texture, bland taste.

"Asshole can order Mom around, but he's not telling *me* what to do. And dig this—he warned me to stay away from rich kids like you."

"Me? Rich?"

"Yeah. After you split that night, he drank beer and bitched about that 'college punk driving a four-thousand-dollar car.' Then laid this sob story on us about how he had to work his ass off in high school to pay three hundred for a piece-of-crap pickup."

She reached for her cigarettes by habit, then shoved the pack aside. "He can't stand college kids. Thinks you're all spoiled hippies screwing up the country."

Reed reflected on the people he'd talked to at Lifelines, seeing them now less as freaks and potheads and more as ordinary kids struggling with some serious shit. "Well, some are, for sure. But not everybody."

He glanced at her wrists, covered again by a long-sleeved shirt. Should he ask about the scars? Or would she freak out?

Outside, a VW engine coughed to life. For a moment Reed mistook it for Jordan's Beetle, but it was an orange Microbus with a bright-yellow bumper sticker: *Ass, Grass, or Gas. No One Rides for Free.*

"Pretty funny. By the way, I *did* remember you from the Pig Farm."

"So...why'd you say you didn't?"

"Thought you were some weirdo, showing up with my work shirt like that. It smelled like pepperoni pizza, by the way."

Reed pushed his tofu away—a little went a long way—and changed the subject. "So what's up with your real dad?"

"Captain Lucas Taylor, United States Army."

He leaned in. "No kidding. Tell me about him."

She was reluctant to say much. Captain Taylor had fought two tours in Vietnam before coming home in the fall of 1968. "Then he up and left."

"Left? Like what, divorce or something?"

She shoved her plate aside. "Forget about him. He just split. Took off."

"I'm sorry."

"Yeah, well, everything was okay until Asshole showed up. Now he's thinking about selling his house and moving in with us. Every time I think about it, I wanna puke."

Reed tried to lighten things up. "Let's have dessert before you do that."

They ordered carrot cake with cream cheese frosting. To his surprise, it tasted great.

While Annabel ate, Reed glanced outside at yet another beautiful day. As often happened when the sun shone and his belly was full, he imagined his father alive in some Asian jungle hellhole. While Reed stuffed his face with cake, Dad gagged on rotten fish heads or rancid meat in a watery gruel. While Reed basked in the sun, Dad languished in a dim cage with spiders, mosquitoes, rats, and snakes crawling over his flesh. Every day, Reed showered with hot water while Dad choked on the stench of his own waste. *How screwed up is that?*

"Hey." Annabel's hand fanning his face sucked him back into the restaurant. "Are you there?"

"Sorry. Kinda spaced out."

"You look bummed."

Rising to pay the bill, he forced a smile. "I'm fine."

—

During the drive back, he asked himself, *What now?* He'd checked on her. Should he offer to take her to Lifelines, refer her to a shrink?

Feeling a nagging sense of obligation, he glanced at the textbook on her lap. "Algebra one?"

"Unfortunately. Flunked it once already."

"Don't worry. It's not hard. Just keep at it."

"Are you kidding me? It's impossible."

"Come on, no way."

"Besides, I'm a girl, and we suck at math."

"That's crap," Reed shot back. "My sister got all As in math. Anybody can if they work hard enough."

His vehemence silenced her for a moment.

"What's the point? Math is worthless. Unless you want a boring job like my mom's."

"What does she do?"

"Bookkeeping over at Dixon's."

He knew the place, a local hardware store, where he'd once bought a set of socket wrenches.

An idea popped into his head. "Look, if you wanna learn, I can help you."

"Like how?"

"Like, maybe some tutoring." She frowned and lit a cigarette. "But hey, if you're not interested, forget about it."

After a few puffs, mercifully blown out the window, she offered him a coy smile. "Okay, Professor. Help me."

Reed suggested once or twice a week for an hour. Annabel agreed, but she didn't want her mother or Ross to know about it.

"Why not?"

Her emerald eyes flashed. "Because I don't need them on my case."

Earlier, she'd admitted to lying to her mother about where she was the night of the Pig Farm party. "Since then, Mom's kept me on a tight leash. I can take the bus straight home, to work, or Tracy's to study. Then I gotta hang around until she or Asshole picks me up. I'm supposed to be less depressed if I'm never alone. The thing is, the bitches I hang around with bring me down even worse."

She suggested Reed pick her up at Tracy's on Mondays and Fridays, drive her to a nearby Kastle—not the one where she worked—for tutoring, then get her back to Tracy's before her mother or Ross showed up.

Although uneasy about what seemed like unnecessary secrecy and the threat of Ross's hair-trigger temper, Reed agreed.

—

Still questioning his decision to tutor Annabel, Reed stepped into his room after dinner on Sunday night and tripped over one of Adam's books, *The Destruction of the European Jews.* Whenever Adam dove into that book, he'd slump at his desk and scribble feverishly in a journal. He became somber, morose. Once, flipping through the book, Reed had noticed text underlined on almost every page and margins thick with notes.

An only child, Adam had grown up in Miami Beach. Most of his family had been murdered in Nazi concentration camps. Before the war, the Gold family had lived in Warsaw, Poland and had included Adam's father Benjamin, his uncle Jacob, his aunt Sarah, and Adam's grandparents. Aunt Sarah and both grandparents had been gassed at the Treblinka death camp. Miraculously, Adam's father and Uncle Jacob had survived.

What Reed knew of the camps, he'd picked up from images in magazines or from the black-and-white newsreels he'd watched before the features started at the local theater. Helpless men, women, and children herded onto boxcars. Skin-and-bone prisoners in striped pajamas, with sunken eyes and shaved heads. Gas chambers disguised as showers. Mounds of confiscated eyeglasses and gold dental fillings. Open mass graves—lime-covered corpses stacked like cordwood.

On a rare frosty January morning, riding in Reed's Mustang, Adam had insisted that the "veneer of so-called civilization is thinner than the coating of ice on your windshield. A single degree warmer would melt any goodness away to reveal the absolute evil beneath."

Thinking about that conversation, Reed collapsed into his desk chair. Moments later, Adam walked in, glumly lugging his organic chemistry book. He wore his blue-and-white Gamma Delta Iota "fraternity" jersey. GDI—God Damn Independent. Adam and other guys on campus wore the imitation frat jersey to express contempt for "juvenile, boorish, clannish" fraternities.

Reed glanced at his watch. "Weren't we running today?"

Besides walking to and from class, Adam didn't exercise. He'd signed up for yoga classes the previous fall but quit after two sessions "because I was the only dude and felt weird." Impressed by Reed's disciplined routines, however, Adam had vowed to take up jogging.

"Sorry. Forgot." Adam tossed the book on his bed. "Had to catch up on this chemistry shit. It'll be a miracle if I pass."

Not bothering to reply, Reed walked into the hallway toward the phone. His mother expected a call after dinner whenever he didn't go home on Sundays. Although reluctant to talk to her after his last visit, he leaned against the wall and dialed the number.

"How are you, sweetheart?"

"Fine." All he could think of was the potential sale of their house, but he managed the usual small talk. Classes were okay. No, he wasn't dating anyone.

Why am I tiptoeing around the issue?

"By the way, is that guy Walker working on the house?"

An uncomfortable pause. "Not yet. Let's talk about that when we're together for Easter."

CHAPTER THIRTEEN

"I was wondering whether you'd turn up," Jordan said as Reed stepped inside Lifelines for the free clinic on Tuesday night.

"If I say I'll do something, I'll do it," he snapped, instantly regretting his sharp tone.

Unfazed, she mock saluted. "Aye, aye, sir. In that case, you can help us turn the front room into a waiting area."

Reed placed folding chairs along the walls and taped a poster above the sofa: *Health Care Is a Right, Not a Privilege.* On the front door, he taped a hand-painted sign: *No Dealing. No Holding Drugs. No Using Drugs. No Alcohol.*

Jordan explained that the clinic's purpose was to help teenagers and others who couldn't find health care—street people, poor people. University students were supposed to use the campus health center unless they had good reason to avoid it. Two volunteer doctors from the university's teaching hospital—one woman and one man—would handle routine exams and tests, aided by a nurse, pharmacist, and lab tech.

Jordan ushered Reed into the largest bedroom, converted to an exam room for the clinic. Olivia was stacking medical supplies in a metal cabinet. A contraption with two metal arms at the end took up most of the room.

"In case you're wondering," Jordan said with condescension, "that's an OB/GYN exam table." She picked up a three-ring binder. "Here's something a bunch of women in Boston are working on. You're welcome to borrow a copy. Might be an eye-opener."

The lettering on the front of the binder read *Women and Their Bodies: A Course.*

"Check out the chapter on abortion," Olivia chimed in. "Do you realize that last year, almost eight hundred thousand women got an abortion? And that most of those were illegal, and that thousands died?"

"No, that's terrible." She sounded like a courtroom prosecutor. How was he supposed to know stuff like that?

Jordan appeared amused by his discomfort. "Okay, let's go. I reckon we're in for a long night."

And they were. Before the clinic opened, nearly twenty people crowded the front room, some sitting on the threadbare carpet. More girls than guys, mostly teenagers, but several adults who looked like they couldn't afford hospitals.

For the first hour, Reed handled intake at a small card table near the door. The form included basic questions such as name, sex, birth date, marital status, address, and medical history. However, Olivia told him not to pressure people for the information. They couldn't verify it anyway, and they didn't want bureaucratic hassles discouraging people from getting help.

Manning the phones for the second hour, Reed overheard clients' complaints from the exam room across the hall. Some were routine—fevers, cuts, bruises, skin infections, general aches and pains. Many kids were strung out—sallow complexions, blank eyes. Several needed showers—Reed resorted to mouth breathing around a few of the more pungent ones.

The most common complaints, though, involved the potential for sexually transmitted diseases: gonorrhea, herpes, chlamydia, vaginitis, and even syphilis. The doctors took dozens of samples for lab analysis and treated possible cases with penicillin. Several female patients told the staff how "far out" it was to be examined by a woman doctor for the first time.

When Reed expressed surprise at the sheer number of cases, Olivia launched into yet another lecture. Many female patients were having sex for the first time and were incredibly ignorant about their bodies. "They're ashamed. They've been preached to—that VD is punishment for sin. 'If you hadn't had sex, you wouldn't have VD. So suffer and repent.'"

Olivia had hitchhiked cross-country to San Francisco in 1967, Reed learned, to work at the Haight Ashbury free clinic. Her perspective on the "Summer of Love" was a far cry from the glorified news accounts. Some kids had traveled that summer to San Francisco for a spiritual awakening—a communal "be-in to spread so-called peace and love." Others came seeking drugs and sex. Unfortunately, predators, thieves, and deadbeats also showed up to rob, rape, and beat up the vulnerable.

"Forget spiritual awakening; forget the 'Age of Aquarius.' It became a circus that turned into a horror show. We treated runaway thirteen-year-old girls who were gang-raped," Olivia told him.

When the hotline phone rang and Reed introduced himself, the female caller asked to speak with a woman.

"Yes, ma'am, how can we help you?" Jordan said as Reed listened in. "No, that would be illegal. But yes, we have a list of doctors who can provide you with counseling." She removed a notebook from the desk drawer. "We can refer you to someone out of state...uh, yes, it's legal, but we'd like you to come in first and talk."

After the call, Jordan slid the notebook back into the drawer, rose, raised her arms high above her head, and stretched from side to side. If she was aware of the erotic effect she was having on Reed, she didn't seem to care.

"What was that call about?"

"How to get an abortion. In most states, they're illegal or restricted. They're technically allowed in Florida, but only if the woman's life is in danger."

She explained that Lifelines planned to set up an unofficial referral service to connect pregnant women to counseling services. "But some ridiculous Florida law makes it illegal to publish or advertise a list like that. Hard to believe, but it's actually a felony."

Felony? Reed envisioned police cruisers converging on Lifelines, imagined himself getting busted, kicked out of ROTC, expelled from college, disowned by his father. Utter disgrace.

"Uh...do you think we could get in trouble?"

"Possibly, but it's unlikely. Then again, if you're uncomfortable with anything we're doing, you don't have to be here."

He regretted his words the second after they tumbled out. "I sort of do...have to be here, that is."

"What do you mean?"

Avoiding her eyes, he mumbled, "My Rot-cee commander figured I needed some community service."

She squinted, hands on hips, like Reed's high school football coach standing on the sidelines, disgusted by his team's performance. "So I was right. Just following orders like a good cadet. I should've known you're not committed."

His face reddened as if on fire. "Yeah, maybe I wasn't. At first." Then he summoned resolve. "But I am now."

"Why didn't you tell me that in the first place?"

"Sorry, I should have."

He sensed the gears turning in her head, trying to figure him out. "Okay." She shrugged. "Come on, then, we've got the perfect job for you."

She led him into the kitchen, where several vaginal speculums lay on the counter. "These have to be cleaned after every use."

Each strange steel device resembled a duck's bill. When Reed gingerly picked one up, Jordan sniggered. "Soak it in disinfectant, boil it, then rinse and dry. When we raise more money, we'll buy an autoclave that uses hot steam to clean them."

Reed cleaned speculum after speculum, grossed out by this proximity to "female problems." During a break, he'd overheard Olivia stressing the need for women to demystify their bodies. "Every woman ought to insert a speculum in their vagina, then use a flashlight and a mirror to examine their cervix."

It took Reed a while to get past the image. Though he'd grown up with two women, he knew precious little about female anatomy, other than seeing packages of Tampax in the bathroom his mother and sister shared. When he picked up girls for dates, they were showered, made up, fashionably dressed, and perfumed.

After cleaning the speculums, Reed wiped the counters, swept the floor, took out the trash, and scrubbed the percolator. Jordan walked in and filled the teakettle.

"What are you doing?"

"This place was a garbage dump."

She inspected his handiwork and cracked a smile. "Hey, maybe you should switch majors to home ec."

For the rest of the shift, when Reed wasn't taking hotline calls, he was signing in new patients, disinfecting everything in sight, or stepping outside to make sure the line of waiting patients wasn't disturbing the neighborhood.

"If we're not careful," Jordan said, "we'll get complaints about dirty hippies taking over the city."

The first clinic turned out to be a resounding success. The doctors treated sixty-two patients in four hours. Afterward, Dr. Carlson gathered the volunteers to discuss what had gone right, what had gone wrong, and what they could do better next time.

"Despite a few hiccups," she said, "you all did an amazing job and should feel proud of what we accomplished. How about some hugs?"

Reed wiped sweat from his face as Dr. Carlson walked up and hugged him. Then she hugged Olivia. Meg hugged Reed. Olivia hugged Jordan.

Jordan hesitated, then gave Reed a perfunctory hug.

Even that brief moment of contact felt electric.

CHAPTER FOURTEEN

After only four hours of sleep, Reed faced his regular Wednesday classes, tons of homework, and another late-night shift at Lifelines. He'd need some speed to get through it or some Quaaludes to fall asleep afterward. Great. Now he sounded like the hotline callers.

Climbing into his Mustang outside the 7-Eleven, he spotted Lude, the guy he'd knocked down at the Pig Farm party, staggering across the street. Lude swerved to dodge a speeding car and scurried around the corner.

Damn. Lude was wasted, gaunt enough now to definitely fail the Army physical. Should Reed apologize for being a dickhead? Or would his presence just rile up the guy again? Besides, Reed's uniform had already attracted the day's quota of derision.

He checked his watch—ten minutes until class. He drove around the corner, pulled up to the curb, and jumped out.

"Hey, Lude…uh, I mean Darryl," he yelled, jogging to catch up to him.

Darryl froze, not recognizing Reed at first. "Huh?"

"Hey, listen, just wanted to say I'm sorry. You know, for what happened at the Pig Farm."

Darryl's ice-blue eyes flared. "Get away from me, man! You're fucking crazy!" He dashed into a bungalow so run-down it made Lifelines look like a mansion. Bob Dylan's "Lay, Lady, Lay" drifted from windows.

Reed walked toward the house, then stopped to recheck his watch. Better not barge in and risk being late to class. Maybe he'd come back later.

Outside the ROTC building, the protesters were back, including Jordan, carrying the sign again—*Bombers Are Killers, Not Heroes!*

Jeezus H. Christ. Reed shot her a nasty look, which she defiantly returned.

A protester shoved a petition in his hands: *Cancel All University Research Contracts with the Department of Defense. Dissolve ROTC Courses Immediately. Get ROTC Off Campus!* He scanned the fine print: *The presence of a militaristic organization on campus violates the foundational goals of our humanistic academic community.*

What utter bullshit. Reed crumpled the flyer and tossed it. Captain Harwood had raised the issue in class weeks ago. "The political left believes that banishing ROTC from campus will reduce the likelihood of war." He suggested the opposite was more likely. "Officers provided with a thorough liberal education are more likely to appreciate peace, and work to avoid war."

—

"Let me guess," Jordan ventured, "you're still ticked off about the protest."

Reed was helping her clean up the garage after a rap group.

"What's the point? Banning ROTC won't end the war a minute sooner."

"It may or may not. But no man is going to tell me what to think or do."

"And I wouldn't be caught dead trying to do that—but it's unfair to pick on Rot-cee."

"Bullshit. You're puppets of the military-industrial complex. This university has two million dollars in Department of Defense contracts, and no one questions it."

"What's that got to do with training officers?"

"Everything. The contracts support the war machine, and the war machine needs cannon fodder. Like you, for example."

Screw it, there was no arguing with her. Just when she seemed to be warming up to him, politics hopelessly divided them again.

Back in the hotline room, Reed yawned and willed his watch to tick faster.

"My name is Reed," he told the next caller. "How can we help you?"

A long silence. It must be the same girl Meg had listened to for weeks, the one who never spoke more than a few words. He sat and waited, reminding her every few minutes, "If you want to talk, I'm here for you."

Perhaps she liked the sound of his voice or decided she was ready. "My name's Robin," she whispered. She was a sophomore from Mobile, Alabama. Reed told her he'd been there once and liked "the cool fort at Dauphin Island."

What was she studying?

"Math. I'm kind of interested in computers."

He complimented her—not many girls were interested in math and science.

After another awkward stretch of silence, Robin thanked him and hung up.

Reed breathed deeply. Something within him shifted—he'd actually connected with someone.

Past midnight, his stomach queasy from too much bitter coffee and reheated pizza, he listened to Jordan take a call.

"Okay, well, if you suspect she's having a bad trip," Jordan was saying, "please call or bring her in. We can help."

Perched on the edge of her chair, she listened. Accustomed to her quirks by now, he noticed her right thigh bobbing (impatient), her left hand raking her hair (annoyed).

"Yes, if it's an emergency, we can call an ambulance. Can I get your phone number and address?" She waited. "Okay, whatever."

About to slam the phone into the receiver, she caught herself. "Please call back if you need us. We're here to help."

After scribbling in the call log, she rushed out. The front door slammed.

Intrigued by this crack in Jordan's cool, ever-competent facade,

Reed followed her outside, handing over his phone line to another volunteer.

She was running down the street, moving surprisingly fast. Sweating in the muggy air, Reed sprinted to catch her. She slowed to a walk, showing no surprise.

"What's wrong? What happened on that call?"

"Some man called to bitch about his daughter. Claimed she was doing lots of drugs, flunking out of high school, and screwing around. He figures she must be crazy, wants to lock her up in a mental hospital. So typical. If men misbehave, they're just 'boys being boys.' But if women dare step out of line, then shit, they must be crazy."

That idea had never occurred to Reed.

"Probably a country-club asshole who cares more about his stock portfolio than his own daughter."

"Harsh," Reed said. "But…shouldn't you have been…maybe a little more professional?"

She froze in the street. "Why?"

"What do you mean, why? You could have been more respectful. After all, he *is* her father."

Her eyes flashed contempt. "Fathers deserve only the respect they earn."

Really? Reed frowned. According to Frank, fathers represented rightful authority and were automatically accorded respect. Or else. It was children who had to earn the respect of authority figures—parents, teachers, priests—not the other way around.

"A father is someone who's always there for you when you need him," Jordan said. "Besides, don't you ever get pissed at yours?"

As a wave of melancholy washed over him, he looked off. Some kids were drinking beer around a foosball table that had been dragged outside. "No…not really."

"Frankly, I find that impossible to believe."

Believe whatever the hell you want. Instead, he said: "What about your father? Do you respect him?"

"The biggest hat in East Texas? Sure, most folks respect big Harlan, all right."

"What does he do?"

"He takes care of business. Everybody's business—whether they like it or not."

Reed suspected that father and daughter had a troubled relationship. Harlan Ellis was in the oil business. Ellis Oil gas stations were scattered throughout the South. When Reed was a kid, his dad had bought him a coveted model of the iconic yellow Ellis tanker truck.

"He's the original 'take charge' guy," Jordan continued. "One of his favorite sayings is, 'I don't *get* ulcers. I *give* them.'"

Reed figured Harlan and Frank would get along just fine. He checked his watch. "We're shorthanded. Let's get back to work."

Driving back to campus after his shift, Reed thought about what Jordan had said. Had he ever been pissed at Dad? Sure. So what? He tried to think about something else—that night's hotline callers, tomorrow's homework—but for some reason, he couldn't shake his gloomy mood and was drawn back to the last night he'd spent with his father.

—

It was a Sunday in the fall of 1966. Frank was set to deploy to Vietnam the next morning. In the garage, Reed was fiddling with the Mustang, searching for the source of the engine's rough idle. His father hovered like he usually did, which made Reed nervous enough to drop the screwdriver.

Grumbling, Frank retrieved it and leaned under the hood. "There's a right and wrong way to do everything. If the idle's rough, the mixture's too rich."

"I know, Dad. I know."

Frank wiped his hands on a rag. "Now make sure you don't screw up anything when I'm overseas. No hot-rodding or letting *anyone* else drive this thing. You understand?"

"Dad, it's gonna be in perfect shape when you get back."

Later that evening, Reed peered into the backyard where Frank sat drinking beer, several empties strewn across the grass. Away from the house. Apart from his family.

Brooding.

About what? Going back to war? Or the latest chore Reed had screwed up?

—

His father's dark moods had worsened that year. Why? Too intimidated to ask him, Reed had turned to his mother. Her reasons offered scant comfort: "He's under a lot of pressure." "Sometimes he just needs to be alone to think."

Reed knew being a fighter pilot was a dangerous profession. In the 1950s and 1960s, nearly one in four military pilots had died during training or test flights, not even counting deaths in combat. Frank had joked about the Navy's definition of an optimist—a naval aviator with a savings account. Once, when a fellow pilot—a close family friend—died in a crash, Dad had curtly shrugged it off: "It's part of the job. I can't afford to think about it."

Given the degree of skill required, supreme confidence was essential, especially for taking off and landing on carriers. "If you stop believing you're the best pilot in the world," Dad had said, "you're gonna get killed."

But that year his father had radiated constant tension, not confidence. Like on that trip to Sebring back in March. At a Waffle House the morning of the race, Reed had wolfed down eggs, bacon, cheese grits, and biscuits. Dad drank only black coffee and flipped irritably through the newspaper, grumbling about "that Texas hick in the White House" or "that Pentagon pinhead McNamara."

That night in their motel room, he was awakened by Dad crying out. From what—a nightmare? Even after his father fell back asleep, Reed lay awake, heart thumping, frightened by apparent fissures in his father's rock-solid facade. Momentarily, he felt the solid base supporting him melt into quicksand.

In the weeks leading up to Frank's departure for Vietnam, his moods worsened. He retreated behind a wall of silence, accompanied by bourbon-and-sodas and cigarettes he let burn until the ashes fell. So far that year—1966—nearly one hundred Navy pilots had been shot down.

Yet Dad refused to talk about the war—until one night at dinner. There were no interrogations. Nothing about Reed's schoolwork, sports, or chores. No assaults on Sandy's left-wing views.

Staring at his untouched meat loaf and mashed potatoes, Dad only muttered, "This damn thing won't be ending anytime soon."

"Why not?" Reed ventured.

Dad refused to answer, waved off further conversation. Still, this hint of pessimism was the first Reed had ever detected. Never in Reed's presence had his father criticized the war's mission or the Navy's strategy.

—

That night before Dad deployed, Reed had picked his way across the yard—craving reassurance and seeking an invitation to share a beer and talk.

Something. Anything.

"Hey, Dad." No response. "Are you okay?"

Reed's gut churned with the familiar, hollow anxiety and frustration of being unseen and unacknowledged. Instead of responding, Frank turned to stare at him with vacant eyes, as if he'd already left.

"Did you put the tools back where they belong?"

Glumly, Reed nodded.

Early the next morning, Frank's parachute bag lay on the driveway. A Navy buddy sat in a Chevy idling at the curb. Because Carol disliked emotional send-offs, she'd refused to drive him to the airfield.

Eyes masked by Ray-Bans, Frank gave Reed a gruff hug. He reminded him to take care of his mother and sister and look after the house, then added with a thin smile, "Don't go soft on me. And don't be a dumbass shithead."

He didn't say "I love you," and neither did Reed.

—

Instead of heading to the dorm, Reed walked through the quiet, empty campus, thinking about that last night, as he had so often over the years. Dad brooding in the backyard—just as he had done when

Grandpa died. Reed never remembered his father crying. Not at the funeral, not after the funeral.

But so what if his father was often remote? So were most of the other fathers Reed knew. Besides, he was just a kid. What did his puny concerns and sissy feelings matter? Dad was dealing with war. Command responsibility. The weight of the world rested on his shoulders as he fought the grand battle of the twentieth century—destroying communism, defending democracy.

Besides, incessantly ruminating was a waste of time, like revving the Mustang's engine in neutral, pistons pounding, the car going nowhere. Dad was alive, and when he came home, there would be more trips to Sebring, more cars to work on, more backyard barbecues.

On February 16, 1967, time had frozen—as if the grandfather clock in the Lawson living room had suddenly stopped. But soon, Reed was sure, the clock's hands would start ticking again.

CHAPTER FIFTEEN

Annabel reached for her Camels and an aluminum ashtray stamped with the Kastle logo.

"Can you please not smoke?" Reed asked.

"Okay already." She picked up her Coke. "But who gives a rip about lung cancer?"

It was Friday afternoon, and they were sitting in a corner booth. Reed checked her homework, an exercise in solving equations. Of the ten problems assigned, she'd finished one incorrectly, abandoned another halfway, and left the rest blank.

"Not great, but it's a start."

"Told you, I'm a retard."

"Not true. You just got frustrated and gave up too soon."

"Because I'm stupid."

"Quit putting yourself down. Things can't be that bad."

"That's 'cause you don't go to *my* school."

"Most kids hate high school. You just gotta power through it."

Her school had been integrated between semesters, causing chaos. Overcrowded classrooms. Fistfights in the schoolyard between Black and white kids. "It's like being locked up in a loony bin," she'd complained.

Reed focused on her math problem. "Start by simplifying it, step by step. First, undo the subtraction. Then undo the multiplication. You end up with x equals minus three, and then you just solve for x. Does that make sense?"

"No," she said, but eventually wilted in the face of his commanding presence. She let him coax her through the remaining problems and got a few correct.

"See? I knew you could do it."

"Yeah, only the easy ones."

"Come on, give yourself some credit."

She offered up a coy smile. "Whatever you say, Professor."

Uneasy, Reed wished she'd stop flirting—he was only tutoring and listening if she felt like talking about her problems. Nothing more.

Reed helped her finish the assignment, then let her surrender to nicotine addiction as long as she smoked outside. They sat on a wooden bench across the street from Second Genesis.

A petite girl materialized—waif-thin, grimy bare feet, faded peasant dress—and displayed an angelic smile.

"Praise Jesus," she said, handing Reed a pamphlet before gliding past.

He glanced at the cover—*Turn On with Jesus. It's a Good Trip*—and showed it to Annabel. "You interested?"

"Nah...don't go to church anymore. Mom's been on my case about it, but I don't believe in God, so going would be hypocritical, wouldn't it?"

"I'm not sure." He glanced at her wrists. Was now the right time to ask? "Those scars...do you want to talk about them?"

She yanked her sleeve down. "No."

"I'm sorry. I didn't mean to upset you."

Reed sensed she wanted to confide in him, but was scared or didn't trust him yet. Like silent Robin, who'd taken so long to open up.

Annabel dropped her cigarette butt and ground it out with the toe of her sneaker. "I gotta get back to jail."

Jail meant home. Earlier, she'd bitched again about Ross. "He's in Mom's bed every other night. Grunting. It's so disgusting."

"Hey, man."

Reed looked up to find Adam holding a bag from Second Genesis. Probably more rolling papers. Adam eyed Annabel curiously until Reed introduced them.

"Do I know you, Adam? You look kind of familiar," Annabel said.

"I don't think so, but it's nice to meet you."

Before Adam could start asking questions, Reed checked his watch and motioned to Annabel. "C'mon, it's time to split."

—

When they rolled up to Tracy's house, several kids approached from the high school a few blocks away.

Annabel grabbed her school bag. "Thanks for putting up with all my whining."

There was a tap on Reed's window.

"Don't talk to her!" Annabel hissed.

A tall girl leaned in and glanced from Reed to Annabel. "Hey, Taylor. Don't tell me *this* is your new boyfriend." Removing dark sunglasses, the girl flicked her long blond hair and smiled seductively. "Hi there. I'm Jenny Palmer. Pleased to make your acquaintance."

Reed granted her a perfunctory nod. He knew the type—precocious flirt, more talk than action.

"Bitch," Annabel mumbled, and scrambled out of the car.

Jenny drew closer and whispered, "Careful with Taylor. She's a total head case."

Repelled by the girl's casual cruelty, Reed was eager to leave and turned on the engine. But Jenny and Annabel were facing off in front of the car.

"Wow, Taylor. What a dreamboat!"

"Who are you, Annette Funicello?"

"Very funny," Jenny said. "How about doing us all a favor and slitting your wrists? And maybe get it right this time!"

What the fuck! Reed switched off the engine, leaped out, and advanced on her. "Hey, you!"

Jenny flinched. "Huh? What?"

He got in her face. "What the hell you think you're doing, talking to her like that?"

Eyes widening in fear, Jenny took a step back. "I didn't mean—"

"Didn't mean *what*, exactly?"

Annabel stepped between them. "Leave her alone."

Jenny stalked away, muttering, "Freaking psychos."

"Just what I need," Annabel said. "The bitch queen, back on my case."

"You can't let people walk all over you like that."

"Yeah…as if I can stop 'em."

She hurried into Tracy's house. Some kids walking past the Mustang gave him a wide berth. *Dammit.* Although his anger was justified, he'd let himself be drawn into Annabel's orbit. Time to back off.

—

Adam watched a dryer spinning at Groomers Laundromat that evening.

"Just remembered where I saw that girl. You were talking to her at the Pig Farm last month. She looked so different today. Younger."

Wordlessly, Reed waited for the dryer to stop spinning, then grabbed their clothes and started folding.

"So what's the deal? You dating her or something?"

"No, I'm not 'dating her or something.' She's in high school, man. I'm tutoring her in algebra, that's all."

"Okay, okay. Sorry. Just surprised you can spare the time."

"You're right. I'm swamped, but I'm doing it anyway."

"You know, when you first volunteered, I figured you'd last two weeks, tops. Now you're also teaching math. We call that *tikkun olam.*"

"Say what?"

"It's a Jewish concept—performing acts of kindness to repair the world."

Reed lifted the laundry basket, doubting he was repairing much of anything. "If you say so."

—

Saturday night, Reed paused outside Lifeline's screen door. Olivia and Jordan were arguing in the front room.

"No way I'm asking Harlan for *anything,*" Jordan said. "Nada."

"Yeah…that would mean actually talking to him and swallowing your pride. Just the rent here costs three fifty a month—but that's chicken feed for you people."

"What do you mean, *you people*?"

"If you ask me, you're being damn selfish."

"And who's asking you?"

Olivia brushed past Reed as he stepped inside. She wore a T-shirt that read *Lavender Menace*. He had no clue what *Lavender* referred to, but the *Menace* part sure fit.

"What was that all about?" he asked Jordan.

"None of your business," she snapped.

Reed recalled Winston Churchill's response when he was asked to describe Russia. The words fit Jordan perfectly: "a riddle, wrapped in a mystery, inside an enigma."

One of Reed's first callers that evening was a girl whose boyfriend had dumped her.

"We'd been dating for six months. He smoked grass all the time. I smoked too, even though I didn't really dig it. But he was obsessed. Basically, it's like he left me for weed...but the thing is, I'm still in love with him. Isn't that crazy?"

Reed listened uncomfortably, thinking, *You're better off without the jerk*. But since he wasn't sure how to respond, he transferred the call to Jordan.

Call after call, visitor after visitor, Reed tried to apply his training—to reflectively listen and empathically respond. More often than not, however, he stumbled ineptly over his words.

At two in the morning, he was ready to leave when a guy named Jason called. The conversation began with the types of complaints Reed had begun to find tiresome.

Jason: "I'm flunking organic chemistry. It's so fucking hard and boring."

Reed: *Suck it up. Study harder.* "You sound like you're really frustrated by it."

Jason: "Half the week, when I need to sleep, my roommate's up late drinking Colt 45s and playing Grateful Dead."

Reed: *Tell him to cut it out or change roommates.* "You feel like he doesn't respect you."

"Yeah...and if I flunk one more course," Jason continued, "my dad's gonna stop paying tuition. It's all a major bummer, man."

He rambled on, talking about the pressure to graduate and get a "straight job" or else be labeled a loser. About not really knowing what he wanted to do in life. About always feeling anxious...until he finally admitted, "Sometimes I think I may as well end it all."

Reed's stomach lurched; his fist clenched. *End it all?* "What...what do you mean by that?" He signaled for Jordan to listen in.

"It's like sometimes...sometimes I imagine falling asleep and never waking up. My roommate's got a bunch of ludes, and I'm thinking about swallowing, like, twenty or thirty."

Not a single word from Reed's training floated into his mind. The solitary ancient window unit wheezed precious cold air through the bungalow, but even if his desk were a walk-in refrigerator, it wouldn't have dried the sweat beading on his forehead.

Jordan gently but firmly took over the call while Reed listened. "Sometimes when people say they want to fall asleep and never wake up, they're thinking about suicide. Is that what you're thinking about?"

A long pause. "Uh...yeah, I guess. Um...actually, yeah, for a while now."

"That must be awfully hard to talk about. Can I ask you a few questions? Would that be okay?"

"I don't know. I, uh...I guess so."

Jordan spoke to Jason for another ten minutes. There was a hectoring voice in Jason's head that told him he was worthless, he was stupid, he'd never amount to anything. He didn't belong at the university; he was "trailer trash surrounded by smart, rich kids." The despair was relentless. Getting high, getting drunk—nothing helped. Life just wasn't worth the hassle.

"It's like you're stuck in thick mud," Jordan said. "Almost like quicksand—you get dragged down and the harder you struggle, the further down you go."

As Reed listened, he tried to empathize, but over the past few weeks, he'd struggled to understand male callers. How could guys whine so openly about their problems? How could they bare their emotions to perfect strangers? It was weak, unmanly. Boys cried; men never did.

Dad would often warn him, "No crybabies in the cockpit. Control your emotions or you will crash and die."

When Jordan asked Jason to toss the Quaaludes or bring them to Lifelines, he agreed to "think about it." He also agreed to call his cousin, with whom he had a close relationship.

Replacing the receiver, Jordan gave Reed a sympathetic smile. "That was tough."

"Sorry, I screwed up."

"No, you're too hard on yourself."

—

On the porch after his shift, Reed thought about Jason. Dad would say life was a gift from God. Suffering was part of the deal. Take responsibility for your problems and get on with it. Suicide was the coward's way out—leaving loved ones behind to juggle an agonizing kaleidoscope of emotions—bewilderment, anger, guilt, grief.

But Dad's views clashed with Lifeline's philosophy. A suicidal person believed they had run out of solutions. Taking one's life was neither a sign of weakness nor moral failure but a last-ditch response to devastating pain.

Jordan joined him on the couch. "You're still thinking about that call, aren't you?"

"Yeah. I just don't understand why anyone would do it. I mean, it's the ultimate cop-out. Isn't it?"

"Is that what you really think?"

He gazed up at the few stars visible beyond the streetlights' glow. "To tell you the truth, I'm not sure *what* I think anymore."

"At least you're finally being honest."

The front door banged open and Olivia emerged. "Are you ready to go?"

"In a while. You can take the car. I'll walk."

Olivia scowled at Reed, then grabbed the VW keys. "Okay, suit yourself."

Reed asked Jordan about their argument earlier that evening.

"Turns out this place will go out of business in a few months if we can't scrape up some more money. Olivia thinks Harlan will write a check for twenty-five thousand just because his 'sweet little princess' asks him. Actually, he's a real cheapskate. Hell, Harlan would squeeze a nickel until the buffalo screams."

Seeming in no hurry to leave, she sat close to Reed, their thighs brushing. She smelled of musk mixed with sweat, and her western shirt's top buttons were undone. A welcome breeze swept through the muggy air. The Doors' "When the Music's Over" drifted from a house next door.

"So, listen," Reed said softly, "I've been meaning to ask—how did you get that scar over your eye?"

"Oh, that...I fell off a horse, hit my head on a rock."

"Funny. You don't seem like the type who'd ever fall off a horse."

She yawned, stretched her arms. "It's a long story." A drop of sweat rolled between her cleavage. Despite his exhaustion, Reed was aroused.

"Okay, enough for one night. I feel like a horse that's been rode hard and put away wet."

CHAPTER SIXTEEN

"Come on, fat shit, move!" Webb berated himself as he labored to keep up with Reed on their weekly six-mile run Sunday.

"You're working too hard. After all, Rome wasn't burned in a day."

Reed suspected Webb's compulsive overeating and girl chasing were motivated by boredom. His father owned a real estate company in Columbia, South Carolina, and expected Webb to join him after graduation. All he needed to do was bring home a business degree.

"But I don't give a rip about profit-loss statements," Webb had griped one night over a pitcher at the Rathskeller. What he truly loved was custom carpentry. He displayed his powerful hands. "These suckers can't throw a football anymore, but they can sure as shit bang wood together."

"Can't you make decent money doing that?"

"Nah. Pops says woodworking is a hobby, not a career. Period. End of statement."

Hanging out in Reed's room after their run, Webb paged through the copy of *Women and Their Bodies: A Course* that Reed had borrowed from Lifelines.

"What a load of horse crap. Listen to this shit: *There will be no more ideology of control and submission. No more objectifying women as sex objects...women are not chicks, but real people...the establishment is more interested in money and power than health. Women have decided that health can no longer be defined by an elite group of white upper-class capitalists, but by women who need the care.* What did I tell you? These libbers are all just undercover commies."

"That's kind of a stretch, don't you think?"

Reed's father believed America was locked in a life-and-death struggle with the Soviets, but Webb's worldview seemed paranoid. He was a member of a conservative organization—Young Americans for Freedom—and his father belonged to the right-wing John Birch Society.

Webb claimed that the Soviets were corrupting the nation from within, especially through its schools. He bitched about Americans who were card-carrying members of the Communist Party of the USA, the thousands who were sympathizers, and the "millions of idiots who don't realize they're being manipulated, right from the Kremlin." All these "traitors" were collaborating—consciously or unconsciously—with the Russians, Chinese, and North Vietnamese to destroy America.

"It's no stretch at all," Webb sputtered. "Read all the lib propaganda. They *say* so."

Reed recalled a recent shift at Lifelines. "Actually, I have."

Jordan, Olivia, and Meg had taken part in a "consciousness-raising" group. Reed had overheard fragments of conversation from the garage, punctuated by howls of laughter.

Curious, he'd wandered in after everyone left. Large sheets of paper had been taped to the walls, scrawled with notes:

Banging, balling, screwin', getting laid, getting your rocks off. Wham, bam, thank you, ma'am. Modern romance or factory work?

Sounded like Webb, Reed thought.

Overheard at a frat party: "Eternity is the time between the guy coming and the girl leaving."

Sad but true.

Sexist insults men exchange: "Pussy!" "Wuss!" "What's wrong, you on the rag?"

Yup, like his high school football coach barking, "Come on, girls! Hustle!"

Female Help Wanted Ad—Waitress. Male Help Wanted Ad—TV Repairman.

What if women want to repair TVs?

Well, who cared, as long as they got fixed?

All men benefit from male supremacy. All men oppress women.

Bullshit. Reed had never oppressed anyone.

Turning to leave, he'd read one more: *Women are alienated from each other and therefore rendered vulnerable to control by the patriarchy.*

Wait a minute—weren't men also alienated from each other?

Webb tossed *Women and Their Bodies* onto Reed's bed. "Forget this garbage. Besides, most of these libbers are dykes."

"Dykes? What? You mean lesbians?"

"Rug munchers, all of 'em."

"C'mon! Where do you get this crap?"

Webb bent over to stretch, grunting when his fingers stopped six inches from the floor.

"The fact is, these libbers wanna cut off our balls. And I mean every goddamn, red-blooded American male."

—

At the Kastle the next afternoon, Annabel poked a french fry into a mound of ketchup. "I gotta stop eating these."

"Why?" Reed asked. "They're the best thing here."

Raking fingers through tangled hair, she complained, "I'm getting fat."

"That's nuts. You look fine."

"You're just saying that to be nice."

Exasperated, he shoved the fries aside. "Okay, so don't eat 'em."

Sulking, she grabbed one and chewed it mechanically—regressing to little-kid mode. What had happened to the smart, self-assured young woman from the Pig Farm who'd acted so much older? Or was that a figment of his drug-addled perception?

Trying to change the subject, he asked if she had any friends in high school other than Tracy.

"Nope. They're all retards. Or bitches, like Jenny Palmer."

"Everyone can't be a retard or a bitch. What about a boyfriend or something?"

"Are you kidding? Compared to the losers at my school, you're a movie star. All *they* do is fart in class and squeeze their zits."

Reed burst out laughing, spitting vanilla shake.

"It's not funny. The cool people with brains don't wanna talk to me. No one gives a shit about me."

"I do. I care about you," he said, realizing he meant it.

She smiled, then turned away. "My dad cared…until I guess he didn't."

Reed set aside his shake. What kind of rotten father—an Army officer, no less—would abandon his family?

Flipping through her notebook for the next assignment, Reed came upon some writing that resembled poetry—lines written, crossed out, and rewritten:

> *I am sewn from cosmic stardust, woven into a tapestry of light…*
> *But my threads are fraying, tearing apart…*
> *And my glow is dimming…*
> *I am a ghost hiding in the shadows,*
> *Surrendering to the darkness suffocating me.*

She grabbed her notebook. "Hey! That's private!"

"It's poetry, isn't it?"

"More like garbage."

"Doesn't look like it to me."

She scanned the crowded restaurant. "Face it. I'm not like the other girls. I worry about atomic bombs destroying the world, people starving in Africa, Black kids murdered in ghettos. All *they* talk about are clothes, finding the right prom date, or who's cuter—Paul Newman or Robert Redford." Her emerald eyes held his. "Why can't I be like them?"

"Why should you? Nothing wrong with caring about the world."

She sighed. "Yeah, as if I can solve any of those problems anyway."

While she worked an equation, Reed glanced outside as a yellow VW Beetle with Texas plates pulled into the parking lot and stopped, idling.

Jordan. Reed had planned to tell her about the tutoring…when the time was right. Otherwise, like Adam, she might get the wrong idea. To his relief, the VW rolled through the lot and onto the street.

On the way back to Tracy's, Annabel nodded off. When Reed gently nudged her awake, her knees knocked against the glove compartment. "Huh? What happened?"

"Nothing. You fell asleep."

She gathered her things. "Damn, I'm wiped. If only I could sleep tonight. You don't have any ludes on you, do you?"

"Heck no." As little as *he'd* slept lately, though, the drug was disturbingly appealing.

—

"What was he doing with that girl at the Kastle?" Olivia asked, with her usual hint of condemnation.

Reed had paused outside the hotline room when he heard Olivia and Jordan talking about him.

"Looked like he was helping her with homework," Jordan said.

"Yeah, well, I don't trust him."

"That's nothing new. You don't trust any man, do you?"

"And I suppose *you* do?" Olivia countered.

"Maybe I'd like to…at some point."

Hours later, Jordan talked Reed into drinking chamomile tea on the porch. Even with honey, it was barely tolerable, but she'd urged him to lay off the caffeine. Getting too wired didn't help anyone stay calm during difficult calls.

Her gray-blue eyes lasered in on his with that hint of suspicion she often radiated. "So what's the deal with you and this Annabel girl?"

"Well, the thing is…she's nearly flunking algebra. I don't know what makes people tick, but I do understand math and figured I could help her out."

"I guess tutoring isn't a bad idea. Just don't go ego-tripping. Remember, you're not a therapist."

"Understood."

"Good." She fingered her tea cup. "It's funny. Math was always so easy for me, but I got Cs on purpose."

Realizing he'd been holding his breath, Reed exhaled, relieved she'd changed the subject. "Why would you do that?"

"Who wants to date a girl who shows you up in math? Not to mention knowing all about the family's oil-and-gas business."

"Which happens to be number fifteen on the latest Fortune 500 list." Responding to her raised eyebrows, he added, "I looked it up."

"Nosy, aren't you? Yeah, we were number twenty before Vietnam. Turns out you can make serious cash by fueling the American war machine."

"If Ellis doesn't sell it, somebody else will, right?"

"Yeah, that's the bullshit justification I try hard to swallow. Shoot, if it were up to Harlan, daddy's little girl wouldn't be worrying her pretty little head about war."

"Still, I'm surprised you'd ever get bad grades on purpose."

"I did back then. When everybody called me Rosemary. I'd never do it now."

"Wait. Jordan's not your first name?"

"My driver's license says Rosemary Jordan Ellis. I hated Rosemary but loved my Grandpa, Elias Jordan. He died when I was thirteen. So when I started high school, I made everybody call me Jordan."

"Cool. It suits you."

—

At Mother Earth the following afternoon, Reed polished off a "veggie burger"—surprised that the weird combination of ground-up lentils, rice, and spinach tasted halfway edible. Adam was paging through yet another new book, *Man's Search for Meaning* by Viktor Frankl.

The author, Adam explained, was a psychiatrist who'd survived the Auschwitz death camp. The psychological theories Frankl had developed as a result of his experiences emphasized the critical importance of finding purpose and meaning in life.

"Frankl is paraphrasing Nietzsche when he says, 'He who has a *why* to live can bear any *how*.'"

"Sounds pretty deep."

"Sure...except you haven't listened to a word I've said."

Adam was right. Reed had been thinking of an article in the paper that day. Families of eighty American POWs had recently received letters from their loved ones for the first time; some of the captives had been imprisoned for four years. Had Mom and Sandy seen the news? If they had, maybe it would rekindle their hope.

Outside, a listless drizzle blackened the asphalt. Reed spotted Jordan climbing out of her VW and watched her stride into Mother Earth. Dressed in her customary hacked-off denim shorts, tight T-shirt, and sandals, she stepped to the takeout counter.

"There she is."

Adam shoved his carrot cake aside, turned to get a good look, and nodded with approval. "Looks like a high school head cheerleader turned bra burner to me. So, go on, make your move already. I'm sick of you obsessing about her."

"You think it's the right time, huh?"

"There's never a right time. In the words of Castaneda, *a man of knowledge lives by acting, not by thinking about acting.*"

"A man of knowledge—is that what I am?"

Adam stole another hungry look at Jordan. "No, you're just a stupid *schlemiel* in love."

Weeks ago, Reed had discovered a stack of *Playboy* magazines shoved beneath Adam's bed and become convinced his roommate was a virgin. To avoid embarrassment, he'd never mentioned it.

"Besides," Adam added, "at some point in life, you gotta say, what the fuck?"

Reed watched Jordan hurry outside. "You think?" He jumped up and tossed a five-dollar bill on the table. "Don't wait around for me."

"Hey, it's raining, man!"

"Take the bus."

Outside, the drizzle was now a steady downpour. Passing car tires hissed; clouds of wet spray rose in their wake. Reed walked over to Jordan's VW, where she was attempting without success to start the car. He tapped on the window.

She rolled it down reluctantly. "Didn't think this was your kind of restaurant."

"Can I take a look?"

"No need. It'll start."

"Probably not in this rain."

She turned the ignition again—another useless click—then stared at the rain streaming down Reed's face with a resigned smile. "You're never going to give it up, are you?"

"Nope." He grinned.

Jordan hesitated, then climbed out. Lifting the rear-engine hood, Reed began to fiddle around. She squatted next to him, and he was soon distracted by the outline of her breasts against her wet T-shirt. She appeared unconcerned about getting soaked.

"Why don't you stay dry?"

She shot him a *Don't patronize me* look. Reed opened the passenger door, leaned into the back seat, and yanked up the cushion to reveal the battery beneath.

"Cool," Jordan murmured. "I always wondered where that was."

Reed suspected the battery was the problem. "Tell you what. I'll drive you home, then come back and fix it."

"Not necessary. But fine, knock yourself out. Olivia hates to reheat this stuff."

He dropped her off at the small house near campus that she and Olivia rented, bought a new battery, and soon had the VW engine purring. Replacing the tools, he discovered two well-worn textbooks in the trunk: *Drilling Engineering* and *Introduction to the Oil and Gas Industry*. What the heck was she doing with those?

The night before, he'd learned that Jordan planned to become a social worker and had a younger brother, Brick.

"He's lazy as hell. Be lucky if he manages a high school diploma. But—get this—Harlan automatically assumes Brick's heir to the Ellis Oil throne, even though he doesn't give a rip about the business."

Reed closed the trunk, opened the glove compartment to replace the owner's manual, and spotted a photograph. Looking about fourteen, Jordan sat astride a horse, wearing one of those fancy riding outfits—polished boots, tight pants, jacket, and black helmet. Smiling proudly, she held a ribbon.

The man on the horse next to her—probably Harlan—looked about fifty. He was a broad-shouldered guy who wore his western denim well. His air of command reminded Reed of the Navy admirals who used to come over for dinner when he was a kid. Worldly, self-assured, accustomed to giving orders and seeing them carried out without question.

Feeling like a voyeur, he shut the glove compartment and drove to Jordan's house.

She appeared at the door toweling her damp hair, wearing an oversized Florida Tech T-shirt that barely covered her butt. "You wanna' come in, dry off?"

"Like to, but I'm kinda late for class."

"Thanks for your help. Can I at least give you a ride to your car?"

On the way back to Mother Earth, he rehearsed what he would say.

Jordan pulled the Beetle into the café parking lot and waited for him to climb out. "Well, thanks again."

"Glad to help. Listen..." he began, then regressed to fumbling like a ninth grader. "I was wondering. Would you be...I mean, are you doing anything tomorrow? Or maybe, uh, some other day this weekend?"

Her thin smile signaled he was in for a hard time. "Hmm...why do you ask?"

"Well, I figured...maybe if you weren't busy, we could sort of go out? Grab some burgers or something, go to a movie?"

Her eyebrows rose. "You mean on an actual date?"

"Something like that."

"Sorry. I don't do dates," she deadpanned. "It's a feminist thing."

He coughed to hide his embarrassment. "Okay. Yup. That's cool."

"But I dig movies, and there's a new one opening tomorrow night. How about I call you later?"

"Great!" Reed practically yelled. "I mean, fine, cool...okay."

Walking to his car, he felt exposed, mocked, but couldn't stop grinning anyway. *An actual date. Hot damn!*

CHAPTER SEVENTEEN

Annabel was pacing the sidewalk when Reed arrived at Tracy's house on Friday afternoon. Distracted by his upcoming date, he'd almost forgotten about tutoring.

"Hey, sorry I'm a bit late. What's wrong?"

What wasn't? She unleashed her usual litany of complaints. The moron who called her a "drug-dealing slut." Her idiotic teachers, who "only want us to regurgitate useless facts." The ongoing clashes between Blacks and whites "that are never gonna end." And Jenny Palmer's gang of "stuck-up country-club bitches."

"At this rate, I'm not gonna last the rest of the year."

Since the Kastle turned out to be too crowded and noisy, Annabel suggested driving to the Black River, not far from town. She directed Reed to a small riverside park, uncrowded on a weekday afternoon.

There were a few picnic tables, fire pits charred black, and a narrow sandy beach bordering the undeveloped shoreline. The riverbank was thick with overhanging cypress, mangrove, and live oaks. A stately pale-gray egret perched on a log. A fisherman at the stern of an anchored Boston Whaler cast a line.

Reed struggled to get Annabel to focus. She stared out over the water, then at a dying oak nearby, clumps of moss clinging to its bare branches.

"That tree looks freaky, like those talking ones in *The Wizard of Oz*. Remember? When Dorothy grabs an apple and the tree slaps her hand?"

Reed nodded. He'd seen the movie on TV every year since he was ten.

"Forgot how creepy this place can be," she said.

He tried to see it from her perspective. Tree branches broken, half-submerged. Water moccasins lurking below the surface. Insects crawling through decomposing leaves. She had a point, but the river seemed tranquil to him.

Later, packing to leave, he caught sight of her wrists, the scars visible beneath the sleeves that had ridden up. She noticed-and immediately covered them.

"Why did you do it?" he ventured, then sensed her weighing how much to trust him, how much to reveal.

"I'm not sure," she whispered. "Even now."

"Are you...are you going to do it again?"

"Don't know. I never really think about anything beforehand. Stuff just happens to me."

"Come on. You can't possibly believe that."

"It's true. Half the time, thoughts just ricochet around in my head. Like balls getting slapped in a pinball machine."

Reed was tempted to lecture—everyone had free will. Like it said in his father's favorite poem, "Invictus": *I am the master of my fate. / I am the captain of my soul.* But the Lifelines training must have taken root.

"I just don't want you to hurt yourself. Promise me if you ever feel that way again, you'll call me. At my dorm or Lifelines. Anytime."

"Okay, but usually I don't know what I'm feeling. Like there's a black hole where my feelings should be."

On the way back, however, without further prompting, she described the past year.

"I started skipping classes. Smoking tons of grass. I couldn't stand walking around with this 'freak' sign on my back. Pretty soon, every day felt gray. Didn't matter how sunny it was, I felt numb, like those zombies in *Night of the Living Dead*."

One afternoon last summer, she'd crawled into the bathtub. "The weird thing is, I didn't exactly wanna be dead. More like just punish myself. I didn't really plan it, as in 'I'm going to do it this way, on this specific day.' That's why it scares me so much, even now. I was *fine* that day. I was *okay*. It's like...something suddenly switched gears in my brain and turned me into a robot who decided, 'I need to kill myself.' I never said, 'I want to die.' I just thought, 'I need to die, and this is how I'm going to do it.'"

Using her father's straight razor, Annabel slit her wrists.

"I would've bled out if Mom hadn't left work early," she said in a flat voice.

Reed squeezed the steering wheel, envisioning blood filling the tub, Annabel losing consciousness, slipping under, black hair floating in red-stained water. What kind of misery would lead anyone to do such a thing? Unable to find words of comfort, he drove silently back to Tracy's house.

"See you Friday?"

She sat motionless. "Yeah...Do you ever see people who aren't there?"

"What do you mean? Like, ghosts?"

"Kind of, yeah."

The vision of his father staggering across a highway came to mind. "Not really, but do you want to talk about it?"

"Never mind. I gotta go."

He watched her walk into Tracy's house, replaying every word she'd said. How could she have lost control of her mind? What if her mother had arrived a moment too late? How could the knife's edge between life and death be so irrational, so random?

—

An hour later, Adam watched with amusement as Reed drenched himself with Brut cologne, rubbed most of it off, and tried on different outfits.

First, he tried the hippie route—faded jeans, one of Adam's worn-out flannel shirts left untucked. *Nah, too affected.* Next, the country-club look—light-blue button-down oxford, chinos, and Bass Weejuns. *Too square.* Finally, he settled into his comfort zone—polo shirt, jeans, and white Adidas.

"You've never spent this long getting ready for a date."

"Yeah, well. This is different. *She's* different." Late the night before, Jordan had called and asked him to pick her up at six.

Driving to her house, he recalled the fantasy that had kept him aroused the night before.

> *He rolls up to Jordan's house.*
>
> *Dressed in skimpy cutoff jean shorts and a low-cut T-shirt, she greets him with a deep kiss.*
>
> *As the Mustang rumbles along country roads, she tosses her windblown hair, laughs at Reed's witty jokes, and praises his well-rehearsed left-wing propaganda.*
>
> *And when they arrive at a lover's lane deep in the woods, they waste no time.*
>
> *Naked, she straddles him as they make passionate love in the front seat.*

Reed waited on her doorstep in the glow of the sinking sun. Despite his fears about Annabel's state of mind, perpetual anxiety about his father's possible fate, and trepidation about talking to his mother on Easter Sunday, life was looking up in his small corner of the universe.

That is, until Olivia opened the door, blew her nose into a handkerchief, and glared at him as if he were a Bible salesman.

"Oh, it's you." She retreated, replaced by Jordan, who was looking sexy in tight jeans and the raised-fist feminist T-shirt.

"Hi, do you mind if Olivia tags along? She's been psyched to see this flick."

Reed managed a polite smile. "Yeah, no problem." But it *was* a problem. *Three's a crowd.* What was she thinking? He wanted to hold hands at the movie, share milkshakes afterward, drive somewhere and make out—your basic, grade A, All-American Date.

Olivia reappeared in her usual baggy overalls and work boots. "Let's split. I want a good seat."

Like air slowly hissing from a punctured balloon, his hopes for the evening dissipated on the way to the theater. Jordan sat in the passenger seat. Olivia sprawled lengthwise in back, the soles of her boots rubbing dirt on the immaculate vinyl.

Reed glanced back a few times before saying anything. "Sorry, but do you mind keeping your shoes off the seat?"

Rolling her eyes, Olivia reluctantly moved her long legs.

Jordan turned on the radio news.

"Yesterday," the announcer was saying, "President Nixon announced further troop withdrawals from Vietnam over the next year, contingent on progress at the Paris peace talks."

"What a load of bullshit," Olivia said.

"Why is it bullshit?"

"Simple. Because the peace talks are bogus, a cover for Tricky Dicky to keep the war going."

Reed scoffed. Everything Nixon did was bogus or outright evil to Olivia. "Why the hell would he do that?"

She leaned forward, head between the front seats, frizzy hair brushing his shoulders. "How naive can you be? Because it's an imperialist war. We claim to defend democracy but undermine it instead. Do you *realize* the U.S. has supported the French colonialists in Vietnam since World War II? Do you *realize* Ho Chi Minh would have won eighty percent of the vote had elections been held in '56? And do you *realize* just who prevented those elections from taking place? *We* did."

"So let me get this straight…according to you, we're the bad guys, and the North Vietnamese are the good guys?"

"That's exactly right. Vietnam's been fighting for its independence for decades, first against the French and now us. Ho Chi Minh is like, you know, their *George Washington*."

"You have got to be shitting me!"

Jordan switched off the radio. "Enough already. It all sounds like a broken record. By the way, I think you missed the turn a few blocks back."

—

The movie was *Midnight Cowboy*, starring Dustin Hoffman and Jon Voight. Reed sat next to Jordan, Olivia on her right. The acting was good but the story was tedious, so he only feigned interest. Mostly he focused on Jordan's thigh—an inch from his own—and mentally rehearsed draping an arm around her shoulder. Just when he finally worked up the nerve to lift his arm, he glanced over at Jordan—who was holding hands with Olivia.

He lowered his arm, slid down in his seat, and prayed for the "date" to end.

Afterward, though, Jordan wanted to drive into the countryside, and he glumly agreed. She inserted a Jefferson Airplane tape, Olivia lit a joint the size of a small cigar, and the car soon morphed into a cocoon of psychedelic music and pot smoke.

Olivia thrust the joint toward him. "Want some?"

"Fuck no," he said, venom in his voice.

"Figures."

Jordan smiled knowingly—must be enjoying his misery. He punched the radio on and twisted the dialed until a newscaster's voice materialized from the crackle of static:

"In related news, the League of Families expressed satisfaction with the president's call for North Vietnam to provide more information on the whereabouts and condition of American prisoners of war..."

"It's just like this lying government to keep calling them 'prisoners of war,'" Jordan said.

"Hold on a minute," Reed demanded. "What the hell *else* would they be?"

She took a deep hit from the joint, held the smoke, and exhaled slowly. "Think about it," she said in a professorial tone. "This is an undeclared war. Never authorized by Congress. In fact, a lot of people think the Gulf of Tonkin Resolution, which gave Johnson the green light for this disaster, was based on fraud. Basically, Johnson and McNamara bamboozled the American people."

"I've heard that bullshit theory," Reed said. "Forget it. Those commie gunboats definitely attacked us. We didn't do anything to provoke them." Jordan shook her head mechanically. "Either way, what's your point?"

"Simple. The North Vietnamese don't feel bound by the Geneva Convention because they view this as an illegal war. So why should they release information about prisoners?"

Reed yelled, "Because they're supposed to! Because it's the god-damn moral thing to do!"

The Mustang barreled down the road.

From the back seat, Olivia scoffed. "Morality? Give me a break!"

Jordan continued calmly. "From their point of view, our soldiers aren't official POWs."

Reed's foot pressed harder on the accelerator pedal. "That's a lot of crap, and you know it!"

The lights of a one-stoplight town grew brighter. Jordan eyed the speedometer, which had edged above eighty. "Hey. You wanna slow down some?"

Olivia piped in. "Either way, if we'd stop bombing the North, they'd let those POWs go."

"We stopped for two years, and nothing happened," Reed countered.

"Is that what Rot-cee teaches you? Bomb Third World countries into the Stone Age?"

"How would you know what the fuck they teach me?"

A police siren wailed, growing louder until red flashers loomed in Reed's rearview.

"The sad fact is the POWs have become pawns in the peace talks," Jordan said.

"More like war criminals," Olivia added.

Reed smashed his fist on the dashboard. "He's not a goddamn war criminal!"

CHAPTER EIGHTEEN

"Who's not a war criminal?" Jordan and Olivia yelled at the same time.

Now the police car's siren and flashers crowded the Mustang's bumper.

"Shit! Son of a bitch!" Reed slammed on the brakes and veered onto the narrow shoulder, gravel flying.

"Fucking pigs," Olivia muttered.

Reed ripped the joint from her hand and tossed it out the window. Leaning across Jordan, he yanked open the glove compartment and grabbed the registration. "Both of you—don't move! Just shut the hell up!"

Unnerved by his rage, Jordan regarded him with a mix of curiosity and concern.

He jumped out, hoping to intercept the cop before he got near the car. What kind of a major dumbass shithead would drive into redneck country in a pot-infused car? Most of the people around here worked at the nearby state prison and hated hippies, drugs, and anything reeking of the counterculture.

Reed's head swirled with panicked visions. Handcuffs clicking on his wrists. Judge's gavel banging down—Guilty of Possession. Jail door slamming shut. Dismissal from ROTC. Eternal shame.

The cop was a baby-faced good old boy, standing over six feet with a sizable belly protruding above his gun belt.

Standing behind the car, Reed handed over his registration and license. Fidgeting, right hand opening and closing, he read a billboard outside a church across the street: *Let the Power of Love Replace the Love of Power.*

The cop studied both documents and took in Reed's neat appearance and his pristine car. He wore a tiny gold lapel pin in the shape of a pig, an attempt at irony by the Florida State Police.

"Son, do you have any notion how fast you were goin'?"

Reed launched into a detailed justification, punctuated by a stream of obsequious *Yes, sirs*, *No, sirs*, and *I'm sorry, sirs*. Yes, of course he'd been speeding and was "very, very sorry, sir." He'd already slowed down when the speed limit changed, "in only two blocks, from sixty-five to thirty-five. Isn't slowing down that fast actually kind of dangerous, sir?"

The cop muttered several "uh-huhs" as he checked the license plate and glanced inside. Jordan's and Olivia's demure smiles beamed back at him.

"Pretty decent bullshit, son. I've heard worse." Then he wrote Reed a speeding ticket and warned him to be careful. "Some folks aren't too happy with you college kids and all this protesting goin' on. If you ask me, it's goddamn un-American."

"Yes, sir. I understand, sir. Thank you very much, sir."

Reed pocketed the ticket and made a cautious U-turn. He vowed to remain silent on the way back and stay well below the speed limit, though he couldn't wait to get home.

Unfortunately, Olivia still felt the need to spew more left-wing sewage. Only Reed's *Leave It to Beaver* clean-cut looks, along with his groveling and ass-kissing, had kept "that redneck Neanderthal from locking us up." Fascists cops like him were "tools of the capitalist power structure, which is all about keeping women barefoot and pregnant, not to mention oppressing the poor and Blacks."

If only he had his boxing gloves, he could jam his fist down her throat.

Jordan, who'd been glancing at him curiously, interrupted. "Before, you said, 'He's not a war criminal.' *Who's* not a war criminal?"

He didn't want to answer, but what was the point of keeping it a secret? The night had gone to hell long ago.

"My dad. He's a Navy fighter pilot. MIA."

"Wow," Jordan said. "For how long?"

"Three years. We don't know if he's dead or alive."

"I'm so sorry. I really am," Jordan murmured.

Olivia said nothing, and they rode the rest of the way in silence. Meanwhile, his mind churned with defensive arguments. Not all soldiers burned villages, shot babies, and raped women. Or shoved enemy prisoners out of helicopters. Or fragged their officers with friendly fire. And, despite commie propaganda, U.S. warplanes didn't drop bombs on "schools, churches, and pagodas."

According to what his father had told him, the bombing of North Vietnam was not a campaign of wanton destruction against innocent civilians like the "goddamn *New York Times* says." Frank and his fellow pilots did everything in their power to avoid civilian casualties. And if that's what Dad claimed, it was good enough for Reed.

Parked in front of their house, he waited, hands sliding over the walnut steering wheel. Olivia climbed out and headed inside.

Jordan turned to him. "Again, I'm sorry. I...we didn't know. Actually, that's kinda the problem. You put up this 'strong but silent' facade. Invulnerable, like the Marlboro Man. Why haven't you ever mentioned your father?"

"Would it have mattered? I'm a warmonger, remember?"

"Point taken. But you don't give me much credit, do you?" He waited for her to leave, but she was in no rush. "I get how three years must be an awful long time to carry such a heavy load."

"Yeah, it feels like forever."

His right hand kneaded the gearshift knob for a moment, then let it all come tumbling out. The notification. How they'd heard nothing afterward, not from any of the letters they'd sent or any of the people they'd talked to. The casualty officer at the base. Navy higher-ups at the Pentagon. Officials at the State Department. Their congressmen and senators.

"That explains a lot," Jordan said. "About you, that is."

"What...what do you mean?"

"Your vibe. This undercurrent of anxiety and repressed anger I always get from you. Which you try to hide, but can't."

Great. Just what he needed. More psychoanalysis. But her attentiveness was bathing him like fresh rain on a steamy day.

"I didn't hide anything on purpose. The thing is…in high school, a lot of kids felt sorry for me. I didn't need that crap. Didn't want people thinking I was different. Some kids gave me shit. This one guy got right in my face and actually said, 'Lawson, your dad deserves to be dead.'"

"That's disgusting."

He was tempted to point out that her *Bombers Are Killers, Not Heroes* sign implied almost the same thing. "I broke his nose and got suspended for a week. Anyway, when I got to college, I figured why talk about it? Why not make a fresh start? You know what I mean?"

Jordan peered into the streetlight beyond the windshield and said, as if to herself, "Yeah, a fresh start. Like *that's* so easy to do." Then she turned to him. "After all this time, you still believe your father's alive?"

"Yeah, I do."

"How can you believe something without any real evidence?"

"Faith, I guess."

"If only I had faith in something," she said. "Anything. You read the news, watch TV. And things just keep getting worse every day. What are we supposed to have faith in?"

"For a long time," he said, "I had faith in the government, but I'm not so sure anymore." Although he'd fought against it, a nagging voice in his head had been whispering lately—America's leaders had lost their resolve. Over beer one night, Webb had compared the administration's war strategy to football. "We're playing not to win, but to avoid losing."

"What about your mother?" Jordan asked. "How's she been coping?"

Reed shrugged. "Pretty much given up hope."

"That must be really tough for you." When he didn't reply, she said softly, "Well, thanks for tonight. Until the pigs showed up, I had fun."

Great. Nice to know someone did. He let the engine idle and peered inside the house.

Jordan walked into the living room, padded to the sofa where Olivia sat reading a book, and leaned in to kiss her on the lips.

Reed rammed the gear shifter into first.

—

Why the hell had she agreed to go out with him if she was getting it on with Olivia? Since he dreaded his dorm room's confinement, he cranked up the volume on a Rolling Stones tape, lowered the windows, and sped into the countryside.

Mesmerized by the headlights carving a path through the darkness, he pushed the car hard. On impulse, he switched off the lights and grinned maniacally as the car hurtled along, the narrow road nearly invisible under the moonless sky.

A presence drew his eyes to the passenger seat.

His father sat there. Ashen-faced, eyes sunken into cheeks drained of flesh, Frank wore filthy black prison pajamas and sandals made of tire rubber.

"Dad?"

Frank leaned forward, squinted into the darkness, then looked—bewildered—at Reed.

"Dad?"

Wordlessly, Frank lifted his finger and pointed ahead—at a white dog trotting across the pavement just ahead.

Reed stomped on the brakes. The car skidded, fishtailed, and slid onto the shoulder, barely missing the animal.

Engine idling, dust settling on the windshield, his right foot on the brake pedal shook. Heart thumping, gulping for air, he glanced at the passenger seat.

Empty.

He switched on the lights and, when his terror eased, maneuvered the car back onto the road.

—

"Driving with no headlights? I don't get it." Adam said. Reed had dragged him out of bed, bought a six-pack, and driven to a deserted strip mall where he often went to drink alone and think.

"Sometimes you just have to do crazy shit like that," Reed said. "I don't know why." But he *did* suspect why—the adrenaline rush, the feeling of being fully alive when flirting with disaster. Unless something more ominous lurked in the "unconscious realms of his psyche," like that Freudian "id-ego-superego" stuff from Meg's psych textbook.

"Sounds self-destructive to me," Adam said. "Shit. Even kind of suicidal."

Reed pitched his beer can into a dumpster, then grabbed another from the six-pack. No way was he was suicidal. Crazy? Possibly. How else to explain Dad sitting in the passenger seat? A hallucination? A ghost? Other than inhaling Olivia's secondhand pot smoke, he hadn't ingested any spiked punch or hash brownies that could explain it away.

"Maybe you're right. I'm a nutcase. Certifiable. May as well order up a straitjacket now."

"I seriously doubt it. But I'm worried about you, man. What happened on your big date tonight?"

"You mean my date from hell?" Reed gave him a rundown of the lowlights. "You're lucky you didn't have to bail me out of jail. As for Jordan, forget that chick. She's into girls."

"Major bummer. Sorry, man."

"Either way, unless I maybe change shifts, I can't go back to Lifelines now."

"Why not?"

"It would be too awkward. I wouldn't know how to act around her."

"So don't. Don't act. Just be yourself."

Self? What exactly was his 'self'? For Dad, the self was about something bigger than the individual—family, community, the Navy, the nation, God.

"Right. Just be yourself. Do your own thing. Find out who you really are. Follow a 'path with heart' like your guy Castaneda. But what does all that shit even mean?"

Adam grabbed the last beer. "Don't ask me. All I know about life comes from books. All I do is analyze it from the outside, too chicken to jump in."

CHAPTER NINETEEN

So, Reed, my man," Webb said the next afternoon, "you ball that blond chick yet?"

"Hardly." Reed lowered the thirty-pound dumbbells he'd been curling and briefly described his "date."

"Sorry, good buddy. But don't say I didn't warn you."

"Screw it. Let's just lift, man."

"Good thing you never fell in love with her."

"In love? Never got to first base." But he was aware, deep down, how hard he'd fallen for Jordan.

"I say you dodged a bullet," Webb said. "Take it from a pro. Once you fall in love with *any* chick, your life is effectively over."

—

From the moment he arrived at Lifelines for his Saturday night shift, Reed was resolute. He'd rehearsed: Act polite and professional around Jordan. Don't mention their date. Stay quiet about her relationship with Olivia. Lesbianism is cool. Women's lib is right on. Sisterhood is powerful. Blah, blah, blah.

It wasn't easy. Jordan walked around barefoot in hacked-off denim shorts that barely covered her crotch. Why couldn't she wear a nun's habit and smother her sexy musk scent with major BO?

The busy shift began with a homeless vet stumbling in and asking Reed to get him some food. The guy had been sleeping downtown in a park when somebody rolled him and stole his ninety-dollar monthly welfare check. *Jeezus.* What kind of scumbag would rob a man who'd honorably served his country?

Around midnight, a young woman shuffled into Lifelines. She'd gotten wasted at a frat party earlier that night. Dank hair stuck to her forehead. Her face was red and bloated, like she'd been crying for hours. Her eye makeup was smeared, and she smelled of alcohol, sweat, and perfume. There were bruises on her upper arms.

Jordan ushered her into the quiet room, then poked her head out. "Can you bring us two coffees, black with sugar?"

Outside the room, holding the coffees, Reed eavesdropped.

"Since then," the girl was saying, "I try to avoid everybody. Don't even know why I went to that party in the first place. I can't stand being around people now."

"It's like there's no one you can trust," Jordan said.

"Yeah, but I hate to be that way. I'll lose all my friends."

Reed knocked softly, then delivered the coffees.

About an hour later, still tearful, the girl left.

Reed followed Jordan into the kitchen. "What happened to her?"

"I don't want to talk about it," she snapped, reaching for a clean mug, which slipped from her fingers to shatter on the floor. "Son of a fucking bitch!"

She stalked out as Meg came in to make tea.

Reed knelt, gathered the slivers of pottery, and trashed them. "Any idea what's up with Jordan?"

Meg dunked her tea bag. "Just know that it has nothing to do with you." On her way out, she touched his shoulder gently.

Dr. Carlson appeared in the doorway. "Reed, when you finish, can you meet me in my office? I'd like a word."

—

"How's everything been going?" Dr. Carlson asked. She met with all the volunteers after their first few weeks.

Reed fidgeted in the chair facing her desk. "Okay, I guess."

"I'm sure you realize by now how tough this work can be."

"Yes, ma'am."

When Reed said nothing more, she continued. "For many of us, working here can bring personal issues to the surface. You might feel powerful emotions, some of which may be frightening. You may discover things about yourself you didn't know and may not *want* to know. That's why most therapists have their own therapists. So, my door is always open, in case you want to talk."

Again she waited, her intense brown eyes boring into the back of his brain, as if certain some neurosis festered there that he was unwilling to explore.

"Yes, I appreciate that. Thank you, ma'am."

—

At one thirty in the morning, a hulking guy appeared in the front room, raving about the police chasing him and rabid dogs roaming the streets. The frightened girl accompanying him said that he'd dropped some windowpane acid.

"Let me talk him down," Reed offered.

"Not sure that's a good idea," Jordan said. "Usually only people who've used acid themselves or have more training do that."

"Understood, but let me try."

When she relented, Reed persuaded the guy, Alex, to step into the quiet room.

A week earlier, Meg had led a training session about LSD with new volunteers. The difference between a good trip and a bad one depended on the expectations each person brought to the experience (set) and the environment in which it took place (setting).

"Most people we're seeing are dealing with a lot of negative personal stuff," she'd explained, "and shouldn't be tripping, especially not without trusted support."

After the session, Reed had asked Adam about his acid trips. Most had been positive.

"One thing I've learned is to accept and dig anything that happens to me, even if it's not exactly what I want."

And Sandy had once claimed that LSD had altered her perception of reality. "For the first time, I could see beyond my ego—how we're all connected, part of a reality far bigger than our conscious minds can grasp."

None of this ethereal stuff applied to Alex as he paced the small room like a wounded animal, refusing to sit or lie down. At one point, he clutched his chest. "My heart's fucking stopped. I'm dying!"

"Your heart's beating," Reed assured him. "The drug's doing this. Not you."

Repeatedly, Alex seized Reed's arm with sweaty hands and cried, "Where are we? Why am I here? I'm gonna die!"

The guy was the size of a football lineman. When he lunged for the door, Reed summoned all his strength to restrain him. When Alex felt like he was "boiling up," Reed fetched him water. When he threatened to piss his pants, Reed guided him to the bathroom.

A police car raced by, sirens screaming, and Alex shook with fear.

"The drug will lose its hold on you soon," Reed said. "You're in a safe place."

He draped an arm around Alex's shoulder to comfort him, realizing later he'd never held another man like that. Not even his father, with whom Reed had seldom exchanged more than a handshake.

At one point, a plastic bag filled with pills fell out of Alex's coat. Reed examined one, which was stamped *RORER 714*—methaqualone, three hundred milligrams. Pocketing the ludes without Alex noticing, Reed planned to flush them later.

At three in the morning, he finally slipped out of the quiet room. Jordan was still on the phones.

"Alex is sleeping. I think he'll be okay."

"Good work. He sounded like a real handful."

—

After tossing and turning in bed for an hour, Reed remembered Alex's Quaaludes. He fished the small bag from his jeans, swallowed one, and was soon out cold.

At nine thirty, foggy-headed after barely four hours of sleep, he remembered it was Easter Sunday. Shit. He would be late for church with Mom and Sandy. His sister had taken the train home Friday night from Washington for the long weekend.

Dressing quickly, he slipped the bag of ludes into his desk drawer, suppressing a pang of guilt. It *was* a prescription drug, and he'd taken only one.

As he sped down the highway, he thought about his chat with Jordan earlier that week.

"Are you going to Houston for Easter?"

"Nope," she'd replied with an edge. "Just my aunt's in Pensacola. Even though my mother's been nagging me to come home."

Reed had been curious to learn more but sensed the subject was off-limits.

When he pulled into the Lawson driveway, a *For Sale* sign was planted on the lawn.

Son of a bitch.

Since Mom and Sandy were still at church, he made coffee and sat fuming on the patio. His mother's assigned novels lay on the table: Theodore Dreiser's *Sister Carrie*, Ernest Hemingway's *For Whom the Bell Tolls*, Vladimir Nabokov's *Lolita*, and T. S. Eliot's *The Waste Land*. Reed had read only the one by Hemingway.

Next to the books was *Paris Match,* a French magazine. His mother spoke fluent French thanks to having lived with a Parisian family in 1947, the summer after her senior year at Mary Washington College in Virginia. Carelessly flipping through the magazine, he recalled her stories about the elegant but grim postwar city.

Moments later her car door slammed, followed by the back door opening and her footsteps on the patio.

"Hi, sweetheart."

Reed gazed beyond her at her stupid pink azaleas blooming in the backyard.

"I know what you're thinking—hadn't made up my mind—but the agent recommended moving fast. I was going to tell you."

"But you didn't, Mom."

She leaned over to make eye contact. "Please, look at me."

"Obviously, you don't care what I think."

"I'm sorry you see it that way." After an awkward silence, she announced that Sam Walker was coming over for lunch.

Great. Just what he needed. Sam freaking Walker. Why was he coming over for Easter lunch?

"Could you please get the grill going?"

In the kitchen, Sandy was making coleslaw. She'd consented to wear a dress for church, one of those baggy peasant ones he associated with fat girls—not a problem Sandy had. Her slender, powerful swimmer's frame matched her mother's. From a distance, people often mistook them for sisters.

"Hey, what's up?" Sandy asked. Reed yanked a Coke from the fridge and slammed the door. "What's wrong now?"

"Did you know about the house?"

"Not until yesterday."

"If you ask me, it sucks."

"Can we talk about it later? We need to get cooking."

Reed found charcoal briquettes and lighter fluid in the garage. When the coals were ready, he laid chicken breasts on the grill. Sandy walked out to join him, a glass of sweet tea in hand.

"What's with this guy Walker?" he asked.

"What's with your shitty attitude?"

"Why's he here? It's Easter."

"Did you know Mr. Walker lost his wife to cancer a year ago?" Reed shook his head. "Did you know he's new in town and could use a little southern hospitality?"

"Okay, okay, I get it."

"So try to be at least halfway polite."

Then she started lecturing, another of her many talents. He should introduce her to Olivia so they could take turns dumping on men.

"You probably forgot how many legal hoops Mom had to jump through even to *think* about selling the house."

Reed flipped the chicken breasts. So maybe a woman *shouldn't* be allowed to sell a house while her husband was MIA, but he knew better than to say so.

Sandy had harped on the legal issues for years. When their father was shot down, his Navy status had become unclear—neither alive nor confirmed dead. Yet the cars, the house, credit cards, even bank accounts remained in his name.

Fortunately, he'd signed a power of attorney before he deployed, so their mother could handle basic financial and legal stuff. Sometimes, however, even a power of attorney wasn't enough. They'd heard about a lady on base who couldn't register her car without her husband's signature, even though he was a confirmed POW.

"Remember how Mom had to nag the Navy for weeks to unfreeze Dad's pay? That's life as a woman—we're treated like second-class citizens. Mom can't even get a credit card in her own name!"

"Okay already, but the fact is—Dad's alive and he's coming home. Just because it's legal to sell the house doesn't make it right."

—

Sam Walker arrived on time, wearing khakis, a button-down oxford shirt, and a navy sports coat. During lunch, he began asking Reed questions, to which Reed gave curt answers:

What was his major?

"Naval engineering."

"Great. I also went to Tech—on the GI Bill. College of Architecture, class of '49."

How were Reed's classes going?

"Kind of a grind, but okay."

What did Reed do for fun?

Fun? What was that? "Run some track, work out, mess around with my dad's car."

Sam proceeded to say all the right things. Steered clear of war, politics, and the fate of the Lawson home.

After Reed yawned for the fourth time, Carol forced a tight smile. "Excuse me, sweetheart. Are we boring you?"

"Sorry." He relented and mentioned his shifts at Lifelines. Sandy was surprised, Carol intrigued, Walker impressed.

"What are some things you've learned so far?" Walker asked.

Just a few weeks ago, Reed would have dismissed most callers as drug addicts, freaks, or losers. Somehow he no longer felt that way.

"People are dealing with heavy stuff. Kids getting too wasted at parties. Vets coming home to be treated like crap. Addicts trying hard to quit. Street people looking for food and a place to crash…"

Surprisingly, talking about it out loud made him feel more committed.

Sam nodded. "In my opinion, this country's in a world of hurt right now. Way more people need to be doing what you're doing."

Uncomfortable with Walker's approval, Reed changed the subject to the free clinic, knowing Sandy would be interested. She'd recently marched in an International Women's Day rally in Boston.

"I'm really glad you're volunteering there," Sandy said. "Tell me more about it."

The kitchen phone jangled, interrupting them.

"Excuse me." Carol hurried into the kitchen, then returned moments later, looking troubled.

"What's wrong?" Sandy asked.

Carol managed a fake smile. "How about some coffee and dessert?"

Over cherry pie topped with vanilla ice cream, the conversation shifted to Walker, and Carol looked relieved.

He was an Atlanta Braves fan, enjoyed fishing for largemouth bass at Lake Seminole, and rebuilt antique motorcycles. His latest was a 1948 Harley-Davidson Panhead.

Super cool. But Reed wasn't about to admit it.

At the front door, Walker said goodbye and offered his hand. "It was great talking to you, Reed."

Grudgingly, he returned the guy's firm handshake.

—

"Okay, what was that call about?" Sandy asked as they washed dishes.

"It was a coordinator with the National League of POW/MIA Families," Carol said. "They're working with some politicians and other VIPs to plan this gathering in Washington. Early in May. Some kind of 'appeal for international justice.' They're inviting wives and families to lobby the government."

"That's great! You can stay with me in DC. You'll love Foggy Bottom."

"I'm not going."

"Seriously? Why not?"

Carol sighed. "Because it's too far and I'm busy with work and school. Besides, what good would it do, anyway?"

"What do you mean, what good would it do?" Reed said. "This is high-level, not just hippies marching in the streets. You could make a real difference."

"Much as I hate to admit it," Sandy piped in, "Reed's right, for a change."

"Can we please not talk about it now?" Carol said, neatly folding a dish towel.

Reed slammed a plate on the counter and stalked out.

Sandy found him in the garage. "I understand why you're ticked off. Let's go to the beach, work off some of that pie."

He couldn't care less about a beach walk but sensed big sister wanted alone time with little brother.

—

They drove east toward the beach. "She's got some legitimate reasons for not going to Washington," Sandy said.

"Really? How could her work and school be more important than helping Dad?"

"Let's walk first. Then we can talk."

Too sleep-deprived to argue, Reed drove to Jacksonville Beach and parked. They left their shoes in the car and followed a sandy path through the dunes. The day was warm but windy; the gray-green surf, with scattered whitecaps, pounded the shore. A few kids braved the chilly water while surfers waited on their boards for a good wave.

Whenever the Lawsons had gone to the beach, Frank would challenge Reed to a race, usually after the receding tide left the sand hard, its polished sheen reflecting the sky. Once Reed started earning money mowing lawns, Frank upped the stakes—the loser had to spring for ice cream at Dairy Queen. It didn't take long for Reed to beat his father. Frank had cussed the first time he had to shell out a dollar for two double-dipped vanilla cones.

They walked south toward the pier, which was obscured by a ghostly fog. With every step, however, a feeling of doom gradually descended. A thin crack splintered the concrete wall of his optimism. He feared never again running on this beach with his father, but labored to shove his feelings aside. They'd run again soon, and Reed would gorge himself on Dairy Queen cones in celebration of more victories.

For a few minutes without speaking, they relished the smell of salt spray and the feel of cool sand against their bare feet. Seagulls squawked above; sandpipers skittered from their path.

Sandy broke the silence. "You know…after Dad disappeared, the constant wondering and worrying wore me down. The anxiety got so bad I couldn't concentrate at school. I felt guilty about having any fun and pushed my friends away."

Had he ever felt that way?

"It wasn't fair," she continued. "And you know what's odd? You're going to think I'm nuts, but it's like Dad was more present when he was no longer around than when he was."

"What the hell does *that* mean?"

Sandy shook her head irritably. "I think, deep down, you know. The point is, I shut down emotionally. To move on with my life, I needed to distance myself from him. You seem to have done the opposite."

"What do you mean?"

"It's like you're on autopilot, marking time, stuck in the same holding pattern for three years. Dad's still barking orders—my way or the highway—and you're still carrying them out."

Somebody has to. "I guess everybody knows more about me than I do."

He surveyed the boardwalk, crowded with well-dressed families coming from church—men in shirtsleeves and loosened ties, women with bright scarves protecting those lacquered hairdos Jordan and her libber friends mocked.

"I don't know about that, but you do seem different," Sandy continued. "Could be the volunteering. Or maybe someone's knocking on that macho wall you hide behind. I'm guessing it's a girl—maybe someone from Lifelines?"

Reed bent over, picked up a perfect conch shell, and brushed off the sand. "Yeah, there was someone I liked, but it didn't work out."

"Wanna talk about it?"

"Nope. Thanks, though."

"Sure?"

Yeah, he was sure. "Let's head back."

Sandy insisted he first drive north a few miles to Neptune Beach. Near downtown, she pointed out a small wooden cottage—turquoise, with white shutters and a *For Rent* sign.

"That's where Mom's thinking about living."

"But it's so small. What about all of our stuff?"

"Who cares about stuff? It's about Mom figuring out how to live her own life. She's played the good mother, the devoted Navy wife. You know what? I think she's sick and tired of it all. I think she just wants to teach literature and sit on the beach drinking vodka tonics."

There it was again—like Adam and so many others trying to *figure out* their lives. "How do you know all this?"

Sandy turned to go. "You don't ask Mom anything. You may not be aware of it, but you take her for granted."

No way. "Yeah, right. Let's split. I got tons of homework to do."

—

Back home, he stepped onto the patio to say goodbye and froze. His mother was nursing a glass of wine, tears staining her cheeks. Somehow she looked older, worn down. He couldn't remember when he'd last seen her cry. Even after Dad went missing, she'd held it together—at least in front of him.

"Mom, what's wrong?"

"I...I don't want our family to fall apart."

The heartbreak in her voice rattled him. "It won't. Why...why would it?"

"Please! Promise me that much."

"It won't, Mom," he mumbled. "I promise."

He steered the Mustang south on Highway 301, then turned off onto English Church Road, the one he'd driven with his father years ago. Its branches arched over the pavement, creating a straight, mile-long tunnel. At the end, where the road curved sharply left, he braked to avoid the massive oak tree crowding the shoulder.

His hand massaged the gearshift as he ruminated about the day. His mother's betrayal in deciding to sell the house. Sandy taking her side and giving up on Dad. Yet despite his frustration with his mother, her tears had hit hard. Maybe Sandy was right—he *had* taken her for granted.

And what about that "macho wall" crap Sandy had dumped on him? More horseshit. He wasn't barricading himself, not from anything or anyone. *Everybody* was an amateur shrink now. Resentment rising, he dropped into fourth gear and gunned the engine.

CHAPTER TWENTY

Still seething about the house sale, Reed sleepwalked through his classes on Monday.

That afternoon at the river, he studied a photograph of Annabel's father taped to the back cover of her notebook. Army captain Lucas Taylor posed in a thick Vietnamese jungle. Rail-thin, M16 rifle in hand, he gazed blankly past the camera lens.

"That was taken during the Tet Offensive," Annabel said. Her dad had led his company of 120 men into a battle in which 40 of them died.

Reed had read all about the Tet Offensive—a series of North Vietnamese attacks on South Vietnam launched in January 1968. U.S. and South Vietnamese forces ultimately held off the enemy, yet public support for the war eroded in the face of rising casualties and the military's subsequent request for over two hundred thousand more troops.

"When Dad came home, he wouldn't talk about it. Didn't talk much at all, like he was a totally different person. Pissed off at everybody. The government, the Army, the president, even Mom...and especially me."

Reed wanted to learn more, but Annabel shut the notebook as if he'd disturbed a private connection between father and daughter.

He'd never told her about Frank. Maybe now was the time. She didn't probe the way Jordan had, which was fine with him.

"Wow. Three years...I can't imagine what that's been like for you. Sorry for asking, but what makes you so sure he's alive?"

Reed shoved aside the nagging tendrils of doubt. "I just am. Dad's way too tough to die."

"Just like my dad. Tough as nails."

"So, have you written any poetry lately?"

"Nothing good." She paged through her notebook. "This one's not terrible, I guess."

He skimmed the poem, then read it slower a second time.

Stardust

I was sewn together from stardust,
awakened into a tapestry of light.
Conscious, aware, eager for life.
Now I float aimlessly along a river of darkness.
In space without stars, existence without consciousness,
life without meaning.
My tapestry is unraveling, stardust blown back into space—
Once more into the void.

The words sounded so depressing. Annabel waited expectantly for him to render judgment.

"Wow, you're a good writer," he managed.

"No way. I suck…but thanks anyway."

She kept yawning on the way to Tracy's house. Must be out of ludes again.

"You can't sleep at all without them?"

"Almost never. You'll think I'm crazy, but honestly, I'm scared to go to sleep."

"Because of nightmares?" Reed thought about his own.

"Yeah, sometimes."

"Do you remember any of them?"

"Just bits and pieces of weird shit."

At Tracy's, she raked her fingers through her raven hair. "Do you ever feel you're only watching your life from far away? Like it's a TV show happening to someone else?"

Did he? "Not really."

"Well, thanks for today. Who knows? I might actually pass the quiz tomorrow."

As Reed drove away, he recalled the words of several hotline callers.

Nothing feels real, except when I get high.

I feel uncomfortable in my own skin.

There's this distance between me and the world.

Dr. Carlson had recently described how depressed people grew detached and dissociated, especially those who'd experienced some kind of trauma. "Sometimes the lethargy of depression alternates with restless activity or even anger. In fact, you might call depression anger without energy."

Could he relate to any of that? Maybe. Probably not. But screw it. His uniform needed ironing, his shoes polishing, and his homework finishing—no time to waste. Enough navel-gazing.

That night, however, sleep evaded every attempt. On a whim, he climbed quietly out of bed to avoid interrupting Adam's snoring, pulled on swim trunks, and sneaked down to the pool. It closed at seven every evening, so he climbed over the locked gate and dove in.

Skimming the bottom, he gazed ten feet up at the streetlight rippling across the surface and held his breath for as long as possible. For a fleeting instant, he imagined opening his mouth and swallowing. How long would it be before he drowned?

Only when panic struck did he claw to the surface, lungs heaving for air.

—

To shake off his gloomy mood the next morning, he ran the cross-country course hard and fast through a drizzle—five miles in thirty minutes. In the weight room, he benched 220 and squatted 260, then punished the heavy bag.

After a long shower, he stepped into the rain-scrubbed spring day and drew a deep breath. Did he feel down sometimes? Sure. So what? Everybody got the blues once in a while. For him, the reason was simple—Dad was missing. Once Frank turned up alive, everything would be okay again.

At dinner that night, Adam and Reed endured dry, overcooked Salisbury steak, lumpy mashed potatoes, and soggy peas. Reed turned to his Thermodynamics assignment while Adam paged through *Existentialism.*

Neither noticed Meg when she materialized, full tray in hand. Form-fitting jeans, tailored white blouse, gold cross hanging from a necklace, auburn hair pulled into her customary ponytail, warm smile revealing perfect snow-white teeth.

"Hi, Reed."

"Hey, Meg. Have a seat."

"I would, but my roommate's waiting for me. See you at the free clinic tonight?"

"Definitely."

Meg looked expectantly at Adam, who was so smitten Reed feared drool would drip onto his Gamma Delta Iota fake-fraternity jersey.

"Sorry," Reed said. "This is my roommate, Adam."

"Nice to meet you." Meg glanced at Adam's book. "What do you think about it?"

Adam smiled shyly. "Uh, it's interesting, but I just started."

"The 'existence before essence' stuff is strange until you dig into it. By the way, love your God Damn Independent shirt. Frat guys can be so annoying."

"Yeah, and they think they run this campus."

"Touché!" She smiled with a hint of flirtation. "Hope I'll see you around."

Adam watched her stride to a nearby table. "Wow! You never told me about *her.*"

"I'm guessing you're interested."

"Forget it, man. She's *way* out of my league."

"Bullshit. I'll get her number and you can ask her out."

"No way! I just met her."

"Don't overthink it. Like your Castaneda guy—a man of knowledge lives by acting, not by *thinking* about acting. Right?"

"Guess so...anyway, where's all this thinking gotten me so far?"

—

Word of the free clinic had spread throughout the city, and Lifelines was packed when Reed arrived that night. The guy who always hung around was strumming a guitar on the porch, mangling "Blowing in the Wind."

The front room buzzed with nervous chatter. Meg was signing in a long line of clients and greeted him with a relieved sigh. "Boy, am I glad you're here."

After taking dozens of hotline calls, Reed stepped into the kitchen to disinfect speculums. For the next hour, he overheard Jordan talking to a girl in the quiet room—muffled conversation punctuated by sporadic crying. Jordan finally came in to make tea and slumped against the counter.

"What's up with that girl?" Reed asked.

Her eyes flashed. "You really wanna know?"

"Yeah, I do," he insisted.

Jordan explained that the girl, Ellen, had been raped months ago—a date gone very wrong. Eight weeks later she'd discovered she was pregnant, and "some Neanderthal pretending to be a doctor cut her up in a dirty van." A few days after that, she went to the hospital complaining of a high fever and severe abdominal pain.

Instead of sympathy, she was greeted with hostility—berated for her hippie clothes and immoral lifestyle. "The nurse said she got what she deserved. The doctor told her to wait, because—get this—he had 'more critical patients waiting.' So she split. Now she's got a horrible pelvic infection."

Reed remembered the time he'd gone to the hospital with a sprained ankle from football. Everyone—nurses, doctors, receptionists—had been so friendly. How would it feel to be treated with such contempt? "I'm sorry. That's awful."

She tossed her tea bag into the trash. "Yeah, welcome to our reality, cowboy."

Obviously she was dumping on him, possibly because of the argument they'd had during their last shift.

A woman had called who'd nearly been assaulted by a truck driver while hitchhiking to Tampa. She'd escaped only by jumping out of the moving vehicle.

Reed made the mistake of asking Jordan how common that was.

"You wouldn't *believe* how many times I've hitchhiked and had guys come on to me. This one asshole was at least as old as my dad. A real square. Even wore a suit and tie. Said I reminded him of his daughter, then asked if I'd go to a motel with him! Can you believe that?"

"Well, if you're going to hitchhike alone, bad things can happen… right?"

Jordan dropped into her "contemptuous coach" posture—feet spread, hands on hips, head cocked. "So help me understand—I have to give up *my* rights as a free person because *men* are assholes?"

"Most aren't, but it doesn't hurt to be careful."

"So what you're *really* saying is—men are predators and women are prey. We either cope with male brutality or live in constant fear. Is that it?"

He hadn't bothered to reply. She ignored him for the rest of the shift.

—

After the free clinic, Jordan caught up with Reed outside. "What's been chewing your ass all night?"

"The way you talked about that Ellen girl, you'd think what happened to her was my fault. It's like the Rot-cee protests. I'm an easy target."

"Come on, you're overreacting."

"I'm not one of your male stereotypes. All men aren't total assholes."

"Okay, okay. Point taken." Chastened, she added, "I guess there might be a few exceptions."

Walking to his car, he felt good about standing up to her for a change.

—

Professor Carnell handed Reed his latest Differential Equations quiz, a C slashed across the top. "I must say, Mr. Lawson, this low level of effort comes as a surprise, given the caliber of your previous work."

Crossing the Quad after class, Reed scanned the boneheaded mistakes circled in red ink. Dad would have blown his top. The last time

Reed had gotten a C was in junior high. Dad had examined his seventh-grade report card, then squinted disdainfully, like Clint Eastwood in *The Good, the Bad, and the Ugly*.

"We don't get Cs in this family."

"It was just one bad grade. Besides, the teacher's a jerk."

"And we don't blame teachers for our screwups."

Frank signed the report card, ripped it into small pieces, and tossed them at Reed's feet. "Now you can tape those together and take it back to your teacher."

Reed kicked the bits of paper. "Shit! That's not fair!"

Faster than he would have imagined possible, Dad threw him against a wall and jammed a forearm into his neck. "What did you say, punk?"

"I'm sorry! I-I-I'm sorry!" Reed gagged until Frank finally withdrew his arm.

"Now you can shitcan the backtalk and get to work."

When his mother walked in, clearly shaken by Frank's behavior, Reed expected her to defend him. Instead, she'd said nothing—just offered him some Scotch tape and a timid pat on his shoulder.

Reed balled up the quiz and tossed it. Sure, he hated being knocked around, but since seventh grade he'd gotten nothing but As in math. Determined to ace his next test, he hurried to the university library.

—

Exhausted from memorizing math equations, he was in no mood to work the hotline phones that Wednesday night.

"This is Lifelines. My name is Reed. How can I help you?"

"Hey, is this the place you call about drugs?" The voice was male and matter-of-fact.

"Yes, can I get your name and phone number in case we get cut off?"

"What for?"

"Uh, never mind, I don't need it right now. I'm here to listen to whatever you want to talk about."

The silence stretched before the guy revealed his name—Steve. Then he got right to the point, like someone who'd made a decision.

Life was "a steaming pile of shit" that wasn't going to change. "I'd be better off dead." The only reason Steve was calling was to get advice. "How do you think I should do it? Been thinking about a bottle of bourbon and a bunch of ludes. How many should I take?"

Reed's mind went blank; his right knee bobbed. Maybe the guy was joking. After all, it was April Fool's Day.

Again he asked for Steve's phone number and address.

"What the hell for?"

"In case we get cut off, or we need to get you some help."

"Fuck that."

Reed signaled Jordan to listen in. He asked Steve whether something had happened in his life recently.

"Yeah, my girlfriend dumped me last month—after she balled my best friend."

"That must have felt horrible."

"No shit."

"Uh...have you been drinking or doing drugs lately?"

"Yeah, both. Whatever I can get my hands on."

"I'm sorry, but I have to ask—have you ever attempted suicide before?"

"Yeah, two weeks ago, but I didn't take enough downers and woke up."

Reed tried to convince Steve to come in right away, or at least give Lifelines his address. Steve refused, insisting his mind was made up.

"This is a total waste of time." Then he hung up.

What the fuck! "Hello? Hello!"

Still gripping the receiver, Reed turned to Jordan. "What's he going to do? I can't believe he hung up. Is there any way to trace this call?"

"Unfortunately not."

He paced the small room. "This is so totally screwed. What if he actually kills himself?"

"We're praying he won't, but at this point, there's really nothing more we can do."

Reed slammed his palm against the wall, shaking bits of plaster loose. "This is total bullshit!"

He stomped outside, leaned against the railing. Who was this guy to lay such a heavy trip on him? If Steve died, it would be partly Reed's fault, wouldn't it?

Jordan appeared by his side. "I get how you feel. And I know you care. Sometimes, though, caring just isn't enough. And that makes us feel helpless. But there's only so much we can do. We're not ultimately responsible for the lives of the people who call us."

"Okay, but I still feel like I screwed up."

Her eyes were warm and held his firmly. "No, you did your best. Just remember—it takes emotional courage for people to open up to a perfect stranger. And it takes courage for us to listen and accept that listening may be all we can do."

Jordan slid her hand over his and let it rest there a moment. Like an attentive friend. Reed ached for more but was certain more would never happen.

CHAPTER TWENTY-ONE

On Friday morning, April 3, Reed's trembling fingers removed a white envelope from his mailbox. He'd missed a call from his mother on Wednesday night. She'd received a letter postmarked Hanoi, Republic of Vietnam. At first she'd suspected a cruel April Fool's Day prank, but it turned out to be the message they'd been yearning for three years to receive.

A letter from Frank.

After three years and forty-four days, the first sign he was alive. His mother had read it to him over the phone and promised to mail him a copy.

Reed ripped open the envelope and removed a copy of a short letter dated June 5, 1969.

Nine months ago.

Wandering around campus, he read and reread his father's words.

Through the crowded, sunny Quad:

> *Dearest Carol, Reed, and Sandy, I am so very happy to write to you and overjoyed to have received three of your letters, for which I thank whatever gods may be...*

Past the pool crowded with swimmers laughing and chattering:

> *I am adequately fed and housed. Doctors have eased the menace of the years of injury to my leg and arm. I have my ups and downs, especially when the cold and rain looms in the shade...*

Through deep shadows beneath Gothic buildings, emerging into the sun's glare:

> *But please remember that, out of the night that covers us, the springtime sun will rise. It will find me unafraid, with the strength to go on, until the day we will all be together again.*
>
> *Do not worry about me. Live your lives normally. Help each other.*
>
> *I love you all, Frank*

Though overcome with relief, Reed was mystified—the sentences were poetic, with odd phrases such as "eased the menace." Except for admonitions to "live your lives normally" and "help each other," it sure didn't sound like Dad.

He knew POWs' letters were censored, limited in length, and that anything challenging commie propaganda was forbidden. But what explained these strange phrases? Reed read it over again.

I am so very happy to write to you and overjoyed to have received three of your letters...

Of all the letters they'd mailed to Dad, the commies had given him only three! How abandoned Dad must have felt! And how many had *Dad* written, only to have this single letter delivered?

With no memory of walking there, Reed found himself in the dorm parking lot. Spreading the letter on the Mustang's hood, he underlined several phrases: *thank whatever gods may be, menace of the years, out of the night that covers us, find me unafraid.*

He drove to the 7-Eleven and called his mother from the pay phone.

"It's coded," he said, pressing his fingers against his eyelids. "From that poem he loves, 'Invictus': *Out of the night that covers me, / Black as the pit from pole to pole, / I thank whatever gods may be / For my unconquerable soul.*"

Carol continued, "*Beyond this place of wrath and tears / Looms but the Horror of the shade / And yet the menace of the years / Finds and shall find me unafraid.*"

"Mom, it's a sign. A sign that he's okay."

"Yes, it is." Her voice was flat.

"Wait a minute. You don't sound too excited."

"Sweetheart, think about it. For three years we hear nothing from the Navy. Nothing from the government. Nothing from Hanoi." Her voice rose. "Then I get a letter stuck between the water and the mortgage bill. It's just a shock, that's all. And now I wonder—*which* three letters did he get? What about all the others we sent?"

"I don't know, Mom."

"Because he would have told us if he'd received them, wouldn't he?"

"I guess."

After a moment, she whispered, "Sorry…I can't talk any more. I love you."

"Love you too," he murmured.

—

Too restless to study, to eat, to sit still, Reed changed into shorts and jogged to the cross-country course. He ran by Webb's frat house, where shirtless guys washed cars or sat in beach chairs drinking beer. Past the courts where the sleek legs of tanned girls stretched to return serves. And into the woods, where blades of afternoon sun sliced through the pines.

Once again, he fantasized rescuing his father, but instead of imagining a ramshackle hut in a jungle, he now envisioned Dad trapped in downtown Hanoi's Hoa Lo prison, a compound originally built by the French colonialists. Encircled by twenty-foot-high walls capped with barbed wire, the prison had been cynically labeled the Hanoi Hilton by its prisoners.

Back in commando uniform, Lieutenant Reed Lawson leads his fellow Green Berets with valor and bravery as they battle their way into the center of Hanoi.

Scale the prison's ocher-colored stone walls.

Gun down the North Vietnamese guards, whose heads explode, spurting blood and brains.

Bust into the cellblock.

Bash in door after door, freeing stunned prisoners.

Until Reed charges down a dim hallway to the last cell.

Kicks in the door.

Skeletal in leg irons and filthy pajamas, Dad lies on a narrow concrete "bed." Flies buzz and brazen rats scurry across the floor. Reed crushes one with the butt of his rifle.

Frank squints blankly at Reed, then rises and staggers a few steps until his son's powerful arms gather him into an embrace.

Reed thundered along the dirt path, layered thick with pine needles, until the enormity of it all forced him to a halt. Hands on his hips, he eyed the row of pines standing sentinel. The trail ahead blurred as tears welled. His stoic armor—constructed layer upon layer over the past three years—finally cracked, like the first rock freeing an avalanche.

His shoulders heaved as he sobbed.

—

"Fantastic news." Adam handed the letter back to Reed. "Thanks for letting me read it. I have to admit, I never thought he'd turn up alive. Guess I'm a fatalist."

They'd finished dinner, and Adam was polishing yet another editorial he hoped the school newspaper would print.

"To have someone you love, someone you must have believed deep down was dead, just turn up alive like that. It must feel like an enormous weight lifted."

Reed nodded, but what was up with Adam? "What's wrong?"

Managing a wan smile, Adam gathered his books. "Nothing to do with you." He placed his hand gently on Reed's shoulder. "See you later."

Surrounded by the cafeteria's clattering dishes and the din of conversation, Reed imagined what his father had suffered over the past three years.

Some of his knowledge came from news reports about American POW experiences during the Korean War. Between 1950 and 1953, the communists had captured over seven thousand U.S. troops. Prisoners were ill-fed and ill-treated. Thousands died or were murdered. Reed had also seen movies like *The Manchurian Candidate*, which showed brainwashed American POWs betraying their country.

When he was sixteen, Reed saw Commander Jeremiah Denton—a POW in Hanoi—on a TV broadcast. It was May 17, 1966. Although Reed hadn't caught on, many viewers noticed Denton blinking constantly. Analysis later confirmed he'd been using Morse code to tell the world *T-O-R-T-U-R-E*.

In July of that same year, Reed watched on TV as hundreds of handcuffed POWs were marched, two by two, along Hanoi's streets through mobs of jeering Vietnamese. Though flanked by armed guards, the prisoners were beaten, kicked, and spit at by shrieking spectators.

Three years later, in September 1969, Reed had read the accounts of a few POWs who'd been released and brought home descriptions of torture. Months, even years, in solitary confinement. Beaten with truncheons and fan belts, fingernails torn off, limbs scarred with cigarette burns. Forced to sit or stand for days without food, water, or sleep. Hung by their arms from meat hooks attached to the ceiling until shoulders were dislocated. Tortured until they confessed their crimes, acknowledged their guilt and shame, and pleaded for forgiveness.

One of these POWs had told reporters, "You can resist only so long. If they want you to make a propaganda statement, sooner or later you're going to make it."

According to the military's code of conduct, Reed knew, captured prisoners were expected to "continue to resist by all means available." They were to "keep faith with their fellow prisoners" and "give no information or take part in any action which might be harmful to their comrades."

Reed remembered when his father had been sent to a weeklong survival school. The Navy wouldn't allow him to say anything about it, but when he came home, bruises had covered his body, and he'd slept for almost twenty-four hours. Yet the next day Dad had seemed fine and shrugged off questions.

Reed got up and poured more coffee from the cafeteria's urn. *So the commies can torture Dad, but he's gonna make it through.*

Then he read the letter for the fourth time, noticing something he hadn't before. Dad had traced over selected letters to make them stand out. He studied those words again:

> *June...nine...dearest...Sandy...to...received...letters...housed...especially...unafraid.*

He wrote down only the bold letters: ***unity over self.***

What did it mean? Clearly, prisoner solidarity was critical—fighting the commies by banding together. But why send this message to his family? What else, if anything, was Dad trying to say?

—

"It's fantastic...unbelievable," Sandy said. "I just hope we get more letters."

"Me too," Reed said on the phone in the dorm hallway.

She had left several messages for him while he'd wandered the campus. When he'd called her back, he'd been tempted to say "I told you so," but realized how cruel that would be.

They talked about prospects for the war's end—for once not arguing. About how their mother had cried Easter evening, fearful their family would fall apart. And about how it was up to Sandy and Reed to make sure it didn't.

Before hanging up, she whispered, "Love you, little brother."

"Love you too." Replacing the receiver, he couldn't remember the last time he'd said that to his sister.

Perhaps the barrier that had separated them for three years—constructed by politics and ideology—was beginning to crumble and the bond they'd shared for years was being reinforced. Like that day at the beach in San Diego, when he was only ten and wandered into the Pacific surf. A vicious undertow dragged him into deep, frigid water, but even before the lifeguard noticed, Sandy had leapt in and begun swimming with superhuman speed to save her little brother from drowning.

Before going to bed, Reed wrote a letter to his father, his first in three months. He was overjoyed Dad was alive, doing well in school (*not well enough*), excited about ROTC (*in truth, not so much lately*), and happy to report the Mustang was in great shape (*except for chipped paint and scratches*). And he prayed his father would be treated well and released soon. The words sounded trite when he re-read the letter, but he'd mail it anyway.

That night, for the first time in months, he sank into a deep, dreamless sleep.

CHAPTER TWENTY-TWO

The dawn air on Saturday was crisp, the path empty. Reed ran the five-mile cross-country course in twenty-nine minutes—a personal record. Legs pumping effortlessly, he felt weightless, euphoric.

Outside the 7-Eleven, he ran into Lude again.

Shaking fingers clutching a Coke, Lude recognized him immediately and backed up. "You're crazy! Get away from me!"

Reed remembered that Lude's order to report for his Army physical loomed just weeks away, and he was more emaciated than ever.

"Please, calm down. I'm glad I ran into you."

Since he'd gotten the news about his father, Reed had felt supremely vindicated—doubters exiled, naysayers vanquished. Adam was right. With the weight of the unknown lifted, Reed now radiated benevolence toward his fellow creatures.

Lude edged away. "You're not going to hit me, are you?"

"Course not. But shit, man, you gotta eat."

"Had a Snickers bar."

"I mean real food. Come on, I'll buy you some breakfast."

Lude wasn't listening. "Been thinking about splitting. Some dude I know is heading to Canada."

"That's a big decision, man."

"No shit. It's not like I *wanna* live there. Why should I have to go anywhere? This is my country too, but I'm screwed if I stay."

"What about your parents? What do they think?"

"Pretty sure Mom would be okay with it. But not Dad. He was an Army Ranger—all John Wayne gung ho. His unit hit the cliffs at Pointe du Hoc. Can't talk to him, man. Thinks whatever Nixon does is right, ya dig?"

"I get it. Hey, listen, I can't help you decide. But hold on." Reed removed his notebook and jotted down Lifelines' phone number. "Why don't you call, and we can talk?"

"What's there to talk about, man? My ass is prob'ly grass."

"Just think about it." Reed pulled a five-dollar bill from his wallet. "For now, go eat some actual food."

Calmed by Reed's soothing presence, Lude pocketed the cash and walked off.

—

Captain Harwood leaned forward in his chair. "Well, that's wonderful, Cadet. After so long, it must be a tremendous relief."

"Yes, sir, absolutely. Sir, I have a question."

"Ask away."

Reed hesitated, glanced at a palm frond scraping against the window. "Sir, do you think the war will end soon?"

Harwood sat back and gathered his thoughts. "Cadet, it's tough to tell."

Then he launched into a quick analysis. That thousands more American soldiers were coming home was good news. Yet South Vietnamese forces remained too weak or unwilling to resist the communists without America's help. Negotiations at the Paris peace talks had ground to a stalemate. The North Vietnamese, rather than retreating, were pouring thousands of troops into Laos and Cambodia and building up supply lines along the Ho Chi Minh Trail to facilitate attacks against the South.

"We need to destroy those supply lines. To be honest, I'm afraid we're in for a long slog."

The captain's outlook was disheartening.

"Getting back to your father—we do have reasons for hope. Ever since Ho Chi Minh died last fall, our prisoners have been treated better. We know that for sure."

"Thank you, sir."

"So, how's it going at Lifelines?"

"Uh, pretty well, sir. It's real busy there, so I think I'm helping out."

"Good. By the way, you haven't knocked down anyone lately, have you?"

"Uh, no, sir."

"Now *that's* progress."

—

Early that afternoon, Reed coaxed Adam to the cross-country course. After jogging slowly about two miles, Adam starting coughing.

"Sorry, I'm holding you back, man. Too much grass."

"Not a problem. Let's knock off and walk over to Lake Ann."

They sat on a bench in the shade of a massive oak. Adam wiped sweat from his face and eyed Reed. "I've never seen you this relaxed. It's like you're a completely different person."

Self-conscious, Reed changed the subject. "So you ask Meg out yet?"

"Uh, no."

"Because she asked me about you," Reed lied.

Adam's eyes widened. "No shit?"

"What's the worst that can happen? If she says no, it's her loss."

Adam looked skeptical but seemed flattered by Reed's confidence. By the time they trudged back to the dorm, he'd agreed to call Meg.

"Good." Reed grinned. "Because she wants to know if you have a big dick."

"You better be kidding."

"I said no, but you'd make up for it with intellectual stimulation."

—

At the gym later, Webb was also happy to hear the news. He grabbed a dumbbell and began curling it.

"Fucking commies. We should order up some B-52s to carpet-bomb the shit outa Hanoi until they surrender."

"Yeah, but what if a bomb lands on the prison and kills my dad?"

"Don't worry. It's precision bombing, man. Believe me, the only thing the commies understand is raw power."

"Easy for you to say."

"By the way, how's it going with that chick Jordan?"

"Nowhere. Like I said, she's into girls, not guys."

"Are you sure?"

"What do you mean, am I sure? Yeah, I'm sure."

Webb leaned against the bench and admired his twitching biceps. "I wouldn't be, if I were you. In my experience—which I have to admit is considerable—women are complicated, emotional human beings. More so than men. Hell, maybe she swings both ways—she might be up for a threesome."

"What the hell are you talking about?"

"Don't tell me you haven't thought of that." Reed hadn't but wasn't about to admit it. "Dude! Get your gearhead outa your car. There's a big-ass world out there." Webb smiled. "Besides, I'd like to know if the chick's carpet matches her drapes."

"Is there even five minutes a day when you don't think about sex?"

"I tend to doubt it."

—

Arriving an hour early for his shift that night, Reed cleaned up the kitchen—wiped the counter, washed the dishes, and scrubbed a grease-caked skillet. Whistling, he finished by mopping the black-and-white checkerboard linoleum floor.

Bemused, Jordan scrutinized his efforts from the doorway. "Tell me, do you cook as well as you clean?"

Reed was still smiling when he stepped into the hotline room later.

"So what happened?" Jordan asked. "Win the lottery or something?"

"Much better. My dad's alive." He told her about the letter.

"That's amazing. You must be awfully relieved."

Once again Reed was about to counter with "I told you so," but she sounded sincere.

"What about your mom? How's she doing?"

"She's in shock, I guess. It happened so suddenly."

"I can only imagine."

He paged aimlessly through the call log wondering about Easter lunch with that Walker guy. There'd been no hint of intimacy between Walker and his mother. Reed had allowed himself to suspect something terrible. Anyway, Walker was history. Dad was alive! Captain Harwood would be proven wrong, the war would end soon, and the commie bastards would free all POWs.

His jubilant demeanor throughout the shift must have impressed Jordan, because she invited him over for Sunday dinner.

"Olivia's vegetarian, but don't fret—we'll have plenty of beer."

—

Reed inspected their well-furnished, neat house. A matching tan sofa and chair crowded the small living room, and a burgundy shag rug covered most of the scarred hardwood floor. A bookshelf made of wood planks and apple crates was packed with books. Reed spotted two that Jordan and Olivia had mentioned: Betty Friedan's *The Feminine Mystique* and *The Second Sex* by Simone de Beauvoir.

When he volunteered to help cook dinner, Jordan handed him a beer. "We've got this, sailor. Relax, celebrate."

Dinner was brown rice, beans, tofu, and corn bread—all of which went down easier with Jordan's proximity and more beer.

In the backyard after dinner, they lounged in wooden Adirondack chairs. Reed drew a deep, relaxed breath. He hadn't bothered to tuck in his T-shirt or wear socks with his running shoes. When Olivia offered him a fat joint, he hesitated. Since getting the news, he'd been floating in a different realm—peaceful as a calm sea. What the heck—he'd encountered far worse pharmaceutical threats at Lifelines.

"Wow, as I live and breathe!" Olivia exclaimed.

Reed inhaled the marijuana smoke slowly and deeply, held his breath, exhaled, and passed the joint to Jordan.

Pot made Olivia's lips even looser than usual. Tonight's lecture was about abortion. Turned out Florida's legislature was debating a bill to increase access. Olivia read from a newspaper article:

"*Opponents of the proposed legislation condemned it, calling it a 'child murder' bill. An abortion proponent noted that 'if we're still discussing whether women shall control their own bodies in 1970, then we haven't come very far since the days of the suffragettes.*"

She tossed the paper aside. "Unfortunately, they're gonna flush this bill down the legislative toilet." She pointed a finger at Reed. "By the way, I know you've handled a few calls about abortion referrals and followed the script, but you've never said where *you* actually stand."

Reed hesitated. "I'm guessing...no matter what I say, I'm gonna get hammered."

"Go ahead, just be honest," Jordan said.

"Okay. I'm not sure where I stand. I've never really thought about it."

"So typical," Olivia scoffed. "Men have the luxury not to care. Women don't."

"I never said I didn't *care*."

Undaunted, Olivia shifted to a diatribe about her favorite nemesis, President Richard Milhous Nixon. "How can so many know-nothing Americans march in lockstep with a hopelessly corrupt administration?" She shot Reed another pointed look. "One reason? People with *your* fascist politics."

She was full of shit, but her harangues—at least tonight—felt like water sliding off a duck's back. Reed plastered on a smile.

"Says you. In my very humble opinion, it's you left-wingers who sound fascist." He turned to Jordan. "What about you? What are *your* politics?"

"Comfort the oppressed. Oppress the comfortable."

"Catchy," Reed said. Did the comfortable include her own wealthy family? Head buzzing, he took another toke and passed the joint to Olivia. "Is it true that feminists hate all men?"

"What we hate is a system run by men to maintain power over women."

"My dad used to joke that women actually have all the power, but men don't want to admit it."

"Nonsense!"

"Either way," Jordan interjected, "I don't need a man to make me happy." Playfully, she poked Reed's shoe with her bare toe. "Even if I did, I haven't met a *real* one yet."

"Ouch."

"Let's face it," Olivia said. "Nothing will change in this country until women take over."

"Or until a bunch of old white men die off," Jordan added.

They were ganging up on him, but he was enjoying the challenge. He was invincible, anchored, in control of life again. "You mean guys like me are doomed to extinction?"

Jordan appraised his lean, fit body—like a horse buyer evaluating a stallion for stud.

"Well, you're not the worst genetic specimen I've ever seen. We might oughta keep you around...strictly as a semen donor, that is."

"Well, it's good to know I have *some* kind of future. In case the Navy thing doesn't work out."

Jordan laughed, heartier and deeper than he'd ever heard.

He sensed something stirring between them. The way her eyes lingered on him during dinner, how closely she'd brushed past him in the narrow kitchen.

It felt real.

—

"After all this time, that's incredible," Annabel said Monday afternoon at the river. "You know, I remember the night we met at that party. You looked really bummed. Kind of reminded me of that actor Montgomery Clift. Super handsome on the outside but all sad inside."

Funny, he remembered being bored and irritable, but not sad.

He closed her math notebook. "Got seven out of ten right. Not bad at all."

Her eyes brightened. Her fingernails—usually black—were painted purple today to match her eyeshadow, and her tangled hair was well brushed. She didn't seem quite as down as she'd been last time, when he'd read her depressing poem. But then she looked off, somber again.

Maybe she was thinking about her own father's absence. They'd finished her assignment early and were soaking up some sun. It was one of those perfect April days—mild and breezy.

He urged her not to give up on her father.

"Forget about him," she said despondently, then gazed across the river. "How far is it to the other side?"

"Probably about two hundred yards or so," he said, comparing the river's width to a football field.

"Is it deep?"

"Deep enough. Why?"

"No reason." She flipped through her notebook. "This one's bad, but not absolute garbage. In case you're interested."

He leaned in to read the poem.

The Ghost
Am I alive? Do I exist?
I smile, but no one smiles back.
I talk, but no one hears me.
I am invisible.
I live between the cracks.
I must be a ghost.
Yet my heart beats, and I bleed.
My lungs beg for air, and I breathe.
I long to escape the shadows someday.
And step into the light of my real life.

Once again, Reed resisted being sucked into her dark well. "I really like the line about escaping from the shadows."

To cheer her up, he suggested vanilla soft-serve at Dairy Queen.

At an outside table, he picked up her latest math quiz—a C. "I told you, this is progress. You were getting nothing but Ds before."

"True, but except for you, everything in my life sucks right now."

Reed dumped the remains of his cone. Was he seriously the only positive thing in her life? If so, that was way too much responsibility. Right then, he made a decision. Finals were looming, and he was behind. He'd tutor another week or two, then find a polite way to end it.

CHAPTER TWENTY-THREE

Reed waits eagerly in the middle of downtown Hanoi, facing the Hoa Lo prison's enormous steel doors, which slowly creak open. Frank stumbles outside, unaccompanied by guards or soldiers. He wears typical Vietnamese dark trousers and a white shirt. The doors clang shut behind him.

To be rescued by American forces, Reed and Frank must reach the Vietnamese demilitarized zone and, beyond it, South Vietnam. Which direction is that? And how can they get out of the city? Especially since they stick out as Westerners.

"Where's the Mustang?" Frank demands.

Reed has parked it nearby for a quick getaway. He leads his father along narrow streets, passing throngs of Vietnamese, who glare at them murderously.

Covered with dust, the Mustang waits in a crumbling garage. Frank climbs in and turns the ignition. Click. Click.

"Dammit! How long's it been sitting here? Didn't I tell you to keep the battery charged? What a dumbass shithead!"

Abandoning the car, they search for a bus stop. Frank stops a tiny, elderly woman with several missing teeth and, in broken Vietnamese, asks for directions to the South.

"Miên Nam?"

The woman points to a nearby bus stop. Moments later they climb aboard. Frank shoves a dollar at the driver, who refuses to accept "filthy capitalist dollars" and insists they pay with Vietnamese dong.

When Frank argues, the enraged driver kicks them off. They decide to "borrow" two bicycles leaning against a wall.

Pedaling into heavy traffic, they're soon hemmed in by hundreds of Vietnamese on bikes and mopeds, who shout and shake their fists and, oddly enough, yell in English.

"Who are these capitalist running dogs?"

"How dare they steal the People's bicycles!"

Suddenly, police materialize, accompanied by the stolen bikes' owners.

Frank and Reed discard the bikes, break free from the mob, dash down a winding alley, and burst onto a major avenue…

Only to find themselves back outside the prison.

The police close in but can't protect them from the Vietnamese brandishing sticks and rocks, one of which smashes Frank's head; blood streams down his forehead.

"Dad!"

But before he can shield his father, a stick bashes Reed in the face—

Reed's eyes snapped open, his heart pounding, his body damp with sweat. Adam stirred and groaned, then rolled toward the wall.

Struggling out of bed, he replayed the nightmare. In the past, he would have dismissed it as bullshit, but a week earlier he'd asked Meg whether dreams meant anything.

"They're super fascinating," she'd said. "I think about mine all the time. My psych professor says some are important—especially recurring dreams or nightmares that are associated with strong emotions."

Mulling over the dream's failed escape attempt as he showered and dressed, Reed concluded that the strong emotions he felt were dread that his father might never be released and abject helplessness to do a damn thing about it.

—

Slumping in class, eyes heavy with fatigue, Reed craved a nap before dinner. When he returned to the dorm, however, Adam was in gym shorts, bending over, fingers stretching to the floor.

"Let's run, man!"

"Now? I'm bushed."

"Come on! I gotta get in shape!"

Reed yawned. "Okay, what's going on?"

"Get this. I asked Meg out, and she said yes!"

"Never had a doubt."

"Well, I might need to borrow some of your clothes. Mine are all thrift-store shit."

"There's nothing wrong with your clothes. Just be yourself. Isn't that what you've been telling me all along?"

"Yeah, but the self I've got now isn't good enough."

—

A Black man who looked about thirty hobbled into Lifelines. Jordan spoke to him for a few minutes, then fetched Reed from the hotline room.

"I'm thinking he wants to rap with a guy," she told him. "His name is Joseph, and he's heard about the new methadone clinic in town and wanted to know more about it." She explained that Joseph had severely injured his hip and legs in Vietnam, suffered through multiple surgeries, and become dependent on painkillers. "When the doctors cut him off, he got addicted to heroin. Lately we're seeing more people go from one drug to another. It's horrible."

Reed walked over, introduced himself, and asked how he could be helpful.

"You guys know where a man could get some work around here?"

"What kind of work are you looking for?" Reed asked.

"Before I joined up, I did some landscaping. Planting trees and bushes and stuff."

"Did you like doing that?"

"Yup. In Nam, all we did was 'defoliate.' That's a fancy-ass word for destroying God's good green earth."

"Maybe landscaping is something you could do again."

"Sure, if my legs can hold out, and if I can get myself clean."

Since Joseph was eager to talk, Reed made coffee and listened. It was like twisting open a rusted spigot.

After returning from Vietnam, Joseph had taken to drinking. "Even now, when I talk about the shit that went down over there, I wanna drink. Real bad. Makes it so I can't remember nothing, feel nothing, *be* nothing. Know what I mean?"

Sort of. Reed nodded. After Dad was shot down, he *had* begun to drink more, putting away a six-pack with the guys after football games or chasing beer with whiskey to help him relax—although he'd always kept it under control.

"For a long time, the firefights were in my brain," Joseph continued. "Not just thinking about 'em but flat-out reliving 'em. Feeling the fear all over again, doin' the actual shootin'. Anytime I'd lay down and close my eyes, they'd come right on back. About the only thing besides booze that made 'em go away was riding my Harley ninety miles an hour."

The nightmares became so bad, he dreaded falling asleep and would stay up all night drinking. "In the morning, my wife would find my sorry ass passed out on the sofa."

Joseph finally fell silent. Unsure how to respond and wishing Dr. Carlson would rescue him, Reed switched gears. "So...do you think we can win this war?"

"No damn way. We'd have to lose hundreds more soldiers every week. The lives of good American boys—Black or white, don't matter—ain't worth helping those South Vietnamese."

Joseph described the decline in his platoon's discipline and morale. "A lot of us lost faith. You had your alkies, your potheads, your smack junkies."

Recently, Joseph had started protesting the war. "You wouldn't believe the crap I get from the antiwar people, even when I'm on their goddamn side. Hell, even the guys at the VFW. You'd think *they'd* understand. Fuck no. All they do is drink and yammer about the 'good war'—Dubya, Dubya Two."

About six months ago, he'd been diagnosed as a paranoid schizophrenic. "Got no clue what that means, but the shrink said there ain't no cure. Seems I'll just get worse until they have to dump me in a nuthouse."

After Reed grabbed coffee for Joseph, he knocked on Dr. Carlson's door. With a couple of phone calls, she arranged to have Joseph admitted to the methadone clinic.

On his way out, Joseph grasped Reed's hands and squeezed—a gesture that felt as intimate as a hug. "Thanks, man. It's a blessing to talk to somebody who actually gives a shit."

In the hotline room, Reed sank into a chair. Although helping Joseph felt good, what he'd said about the war was depressing. How could America win with troops as demoralized as those Joseph had described?

Jordan looked up from her sociology textbook. "I really hope he makes it." She leaned back and stared at the ceiling. "You know, there was this guy in high school. Two years older. We went out once or twice—he'd bring me daisies before our dates. Then he was drafted. After only a month, he got blown to bits." She shut her eyes. "He was so gentle. Wouldn't hurt a fly."

"I'm so sorry." He tried and failed to stifle a yawn.

"You look plumb tuckered out. Why don't you take a nap? Meg can fill in."

"Okay, maybe just a few minutes."

Reed escaped into the quiet room, yanked off his sneakers, and fell facedown on the bed. Within moments, he was asleep.

When the door creaked open, he stirred. Moonlight seeped through the blinds. Jordan stepped inside, kicked off her sandals, climbed onto the single bed, and straddled his lower back.

"Huh? Wh-what?"

"Stay still!" she whispered, thighs locking him in place. Her hands slid beneath his T-shirt; her fingers expertly kneaded his upper back, shoulders, and neck.

Mystified and aroused, Reed tried to roll over to face her, but her thighs squeezed harder. "Don't move!"

For what felt like a delicious eternity, her palms glided expertly over his skin. He shivered from her touch. Then, as abruptly as she'd appeared, she climbed off. All business again.

"Let's go. Back to work."

Remaining facedown to hide his bulging erection, he muttered, "Give me a minute."

"Take two."

For the blessedly brief remainder of the shift, Jordan acted friendly yet oddly shy around him. What the heck was going on?

When Reed staggered painfully into the dorm room, Adam was immersed in his *Existentialism* book. "What's wrong?"

"The worst case of blue balls ever."

"Want some privacy?"

Reed groaned and collapsed in bed.

—

"Dig this, man," Adam said at breakfast on Friday. He shoved the school newspaper across the table, open to the Advice and Dissent page. "They published my letter! It's not much, but hey, it's a start."

"Nice work. I'll read it later this morning."

At the library after class, Reed took a break to read Adam's letter to the editor:

We're All in This Together

Brothers and sisters, let's face facts. The richest, the most powerful, the most technologically accomplished society known to mankind is mired in racism, sexism, environmental destruction, and a tragic war in Southeast Asia.

How did we get here, and what do we do next?

Twenty-five years ago, America emerged from World War II as the biggest winner. Smooth sailing ahead. No more Depression. A good job, a split-level in the suburbs, two cars, two-point-four kids, and endless consumer goodies. Let's rock and roll, get high, get laid, get stuff, get rich.

Beneath the shiny surface, though, lies plenty of hardship and anxiety. In the midst of rising wealth, thousands go hungry and homeless. Black people, women, and gays are smothered by discrimination and inequality.

We spend millions landing on the moon while choking Planet Earth in garbage. And all of us remain terrified of a Cold War that could turn hot at the push of a button.

Finally, though, we're waking up and starting to ask the tough questions. Isn't there more to life than militarism, materialism, and menace? Is this the best America can do? Of course not.

But folks, only by coming together can we find solutions and win the struggle for freedom and social justice. Everywhere, you can feel a yearning for more community and greater trust.

Now's the time for action, not apathy; the time to commit, not drop out. Straights and freaks, Black people and white people, men and women—let's make it happen! Join the protest against the war on April 15!

Adam Gold, Class of 1972

Reed shoved the paper aside. Lofty rhetoric but scant on details. And the clarion call for involvement sounded odd coming from Adam, who was so often fatalistic and alienated. Perhaps he was warming in the glow of Meg's sunny outlook.

The reference to the Cold War dredged up memories of the Cuban missile crisis in '62. Reed had been only twelve, but he'd sensed the swirling undercurrent of fear as his family gathered to watch President Kennedy deliver his blockade speech. His father leaned toward the TV, his expression grim, when Kennedy stated, "It shall be the policy of this nation to regard any nuclear missile launched from Cuba against any nation in the Western Hemisphere as an attack by the Soviet Union on the United States, requiring a full retaliatory response upon the Soviet Union."

He remembered all those civil defense sirens in elementary school. Being ordered to crawl under his desk during safety drills for protection from mushroom clouds of radioactive death. By middle school, however, cynicism had set in, and his buddies joked about a more realistic drill—in case of a nuclear attack, spread your legs wide, bend over, and kiss your ass goodbye.

None of it was a joke for his father, who'd indoctrinated him about the threat posed by the Soviet Union and Red China. More than other kids, Reed felt the prospect of nuclear annihilation as a constant, low-level hum of dread—not loud enough to prevent him from partying, playing football, or trolling for dates, but present nonetheless.

As he walked out of the library, a girl thrust a flyer in his hands, a notice about the April 15 protest Adam had mentioned in his article.

—

At the river that afternoon, Reed tossed his pencil in the air after explaining the same problem to Annabel three times. "I don't know where your head is, but it's not here."

"I can't believe it. Asshole's moving in. There's no way I'm living with that loser. Get this—he unloaded all his clothes and crap. Then he marched into the garage, bitched about the mess, and says he's gonna throw out Dad's tools. No way *that's* gonna happen!"

"What about your mother? Have you talked to her?"

"Yeah, well, I tried. But she doesn't care what I think."

Neither did his mom, who wanted to sell their house no matter what he thought. "I'm sorry."

"Besides, Mom just sweeps every problem under the rug. As if *that* could make bad shit go away. After I cut my wrists, she was afraid of me—treated me like some kinda monster who might go crazy any minute."

He empathized, but knew he needed to extricate himself. Still, he worried—would ending the tutoring now propel her back to hanging around with losers, popping pills…or worse?

CHAPTER TWENTY-FOUR

"Let's go. I think I can do five miles." Adam was in a great mood Saturday morning, awake hours earlier than usual, dressed in sneakers and baggy shorts.

Still in bed, Reed yawned and stretched. "Good date?"

"Yeah, Meg's great. We scratched the movie and talked for hours."

Reed got up and rummaged for clean shorts. "Cool. What about?"

"Well, we started with routine stuff—our majors, family backgrounds, what we're into. But we wound up talking about the existence of God. It was yes for her, no for me. The whole night was awesome, although I drank too much Ripple. She wouldn't touch the stuff—that crap is worse than the Mogen David we drink at Passover."

As they walked toward the cross-country course, Reed recalled a conversation they'd had over beer and pizza weeks earlier.

"My Rabbi says it's not for me to question God, since he knows what he's doing. If that's true, how could an all-knowing, all-powerful, all-merciful God allow the industrialized slaughter of millions?"

Reed hadn't been able to think of a rational answer, nor recall anyone at Saint Agnes in Jacksonville ever asking that question.

After three miles, Reed suggested they walk over to Lake Ann. Uncharacteristically quiet, Adam said nothing when they sat on a bench and watched mirrored cloud patterns on the water's surface.

"To heck with a penny," Reed said. "How about a quarter for your thoughts, since they're apparently so valuable."

"You know, I've been trying to figure out how I feel…and actually, right now, I feel happy."

"Good. Why shouldn't you?"

"Because I'm supposed to suffer."

"Suffer? Why?"

"I don't know exactly. Dad and Mom are always telling me to be happy. 'It's Florida. Don't be so somber. Quit all that deep thinking.' Yet most of the time they're so down. So I feel guilty about feeling happy. Like I don't deserve it."

Adam talked about spending Sundays with his parents at South Beach. He would swim, eat corned beef sandwiches, and scour the sand for discarded Coke bottles, which he'd load into the family station wagon and turn in for a nickel apiece at the grocery store.

Occasionally he'd discover his father staring at a Jewish person's forearm, where, beneath the zinc oxide suntan lotion, the crudely tattooed death camp numbers were still visible.

"Whenever Dad looked up and down the beach, he got this weird faraway look in his eyes. I swear I could read his mind. It's like he expected his sister—my aunt Sarah—to magically show up alive after so many years. She'd just become a doctor when the Nazis killed her. I guess that's always on Dad's mind."

Adam's parents had invited Reed for lunch when they visited in January. More formal than most parents, Mr. Gold appeared in a dark suit and black tie. Mrs. Gold wore a conservative green dress.

Mr. Gold had peppered Adam with questions about his classes and lectured him to earn the highest possible grades so he could get into the best medical school.

After lunch, Reed had asked Adam, "When are you gonna tell them you wanna change majors to philosophy?"

"Ha! Probably never. I'm too chicken."

"Really? To stand up for yourself?"

"Yup. They're working so hard they can't handle another burden. I need to keep my nose to the grindstone and not upset them. Besides, Mom would accuse me of being ungrateful for all they've done for me."

Adam stretched against the bench and gazed at the lake. "You know, I never remember being just a kid—carefree, nothing to worry about except the next fun thing. What about you?"

Reed shrugged. Sure, he must have had fun as a kid, but carefree? He remembered waking up most days with lots to do and not enough time to do it. "Never thought about it. We were your basic Navy family—moving around, going to different schools…" He checked his watch. "Let's split. Can't be late for class."

Adam sighed. "Yeah, I got a big organic chemistry test tomorrow. If I flunk, maybe you or Meg can score me some awesome mushrooms."

—

That night at Lifelines, Reed took a call from an older man named Walter. He owned a farm outside of town and admitted he'd just gotten divorced. His ex-wife had "turned hippie" and taken off with their fourteen-year-old daughter to "one of those damn communes in Taos, New Mexico. I miss her something awful. The wife won't even let me talk to my own daughter. Can you believe it?"

"It's like you feel abandoned," Reed said. "Like your wife doesn't realize how much you love your daughter."

"Yeah, that pretty much sums it up." Reed heard Walter exhale and waited.

"Lemme ask you, son, what do I have to live for? What's the purpose of life?"

Reed was speechless. He'd turned twenty in January. What did a kid know about the purpose of life?

"Uh…I'm sorry, sir…"

"And I gotta tell you, all those prayers and sermons at church sound like gibberish lately. My pastor keeps saying that God is right by my side—not just when things are good but all the time. To be honest, I just don't feel his presence right now."

"It seems like the comfort you used to get from church is feeling hollow now."

"Yeah." Guitar strumming filtered in from the front room. The other phone rang, and Jordan answered. "And you know…driving home today," Walter said, "I was thinking how easy it would be to steer off the road and wrap myself around a tree. Pretty crazy, huh?"

Heart pounding, Reed took a deep breath. "So...you've been thinking of taking your life, sir?"

"Once every so often. Guess I never figured I'd ever do anything like that. But today, somehow, it seemed like a possibility. Like I could actually go through with it, you know?"

"Have you made...have you made a plan?"

"Maybe just eat a gun. Still got my forty-five from Korea."

Reed asked Walter whether he had any friends he could call.

"One or two. But we kinda drifted apart—you know, family, work, the usual stuff."

"Is there *anyone* you could talk to right now?"

Walter mentioned a friend he'd played pool with and promised to call him right after their conversation. Reed wrote down Walter's phone number and address, then asked him about his farm.

Brightening, Walter described the herd of Cracker cattle he was raising, launched into the breed's history and how it was threatened by crossbreeding with cows less suited to Florida's heat.

After the call, Reed turned to Jordan. "What do you think?"

"I'd like to think he'll be okay, but I'm not sure."

On the porch at two in the morning, Jordan ticked off the red flags from Walter's call. "Middle-aged man. Isolated. Has a gun. Has a plan. Drinks too much. Worse, thinks he needs to 'tough it out.' I doubt he's gonna ask for help."

Reed's right knee bobbed. Jordan clamped her hand on it and smiled. "Don't feel bad. You did well. Besides, I may be wrong."

She'd been friendly all night, but there'd been no hint of a change in their relationship. What was the deal with that massage? Had it turned her on too? Or was she just jerking his chain?

Jordan yawned and pointed to his ever-pristine Adidas. "Do you just wear those for show, or do you actually run?"

"Is that an invitation or a challenge?"

"Let's get some shut-eye and find out. Sitting on my ass all the time, I'm getting out of shape."

—

Jordan joined him at the cross-country course wearing well-worn track shoes. Weeks ago, she'd run fast, but that was only a few blocks in the Lifelines neighborhood, not five miles. Yet she easily kept up with his seven-minute pace.

At the trail's end, they slowed to a walk. She lifted the hem of her T-shirt to wipe sweat from her face, revealing a sky-blue bra underneath.

"Where'd you learn to run like that?"

"Why are you surprised?"

He grinned. "Because I'm a misogynist jerk."

"Your words, not mine. I ran cross-country in high school."

Walking back to the Mustang—figuring nothing ventured, nothing gained—Reed steeled himself for more rejection. "By the way, you doing anything for dinner?"

"Nothing special. What'd you have in mind?"

"How about we grab some pizza and beer?"

"Sure. I'm starving." She pointed to the *DASH-1* license plate. "By the way, I've been meaning to ask. What's that all about? Dash? Like, what, running?"

"No. It's my dad's nickname. Stands for Dumb Ass Shit Head."

"What on earth…?"

"It's sorta funny. Back when Dad was young, he got totally plastered once and puked all over his CO—commanding officer. So the CO started calling him a dumbass shithead, and it stuck. The thing is, every time I screwed up—which was almost every day—he'd call me that."

"C'mon, you're too hard on yourself. You probably only screwed up every *other* day."

CHAPTER TWENTY-FIVE

At Rossetti's Pizza, they were lucky to grab a table on the covered porch next to the sidewalk. An overhead fan churned humid air as the setting sun turned the sky a pale pink.

Jordan wore tight jeans, a yellow V-neck that plunged low enough to distract Reed, and dangling silver earrings. They ordered a large pizza with mushrooms and peppers and a pitcher of beer.

"Can you go easy on the cheese?" Reed asked the waitress.

"That's funny," Jordan said. "I'm not into much cheese either."

When the beer came, she took a sip, aimed those piercing eyes at him, and skipped any small talk.

"So, if you don't mind my asking, how did your dad get shot down?"

Taken aback, Reed set his beer mug down. He had assumed she wasn't interested in the details. He told her what the Navy knew about Frank's last mission.

"They were supposed to bomb some worthless bridge. Actually, for the second time."

"Wait a minute. Since we're wasting millions of dollars every day bombing a Third World country, why bother with worthless targets?"

"It's a long story." Reed started describing Operation Rolling Thunder—the aerial bombardment of North Vietnam from 1965 to 1968—until Jordan cut him off.

"That stuff is old news."

"Yeah, but there's more to it. I've been reading about it for years. It was a screwed-up strategy." He explained how valuable targets, such as fuel depots, airfields, and antiaircraft missile sites—targets whose destruction could really hurt the enemy—were designated off-limits to bombing. "I still can't figure out why."

Other targets that *were* approved for bombing were heavily defended by the enemy because "the commies could tell we were coming. The White House was directing the bombing. Johnson supposedly said pilots couldn't bomb an outhouse without his permission. How stupid is that? They should've listened to people like my dad who knew what was happening on the ground."

His throat suddenly dry, he swallowed hard. "So the commies shot down hundreds of planes, and way too many pilots died."

"Wow…that's even more immoral than I thought."

His chest tightened; so did his stomach. Why'd she have to ask about Dad? "That's…that's basically why my dad was shot down."

"Because the targets were heavily defended?"

The pizza's arrival interrupted his reply. They chewed in silence for a moment. Though Jordan looked sincerely interested, Reed was reluctant to dredge it all up again.

"No. Because Dad took somebody else's place."

Jordan leaned in. "What do you mean?"

Staring past her into the street, Reed haltingly told her what happened. How his father wasn't scheduled to fly that day, since his Vietnam tour was officially over. How he'd been reassigned to the Pentagon and was due back home in a few days.

"We could hardly wait to see him. Mom was even planning a party. Instead, Dad walked onto the carrier deck. He knocked on the cockpit of an A-4 getting ready to take off and ordered the pilot to get out. Then Dad took his place."

"I'm so sorry. Not to pry—and I'm sure you've asked yourself this same question a million times—but why would he do that?"

"Who knows? Because the pilot was inexperienced. Because they changed the target at the last minute and the mission was risky. Or because the weather sucked that day. All kinds of reasons make sense, but…"

A police car barreled past, siren wailing. Reed's stomach churned. Feeling flushed, he gulped more cold beer.

Jordan reached across the table and squeezed his hand. "Sorry, I didn't mean for you to relive all this."

"That's okay."

But it wasn't. His brain couldn't help but plunge down the eternal *What if?* rabbit hole again. What if Dad hadn't climbed into that plane? What if he'd dodged the antiaircraft fire that hit him? What if the Navy had rescued him? What if…?

"I guess what he did was pretty heroic," Jordan said.

"I thought so, but my sister said it was foolish. Mom refused to talk about it."

Jordan refilled their beer mugs, and they drank in silence for a moment. Then she gave him that familiar probing look—the social worker eager to examine the rocky terrain of his psyche.

"Sorry, but I've got to ask…aren't you angry at your father for getting in that plane when he didn't have to?"

Had he been angry? Sure, he'd been pissed, especially when he first found out what had really happened. After two tours, hadn't Dad risked enough? Hadn't he flown more than fifty missions already? But he didn't need Jordan playing Freud.

"No, he was just doing his job. All pilots understand the risks."

Jordan nodded politely, but looked unconvinced. "Okay, I think I get that."

"Hey, Reed," a familiar voice called.

It sounded like Annabel because it was. In a baggy Grateful Dead T-shirt, she staggered over and grabbed the railing next to their table.

"Oh hey, Annabel." *Shit.* Obviously high.

Her smoldering emerald eyes sized up Jordan's *Can't be bothered to comb it* hair, earrings, and low-cut blouse.

"This is Jordan. I'm sure you don't remember her from the Pig Farm."

"Nice to see you, Annabel. Would you like to join us?"

Reed forced a polite smile. "Yeah, have some pizza."

Annabel shot them a *Three's a crowd* look. "Thanks, but I got people waiting for me."

As she shuffled down the sidewalk, Reed rose. What kind of people could be waiting for her on a Sunday night? "Be right back."

He caught up with her outside Second Genesis. "Wait up! Where you going?"

"What do you care?"

"Are you okay getting home? You look totally wasted."

"What difference does it make how wasted I am?" She gazed inside the head shop's display window, where orange blobs floated in a lava lamp. "What difference does *any* of it make?"

"Is this about Ross moving in?"

"No, it's not about *Asshole* moving in. He's *already* moved in."

"Does your mother at least know where you are?"

She shrugged. "You'd better get back before your pizza gets cold."

"Wait a minute. Will I see you at Tracy's tomorrow?"

She rushed off without answering and jumped into a dust-coated station wagon adorned with lime-green flower decals. Reed recognized it from the Pig Farm and prayed she wasn't headed there.

"What was *that* all about?" Jordan asked after Reed sat down. "She was clearly strung out."

Reed talked about how Annabel's father had abandoned the family, described her attempted suicide, and explained that she hated her mom's boyfriend, who'd just moved in.

"That's an awful heavy load for anyone, much less a teenage girl. I know you want to help, but it's ultimately up to Annabel and her mom to work things out."

"Guess you're right," Reed said, then changed the subject. "So… how often do you stay at your aunt's house?"

"Aunt Lilly's? Holidays and summers."

"Since high school?" She frowned. "Sorry, uh…that's none of my business."

"No, it's okay. The thing is, I couldn't stand living in Texas anymore. I was sick of Harlan trying to run my life. Besides, I hated the debutante crap. It's all about externals—what you should wear, how you should look, how you're supposed to act. Not about who you are inside—what you really think and feel."

"You, a debutante? Kinda hard to picture."

"Oh yeah? Watch this." She pushed her chair back and stepped around to the sidewalk. "This is the Texas dip. Come on, hold my hand."

Joining her, Reed self-consciously took her right hand. Passersby stopped to watch. Jordan crossed her ankles, bent her knees, and sank into a curtsy lower than any he'd ever seen, her cheek just inches from the pavement.

Scattered applause greeted her performance as they returned to their table.

After Reed asked for the check, they drank the remaining beer and watched people pass. Jocks pranced as if they owned the street. Freaks ambled, trailing scents of grass and patchouli in their wake. Townies spilled from a nearby church after late mass.

"Shakespeare was right on when he said all the world's a stage. We're just actors, looking for the roles society dictates for us. Take my parents, for example. They expect me to become an obedient, well-bred heiress." She shot him a pointed look. "You have a role to play too—your body and soul for the Stars and Stripes. But what's it all for?"

Reed could have listed many answers. To serve the public. To protect the nation from its enemies. To honor tradition. To keep faith with his father and grandfather and all the fathers before them. But he was too buzzed and too happy to be with her.

"Say you *did* become this obedient daughter—how bad could that be?"

Jordan brushed crumbs off the table. "I'd probably end up like my mom. She got her MRS degree at twenty-one, got married, and had two kids in three years. Now she manages the help, organizes charity luncheons, and drinks lots of gin and tonics at the club."

"Nobody twisted her arm, did they?"

"Yeah, they did. Our male-dominated society dictated her predetermined role in life."

"Predetermined? Bullshit. People can change, can't they?"

"I don't know. Can *you*?" She displayed a rare smile, showing off radiant white teeth. "Come on, let's find out."

When he fumbled for his keys in the parking lot, she grabbed them. "Step one. Let the woman drive."

He slid an arm across her shoulder. "Forget it. You've had too much beer."

"Nonsense," she said, climbing into the Mustang. She drove roughly, grinding the precious gears, stomping on the brakes. "Step two. Let's be honest. My first period started during sixth grade, in math class. Because Mom never told me what to expect, I thought I was bleeding to death. Okay, now it's your turn. How old were you when you first jerked off?"

"Wh-whaaat?" he stammered.

"Come on, don't be such a wuss."

Embarrassed, he mumbled, "Uh…in the shower. I think I was eleven."

"My mom told me being bossy was unladylike."

It took him a moment to figure out her game. "It's up to men to give orders."

"Men don't like muscles on girls, so forget about sports."

"Do good in sports so girls will think you're hot shit."

"Forget about a career. Stay home and raise polite kids."

"Work hard, succeed, provide for your family," Reed said.

"Women depend on men," Jordan said.

"Men depend on no one."

"Ha! Even if men's brains were dynamite, they couldn't blow their own noses."

Reed burst out laughing.

Jordan pulled in front of her house. "Has any of this feminist stuff sunk in? Or are you just saying what you think I want to hear?"

"That depends," he said. "Which answer will get me another date?"

She handed him the keys. "Thanks for telling me about your dad. I know that was tough. You know, at first, I reckoned you were all hat and no cattle. But there's actually more to you than I expected."

"So is that a yes to another date?"

"How about a definite maybe?"

CHAPTER TWENTY-SIX

Reed was sure Annabel would mention meeting Jordan. Instead, at the river on Monday, she eagerly exhibited her latest math grade—an A.

"Didn't I say you could do it?"

She eyed his starched ROTC uniform; he hadn't had time to change. "I swear, you look like the guy on the Navy recruiting poster."

"What happened last night? You didn't go back to the Pig Farm, did you?"

"No way," she said, although he didn't believe her. "Anyway, you're not responsible for me, but I love it that you care."

She dragged him into a fierce, clinging hug. "You're the only person who believes in me."

He patted her back, big-brother-like. She'd gotten the wrong idea. *Dumbass shithead.* It was past time to disengage.

Gently, he pulled away. "You need to believe in *yourself*."

She jammed the test into her backpack. "Gee, Professor, that's *so* profound!"

—

At the free clinic, Jordan mentioned the protest planned for the next day—April 15. It had been organized by the national Student Mobilization Committee, of which Jordan and Olivia were members. Protesters would march from the Quad to the Federal Building downtown. SMC members would each carry a white cross to honor a local Vietnam vet killed in action.

"There are fifty-one crosses so far," Jordan said to Reed.

"Way too many." Nothing wrong with honoring fallen veterans.

"Are you planning to go?"

"Nope."

"So the fact your father's alive hasn't changed how you think about the war?"

Since her tone wasn't judgmental, he replied cautiously, "I don't think it changes anything."

"Okay, it's your decision," she said, in a tone flat with disappointment.

Yeah, the decision was simple. Don't protest. Don't reinforce commie propaganda. But maybe she had a point. Now that his father was alive, would protesting help or hurt? Would it make any difference either way? Maybe not, but Reed couldn't shake the feeling that if he joined the march, he'd be betraying Dad.

—

Curiosity, though, propelled him downtown the next afternoon. The marchers were approaching the Federal Building. He parked the Mustang a block away, walked over, and joined the crowd lining Broad Street.

The protesters were chanting and carrying signs. One demanded *Bring All Our GIs Home NOW!* Olivia and Jordan appeared about fifty feet away, carrying a banner—*Women Unite Against the War!* Reed drew back, out of sight.

A black Cadillac hearse rumbled past, *Amerika Lies in State* painted on its side. Three protesters sat on the car's roof, including a girl wearing a black cape and vampire's teeth.

Counterdemonstrators had also shown up: *America Is Worth Saving! Put Victory Back into Our Vocabulary! Communism Is the Enemy of Freedom!*

Loud cheers clashed with scornful catcalls, reminding Reed of frenzied Friday night football games.

A girl in a Che Guevara T-shirt passed, waving an American flag in which the peace sign had replaced the fifty stars.

Desecrating the flag is a disgrace! Back in high school, his family had watched protesters on TV tearing up an American flag, and Dad had gone ballistic. "That flag represents everything we stand for, everything we've fought and died for! Rip it up and you may as well tear up my goddamn heart!"

Several protesters broke into a chant: "Ho! Ho! Ho Chi Minh! The National Liberation Front is gonna win!"

Rooting for the enemy! Screw that shit! Reed recalled Ho Chi Minh's prediction—the war would be won not on the battlefield but on the streets of American cities.

Another protester waved the flag of North Vietnam—a yellow star on a red background.

Commie-loving traitors! Seeing that flag waved so openly drained any sympathy Reed had for the antiwar movement.

Charging back to his Mustang—he'd wasted enough study time on this shit—he spotted a familiar truck idling at the cross street. It was Ross Decker's white Ford pickup, stuck in blocked traffic. Armed police wearing helmets and wielding billy clubs had cordoned off the intersection.

Ross pounded on the steering wheel, revved his engine, and yelled at the protesters.

"Hey, why don't you goddamn sons of bitches get your asses back to class!"

A grinning protester gestured. "Why don't you join us, man?"

"Fat chance. Fucking traitors!" Ross made a U-turn, then braked when he spotted Reed and pulled to the curb. "What the hell are you doing here?"

"Actually, I was just leaving."

Ross shook his head. "Lemme tell you something. Twenty years ago I was at Chosin Reservoir. Humping in the Korean snow, thirty-five below zero. Losing thousands of good American boys your age. Feels like yesterday. I got a mind to grab my Remington and take care of business—right here, right now!"

Without waiting for a reply, the pickup roared off, nearly running down two protesters crossing the street.

—

"By the way, I spotted you downtown. Didn't think you'd show," Jordan said at Lifelines that night.

"I was just checking it out."

"But not participating."

"No way I'm marching with traitors carrying commie flags."

"You can't dismiss everyone because of a few stupid radicals. Every movement has its extremists. Maybe you're just looking for an excuse not to take a stand?"

He started to argue but checked himself.

The front door slammed around midnight, followed by a thud. Reed rushed into the front room, Jordan behind him, to find Lude curled up in the fetal position on the carpet. His moans filled the air, and the stink of whiskey oozed from every pore.

Shit. He should've followed up with Lude after giving him money outside the 7-Eleven.

A guy kneeling next to Lude looked terrified.

"I know this guy," Reed said. "What happened?"

"I was getting coffee down the block and almost tripped over him."

Reed checked Lude's respiration, which was faint. "He's barely breathing. You got any idea what he took?"

"Mumbled something about a bunch of Sopors and a bottle of bourbon. Unbelievable."

Fuck. A combination of Quaaludes and alcohol could cause convulsions, even coma.

Meg appeared. "I'll call an ambulance."

Reed tilted his chin, checking for a blocked airway.

"Keep him awake and sitting up," Jordan instructed. "He might have a seizure."

"You gotta stay awake, man," Reed urged. Over the next few minutes, Lude's breathing improved, but he remained too groggy to sit without help.

When the ambulance arrived, Reed and Jordan volunteered to follow it to the hospital, leaving Meg to handle any calls.

—

At the hospital, the doctors pumped Lude's stomach but warned that the drug could stay in his system for days. "Any way to contact this kid's parents?"

Reed emptied Lude's wallet and found a phone number with an out-of-state area code. Lude had mentioned being from Montgomery, Alabama.

He dialed from a pay phone in the hallway, Jordan hovering. He got lucky—the number belonged to Darryl's father.

"Sir, I'm a friend of Lude's...Darryl, that is."

"Christ, what's wrong now?" Mr. Warren said, sounding more irritated than concerned.

Reed told him what he'd learned about Darryl. His fear of getting drafted, his hunger strike, and the suicidal quantity of drugs he'd ingested.

"What are the doctors saying? Is he going to pull through?"

"They think so. He's awful lucky, sir."

"That's a relief. You can't imagine how many times we've tried to talk sense into that kid, but he won't listen to reason. It's the drugs. They've destroyed his mind."

"Sir, the drugs aren't the point. The thing is, he's been afraid to talk to you."

"Why? We've been doing all we can to help him. Nothing's worked."

"I understand, sir, but you've been judging him. Fact is, he doesn't want to be in the Army."

"That's none of your business, young man. And I frankly don't appreciate your attitude."

"Who cares about *my* attitude? This is about Darryl, not me."

"It's about obeying the government. It's about doing your duty, honoring your country."

"*Duty's* not the point!" Reed yelled. Jordan flinched. "*Honor's* not the point! Your son tried to *kill* himself! Do you hear what I'm saying? You need to get down here right away."

"Of course. We can be there tomorrow night."

"He needs you now! This is your son—you can't just quit on him!"

"I don't have to listen to this nonsense. Get me the doctor in charge!"

Reed passed the receiver to Jordan and stomped off.

—

By the time they stepped into the hospital parking lot an hour later, his anger had given way to shame at the way he'd spoken to Darryl's father.

"Wow, you really unloaded on him," Jordan said.

"You said it yourself—fathers deserve the respect they earn."

"That's right, but you've never *been* a father. You've never gotten a call about a child who OD'd."

"Understood," he muttered.

She regarded him thoughtfully. "You know, you carry so much pent-up anger. Sometimes you scare me."

"Sorry. That's the last thing I want to do."

On the drive back, they listened to the ethereal harmonies of Crosby, Stills & Nash's "Wooden Ships."

After the song ended, Reed admitted to knocking Lude down at the Pig Farm. "I just lost it that night."

"Don't feel too bad. You know how bitchy *I* can get. The hard part is figuring out who I'm really angry at, and what I should do about it."

Outside Lifelines, moonlight streamed through the windshield as Jordan leaned over to kiss his cheek. "Good night," she whispered, her lips lingering.

Reed turned his head; their lips met. She didn't pull away. He slid his lips beneath her earlobe and traced the nape of her neck. She shivered.

When his hand drifted up her inner thigh, she pushed it away. "Whoa, cowboy."

They exchanged an intimate look—his questioning, hers considering—until...

"I don't know about you," she said, "but I need a break from all this heavy shit. What're you doing Sunday morning?"

"Depends. What did you have in mind?"

"You'll find out. How about I pick you up at nine?"

"Perfect."

Reed drove away, dazed from the night's emotional roller-coaster: Battling to keep Lude alive. Pacing the emergency room. Losing his cool with Lude's father. And now, finally, a promise of intimacy with Jordan.

—

Stalking out of Tracy's house on Friday afternoon, Annabel hopped into Reed's car and slammed the door.

"Let's get the hell out of here!"

Now what? All week he'd been rehearsing how best to end the tutoring.

Annabel rummaged in her backpack. "Got a present for you." She handed him a folded-up straight razor.

It didn't register at first. "What? Whose is this?"

"Who knows? Some cocksucker left it in my locker, with this note." She unfolded a sheet of notebook paper and read, "*Next time you decide to off yourself, do it right. Use this.*"

"Holy shit!" How could even moronic high school kids be so cruel?

Annabel said her English teacher had discussed a British author, Virginia Woolf, that day in class. "One of her books has this cool quote: *A woman must have money and a room of her own if she is to write fiction.*

"Turns out Woolf killed herself by sticking rocks in her coat and walking into a river. The bitches must've heard me talking about that writer at lunch. They hate anything they don't understand, anybody who's different."

Last fall, after word of Annabel's suicide attempt got around, a few kids had made mean comments, although most offered awkward sympathy or just avoided her like she had some contagious disease.

"You gotta ignore them. They're stupid kids who don't know any better."

Annabel groaned. "I can't take much more of this."

At the river, Reed persisted until Annabel got every problem right. Obviously, now wasn't the time to quit on her.

CHAPTER TWENTY-SEVEN

Sunday morning took forever to arrive. Reed sat on the lawn in front of the dorm, reading the day's newspaper. Enemy gunners had shot down twelve more American aircraft, bringing the number of American aircraft reported lost in Vietnam and Laos since 1961 to 6,689.

The weekly death toll of American soldiers had risen to 141, the highest in seven months. The previous week it had been 138. These numbers brought American casualties in the war so far to 41,516 killed and 273,436 wounded.

Sickened, Reed set the paper aside. In just two weeks, 279 American men—heroes all—had been lost. Meanwhile, his banal existence amounted to memorizing textbooks and pursuing Jordan.

Precisely at nine, Jordan's VW puttered to the curb. Reed jogged over and hopped in.

She wore faded jeans and a long-sleeved denim shirt, though the day was already warm. Driving out of town into rolling farmland, she refused to say where they were going. Reed imagined skinny-dipping together in a secluded lake. Instead, the VW pulled into the dusty parking lot of an equestrian center.

She removed riding boots and a battered cowboy hat from the trunk. Noticing his wary look, she grinned. "Come on, this will be fun. Leave your wallet in your pocket. This is on me."

Moments later, they waited for a stable hand to lead two horses from a cavernous red barn. Reed knew zilch about horses. These particular specimens were chocolate brown—large and restless.

Jordan mounted hers smoothly. Reed's foot slipped on the stirrups; the skittish horse pawed the ground.

"Haven't you ridden before?"

"Couple of times." He managed to scramble into the saddle but couldn't control the animal until Jordan grabbed the reins.

"Follow me."

Not that he had a choice—his horse followed Jordan's lead. He'd never ridden or even sat on one before. How did Clint Eastwood and John Wayne do it in the movies? Prod the beast with your heels, shake the reins, look tough, look cool.

At first, as the horses clopped side by side along a dirt trail, it was easy. Yet with each stride, Reed struggled to keep his groin from hitting the hard saddle. They rode a while without talking until Jordan sensed he was more comfortable.

"You never answered my question back at Rossetti's. What's your plan after college? Fly Navy planes?"

"I'm not sure yet." That he would follow in his father's footsteps had always been an unspoken expectation. Dad had never raised the topic, but Reed understood, deep down, that he lacked the single-minded obsession required to be a naval aviator. Better to stick with something he could do well, like keep the ships running, but that sounded too boring to impress Jordan.

"What about you?" he asked. "How come you quit horse jumping?"

"I stopped caring about competing. It became less about having fun and more about my parents' plans for me—major in something useless like art history, then marry the right guy, ideally rich. Then pop out two kids and make sure my mascara never smears."

"Doesn't sound like someone who reads *Drilling Engineering*."

"What? Oh yeah … those books are still in the trunk. Nosy, aren't you'?"

"Yup, but if you hate the oil business so much, why keep 'em around?"

"I confess. You've discovered my dirty secret. It's not what they do with the oil; it's the actual work. I love everything about it. The oil rigs drilling in the Gulf, the endless fields in West Texas—the hypnotic way the derricks pump, like birds pecking at the ground. It's all so real, so visceral." Her smile vanished. "Of course, Harlan never let me get too close. Too many roughnecks, too much cursing for the tender ears of his princess."

"Bummer. I could see you running an oil rig someday. After all, you love to order men around."

"Ha! A female boss? Over Harlan's dead body."

Jordan guided her horse to the shore of a small lake, where a great blue heron greeted them with flapping wings.

Her father had called the day before, demanding to know about her summer plans. "Harlan said my mom misses me. But he never says *he* misses me. Olivia wants me to go to Boston and volunteer with the Women's Collective. They're publishing a book from that binder, *Women and Their Bodies.*

"Dad wants me to work at the company. Mom just wants me home so she can ride herd over my life. She thinks Aunt Lilly's a bad influence—been married twice and hunting for number three."

"And what do *you* want?"

"Not sure. Those women in Boston are making a difference. Besides, the only job Harlan will ever give me is receptionist. I'll be stuck in an office making coffee, answering phones, getting my ass pinched by horny engineers."

Her father's corporate jet was due in Jacksonville in a few weeks, and he wanted to have dinner. "I told him I'd think about it. Dinner, that is."

"If you're interested in the oil business, why not ask him for a real job?"

Her jaw set. "I'm not asking him for anything. Nothing. Nada."

Familiar anguish struck in his chest—at least she could talk to her father anytime she wanted.

She led him back onto the trail, then nudged her horse into a canter. As Reed struggled to stay in the saddle, he admired how well Jordan rode—as if rider and horse had fused together.

"Time to get back. Be sure to sit tall on your seat bones and let your legs relax."

Then she galloped off. Despite his desperate attempts to rein in his horse, it followed her lead. He winced as his privates slammed against the stiff leather. Mercifully, she slowed to a walk until he caught up. Thank God. Any more of that and he'd surely lose the ability to father children.

"Tell me something. If I were a male friend, would you admit you'd never ridden a horse in your life?"

"I don't know. Maybe."

"So why is it different with a woman friend?"

If only she'd stop using the word *friend*. "I guess I wanted to impress you."

"By being someone you're not? Some macho John Wayne character, riding into town to gun down the bad guys?"

"How about a macho Clint Eastwood instead?"

"Dream on, cowboy."

They dismounted at the stable. Jordan squinted into the barn's inky darkness, ran fingers nervously through her hair, and scraped a patch of dirt with the toe of her dusty boot.

Suddenly on edge, she demanded, "Where the hell is the help?" Her tone was haughtier than any he'd yet heard.

A stable hand appeared, leading a horse to a waiting rider, and glanced at Jordan. "Do you mind walking yours in?"

"Yes, I *do* mind!"

She dropped the reins and rushed toward the parking lot as the stable hand rolled his eyes. Reed could read his mind: another spoiled rich kid. But clearly something had spooked her.

Moments later, with Reed uneasy in the passenger seat, Jordan drove them away. Wordless, stern, retreating inward.

"Are you okay?"

"Fine." But her hand on the gearshift trembled.

Obviously not, but why? He slid his hand over hers. She let it rest a moment before gently pushing it away. He looked away to hide his dejection.

"Sorry," she mumbled. "This was kind of a mistake."

"Me? Today?"

"No." They drove for miles, locked in awkward silence.

Jordan turned the radio to a country-western station. Merle Haggard sang "Okie from Muskogee."

"How many times do they have to play this bullshit song?" She switched to a Sunday sermon, listened for a moment, scoffed, and shut off the radio.

Back at his dorm, she managed an apologetic smile. "I'm sorry. You did nothing wrong."

"It sure feels that way."

All the uncertainty in their so-called relationship was driving him nuts. He'd had enough. "I just want you to know...the thing is...well, I'm crazy about you. But you already know that, don't you?"

A flush crept up her neck. Avoiding his eyes, she jammed the car into gear and revved the engine. "I'm sorry, I care about you, but I can't deal with this now. Sorry...I just can't."

—

Frustrated and restless, Reed ran the cross-country course. Face it, they would remain friends, nothing more. He stopped at a Rexall drugstore and bought a package of condoms. At a pay phone, he dialed Candy's dorm. After the usual wait for someone on the floor to find her, she sounded pleased to hear from him.

"I know it's last-minute, but how about dinner at Crescent Beach?"

"Sure! Gimme about an hour."

When he rolled up to her dorm, Candy hopped in. Her gleaming brown hair was pulled into a ponytail and she wore a thin summer dress—the kind girls threw on after swimming.

"Hey there. Long time no see!" She gave him a quick peck on the cheek.

With the sun sinking behind them, Reed listened to Candy's chatter on the drive east. Classes she loved, classes she hated. How she might switch majors to biology and become a physical therapist. How superficial the bitches were in her sorority and why she shouldn't have pledged.

At a cheap diner near the beach, Reed picked listlessly at meat loaf with gravy slathered over lumpy mashed potatoes. Candy had a Cobb salad drowned in Thousand Island dressing, most of which she scraped off. He had to admit—she was in great shape.

Afterward, they bought a bottle of Boone's Farm red and padded barefoot to the shore. They eventually had perfunctory sex on the beach. Sensing her vague disappointment, Reed knew it was his fault. On the drive back, it bugged him how forgiving she was.

"You're sweet," she murmured, running her fingers through his hair like they were actually dating or something. He felt awful about using her—she was a nice girl and didn't deserve it.

And he felt empty and guilty, as if he'd somehow betrayed Jordan.

CHAPTER TWENTY-EIGHT

Reed tried to focus on Annabel's homework on Monday at the river, but he kept thinking about Jordan. What had spooked her on their date?

"What's wrong?" Annabel asked.

"Nothing. Just tired."

Once again, he'd rehearsed what he'd say. Since she was doing better in math, she could now succeed on her own. His finals were coming up and he was too swamped to continue tutoring. In his head, it all sounded perfectly reasonable.

On a break, they hiked down a narrow path along the river. Annabel stopped to stare at the water. "Are there gators in there?"

"Maybe a few."

"When I was little, we lived at Fort Benning, up in Georgia. Dad loved driving all the way to Tybee Island. The ocean scared the shit out of me, but he forced me to learn how to swim. I hated dunking my head under, afraid I'd swallow water, but he'd always say, 'No way will Daddy let his little girl drown.' It's stupid, but I'm still scared to swim."

After they finished her homework, she showed him another poem. "This is just a first draft."

Escape

Am I a real person?
Someone who can cry, laugh, be happy?
Or am I only the sum of my pain and tears?

Am I all of this or none of it?
Am I a worn-out idea of the person I could become?
My scattered mind is a prison, not an open door.
How can I ever escape?

Again he offered a bland compliment. Her mind was a prison? He'd hoped her depression would have somehow eased by now.

For once, she didn't smoke on the drive back. Instead, she described her father's Jekyll and Hyde personalities. There was the "always patient" Lucas Taylor, the one who painstakingly crafted an elaborate dollhouse, helped her with homework, even took her fishing. The sweet dad who read poetry to her—like Robert Louis Stevenson's "My Shadow"—before tucking her in.

"*I have a little shadow that goes in and out with me*," she recited, "*And what can be the use of him is more than I can see.*"

Precious little of that loving father survived his final tour in Vietnam, which lasted until October 1968, when Annabel was fourteen. A complete stranger came home.

"In a restaurant, he'd sit with his back to the wall so he could check out everybody coming in. If we couldn't get the right table, forget it. We'd have to split."

Loud noises startled him—fireworks, cars backfiring. "He'd spend hours messing around in the garage, cleaning and oiling his guns. It's like he didn't belong over in Nam *or* back home."

At dinner once, he asked Annabel and Louise, "Can anyone tell me why I'm alive when the real heroes—my men—are all dead? Can *anyone* explain why?"

There were days when he scarcely spoke, but on other days "he'd just lose it and yell at everybody. Especially me." Nothing Annabel did was right.

The way she dressed. ("Freaking basketball shoes on a girl?")

How she looked. ("Cut them damn bangs off so's you can see!")

The kids she hung around with. ("Nothing but white-trash losers and hippie dopeheads.")

Jagged anger punctuated Captain Taylor's dour silences. To

Reed, Taylor's anger resembled his father's—unpredictable rages that exploded only to melt quickly. Like those late-afternoon thunderstorms that unleashed torrents of rain, only to be followed by steam rising from sunbaked streets.

"It's not like he was wrong," Annabel admitted. "I turned into a little bitch and drove him crazy."

"Still, the fact he took off wasn't your fault."

"It sure as shit is." Then she smiled shyly. "But hey, thanks for listening. I've never talked about this with anybody before. I know I must sound like some dumb kid."

"You don't. Not at all."

He glanced over to find her staring at him with longing. "I feel like I can trust you." She leaned over and kissed his cheek. "I love you."

Reed pretended to check his side mirror to hide his panic.

"I don't think I could live without you," she whispered, spilling warm breath on his cheek.

"Come on. *Please*."

"No, really." She slid her hand across his thigh to his groin and started massaging him.

"Hey! Wait a minute!" She fumbled for the zipper of his jeans. "Stop it, dammit!" He fought to keep from swerving into oncoming traffic on the two-lane road as he shoved her hand away.

"Ow! That hurt!"

He managed to pull onto the shoulder beside a cattle farm—a split second before a truck barreled past, horn blasting, inches from ramming them.

His foot shook on the brake pedal. "Are you out of your fucking mind?"

Another truck thundered past, spraying pebbles against the hood.

"I thought you liked me."

"Sure, I like you. But not in *that* way."

"What do you mean? We've already *balled*, haven't we?"

Yes—in a drug-induced fog he'd labored unsuccessfully to forget. "I'm sorry. It was a mistake."

"Right, I'm a mistake—a loser, totally worthless!"

"Of course you're not a loser. We're friends. But that's it. You get that, don't you?"

"Yeah, friends. Not like your gorgeous girlfriend."

"What are you talking about?"

"The hippie chick at Rossetti's, the one you were drooling over. Who else?"

"She volunteers with me at Lifelines, that's all."

"Bullshit. I saw the way you were looking at each other. You're probably fucking like rabbits."

Reed twisted the ignition. "You have no idea how wrong you are."

"Lemme out!"

"Wait. I'll drive you home."

She leaped out of the car and jogged toward a gas station down the road—which ironically displayed the yellow *Ellis* sign.

Reed ran after her. When Annabel arrived at the station, she stuck her thumb out to hitch a ride.

"Don't do this," he begged when he caught up to her. "Please! I'm sorry."

"Fuck off!"

A pickup truck pulled over, and a burly guy leaned out. "Where ya headed, sweetheart?"

That's all he needed, some redneck picking her up. He shuddered to think how he'd explain the mess to Annabel's mother if something awful happened.

Reed tried to block the truck's passenger door. "Get back in the car. Please!"

"Hey, honey, you got a problem with this guy?"

Annabel reached up to grab the truck's door handle, muttering, "Fuck yeah, I got a problem."

The truck driver grinned. "Hop in, then."

"Please!" Reed shouted. "Can't we just talk?"

She froze, then slammed the truck door shut. "Just get me to Tracy's!"

She ran back toward the Mustang. Reed followed, sick to hell of the whole thing. Next to the car, a cow chewed its cud obliviously behind a wooden fence.

"What're *you* looking at? You'll be pot roast next week."

—

She made a point of chain smoking on the way back, carelessly tapping the ash in the vague direction of the ashtray, daring him to object. Reed tried to break through her wall of anger: He understood what she'd been going through. Was sorry she'd gotten the wrong idea. Wanted only to help.

They pulled up to Tracy's house. "I'm your friend. Please! Just talk to me."

"Get the hell out of here and leave me alone!"

—

Back on campus, he marched to the gym, determined to bash the shit out of the heavy bag.

Jab. *How naive can you get?*

Jab, left hook. *Leading her on, ignoring the obvious—troubled high school girl falls for slick college dude.*

Jab, left hook, right cross. *Sounds like a lame plot from one of those California beach party movies.*

Bam, bam, bam. *Dumbass shithead!*

CHAPTER TWENTY-NINE

Reed joined others at the student union that evening, April 20, to watch President Nixon's speech. Too busy ruminating about Annabel and why his date with Jordan had gone sour, he paid little attention to Nixon's description of his latest war strategy.

No matter. The kids around him provided predictable commentary.

Nixon: "South of Laos, almost forty thousand Communist troops are now conducting overt aggression against Cambodia..."

Student: "Which you're bombing the shit out of, asshole!"

Nixon: "We have offered repeatedly to withdraw all of our troops if the North Vietnamese would withdraw theirs..."

Student: "Bullshit!"

Nixon: "It is Hanoi and Hanoi alone that stands today, blocking the path to a just peace for all the peoples of Southeast Asia."

Student: "More lies!"

Reed tuned in when Nixon spoke about the plight of the POWs.

"The callous exploitation of the parents, the wives, the children of these brave men, as negotiating pawns, is an unforgivable breach of the elementary rules of conduct between civilized peoples.

"We shall continue to make every possible effort to get Hanoi to provide information on the whereabouts of all prisoners, to allow them to communicate with their families, to permit inspection of prisoners-of-war camps, and to provide for the early release of at least the sick and the wounded."

Hopefully the commies were listening to the speech and his family would now get more letters from Dad. Heartened by Nixon's words, Reed walked out as the president's rhetoric faded behind him:

"We are not a weak people. We are a strong people. America has never been defeated in the proud one-hundred-and-ninety-year history of this country, and we shall not be defeated in Vietnam."

Might be too late for that, Reed thought, then felt instantly ashamed. If America lost the war, what purpose would his father's imprisonment serve?

—

On his way to class, Reed paused among a crowd at the Quad celebrating the first-ever "Earth Day environmental teach-in." A biology professor was lecturing about pollution's devastating effects, but Reed left after a few minutes. How many issues could you get pissed off about at the same time?

Back at the dorm, Adam was reading Alan Watts's *The Way of Zen.* He'd just gotten back from visiting his parents in Miami Beach for Passover.

Reed crossed to his desk. "How'd your Seder go?"

"A downer, as usual."

"I don't get it, man. Charlton Heston parts the Red Sea and the Jews escape the evil Egyptians—it's a movie with a cool chase scene and a happy ending, right?"

"Not around my house. It's all about mourning our family and the millions killed in the camps. Like sitting *shiva.*" Adam closed his book. "As usual, they asked if I'd met any nice Jewish girls yet. They're gonna go apeshit when they find out I'm dating a shiksa—a Catholic, no less!"

"Jeez, you've only been on three dates. It's not like you're ready to pop the question."

"I keep thinking she's going to dump me."

"Are you kidding? Why on earth would you think that?"

Adam shrugged. "I don't know. It's like my life consists of always expecting something bad to happen."

Not knowing what to say to that, Reed opened his Naval Engineering book. "So I'm guessing you didn't tell them about changing majors."

"Actually, I did, and Dad freaked out—as expected. Why should he pay tuition for nonsense like philosophy? How could I waste my precious brain on something so useless?"

Adam glanced at Reed's right knee bobbing. "Look, man. Forget about me. You're obviously bummed about something. Like I said, I'm here to listen if you wanna talk."

Part of him wanted to spill it all—everything that had happened with Annabel and Jordan. Instead: "Thanks, man. I'm swamped right now. Maybe later, okay?"

—

Jordan was reserved and uncomfortable around Reed that Wednesday night. As their shift wore on, he became increasingly embarrassed about laying bare his true feelings for her.

When he walked outside for a break, there was Eric, the speed freak, leaning against the Mustang. What the hell? Why was this total loser always hanging around Lifelines? He'd actually bragged about how much heroin mixed with speed he could inject and still survive. Talk about a bad influence.

"Hey!"

Startled, Eric froze. "Huh? What?"

"Didn't I tell you to stay the hell away from here?"

Eric scratched and picked at his arms, at the "crank bugs" he'd described living beneath his skin.

"Why? It's a free country, man."

Reed shot him a dead-eyed stare. "Yeah, and I'm free to kick your ass."

Eric shuffled off. "Fascist pig."

Jordan was standing on the porch when Reed walked back in.

"What a scumbag," he said.

"Granted. But threatening to beat up people? Not cool. So, listen, about last Sunday…"

"You don't have to explain anything."

Jordan raked her hair. "No, I wanna apologize. I gave you a hard time, and you didn't deserve it."

"It's okay; I had fun."

"Watching you on that horse, I doubt it."

He waited, sensing she wanted to say more, but she offered him only a wan smile. "Well, see you Saturday."

—

He didn't have to wait that long. Around eleven Thursday night, there was a knock on their door.

"Yeah?" Reed yelled, deep in Naval Engineering homework. No reply. "Can you please get that?" he asked Adam, who was reading in bed.

Somber, Jordan stood at the door, wearing her wrinkled Texas Longhorns T-shirt and cutoff shorts.

"Hi, is Reed around?"

She wanted to talk, but not in the dorm, so Reed suggested Burnham Pond. They sat side by side on the grassy embankment—Jordan seemed more comfortable talking that way. In faltering bits and pieces, she told Reed what had happened almost two years ago.

"There was this guy, Wayne. A stable hand. He was great with the horses. Handsome but kinda rough—like he'd fallen off one too many broncos, you know? Anyway, he was a couple of years older than me. A good listener. The first guy who took me seriously. Didn't treat me like a spoiled rich girl. Didn't suck up to me or talk down to me, know what I mean?"

Reed nodded.

"Things were good for a while. We used to talk a lot. Actually, I did most of the talking. Anyway…one Saturday night, we were in the horse barn real late. Somehow, a kiss got out of hand. I joked at first. Told him I wasn't into that. He said I'd been leading him on. We argued…" Jordan's breath quickened, as if she was about to hyperventilate.

"I tried to push him away, which really pissed him off. Then I started screaming. The next thing I knew, his big hand was covering my mouth. I couldn't breathe, felt like I was suffocating. I panicked, then tried to fight, but he was way too strong…so I just froze. Just absolutely froze."

She fell silent as some students passed by, talking and laughing.

"I still remember how he smelled of sweat. And that horrible Red Man he chewed."

"I'm so sorry," Reed said.

"I never knew how Mom and Dad found out. In some ways, Wayne was dumb as a post; shoot, he probably bragged about it."

A week after the rape, Jordan had overheard her parents arguing in the living room. "Harlan was complaining—how many times had he warned me to stay away from the goddamn help? He practically said I had it coming. Like it was *my* fault and *I* should be ashamed. That's when I rode off on my horse. That's when I fell off and almost lost my damn eye."

Reed glanced at her scar—she'd been lucky.

Harlan had vowed to take care of it quietly. Only later did the news filter back to Jordan. "Wayne just up and disappeared one day. Harlan had him beaten and dumped in scrubland miles from nowhere. I still don't know whether he got out alive. No one's ever seen him since.

"It was just like Harlan," she added bitterly. "The most important day in his life wasn't when he made his first million—it's when he became an honorary Texas Ranger. He's all about law and order. *His* law, *his* order."

As they sat in silence, watching ripples spread across the pond's surface, Reed tried to digest it all.

"Harlan called all the shots. What I could and couldn't say. Which family doctor—sworn to secrecy—would check me out. No police, of course. *That* would've been a major disaster. After all, he wasn't about to let a family scandal tank the Ellis Oil stock price."

Reed was reluctant to defend Harlan, but…"I get it, but I wonder if that was the only way he knew to protect you."

"More like protect his reputation."

He ached to hold her, to comfort her, but sensed she needed space. "I can't imagine what you've been through."

Music seeped from a nearby dorm room window—Crosby, Stills & Nash's "Guinevere."

"I figured I was finally over it, but I'm not. Don't know if I'll ever be. It's like there's a 'before' Jordan and an 'after' Jordan. The 'before' Jordan was happy. Confident. Trusting. Not scared of anybody or anything…

"The 'after' Jordan is totally different. I pretend to laugh at jokes, pretend I'm happy. I avoid parties. It's tiring to make conversation. I push people away. Everyone thinks I'm aloof, unapproachable…a bitch.

"I don't like to be touched. I freeze up whenever anyone hugs me, even friends. And I don't want *anything* to do with men. So you're absolutely wasting your time hanging around me."

"Not true," he whispered, and reached for her hand. She gave it a perfunctory squeeze, then rose.

Another Crosby, Stills & Nash song, "You Don't Have to Cry," played as they walked off. Reed would remember those two songs for a long time.

—

He woke up Friday morning feeling more physically and mentally drained than ever. Managed only fourteen pull-ups. *Weak.* Shuffled along the cross-country trail like an old man. *Slow.* Examined the C on his Thermodynamics quiz. *Stupid.*

Craving caffeine and sugar after class, he stepped inside the Krispy Kreme on Broad Street. Ordered a large coffee and three glazed doughnuts. Sat by the window, savoring the mix of sugar, flour, and fat.

None of it helped. Outside, students rushed to class, businessmen strode past sweating in shirts and ties. Across the street, mothers juggled kids and grocery bags at the Winn-Dixie. Everyday life rolled on. So why did he feel apart from it? Though the weight of three years had lifted from his shoulders, a formless dread refused to budge. What the hell was wrong with him?

—

At three thirty, the time Reed usually collected Annabel for tutoring, his Mustang idled in front of Tracy's house. On a whim, he'd driven over, yet he hesitated now, wondering what to say to her.

He was about to leave when she rapped on his window. "What the heck are you doing here?"

"Look, I still care about you as a friend. I was hoping you'd changed your mind about the tutoring."

Her hair was straggly, and dark smudges hung under her eyes. "Fuck math. It's all a waste of time."

"You were finally doing better. How can you just quit?"

Her emerald eyes flashed. "I'm done with math, just like I'm done with you."

—

Reed leaned against the living room wall at Webb's Sigma Alpha Nu frat house Saturday night, drinking grain-alcohol-spiked grape juice. The late-April party had been billed as the last blowout before exams. In the adjoining room, a live band butchered Creedence Clearwater Revival's "Keep on Chooglin."

He'd decided to check out the party before his Lifelines shift, figuring a few cups of jungle juice might lift the foul mood he'd been unable to shake for the past two days.

The frat brothers were mingling with sorority girls, some triumphantly escorting them upstairs to their rooms. Earlier, one girl had sidled up to Reed with an inviting smile. He'd smiled back, then offered nothing but polite, obligatory small talk until she realized he wasn't interested.

Webb materialized by his side. Drink in hand, eyes bleary, shirt wrinkled, barefoot. "Hey, good buddy, howzit hanging?"

"The grape juice is helping," Reed yelled over the lead singer, who'd now moved on to slaughtering "I Can't Get No Satisfaction."

Webb indicated the stairway. "In case you're interested, little Miss Susie Q is ready for you upstairs."

The last thing he needed. Reed grimaced. "Thanks, but no thanks."

"Come on, I guarantee no sloppy seconds for my buddy."

Reed watched a guy coaxing a girl upstairs. "You know, you can stop this shit if you want."

"What for? Nobody's forcing these chicks to hang around here."

"Oh yeah?" He pointed to the girl on the stairs. "How many ludes has *she* chased with grape juice?"

Webb recoiled. "What's with your downer attitude, Lawson?"

"*My* attitude?"

"You hang out with some libbers and suddenly you're Mr. Holier Than Thou. Maybe what goes on around here is none of your freaking business."

Propelled by impulsive rage, Reed weaved through the crowd. "Maybe I'm gonna *make* it my business."

"What the fuck!" Webb yelled.

Reed made it halfway up the stairs before Webb's enormous hands grabbed the back of his jeans and yanked hard.

"I don't think so, asshole!"

"Leave me alone!" He thrashed, aching to hit somebody, before realizing Webb had helpers—several beefy frat brothers.

Next thing he knew, Reed was frog-marched down the stairs and outside, then dumped unceremoniously on the lawn. It was still damp from an evening rain.

Brushing himself off, he stalked back to the dorm and showered, trying in vain to sober up. He'd been at a party last fall where they'd also had girls upstairs, including a few high school kids. Why had he shrugged it off back then? Considering his night at the Pig Farm, though, who was he to point fingers?

Still reeling from the alcohol, he sleepwalked through a blessedly quiet Saturday night shift. Jordan was friendly and professional, nothing more. A knot of dejection took root as the evening wore on.

—

Reed woke up at seven on Sunday. He needed to study, exercise, do the laundry, iron his uniform. But lethargy overwhelmed him. Screw it all.

He yanked on a pair of jeans and grabbed a clean T-shirt.

Adam stirred. "Jeezus, where you going this early?"

"Couldn't sleep."

He'd surprise his mother, knock off a few chores, and take a nap. With no traffic, he arrived home in only seventy minutes.

The *For Sale* sign was gone.

But Sam Walker's white truck was parked in the driveway.

CHAPTER THIRTY

Reed checked his watch—the Abercrombie & Fitch Shipmate Dad had given him so many years ago.

Yup, eight thirty on a Sunday morning.

He imagined kicking in the door, his fist colliding with Walker's square jaw. He stalked around back and stepped into the kitchen. Silence, except for the grandfather clock ticking in the living room.

Too quiet. Time to make some noise. He yanked the can of Maxwell House from the pantry. Banged the door shut. Slammed the can on the counter. Dumped water into the percolator.

Must have done the trick. Within moments, his mother appeared in the kitchen, sleepy-eyed, hair mussed. Her robe hung open, revealing a lacy nightgown and bare feet. Noticing his embarrassment, she tightened her robe.

"Sorry, I didn't expect you until next weekend."

"Yeah, well. Here I am." In the silence that followed, he whipped open the cabinet. "Where's the *damn* sugar?" Purposely emphasizing the vulgarity she abhorred.

Barely three weeks had passed since they'd gotten the news about Dad. After years of agony. Yet here she was, *fucking* Sam Walker—a wuss pretending to be a real man, with his bullshit bass-fishing gear and piece-of-shit Harley.

"Look, just give me a few minutes. Then we can talk." She padded back toward her bedroom; Reed retreated into his.

It felt like a stranger's room now. His high school letter for track and field. A football autographed by Baltimore Colts quarterback Johnny Unitas. Little League baseball trophies. A stack of well-thumbed Superman and Batman comics.

Sandy, Jordan, and Olivia were right. He was a square, clueless kid whose childhood was a *Leave It to Beaver*, *Father Knows Best* TV fantasy. Avuncular father arriving home for dinner. Well-scrubbed son and daughter politely waiting. Adoring wife, freshly made up to appear alluring despite surviving a day of tedious chores and recalcitrant children.

What a steaming pile of horse dung.

When Sam's truck roared out of the driveway, he walked outside, where his mother sat—dressed—on the patio. Coffee mug in hand, she was looking at her stupid azaleas and hummingbird feeder.

Reed sipped coffee and waited sullenly.

"This is painful for me, but you're grown up now, and we need to be honest with each other."

"Honest? While Dad's trapped in a prison cell, you're in *his* bed with some other guy. That's what you call being honest?"

She winced. *Serves her right.*

"You know, you're like your father in so many ways. All straight lines, right or wrong, black or white. When real life is nothing but messy shades of gray. Besides, son, there's a lot you don't know."

He could not make eye contact. "Okay, Mom, just what is it I don't know?"

"Remember the November before your father was shot down? When he took leave and we met at a hotel in the Philippines?"

"Yeah, what about it?"

"He told me he no longer believed in the war."

Total bullshit. "Come on, how is that possible? He never said anything like that to me. No way."

"Your father had begun to believe the bombing was wrong. Too many civilians were dying."

"That's rough, but Dad would never bomb civilians. No way."

"Of course he wouldn't, not on purpose. Yet he insisted they were being killed and it was immoral. In fact, he was thinking about turning in his wings."

"What? No way would Dad ever do that!"

"He was seriously considering it."

Reed stalked inside to get more coffee. Sure, there were valid reasons that pilots quit flying. If their eyesight deteriorated. If they could no longer make carrier landings safely. But Dad was a naval aviator—tip of the spear. Reed had always suspected that nothing, not even his family, mattered as much to his father as flying.

Yet he remembered Dad talking about Clausewitz's *On War*. The author had described war as a clash of moral forces, not bullets, bombs, and tanks. "Once you've lost the moral high ground," Dad had argued, "you've ultimately lost the war."

He stepped back outside to find the morning coolness giving way to dank humidity.

"So what does that stuff with Dad have anything to do with you and Walker?"

"Just hear me out. *Please.* Can I make you some breakfast?"

"Not hungry."

Carol sighed. "You should know that the real issue between your father and me wasn't ever the war. It was our marriage. In fact, when we were in Manila, I asked your father for a divorce."

Divorce? The word hung in the air between them, vibrating like a hummingbird's wings.

"He asked me to wait until he was home to deal with it—which was only supposed to be a few months."

Months that had metastasized into three long, agonizing years.

In the adjacent yard, a young girl laughed as her mother pushed her on a swing set.

"But why, Mom? *Why* do you want to get divorced?"

"Sweetheart, it's too complicated to talk about right now. As I'm sure you must have noticed, it's no secret that your father and I are very different people…and we drifted apart a long time ago."

No, he hadn't noticed. Was he supposed to have? "So why didn't you ever say anything?"

"Fair question. Maybe I should have. But we were trying to protect you and Sandy. And then, when your father disappeared…well, it didn't seem right somehow. Talking about it would have just added salt to the wound. I don't know. I might have made the wrong decision."

They sat for a moment in silence. Reed willed the kid next door to either shut up or fall off the swing.

"Besides, if I said anything..." Her voice was tinged with resentment. "I was sure you'd blame me."

"For what?"

"For everything. For being a bad wife. A lousy mother. But mainly because, no matter what happened in our family, you saw the world only from your father's point of view. And always took his side. Now I need you to understand mine."

He fought to find the right words. "But it's like...it's like you're asking me to choose. You or Dad. That's not fair."

Clearly uneasy—as if she'd revealed more than a parent ought to—Carol rose. "I'm *very* sorry you see it that way."

They tiptoed around each other for another awkward hour. Jarred by her bombshell, anxious to leave, he wolfed down some toast, then rushed through a couple of chores.

His mother stood next to the Mustang. "I'm terribly sorry it all came out like this. I know how you must feel."

He couldn't reply. There were no hugs, no goodbyes.

—

Lost in thought, Reed drove slowly back to school. Angry drivers honked as they passed him.

Divorce? It seemed inconceivable. His parents had met on a blind date in Annapolis. She'd been a senior at Mary Washington and Dad had been a midshipman first class at the Naval Academy. They'd gotten married right after graduation, and Sandy was born nine months later.

Reed tried to purge the image of his mother having sex with Sam Walker. The notion she had *those* needs—that she hadn't been with a man for over three years—had never occurred to him. At a party once, he'd overheard hushed comments about a woman who'd had an affair with a Navy officer only months after her husband became a POW. She was reviled as a "homewrecker," a "slut," a "cheap whore."

Suddenly he remembered a night last year—January 1969. Dad had been missing for almost two years. Reed was at home drinking beer and watching TV news about Nixon's inauguration. At eleven thirty, his mother tiptoed inside, then turned to whisper and wave to someone out of view. *Who?* She'd said she was going to a movie with friends. But when she noticed the TV still on, she flinched. And what about that lime-green dress she wore that night? It was the first new one she'd bought since Dad disappeared.

Reed had shut his eyes and pretended to be asleep.

He pulled into a rest stop and guzzled a Coke as he strained to recall the years before his father was shot down. Heated arguments had often seeped from his parents' bedroom—sometimes about Dad drinking too much at the officers' club.

Whenever Dad came home late from work, Reed had assumed he was "tied up at the base." At least, that's what his mother had said whenever he'd asked, "What's up with Dad?" Her tone was always dismissive, as if to discourage further conversation. *Why?* Maybe Dad had been somewhere else. *With* someone else.

No way. That wasn't his father. Hadn't he lectured Reed enough about sex and marriage? "Sow whatever wild oats you want, but when you slip that engagement ring on her finger, that's it."

Reed tossed the Coke bottle and drove off. How could he possibly accept his mother's relationship with Walker? How could she have begun to see him when Dad was still missing? And *continue* to see him even after Dad turned out to be alive and living in a hellhole? It was so wrong!

Yet...how could he condemn her now, knowing how long she'd suffered? And the way she'd cried on the patio at Easter, fearing their family would fall apart?

—

Arriving back at the dorm midafternoon, Reed realized he'd eaten only toast all day. "Hey, you wanna go to Sonny's? I'm starving."

Adam tossed his book on the floor. "Kosher pork? Count me in!"

At a stoplight, Reed idled next to a chopped Harley. Along with the requisite black work boots and sleeveless denim jacket, the biker wore a World War II–era German army combat helmet.

Adam rolled down the window, raised his middle finger, and muttered, "Nazi scum."

Still preoccupied, Reed noticed the enraged biker only when he veered in front of the Mustang, looking to block them in.

"Let's split!" Adam yelled. "Now!"

The signal turned green; Reed swerved around the guy and sped off. After a few blocks, he checked his rearview. No sign of the biker.

"Are you out of your freaking mind!? Guys like that would eat both of us for breakfast! Not to mention he's probably packing and could blow your head off."

"Sorry, man. I admit it, that was idiotic."

Anything about Nazis set Adam off. He was convinced America had been overrun by former Nazis who'd emigrated to the U.S. after the war. "It's not paranoia if they're really out to get you," he would insist.

At Sonny's, Reed ate his barbecue and said very little.

"So what's wrong now? And please don't tell me 'nothing.'"

Reed shoved his empty plate aside. "Okay, I'm sick and tired of it."

"Of what?"

"Family. Women. Relationships. Lifelines. The war. *All* of it."

"So let's talk about it."

"I would if it could change anything, but it's complicated. Let's split. I got tons of shit to do."

He spent the rest of that Sunday afternoon checking off his to-do list. Caught up on homework, more or less. Ironed his ROTC uniform, polished his shoes. Dragged the laundry to Groomers, where he sat reading a paper while the dryer spun. The news was bad everywhere. Fighting along the South Vietnamese–Cambodian border. Tensions rising between Arabs and Israelis. Trouble between Blacks and whites in apartheid South Africa—not to mention in the U.S.

At the cross-country course later, Reed jogged slowly and ruminated. This was what happened when you got trapped in a spiderweb of relationships—burdened by conflicting emotions, confusing expectations, and long-buried secrets.

He could have avoided the entire mess.

If he hadn't lost his temper at a stupid protest, he wouldn't have fallen for Jordan.

If he hadn't mindlessly ingested hash brownies, he wouldn't have screwed an underage hippie in a closet.

If he hadn't knocked down a draft dodger, he wouldn't be stuck at Lifelines, listening to people whine about their problems.

Forget Annabel. She needed a real shrink.

Forget Jordan. She had a girlfriend and a past he was powerless to erase.

Forget his mother? No, of course not. But should he condemn her or forgive her?

Running harder and faster, he prayed movement alone would banish his funk and magically usher back his well-ordered, spit-shined life.

Utterly drained, he slowed to a walk and gazed up at billowing, swirling clouds that raced across the sky.

Somber and threatening. Primed to unleash a thunderstorm.

PART THREE: COMMITMENT

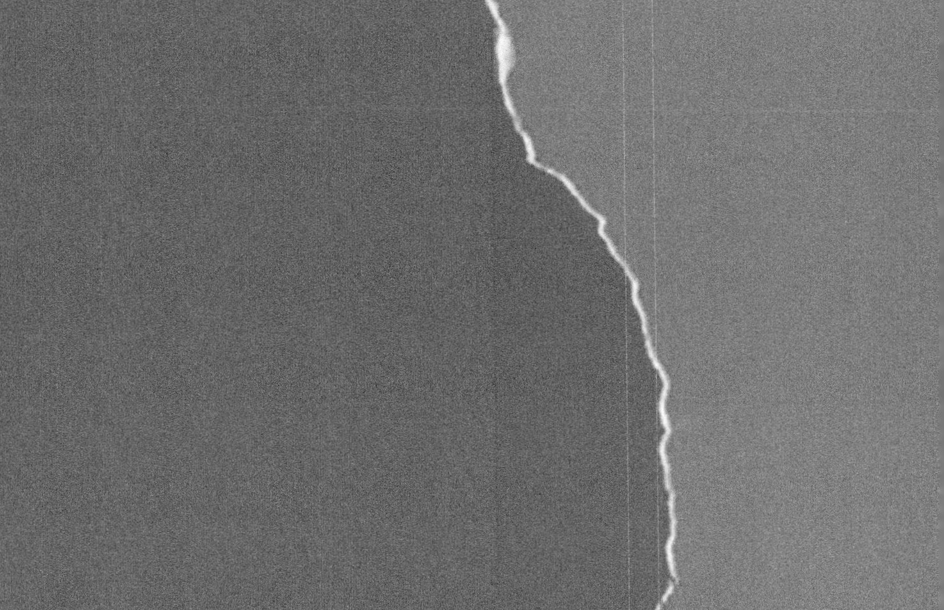

CHAPTER THIRTY-ONE

On Monday afternoon, Reed's Mustang sat high on a lift at Decker Motors. The place was located a mile from downtown on what had been the primary route for travelers before the interstate opened. A shabby railroad car diner and a run-down motel stood across the street. The garage looked tired too, but with three cars on lifts, it buzzed with activity.

Reed wasn't sure why he was there, other than a compulsion to check on Annabel under the pretext of needing an oil change. He'd awakened that morning unable to stop worrying about her. What was she doing now? Flunking math? Smoking more grass, popping more Quaaludes?

Reed hadn't known what to say when he handed Ross the Mustang's keys. Nor when he gulped burnt coffee in the tiny waiting room, flipping through a *Popular Mechanics* magazine. Nor when he watched Ross finish greasing the suspension.

"Everything okay?" Reed asked.

"Yup." Ross twisted a lever. The lift hissed and descended. "Didn't think you'd come by."

"Been kinda busy."

Ross shot him an icy stare. "The thing is, you didn't need no oil change. So why are you here?"

"Uh…figured you could use the business."

Ross shoved the lever. The lift jerked to a halt. "Yeah, well, we don't need *your* kind of business."

"Sorry, I didn't mean it like that."

"Just like we don't need you 'helping' Annabel." The Mustang sank to the floor. "Like I'm some retarded grease monkey never heard of algebra."

Reed was relieved—the tutoring was out in the open.

"I don't get it. A military kid like you—all squared away—messing around with hippies and traitors while your dad's rotting away in some gook shithole. The fuck is wrong with you, son?"

Then he paused, regarding Reed with a trace of sympathy. "Yeah, I heard about your dad. Sorry, it's gotta be tough. I get that, believe me. But you got no right messing in family business you don't understand."

"We're friends. I'm just worried about her, that's all."

"Friends my ass. She's a kid, and she'll be fine once we knock some sense into her head." Ross threw his rag on a tool bench. "Now, I got people waiting. You can pay up front."

—

Reed sped out of Decker Motors and headed to the library, since his homework wasn't going to finish itself. A block away from campus, he pulled to the curb. *Knock some sense into her head.* What was that about? He turned around and drove to the Kastle, suspecting Annabel was *not* okay.

"Taylor?" The shift supervisor shook his head. "Called in sick again. If you see her, tell her she'd better get her ass in gear if she wants this job."

Knowing Ross and Louise would be at work, Reed called their house. No one picked up. Where else could she be? He wasn't about to barge in on Tracy. A nagging suspicion pointed him to the Pig Farm, only a half-mile walk from the end of the bus line.

He rolled down the gravel road to the farmhouse. The usual stoner was rocking on the rusted porch swing.

"Who?"

"She answers to Summer," Reed said.

"Oh yeah, that chick. Man was she freaked. Bought a lid, some ludes, and split. Said she was gonna get totally wasted."

"Did she say where she was going?"

"Dunno, but she was lugging a duffel bag."

Shit. Annabel had threatened more than once, *Mom needs to decide: Ross or me. If it's Asshole, I'm splitting for good.*

Reed figured her cheapest option would be the bus, so he raced to the Greyhound station, a squat building downtown. Two silver-paneled buses idled out front, spewing diesel exhaust.

Annabel was perched on a scarred wooden bench in the crowded, smoky waiting room, legs draped over an Army duffel bag. She looked ashen in her black Grateful Dead T-shirt and ragged jeans.

"You don't listen too good, do you?" she said.

He sat next to her. "Where're you headed?"

"How'd you find me?" Her voice rose. "It's like you're some kind of pervert or stalker—or both."

"You know that's crap."

"Bullshit!"

Two businessmen in suits overheard and eyed Reed suspiciously. To avoid a scene, he persuaded her to step outside. Pacing the sidewalk, Annabel said she was "done with Asshole" and was going to live with her grandmother in Atlanta.

"Thanks to you, I got an A in math. Asshole said I must have cheated. When I told him to shove it, Mom slapped the shit out of me."

The diesel fumes, mixed with the stifling humidity, were suffocating. Annabel was thirsty but refused to dip into her cash, so Reed bought her a Coke, which she gulped like she'd been crawling for days through a desert.

He listened impatiently to her bitch about Ross. "He drops greasy clothes everywhere, expects us to clean up. Yells about lies on TV, as if Cronkite was actually listening. Doesn't even talk to me unless he's on my case. It's like I don't exist."

Reed glanced at passengers boarding the bus. "Look, about Atlanta..."

"You're not my dad, so don't even start. Grandma's super cool. Even smokes some weed."

"Great. Just what you need."

"Who are you to tell me what I do or don't need?"

Maybe she was right. After all, it was her life, wasn't it? Yet on some level he felt responsible. Why? He'd never intended to become her friend, but that's what they were. And you couldn't just quit on a friend. It would be like leaving a wounded soldier on the battlefield.

"Look, what if I found you a place to crash? Just for a while. It would give you some time to cool off. Right now you're not thinking straight."

Finishing her Coke, Annabel grimaced. "I think I'm gonna puke."

Ten minutes later she stumbled out of the ladies' room. "Okay, you win. Lemme at least get my money back for this stupid ticket."

—

In the Mustang, she balked when Reed mentioned their destination. "No way I'm hanging around that blond chick of yours."

"Please, just give her a chance. At least for one night."

Annabel grumbled but eventually relented. Thankfully, when they arrived, Olivia wasn't home to dish out unsolicited advice.

"You can crash here, at least for now," Jordan said. "But we'll have to call your mom."

Annabel pouted. "Why? What for?"

"So she knows you're safe and not here against your will."

"Can you not tell her where I am?"

"No. You're a minor and a runaway. We'd get into legal trouble."

Annabel was about to object but wilted in the face of Jordan's commanding presence. "Okay, okay. Where's your bathroom?"

"Down the hall, first door on the right." Jordan turned to Reed. "Now you see why this town needs a runaway shelter?"

—

Fifteen minutes later, Annabel and her mother were arguing in Jordan's front yard. Reed lingered close enough to hear.

"Ross is sorry he insulted you," Louise said. "He was only joking."

"He's never sorry about anything."

"Why didn't you tell me about the tutoring? Don't you trust me?"

"Why should I? You don't trust *me*."

"*You're* the one who's keeping secrets, sneaking off, doing drugs behind my back. Now I need you to come home, right now!"

"Not if *he's* there."

"I'm your mother—it's not for you to give me ultimatums. Besides, why can't you give him a chance?"

"Because you can do a lot better than that white-trash redneck."

"He's no such thing! Ross owns his own business. He was an Army sergeant in Korea and came home with a Purple Heart!"

Annabel's shoulders slumped. "Mom, don't you get it? With him around, it's like I can't breathe in my own house."

Taken aback, Louise gazed off pensively. "Can't breathe..." She sighed. "Okay...so how exactly are you going to get to school?"

"Don't worry. I'll figure it out. Maybe Reed can give me a ride."

Louise glanced at Reed, who nodded. Then she pulled car keys from her purse.

"My goodness, you're so damn hardheaded. Just like your father."

After Annabel walked inside, Louise motioned to Reed. "As for you, we need to talk. Please."

—

They sat drinking coffee in Jimmy's 616—the sort of steak-and-potatoes place where parents visiting campus took their kids for a "decent meal."

"The last thing I wanted was to get her in trouble," Reed said.

Louise frowned, only slightly sympathetic. She looked exhausted, dark crescents hanging beneath her eyes. Her nails, polished pink, rapped on a coffee cup. "What has she told you during all this tutoring?"

He glanced at the gold cross glinting on a chain around her neck. Hesitant to betray Annabel's confidence but not knowing how to avoid it, he summarized what she'd revealed to him.

"I'm her mother. I don't understand—why won't she talk to me? All she does is blame Ross. But he's not the problem. Lately he's been under a lot of pressure. Business is slow, and he's blaming it on everyone and everything. Besides, that Lifelines place has a bad reputation around town. Ross thinks they're selling drugs and the free clinic's up to no good."

"Ma'am, with all due respect, that's just not true. Drugs aren't allowed anywhere near the place. And the clinic's run by doctors from the hospital."

"Maybe so, but plenty of ordinary people around here feel threatened, especially with all these protests going on. It's not just this war—they're attacking our entire society. Parents know nothing. Our leaders are corrupt. Even questioning our basic values—God, country, hard work. So tell me, what's the answer? Toss morality out the window? And replace it with what? 'If it feels good, do it'?"

Not waiting for him to respond, she pressed on. "The thing is, you people don't speak for us. We're just working folks, following the rules and trying to get by. No one puts *us* on TV. No one's interested in *our* opinions. No one cares what *we* think."

Though resenting being lumped in with "you people," Reed had no idea what to say, so he nodded politely and murmured, "I'm sorry, ma'am."

Louise sighed. "Annabel and me, we used to be able to talk. About anything. But now she's shutting me out. Punishing me. She knows Ross will never take the place of her father."

"Where is he now, ma'am?" Reed ventured. "Uh...Captain Taylor, that is."

Louise shrank from the table. "What do you mean, *where* is he? What in our good Lord's name has that child told you?"

"Just that he's not around. That he took off."

Abruptly, she signaled for the bill. "I just don't understand why she has to lie about everything. Even something like this."

Reed fumbled in his wallet for cash. "Let me pay."

"Forget it." Angry emerald eyes locked on his. "The fact is, my husband is *dead*."

CHAPTER THIRTY-TWO

"Why didn't you tell me your dad died?" The Mustang idled at a traffic light near Annabel's school on Tuesday morning.

"I don't want to talk about it."

"You know you can trust me, right?"

"No, I don't! Just get me to school."

Reed wanted to argue but could tell she'd shut down. In the drop-off circle, she jumped out without a word. Jenny Palmer appeared, shot Reed a flirty smile, and gave Annabel a thumbs-up. Annabel lifted a middle finger in response.

Reed sighed. Some things never changed—teenagers and the reckless torments of high school.

—

"You're sweet to do all this driving," Jordan said when Reed dropped off Annabel after school. "How about you come over for dinner tomorrow night, before our shift?"

Reed eagerly agreed. As long as she was around, he didn't care how much tofu and brown rice he had to choke down.

The next evening, it didn't take long for Annabel to start bitching about Ross and for Olivia to jump on her soapbox.

"Do you *realize* this guy, Ross, is a chauvinist pig?"

"He's a pig all right," Annabel agreed.

"Do you *realize* your mother needs some serious consciousness raising?"

Annabel frowned. "What are you talking about? She's got a conscience."

"Okay, but do you *realize* she doesn't have to surrender her power to any man?"

Jordan raised her coffee mug. "Do you *realize* we're out of coffee?"

Reed stifled a chuckle.

"Very funny," Olivia muttered. She rose to fetch the coffee and was still pissed when she returned.

"Seriously, Annabel, people like me grew up around women like your mom. They work their asses off all day, take care of kids, cook dinner, and do laundry—while their lazy husbands drink beer and watch football. And they still find bullshit to whine about."

Jordan nodded. "Yeah, I know plenty of women like that."

"Oh, really?" Olivia looked at her contemptuously. "I'm talking about women who actually have to *work* for a living. Not go to cocktail parties while maids and nannies raise their spoiled kids."

"Who are you to call me spoiled?"

"Come on, as soon as you turn twenty-one, you get your five-million-dollar trust fund."

Jordan looked blindsided. "First of all, it's when I'm twenty-five, and I get *one* million. Which I don't want, and won't accept."

"Don't make me laugh."

"So wait a minute. Let me get this straight. You have to be poor to understand the problems of working people? Is that what you're saying?"

"What I'm saying is that you need to wake up and decide—are you gonna feed the Ellis Oil war machine or help your sisters?"

The two women glared at each other, a torrent of the unsaid flowing between them.

Jordan leaned back and crossed her arms. "I don't get it. We're just trying to have a relaxed dinner here. What's really going on?"

Olivia glowered at Reed. "Why don't you ask Rot-cee here?" Then she stomped into the kitchen.

Jordan rose. "Excuse me, I need some air."

After the front door slammed behind her, Annabel broke the silence. "What the heck was that all about?"

Reed shook his head, trying to decipher the evening's snarled emotional terrain. "Not sure, but it's got nothing to do with you."

—

That night's shift was hectic. Only later did Reed find a moment to talk to Jordan. "Why was Olivia giving you such a hard time?"

Jordan stirred sugar into her iced tea. "It's complicated. Sometimes she can be a real bitch. Just like me, I guess."

"Don't be so hard on yourself."

The kitchen was stifling; the barest tendrils of cold air floated from the front room. Jordan lifted her hair to cool her neck. "Damn, it's hot. If you threw me up against a wall right now, I'd stick. By the way, what are you doing tomorrow after you pick up Annabel?"

Tons of homework, but... "What did you have in mind?"

—

Bright sun splashed through billowing cumulus clouds. Jordan and Reed were floating on inner tubes and drinking beer at Ginnie Springs, twenty miles from campus.

"Yum. Just what the doctor ordered," she purred, eyes closed. Her face and hair were damp from the aqua-blue water, her tanned skin set off by a yellow bikini.

Reed held her inner tube against his so they could talk. To his surprise, Jordan was an expert on Florida's geology and relished talking about it. The crystal-clear spring—one of hundreds in the state—bubbled up from a limestone maze of caverns and underground rivers, part of a vast freshwater aquifer.

Jordan trailed her hand through the water—seventy-two degrees all year—and admired the sandy limestone bottom fifteen feet down. "Billions of gallons flow from these springs every day. I figure at least fifty million from this spring alone."

"Amazing. And here I figured you were just an oil expert."

"Nope. I'm really interested in geology and the environment, especially how Ellis Oil is screwing up Mother Nature. Remember that Santa Barbara oil spill last January?"

"Vaguely, but tell me more about it."

The spill had occurred because one of Union Oil's underwater rigs blew out, she explained. It spewed three million gallons of crude oil into the Pacific. The slick spread thirty-five miles, killing thousands of birds, fish, and seals. "It was a massive fuckup that finally shook people from their stupor."

Reed remembered the TV images: blackened California beaches, birds covered in oily muck, seal corpses washed ashore.

"If I actually end up in the oil business, I'm gonna make sure nothing like that ever happens again."

"I don't doubt it one bit."

Jordan reached over, squeezed his hand, and gazed longingly at the late-afternoon sky. "Must we go back to the real world? I could stay here for the rest of the year."

He wasn't sure where he stood with her, only how he felt. He pulled her inner tube closer, slid his arm around her waist, and drew her in. She pressed against him and he kissed her lips, which parted tentatively, but not enough to welcome him fully. Her heart drummed against his chest.

—

That night, Sandy called and got right to the point. "Mom told me what happened last Sunday morning."

"You mean when I showed up and surprised them?"

"I'm sorry. I should have warned you."

"Don't tell me you already knew about it," Reed said.

"I suspected they were dating, but not that it had gone that far."

"What about divorce? You knew about that too?"

"Mom never outright told me, but I saw it coming. It was obvious."

"Not to me."

"Maybe that's because you never saw the signs. Or didn't want to. It's like that day at the beach, years ago, when we came home late and Dad dumped that shit on you for no reason. Mainly because he was taking out his problems on you…as usual."

What day at the beach? "I don't know what the hell you're talking about. This is not about me—we're talking about Mom!"

Sandy sighed. "Okay, never mind—"

"The point is, Dad's coming home soon, and Mom's screwing some other guy. But I guess you're okay with that."

"It's not about whether we're okay with it. This is about *her*. We've got to give Mom some space right now. For once, could you be *slightly* less judgmental?"

He'd had enough of Sandy hammering him. "Okay, listen, finals are coming up. I gotta go."

"I hear you. Otherwise, you doing okay?"

"Fine."

"I wish I believed you, but we can talk about everything when you're ready. By the way, you gonna catch Tricky Dicky's speech tonight?"

"What speech?"

"Today's April thirtieth—it's been in the news all week."

Reed glanced at his watch. "Yeah, probably."

—

Walking over to the student union, he recalled the day Sandy had mentioned.

It was a Saturday, about four or five years ago. Dad had given him a list of chores to be done by dinnertime. But Mom and Sandy insisted he go to the beach with them—just for an hour or two. The day was gorgeous, and they got lost in discussion about James Michener's *The Source*, fascinated by the book's blend of biblical history, archaeology, and religion.

When they finally got home at six, Dad ordered him to finish his chores before dinner. "I don't give a damn how long it takes."

"What's the point of punishing him like this?" Mom argued. "Why on earth can't it wait until tomorrow?"

"Because I told him to do it today."

Mom then refused to cook dinner and drove Sandy to their favorite diner. After Reed finished his work, he and Dad ate TV dinners and watched *Gilligan's Island* in tense silence. Dad's jaw twitched with rage throughout. He dumped the aluminum trays in the trash, tossed the dirty silverware in the sink, and stalked into his office.

Mom and Sandy came home laughing an hour later, then Mom escaped to the patio with a cocktail. Later that night, Reed listened to angry hissing from his parents' bedroom.

Mom: "Don't you dare take out your anger at *me* on the kids."

Dad: "If you didn't coddle him like a baby, I wouldn't have to deal with this shit."

Convinced it was all his fault, Reed had squeezed the pillow over his head.

—

Stepping inside the student union, Reed recognized that Sandy was probably right—his parents had marital problems. And maybe Dad *had* sometimes taken it out on him, but why dredge up all that shit now? Nothing could justify Mom having an affair while Dad rotted in prison.

On TV, the president was speaking from the Oval Office. "North Vietnam has occupied the Cambodian frontier with South Vietnam," he revealed, then explained the U.S. response. "Attacks are being launched this week to clean out major enemy sanctuaries on the Cambodia-Vietnam border."

Nixon assured Americans, however, that he wasn't invading Cambodia but protecting American lives. "We will not allow American men by the thousands to be killed by an enemy from privileged sanctuaries."

He concluded the twenty-two-minute speech by claiming, "We live in an age of anarchy, both abroad and at home," referring to "mindless attacks" on institutions, including "American universities that are being systematically destroyed." And he warned that if America "acts like a pitiful, helpless giant, the forces of totalitarianism and anarchy will threaten free nations."

Reed walked out through a swirl of outraged students, nearly all of whom condemned the speech and assumed Nixon's real purpose was simply to expand the war. But what was so wrong with shutting down North Vietnam's supply lines that aided their commie allies in the South? According to Captain Harwood, it was a legitimate tactic and long overdue. Rather than extending the war, it might end it sooner.

—

Louise was arguing with Annabel on Friday morning when Reed arrived to drive her to school. Killing the engine, he lowered both windows to listen. It was the first of May and a perfect seventy degrees.

"Sweetheart, it's been over a week now. Can't you give Ross another chance?"

"No way. He's a male chauvinist pig."

"A male what?"

"Never mind. I'm not going back home until he splits for good."

"I could call the police right now, say these girls have kidnapped you."

Jordan stepped in. "Wait a minute. We're not keeping her against her will. She's absolutely free to leave anytime."

"Besides," Annabel said, "if you make me go home, I'll just run away again."

Louise rubbed her forehead, trying to stay calm. "Look. I'm late for work. Are you coming home after school or not?"

"No way." Annabel hurried toward the Mustang.

Louise shot Jordan a contemptuous look. "Just what do you girls think you're doing?"

"For one thing, we're not *girls*."

"Male chauvinist pigs, women's lib. They're just slogans to you, aren't they?"

"They're way more than that."

"How old are you, if I may ask?"

"Twenty."

"When I was twenty, I was married and pregnant."

"And that makes you an expert?"

"No, but it makes me an adult."

Louise walked off.

Annabel jumped in the Mustang. "Let's split."

Traffic was at a standstill on University Avenue. Protesters streamed across the street, heading toward the Quad. After detouring through neighborhood streets, Reed pulled into the school parking lot.

"Look, she *is* your mother…and you're not eighteen, so she's still responsible for you."

"Whose side are you on, anyway?"

"Yours. Isn't it obvious?"

She reached for the door handle. "I should've taken that freaking bus to Atlanta."

CHAPTER THIRTY-THREE

The protest on campus against Nixon's speech had swelled to several thousand by the time Reed found himself wandering among the milling, angry throng. Signs carried or tacked on trees proclaimed:

Nixon Declares All-Out War on Southeast Asia!
Immediate Withdrawal of All U.S. Troops!

But something was different this time. Amid the usual longhairs and freaks were professors, townies, even a few ROTC cadets.

Counterprotesters also carried signs:

Stand Up for America!
Don't Lie Down With The Vietcong!
These Colors Won't Run!

The last one had been printed beneath a hand-drawn American flag.

There was no podium. Protesters instead climbed a low brick wall, bullhorns in hand, to speak spontaneously.

The student body president shouted, "Nixon is practicing the same genocide in Vietnam that we condemned in World War II. First the entire Vietnamese population was the enemy. Now it's also the Cambodians! It's way past time to stop this criminal war!"

A gray-haired professor in a suit and tie spoke next. He insisted the political left was to blame, not the Nixon administration, nor the military: "The left isn't interested in peace, but in promoting violence for violence's sake. We've had over a hundred bombings on campuses just this past year. How can this kind of anarchy possibly stop the war?"

Scattered boos punctuated his remarks.

Restless, Reed turned to leave just as Olivia's booming voice erupted. She was standing beneath a *Women Unite Against the War!* banner. He maneuvered closer to listen.

"Why are women united against the war?" Her curly black hair bounced with the fury of her words. "Because the immorality of Vietnam reflects the evils of capitalism. A system based on male supremacy—"

Amid scattered applause, a guy shouted, "Total bullshit!"

"Women are the largest oppressed class in this country! Exploited as sex objects, breeders, domestic servants, cheap labor—"

"Fucking commie bitch!"

Startled, Reed recognized Webb, standing a few yards away.

Olivia raised her arm, palm out, as if to keep hecklers at bay. "All forms of exploitation and oppression, including this criminal war, are nothing but extensions of male supremacy. Men control all political, economic, and cultural institutions and use their power to keep women in inferior positions—"

"If you weren't so butt-ugly," Webb barked, "we'd get *you* in an inferior position, all right!"

The comment ignited a sickening ripple of laughter and catcalls: "Shut up, bitch!" "Women's lib sucks!"

Undaunted, Olivia pressed on. "... and it's *this* system of exploitation America is exporting to the Third World. All of us—women *and* men alike—can *end* male supremacy, *end* oppression, and *end* this war!"

Amid scattered applause, Webb yelled, "Drag her ass down and get her laid!"

Enough already. Reed had gotten to know Olivia better over the past several weeks. In San Francisco, in '67, she'd toiled at the Haight Ashbury free clinic. She'd endured vicious taunting while protesting at the Miss America pageant in '68. Though he didn't always agree with her ideology, she at least had the courage of her convictions.

He charged over to where Webb was laughing with his frat buddies. "Hey!"

"Reed, my man!" He was drunk, high, or both. "Where you been hanging? Sorry we had to kick your ass out last week." He stuck his hand out. "No hard feelings?"

"Forget that shit." Reed pointed at Olivia. "Did you hear what you just said to her?"

"Huh? What did I do?"

"Did you actually *listen* to the garbage coming out of your mouth?"

"What the hell are you talking about?"

"Never mind. From now on, find yourself another workout partner."

"Wait, don't tell me you know that chick?"

"Doesn't matter if I know her. We're done, understand? Done!"

He marched across Broad Street to escape the mayhem, only to step into another sign-carrying crowd outside Krispy Kreme. A construction worker (*Support Our Boys in Vietnam!*) was facing off against an antiwar student (*End Nixon's Cambodian Genocide!*).

"Dammit, get that sign outa here!" the construction worker yelled.

"We got as much right to be here as anyone else."

"If you hate America, why don't you up and move to Vietnam?"

"If you love this country, you'd agree with us."

An older man stepped between the warring sides. "Look, let's all calm down. Certainly we can agree—we're *all* patriotic Americans. Can't we have a civil conversation?"

Grumbling, the students and workers moved off in opposite directions.

The gentleman turned to Reed. "What do *you* think about all this, son?"

One of his father's favorite acronyms popped into his head. FUBAR. Fucked Up Beyond All Repair. "I don't know, sir. It's pretty messed up."

"That it is, son. That it most certainly is."

Even at Annabel's high school, kids were staging a walkout and protesting on the sidewalk, carrying hand-scribbled signs:

Stop the War!
Get Out Now!

As he waited for her, car horns honked and drivers yelled for and against the war: "Down with Nixon!" "Go back to class, commies!" "Stop the genocide!"

Among the last students to emerge was Annabel. She glared at the protesters, then trudged to the Mustang.

"There's something I need to show you. Don't wanna talk, just drive."

She directed him through a new suburban development and into a cemetery. He parked next to a massive live oak. Several headstones clustered beneath its sprawling branches. Having guessed what he was about to see, he took a steadying breath.

Annabel led him to a white marble stone.

Lucas Benjamin Taylor
Beloved Husband and Father
January 11, 1930—May 2, 1969

At its base, a ceramic vase held wilted daisies. Next to the vase was a small American flag stuck in the ground, the kind hardware stores sold for July Fourth.

Kneeling, she brushed aside a layer of moss and fallen leaves. "Need some more daisies and another flag. There used to be three. Somebody must have ripped them off."

She stood up, and stared impassively at her father's stone. Reed waited in silence, filled with questions he wasn't sure how to ask.

"Let's get outa here," she said.

—

At a nearby McDonald's, he bought Cokes and fries. They sat outside, across the street from an elementary school packed with kids scampering around the playground, and ate mechanically in silence.

If Captain Taylor hadn't died in the war, then how? "Do you want to talk about him?"

"It's about what happened over there. During that Tet thing. Dad lost forty men in a single battle. For revenge, I guess, he ordered a raid on this little village to capture any Vietcong hiding there. But he said his men killed a bunch of innocent men, women, and children—even babies. Kept saying it was all his fault but never explained what actually happened."

Annabel had tried to patch the story together from bits of information in newspapers and the few details her father would let slip when he was drunk. Then, on November 12, 1969, the news broke about the Mỹ Lai massacre.

Reed had read the story. Mỹ Lai had taken place in March 1968, during the Tet Offensive. The North Vietnamese Army and its Vietcong allies attacked targets throughout South Vietnam. U.S. and South Vietnamese armies counterattacked. In response, the Vietcong hid in villages, and the U.S. military led search-and-destroy operations to root them out.

In one incident, American troops descended on the village of Mỹ Lai and killed hundreds of unarmed South Vietnamese civilians. Those killings took place at the same time—and in roughly the same area—where Captain Lucas Taylor's company had been fighting.

"But Mom said no way would Dad ever do something like that."

"I'm sure your mom's right. I don't believe your father would have deliberately ordered the death of innocent women and children."

"Me neither. But one day, I begged him to tell me what was wrong. I'll never forget what he said: 'The blood of innocents is on my hands. It can't ever be washed off. And for that, I will never be forgiven and I will go straight to hell.'

"I think that's why he did it," she added in a choked whisper.

CHAPTER THIRTY-FOUR

"Hard to believe it's going to be one year tomorrow," Annabel said. Leaning against the fence that surrounded the playground, her voice wavering, she explained what had happened.

On a sunny day a year ago, Captain Lucas Taylor walked into the garage, draped a thick rope over a ceiling beam, and tied a noose. He climbed a stepladder, slipped his head through the noose, and kicked the ladder aside.

Annabel was the one who discovered him swaying.

"I'd never seen a dead person. He was looking right at me, mouth hanging open, eyes all bulging out. I swear those eyes were staring at me! I still see 'em all the time. When I'm dreaming. In class. Walking around. He'll pop up outa nowhere."

Realizing he'd been holding his breath, Reed exhaled.

"I can't get him out of my head," she cried. "I just can't!"

Annabel explained that her father had left a note with instructions for his funeral. "At the end, he wrote, *None of this is your fault. I love you both more than my life.*

"But it *was* my fault! That morning I was wearing my headband and moccasins. He said I looked like a drugged-out hippie, ordered me to change my clothes. I yelled at him to get off my back.

"Then I didn't come straight home after school. Smoked tons of grass and got home late. If we hadn't argued or I hadn't gotten high, then maybe he wouldn't have done it. Or I could have stopped him or something."

"You can't blame yourself," Reed said. "Your dad even said so in his note. And you told me how different he was when he came back from the war. That had nothing to do with you."

She shook her head, resolute. "When I go to sleep, he's always there. Hanging, but not dead yet. Yelling at me, 'Get me down from here! Look what you made me do!'"

Fighting back tears, she ran to the Mustang. Instead of getting in, she banged her forehead repeatedly on the roof—hard.

Alarmed, Reed rushed over.

"What are you doing!?" he yelled, dragging her away from the car.

She gasped for air. "Lemme go!" Her eyes were puffy, and red welts had appeared on her forehead. After a moment, she stopped shaking and got in the Mustang.

Rendered mute by what he'd heard, Reed drove by rote back to Jordan's.

For the rest of the day, he couldn't concentrate on homework. Looking up from his Thermodynamics book, he suddenly remembered the time Grandpa Jack had offered to teach his Sunday School class—a big deal for "a hero of the Battle of Midway."

Grandpa had selected an excerpt from Ezekiel, verse 18:20: *The son shall not bear the iniquity of the father, neither shall the father bear the iniquity of the son.*

Grandpa had emphasized that "one generation is certainly tied in complicated ways to the next generation. But ultimately, each soul is directly responsible as an individual to God."

Obviously, Annabel wasn't responsible for her father's actions. Captain Taylor hadn't committed suicide because Annabel wore the wrong clothes or smoked some pot. So why in hell did she blame herself?

—

"You got to watch this shit, man," Adam said. "It's wild."

Reed had arrived at the student union, where Adam and Meg were watching the Friday night news. Demonstrations had erupted across the country protesting Nixon's actions.

Earlier that day at Ohio State University, 1,200 National Guardsmen and police had responded to protesters by deploying tear gas. They wore gas masks, carried clubs and rifles with fixed bayonets, and were backed by armored personnel carriers. Seven people were shot and wounded, seventy-three injured, and about three hundred and fifty arrested.

"What's going on?" Adam was staring at Reed.

Unable to focus on the news, Reed kept replaying the image of Annabel's head banging repeatedly against his car. He shuddered. "Huh? Oh, uh, nothing. Just these protests."

Adam and Meg exchanged a look of concern.

Reed rose. "Look, I gotta study."

Yet, even heavily caffeinated, he couldn't focus. At this rate he'd be lucky to *pass* his finals, much less get As.

Adam burst into their room an hour later, giddy with excitement. Quickly undressing, he rushed down the hall to the showers. When he returned, Reed noticed he'd even shaved and tried to tame his frizzy hair.

"Hey, can I borrow some of your Old Spice?"

"Don't you hate the smell?"

"Yeah, but Meg likes it." Adam inspected a wrinkled oxford shirt. Yanked his only decent jeans from the closet. Rubbed his sneakers clean. Patted on some cologne.

Stuttering and stammering, he explained that Meg's two roommates were away for the weekend and she'd invited him over. "Hey, uh, Reed...you wouldn't happen to have any...uh...protection?"

His nervous anticipation offered a welcome break. Reed remembered how awkwardly he'd fumbled losing his cherry with Susan after senior prom.

"Relax, I got you covered, so to speak." He reached into his desk drawer and handed Adam two small condom packets. "You ever use one of these before?"

"Well, sort of. Actually, not exactly."

"Okay, just be careful—this size might be too big for you."

Adam's fingers shook as he pocketed the condoms. "Very freaking funny."

—

The next morning, Reed drove to Crescent Beach to escape his inner turmoil and the chaos on campus. Tempted to stop and buy a six-pack, he ruled in favor of caffeine.

Cars and pickup trucks already blanketed the hard sand. Fishing rods sprouted from sand spikes; their lines stretched into the roiling surf. Kids shouted, jumped waves, and sculpted elaborate sandcastles. Adults tossed tennis balls for dogs to fetch. Others lounged in beach chairs, reading and drinking beer, their skin slick with suntan lotion.

A typical, idyllic eighty-degree Saturday in May. No one seemed to have a care in the world.

As Reed's bare feet slapped the wet sand, images flashed through his mind. His mother in bed with Sam Walker. Dad wasting away in a dank cell. Lude sprawled unconscious on the carpet at Lifelines. Annabel lifeless in a bathtub, blood staining the water. And Captain Taylor, eyes bulging, dangling from the ceiling of his garage.

He kept walking into the distant haze, as helpless to control his world as the sandpipers scampering away from the relentless tide.

—

"Nice night?"

Adam was sitting at his desk, exuding the self-satisfied air of a guy who'd gotten laid for the first time. "Yeah, it was great. But man, your mom called twice already."

Reed didn't want to talk to her, especially about Sam Walker. He'd call her later.

At the library, he scanned the papers for news about the war. The *Washington Post* had reported on the gathering his mother had refused to attend—the Appeal for International Justice.

Vice President Agnew, Senator Barry Goldwater, and other members of Congress had spoken to over a thousand people, including hundreds of POW/MIA wives, who'd crammed into Washington's DAR Constitution Hall on Friday. A resolution passed by Congress earlier that week had designated tomorrow—Sunday—as a National Day of Prayer for the POWs.

Reed was buoyed by the success of the event. Maybe the commies would finally pay attention and do something—even let all the prisoners go home.

—

"Were you on the Quad yesterday?" Jordan asked that night at Lifelines.

"Yeah, and I heard Olivia's speech. Pretty strong stuff."

"Some pigs heckled the shit out of her."

Reed was tempted to claim credit for shutting Webb down. "Yeah, it was way out of line."

Sitting on the porch after a busy shift, he told Jordan and Meg all about Annabel's father—how she'd found him hanging, how she felt responsible. Although Reed knew he was betraying Annabel's confidence, he yearned to unload the burden.

"Thanks for sharing that," Jordan said. "Olivia and I have been trying to get her to open up. So far, she's been keeping everything in."

Meg had been pacing nervously as Reed talked. She paused to gaze into the yard.

"That's a terrible weight she's been carrying. I can't begin to imagine the kind of pain people like Captain Taylor experienced. And so many other veterans. I sometimes wonder whether our country is simply scapegoating our soldiers so the rest of us can avoid accepting moral responsibility for this war."

—

At Mother Earth on Sunday, Adam poured cane syrup on a stack of blueberry pancakes and scanned the newspaper. "Listen to this crazy shit. *Last night, at Kent State University in Ohio, protesters burned an ROTC building to the ground.*"

Reed jabbed at his tofu scrambled "eggs." What if something like that happened while he was in class?

"I don't get it. What's the point of burning buildings? What're they possibly hoping to accomplish? It's so fucking stupid."

"I don't know. Maybe you shouldn't go to ROTC for a while."

"No way I'm hiding in some foxhole. That's exactly what these assholes want."

After breakfast, Adam stood next to the Mustang, scraping the toe of his sneaker against the asphalt. "I just want to ask you something… uh, I know it might sound weird."

"Yeah?"

"Do you think we're friends…or just roommates?"

Caught off guard, Reed thought about their relationship—how much better they'd gotten along lately. And how he'd made no real guy friends in high school or even in college so far. *Why not?*

He nodded. "Yeah, sure, man. We're friends."

"Cool." Adam coughed self-consciously. "Because friends trust each other. I know you've been dealing with some really heavy shit. So whenever you wanna talk, I'm ready to listen."

To cover his embarrassment, Reed tossed him his car keys. "Here, you drive."

Adam looked dumbfounded. "Me? Are you serious?"

"Yeah, I'm beat. Let's burn some gas."

Although eager, Adam did no better at first than Jordan—stomping on the heavy brakes, muscling the steering wheel, grinding the gears, stalling at stoplights—until they hit an open stretch of highway, where he finally found his groove.

"You're driving like a grandma!" Reed yelled. "Haul ass, man!"

"What if I get a speeding ticket?"

"Gold, you worry way too damn much. Just drive."

Grinning, Adam stomped on the accelerator. The car lunged forward. "Awesome!"

Reed leaned out the window, closed his eyes, and inhaled the pine-scented breeze.

—

He finally called his mother that night.

"Didn't you get my messages?" she asked.

"Sorry, been super busy."

"With all those protests going on, I've been worried. Are you okay?"

"I'm fine, Mom." The Doors' "Light My Fire" reverberated down the hall.

"I understand you're angry at me." When Reed didn't respond, she continued. "Just know...just know that whatever happened between your father and me, and whatever happens in the future, I love you very much."

The expected response stuck in his throat.

After an uncomfortable pause, Carol said, "Will I see you next Sunday?"

"Not sure. Finals are coming up and I'm way behind."

"Of course, I understand. All right, sweetheart. Good night."

There was dejection in her voice. Reed hung up and headed back to his room, feeling the familiar churn of anxiety in his gut.

Adam sat on the floor in the lotus position, eyes closed. Meditating and chanting. "Om...shanti...om...shanti, shanti..."

Reed lay down. Maybe he should give Adam's meditation thing a try. He closed his eyes, focused on his breath, and tried to calm his mind. After several minutes crawled by, he gave up and grabbed his car keys. Screw it, better to go get buzzed.

—

At the Rathskeller, he huddled at the bar and nursed a large draft—thinking about his mother, recalling a night two summers ago.

She'd gone to English lit class, leaving him alone to watch TV. On those days she seemed happier, more carefree. According to Sandy, throwing herself into coursework was a welcome escape. In class, no one knew Mom's background, and there was no obligation to play the role of a Navy commander's wife. No awkward questions about her missing husband. She was just an older student working hard to earn a degree.

Reed had popped the last beer of a six-pack while watching reports of the chaotic 1968 Democratic National Convention. Thousands of protesters in Chicago taunted police, hurled rocks, and chanted, "The whole world is watching!" They were clubbed by beefy police and assaulted by mace and tear gas sprayed by National Guardsmen.

Craving fresh air, he had stumbled into the backyard, collapsed on the lawn, and fallen asleep. Curled up in a fetal ball on the damp grass, he became dimly aware of his mother approaching. Kneeling in her robe, barefoot, she caressed his hair and stroked his cheek. When she shook him gently and whispered, "Come to bed," he'd pretended to be asleep, embarrassed yet also comforted by her touch.

Now he scanned the row of whiskey bottles behind the bar and remembered how things used to be between them. As a little kid, he'd loved to walk the beach and swim with her. She always wore a white rubber bathing cap to protect her honey-colored hair from the salt water. Afterward, sipping sweet tea, she'd read him book after book. They acted out the characters from *The Cat in the Hat* or *Alice in Wonderland*. When he was older, they probed disturbing themes in *Lord of the Flies* or *Fahrenheit 451*.

At some point, books and beach walks began to seem vaguely sissy. Instead he was drawn inexorably into his father's orbit, one of rigid masculinity—grease-stained fingers tightening wrenches, the collision of sweat-soaked football pads. The bruises, blood, and bravado of teenage boys pretending to be men had beckoned him, and he'd toiled to respond.

"Hey, kid, you done for the night?"

Reed flinched, then nodded at the bartender and paid up.

Sandy has begged him to give Mom some space. Sure, made sense. But bridging the divide with his mother wasn't just up to *him*, was it? Why couldn't she simply end it with Walker?

CHAPTER THIRTY-FIVE

"Sorry I'm late," Reed said as Annabel jumped into the Mustang. "How was your weekend?"

"Forget my weekend. Why'd you have to blab about me? Now they think I'm a wacko!"

"I'm sure they don't. You're dealing with heavy stuff right now and need some help, that's all."

"Forget that shit. Mom dragged me to a doctor last year. He laid some crap on me about having an anxiety disorder. Gave me a bunch of Librium, which just made me sick."

Flipping down the sun visor, she inspected the dark circles beneath her eyes. "Dammit, forgot the concealer—I'll look like a corpse all day."

Reed tried to change the subject. "By the way, have you written any poetry lately?"

"Fuck no. Gonna burn all my notebooks."

"What! You can't do that."

"Who says? Not like anyone's gonna read that garbage anyway."

"Wait a minute. You can't just get rid of creative stuff like that. Besides, it's really good."

"Says only you."

"I don't get it. I thought you wanted to go to college and become a writer."

"Another stupid pipe dream."

Clearly, nothing else he could say was going to make a difference.

—

That same day—Monday, May 4—Ohio National Guard troops were summoned to restore order at Kent State University. In the confrontation with protesters that ensued, Guardsmen opened fire, killing two students and two bystanders. Nine others were wounded. News of the Kent State killings quickly spread nationwide.

In the crowded TV room, Reed and Adam fixated on the evening broadcast—Guardsmen firing, students screaming. And a photo of a young woman pleading for help, kneeling next to a guy lying on the pavement, his head in a puddle of blood.

Adam raised his voice above the angry clamor. "I guess American citizens are now no safer than the Vietnamese we're killing."

—

The next morning after drill, Reed stood in the ROTC parking lot and spread the newspaper across the Mustang's hood. According to the front-page article, the Guardsmen had lobbed tear gas at protesters in attempts to break up the rally. Some protesters threw the smoking canisters—along with stones—back at the Guardsmen, who retreated, except for twenty-eight, who suddenly turned and fired into the unarmed crowd. Over sixty rounds in thirteen seconds.

As he finished the article, students slowed and leaned out of passing cars to jeer.

"Fuck you, ROTC!"

"Fascist pig!"

Reed stiffened but didn't bother to respond, then walked into class.

Captain Harwood joined the class that day to discuss the killings. He began by reading excerpts from articles: "*According to the Ohio National Guard, the Guardsmen had been forced to shoot after a sniper opened fire against the troops from a nearby rooftop. Others claimed there was no sniper fire…the brigadier general commanding the troops admitted students had not been warned that soldiers might fire live rounds…a Guardsman always has the option to fire if his life is in danger.*"

The captain scanned the room. "So, what do you all think?"

"Seems to me, sir," a cadet responded, "it was self-defense."

Reed raised his hand. "Sir, why couldn't they have just fired warning shots?"

Harwood was about to speak when he was interrupted by shouting from protesters outside: "Down with ROTC!" "ROTC off campus!" "Burn it down!"

He pressed on. "Once weapons are loaded, Guardsmen have a license to fire. These guys were inexperienced, afraid, and poorly trained."

As another cadet raised his hand, bricks crashed against the classroom windows, cracking a few panes.

Reed dove to the floor and crouched under his desk. *Son of a bitch!*

More bricks, glass breaking, and chanting continued until Harwood was able to shepherd the cadets into the hallway amid pounding on the front door.

Sirens wailed in the distance. Campus police soon arrived to clear the front lawn and sidewalk, cordon off the area, and direct the cadets outside.

Reed escaped to his Mustang. It was all too freaking crazy. He drove across the lot, but protesters blocked the exit. Gunning his engine, he envisioned knocking the assholes down like bowling pins. Moments later, the police cleared his path and motioned him through.

Back at the dorm, he ripped off his uniform and rummaged for a clean pair of Levi's. Adam sat at his desk, furiously scribbling notes.

"Don't you have class?"

"Walked out," Adam said.

"Why?"

"Because of what my fascist teacher wrote on the blackboard: *Lesson for the Week—He who stands in front of soldiers with rifles should not throw stones.*"

"Harsh."

"Screw it. I'm not going back."

"Wait a minute. What about finals next week?"

Adam shoved his notebook aside and stepped toward the door. "Who gives a shit? It's like that saying, *To sin by silence when they should protest makes cowards of men.* At some point in life, you gotta take a stand."

In Political Philosophy class, Reed's professor was drowned out by shouting from the hallway. "Strike, strike, strike!"

Several students burst into the classroom.

"They murdered four people!" a girl cried. "How can you sit there like nothing's going on? Strike!"

"Get lost. We're trying to study!" a guy yelled.

"They were students, just like you and me!"

As Reed tried to focus, more protesters interrupted the class. Several kids got up and walked out.

The professor stopped writing on the blackboard. "All right, who *else* wants to leave? If you do, please do so now."

Should he stay or go? Of course, the killing of the students at Kent State was horrible. Jeffrey Miller wasn't an activist, just a concerned kid. Sandy Scheuer had been walking to speech therapy class, paying no attention to the surrounding chaos. Allison Krause had put a flower in a Guardsman's rifle on Sunday. On Monday, she was dead. William Schroeder, age twenty, was in ROTC. *Just like me.*

Adam's quote echoed in his head: *To sin by silence when they should protest makes cowards of men.* Yet what was a strike actually supposed to accomplish?

Reed surrendered to inertia and stayed in class.

Afterward, he drove to the 7-Eleven, yet found no respite from the mayhem. When he walked out, a tearful woman about his mother's age, wearing a peasant dress, leaned against the Mustang holding a sign: *48,700 Dead Soldiers. Four Dead Students. America—What Are We Doing to Our Children?*

Back on campus, a guy shoved a leaflet into his hand: *Strike to End the War. Strike to Take Power. Strike to Smash Corporations. Strike to Set Yourself Free!*

Reed crumpled and tossed it. Strike for *whose* power? Smash *which* corporations? Set yourself free from *what* exactly?

At Annabel's high school, tensions ran nearly as high. Kids had commandeered the sidewalk. White-helmeted police officers lined the curb, clenching batons and shielding protesters from passing cars.

"Can you believe it?" Annabel said. "One minute you're waving some sign, the next minute you're dead."

On the way to Jordan's, traffic was stalled by hundreds of protesters spilling across the road in front of the university's administration building. When Reed tried to make a U-turn, the police signaled him toward a side street.

Annabel poked her head out the window. "Come on. Let's park and see what's going on."

They walked to the administration building, where a school official stood blocking the front door, trying to calm the crowd.

"I appeal to everyone to use reason. A mob has no reason. Let's not create a situation that invites the very same violence we all deplore!"

His words were met with a mix of approval and derision.

The next speaker, no older than the students, wore a military fatigue jacket despite the heat and introduced himself as a member of Veterans for Peace. "I experienced enough violence, blood, and death at Khe Sanh for a lifetime. I vowed, never again!"

At the mention of Khe Sanh, Reed glanced at Annabel. She had a faraway look in her eyes. Must be thinking about her father.

The vet continued, "Now that killing is happening here, the time for complacency is over! I'm not a leftist. I'm not a communist. I'm a patriot. I love America." He concluded by reading from a petition: "*We believe in life, not death, love not hate, peace not war. Join us and demand that President Nixon stop this war now!*"

Annabel turned away. "I gotta get the hell out of here."

She remained stone-faced and silent until Reed dropped her off at Jordan's.

Too agitated to study, Reed parked at the dorm and walked into the student union. On TV, a reporter was asking a middle-aged woman from Kent, Ohio, about the dead students.

"They're traitors!" she hissed. "They deserve everything they got!"

The news program cut to the streets of Manhattan, where helmeted construction workers hoisting American flags fought antiwar protesters with fists and lead pipes. At least twenty people had been hospitalized. In Seattle, members of a vigilante group ironically called HELP—Help Eliminate Lawless Protest—had also attacked demonstrators.

Reed had had enough and left. Maybe Olivia's warning of a nation sliding toward another civil war wasn't off base after all.

—

When Reed arrived for the free clinic that night, he discovered it had been canceled due to the protests. On the porch, Jordan, Olivia, Meg, and other volunteers were donning red-and-black armbands emblazoned with the number *644,000*. Reed now understood it referred to the total estimated casualties so far—soldiers and civilians, both Americans and Vietnamese.

He watched uneasily as Meg distributed white candles. A candlelight vigil march had been planned to honor the Kent State deaths.

Olivia beckoned them to leave, but Jordan lingered and said to Reed, "Are you coming with us?"

He was relieved by her tone—gentle, not accusing. "I don't know."

"You realize what's at stake, don't you? You can't stay on the sidelines. Not anymore."

"Maybe not. But if you're right and the war *is* immoral, that means my dad must be a criminal."

He expected her to argue, but she remained sympathetic. "It's not for me to judge your father. I'm sure he's suffering horribly, but what's happening now all over the country is bigger than one person. Much bigger."

Reed hesitated, thinking about an argument between Sandy and Mom last fall. Dad had been MIA for two years, but Mom had refused to participate in any protests.

"What if your father really is alive and in prison?" she'd asked. "What if the North Vietnamese saw a newspaper article quoting me as criticizing the government? What if they showed your father a picture of me protesting? It would completely destroy his morale."

Down the street, Olivia and the others were joining protesters gathering on University Avenue—students and locals, all carrying flickering candles.

What to do? His mother was right, but Jordan was too. He felt his father's presence—watching, judging—as if they were tethered by a nine-thousand-mile cord. Yet Reed heard no voice in his head, no command, no advice. Nothing.

After a long moment, Reed nodded at Jordan, who'd been waiting patiently. She handed him a black armband. They picked up their candles and caught up with a crowd now numbering well into the thousands.

Like a train slowly leaving a station and gathering steam, the protesters began to march. Several strummed guitars and sang "Give Peace a Chance." Hundreds more picked up the refrain.

—

Annabel looked ill when Reed picked her up Wednesday morning for school.

"You okay?"

"Yeah, just had to puke. Must be that weird cereal those girls eat—granola or something." She rolled down the window and inhaled. "I'm sorry for being so mean yesterday."

"Don't worry about it."

"That guy talking about Khe Sanh. I couldn't handle it."

He was tempted to reassure her that she wasn't responsible for her father's suicide. "I understand."

Back on campus, Reed was one of six guys left in Thermodynamics class. Outside, angry mobs of students roamed the campus carrying signs:

Avenge the Kent State Massacre!
They Can't Kill Us All!
In Solidarity with Kent State, Cancel Classes!

After class, Reed walked past a poster-sized image of Nixon burning in effigy. Four wooden crosses bearing the names of the slain Kent State students had been pounded into the grass.

Reed felt part of, yet alienated from, everything happening around him. Like he was watching it all on television.

A vague sense of betraying Dad remained even after the hours-long candlelight vigil the previous evening. As he'd marched alongside Jordan, their hands had brushed. Occasionally she'd clasped his and squeezed.

When Reed finally permitted himself to sing "Give Peace a Chance," Jordan smiled, and he basked in her approval. Yet the ritual of marching and singing had cloaked his personality in an unfamiliar garb. Did it fit? Was it authentic?

—

The university president had declared Wednesday a day of mourning and promised to address the student body at the Quad. Moments after Reed arrived, a minister raised his arms to quiet the crowd.

"Almighty God, kindle in the hearts of all people a true love of peace. Give us the moral courage to foreswear violence. Guide those in despair, and comfort those who suffer in pain. Fill the earth with knowledge of your love so that, in tranquility, your kingdom may grow."

He called for a moment of silence, which was broken only by the hum of traffic, scattered coughing, and the staccato cries of wrens among the trees.

The university president spoke next. "It is a sad day when American campuses—havens for free discussion and reasoned dissent—degenerate into open warfare, regardless of the provocation. This is wrong. We must *never* allow sorrow to give way to rage and violence..."

Next came the student council president. "We believe the majority of students oppose violence in America *and* deplore violence abroad. We reject policies that aim for peace, yet do so through instruments of war. We reject government actions that lead not to unity, but division and polarization in America."

After several more speeches, Reed had heard enough. Although he agreed with most of what they said, could all those lofty-sounding words actually accomplish anything?

The atmosphere on campus was surreal. Away from the booming loudspeakers, every tennis court was in use, every swimming lane occupied. Frisbees spun across the lawn like colorful flying saucers.

At Burnham Pond, kids slid down the muddy bank into the water as usual. Several girls were topless, and when they scrambled out smeared with mud, guys leaned from nearby dorm windows. "Hey, babe, come on up, and I'll wash you off *real* good."

Weird. War, politics, and sex. All tangled together.

—

"Is Annabel ready?" Reed asked Jordan Thursday morning. "We're running late."

"She's sick. I need to call the school."

"What's wrong?"

"At first, I figured it was some kind of flu. But now I think it's something else."

"Like what?"

Jordan drew a deep breath. "Like, maybe she's pregnant."

CHAPTER THIRTY-SIX

Mind racing, Reed sped toward campus. Jordan had insisted he go to class—she and Olivia would ditch theirs and convince Annabel to be tested at Lifelines. He drove three blocks before realizing he was heading in the wrong direction. Turned around. Stopped at a traffic signal and, when it turned green, just stayed put until cars honking nudged him forward. Then veered into the Winn-Dixie parking lot and sat there, engine idling.

What if she *was* pregnant? Whose fault was that if not his? Obviously, it'd happened over two months ago, back in that foul psychedelic closet. But why assume? She could've been with lots of guys since then. Especially given the expert way she'd seduced him—like the eighteen-year-old he'd believed she was.

No, it couldn't have happened. He was always careful—there was a permanent circular bulge etched into his wallet from the condom he always carried. He must have used one that night. But what if he hadn't? Scouring his memory, he came up empty-handed from that damn memory hole into which he'd plunged at the Pig Farm.

In Naval Engineering class, he tried to decipher the intricate details of nuclear propulsion but found it impossible. He decided to skip Political Philosophy—who gave a rip about James Madison and his *Federalist Papers*?

He drove to Lifelines instead.

"What are you doing here?" Jordan asked.

"Just checking on her."

"Okay, but it'll be a while." She looked puzzled. "Don't you have tons of work to do?"

"Yeah, but it can wait."

He paced the front room. Picked up a *Time* magazine with the cover headline "Who Rules Russia?" Who cared? Every time the phone jangled in the hotline room, he flinched. He drank enough bitter coffee to wire him for days. Scrubbed the kitchen counter. Anything to keep moving—to stop the ping-ponging between guilt, denial, and fear.

Until Jordan walked into the kitchen with the results. Positive. He crushed the wet sponge into a ball and swallowed hard.

Jordan called Annabel's mother, and fifteen minutes later, Louise burst inside.

"Where is she? Where's my baby?"

Reed led her into the quiet room, where Annabel was lying on the bed, curled against the wall, Jordan sitting beside her.

"Sweetheart," Louise cried. Jordan left and shut the door.

Reed returned to pacing, checking his watch, stomach churning. What were they talking about for so long?

The front door banged open, hard enough to shake the glass panes. Ross stomped inside, face smudged with grease, shirt sweat-stained.

"Somebody better tell me what the hell is going on! Where are they?"

"They're okay," Reed said. "Please, wait out here."

"Fuck that." Ross stepped past him toward the hallway, where Jordan appeared and blocked his path.

"Please. They need to be alone."

Ross knocked her backward with the butt of his hand. "Shut up, *cunt*!"

Rage exploded like a grenade in Reed's chest. His right fist—with a life of its own—smashed into the man's jaw. The blow propelled Ross against the wall, knocking a small mirror to the hardwood floor and shattering it. Before Reed could land another punch, the bigger man swung a steel-toed boot into his groin. Reed doubled over, gasping in pain.

"Stop it! Now!" Louise screamed, ushering Annabel into the front room.

The phone rang from the hotline room, and Jordan headed down the hallway to answer it.

Annabel's face was a closed-off mask until she noticed Reed. She stepped within inches of him, emerald eyes flashing.

"The worst thing that ever happened to me was the day I met you."

Louise shepherded her outside.

Ross jabbed a finger into Reed's chest. "I see you again, I'll blow your fucking head clean off."

Groin throbbing in agony, Reed staggered to the sofa and collapsed.

Moments later, Jordan appeared from the hotline room. "Are you okay?"

"Yeah." He grimaced. "What about you?"

"Fine. But what on earth were you thinking, hitting that guy?"

He stumbled to the bathroom and swallowed three aspirin.

Outside, as he fished for his car keys, Jordan intercepted him. "Sure you're okay? Because you look awful whupped."

Reed rubbed the bruised knuckles of his right hand and squinted into the sun's glare, unable to meet her eyes. "What's gonna happen now?"

"I'm really not sure. If they get in touch, which I doubt they will, we can refer her to a clinic. New York's her best bet at this point. They just passed an abortion bill."

Needing time to think, he drove to a park and eased painfully onto a bench. Would this latest disaster push Annabel over the edge? And when she'd said meeting him was the worst thing that had ever happened to her, had she meant it?

—

The university president finally called off classes for Friday, which suited Reed, since he was pathetically behind in preparing for finals. Instead of going directly to the library, he grabbed coffee and drove around aimlessly, thoughts pelting his brain like a hailstorm.

Though he'd been surrounded by women at the free clinic—some of them pregnant—their dilemmas hadn't touched him personally; *Women and Their Bodies* was just ink on paper. Wasn't it wrong to kill a baby, the beginning of a human life? What if Annabel decided to keep the child? Could he imagine himself a father at twenty?

He remembered a girl in high school who'd dropped out during junior year amid rumors she was expecting. She'd been popular, a drum majorette—Marianne somebody. Reed had never thought about where she'd gone, or what had happened to her.

If Annabel wanted an abortion, he'd help her get to New York. He wouldn't let her do anything desperate like those women Olivia had talked about. Sticking coat hangers or knitting needles inside themselves. Douching with Lysol, toilet bowl cleaner, even turpentine. Getting horribly sick or maimed or even dying.

As he sat in his car back at the dorm, Annabel's contemptuous words reverberated in his mind: *The worst thing that ever happened to me was the day I met you.*

"Hey!" Adam was leaning into his window, Meg by his side. "You okay?"

Obviously not. "Yeah, I'm fine."

"Weren't we gonna run before dinner."

"Shit. I totally forgot. Sorry."

"It's cool, man. We're heading over to Rossetti's. Why don't you come along?"

"Thanks. Not really hungry."

Clearly frustrated, Adam turned to leave. Meg lingered, radiating that perpetual concern of hers that was starting to grate on his nerves. "Just between you and me, I heard about Annabel's pregnancy. I'm so sorry. Hopefully she'll agree to let us help her."

"Yeah, hope so." *Damn.* Just what he needed, the rumor mill spinning at Lifelines. Forgoing a decent meal, he headed to the 7-Eleven for a six-pack and their biggest bag of Doritos.

—

Reed's head throbbed with each step as he ran Saturday morning. After a mile, he gave up trying to push through the hangover, washed down three aspirin with coffee, changed, and shuffled to the library.

Despite obsessing about Annabel, he couldn't resist the

newspapers. The previous day, the National Guard had bayoneted eleven protesters at the University of New Mexico. Thousands of protesters had converged on Washington. Most marched peacefully, but some had smashed store windows, dragged parked cars into intersections, and tried to overturn buses. One protester roped himself to a thirteen-foot cross to "show how Nixon was crucifying the American people."

More than fifty thousand American troops, supported by tanks, armored personnel carriers, and jet bombers, had stormed into Cambodia in the past week. Reed scoured every article he could find, desperate to know: Was the invasion going to prolong the war or end it?

Trying to focus on physics, he found his mind wandering instead into fantasy.

The North Vietnamese capitulate at the Paris peace talks.

The war ends in weeks.

All POWs are released immediately!

The Lawson family races to the airfield to welcome them home.

An Air Force C-47 settles on the runway.

The POWs hobble off the plane, many injured but all triumphant.

Frank emerges—thin, pale, limping, yet commanding in his uniform.

Carol, Sandy, and Reed sprint across the tarmac to crush him with joyful hugs.

Reed fixated on the dust dancing in the rays of sun streaming through the library's windows. Was he being childishly naive? Probably, but he marshaled his last ounce of conviction that the war's final chapter was now being written.

—

Jordan placed a hand gently on Reed's shoulder in the hotline room that night. "How are you feeling?"

"I'll live."

He kept to himself during the shift, dreading what he would say to her and when he would say it. He caught her eyeing him often, puzzled.

Luckily, the call volume was light. A redneck called to unload about Kent State. "Those hippies got what they deserved. They're running this country into the sewer."

"Okay. Call back when you have a real problem." Reed slammed down the handset.

A girl called to whine about her stoned boyfriend, who'd cheated on her with her best friend. His right fist opening and closing compulsively, Reed feigned empathy until she hung up.

After the shift, he fidgeted next to Jordan's Beetle, waiting. Moonlight revealed a layer of dust coating the hood. Even at four in the morning, kids were partying across the street, their laughter accompanied by the Doors' "Shaman's Blues."

When Jordan arrived, Reed took a deep breath. "Hey."

"What's wrong? You've been a zombie all night."

Mouth parched, he could barely spit out the words. "It's probably my fault."

"What's probably your fault?"

"Annabel."

"What are you talking about?"

"The week before we found her, the party I went to…at the Pig Farm."

"What about it?"

"Annabel was there." He focused on the gravel beneath his feet. "Well, she and I…uh…"

She cocked her head. "What exactly are you trying to say?"

"It was late, and I…well—"

"You mean the party where you 'may have seen her' but 'couldn't remember'?"

"She was tripping. I was high—"

"But you *fucked* her anyway."

Like white-hot bullets, her words found their target. "I'm sorry. I know I screwed up."

She looked past him, her expression bitter, disillusioned. "And here I was so sure you were different."

"It happened only that once. It was a mistake—"

"No!" She slammed her palm against the VW's hood. "You're just like every other asshole on this campus. You raped a drugged-out teenager!"

"Wait a minute, let me explain...it wasn't like that, not at all!"

"Don't bother. I can't believe I was beginning to trust you." Tears welled in her eyes. "To have real feelings for you." She turned to leave.

He stepped closer. "Wait. Please! Can't we go somewhere and talk?"

She pivoted. Reed flinched, anticipating a hard slap.

"I don't want you in my life. Do you understand? Dammit! Change shifts. Better yet, quit. I couldn't give a shit, as long as I don't see you again!"

CHAPTER THIRTY-SEVEN

After lying in bed forever counting ceiling tiles, Reed hesitated, then swallowed a Quaalude he'd taken from Alex in the quiet room weeks ago. He dozed a fitful five hours and awoke with brain fog at eleven. Adam had already left, probably to hang around with Meg.

Even after two large coffees at Krispy Kreme, the brain fog refused to lift. Must be the Quaalude. He'd dump the rest of the bag later.

At the gym, he hit the bag half-heartedly. Lifted a few weights and dropped them.

At the library, his math equations blurred into hieroglyphics.

He skimmed the papers. In New York City the day before, more helmeted construction workers had beaten up protesters while chanting "America—love it or leave it!" and "Kill the commie bastards!"

To honor the Kent State victims, the city government had lowered the American flag to half-mast. But Nixon's supporters, singing "God Bless America," had stormed City Hall and forced officials to raise the flag back up.

Reed read the transcript of Nixon's news conference from the day before. It ended with the president's warning that, if the U.S. were to withdraw from Vietnam, "America is finished, insofar as a peacekeeper in the Asian world is concerned."

That evening he watched the TV news. By now, the nation's capital resembled an armed camp. Over a hundred thousand demonstrators demanded immediate withdrawal of all U.S. military forces from

Cambodia, Laos, and Vietnam. A ring of fifty-nine buses, parked bumper to bumper, barricaded the White House from the crowd, and thousands of Army troops waited on high alert.

Reed hoped Sandy wasn't among those idiots throwing rocks and bottles, breaking windows, getting blinded by tear gas.

—

Determined to talk to Annabel, Reed parked at her school Monday afternoon and waited until she appeared beneath the portico. She looked like shit: black hair uncombed, wrinkled T-shirt. Lifeless eyes framed by deep smudges.

"What the hell do you want now?"

"Do you need a ride? Can we at least talk?"

Some kids stopped to watch them. "You're embarrassing me. Asshole's on his way. If he sees you, he'll blow your brains out."

"I don't care. I'll wait." He strode back across the lot and leaned against the Mustang's hood. After glancing his way several times, she walked over.

"Okay, so talk. But make it quick."

"Look," he began, dreading the subject but knowing it would be worse to avoid it. "Is this my fault?"

"Is what your fault?"

"You know what I mean. How do you know for sure it's mine?"

"Right. So now I'm a slut, not just a wacko. Is that what you're saying?"

"No, I didn't mean that at all." Because her face remained a stone wall, he assumed the baby must be his. "What did you tell your mom about us?"

"Wouldn't *you* like to know."

"Have you...have you decided what you're gonna do?"

"Everybody's telling me what to do. Mom says abortion is a horrible sin, that I gotta go see the priest at our church for counseling. She wants me to have the kid, then get some family to adopt it. Like *she* knows what's best for me."

Reed's heart pummeled his chest. So she'd give birth to their child and he'd never see the kid again? He'd never considered that possibility, couldn't imagine it.

"I'm not telling you what to do," he said. "I just want to help."

"Hurray for you."

"If you decide to...you know...at least, can I pay for it?"

"I don't know what to do." She pouted. "Do *you* know what I should do?"

Was she really asking him to decide? Did it even matter what he thought? "I'm sorry. I don't know. I'm not sure."

Annabel shook her head dismissively and marched into a grove of pines dividing the school grounds from a new subdivision. He followed and waited for her to break the silence.

"You know, you were the first thing that felt real," she said. "I was happy for a while, never cared about algebra anyway. Just wanted to be with you. It's like I was the desert and you were my oasis. But it was all an idiotic fairy tale. Me as Cinderella and you as Prince Charming. What a joke. Let's face it, no matter what I do, everything always turns back to shit. And nothing's ever gonna change."

She turned to leave as he searched for the right words.

"Asshole's here."

Reed retreated farther into the shade and watched her jump into Ross's truck.

Too upset to drive, he walked into the neighborhood, recalling a conversation they'd had weeks earlier.

"If you're born screwed up, you're gonna stay screwed up," Annabel had insisted.

"I can't believe that. It's hard, but people can change," he'd argued.

The checklist of suicide warning signs at Lifelines came to mind. Feelings of hopelessness and despair. *Check.* Severe sleep disturbances. *Check.* Drug abuse. *Check.* Previous suicide attempt. *Check.* Recent severe stress. *Check.* Current plan to commit suicide. *Unknown.*

—

The next afternoon, Reed drove downtown to Dixon's Hardware. Annabel's mom was going to be pissed big-time, but it no longer mattered.

Just as he expected, Louise Taylor stormed out of her office. "Follow me," she demanded. Grabbing sunglasses, she led him outside through the back door. Cigarette butts littered the cracked asphalt. The smell of garbage seeped from overflowing cans.

Without preamble, she pounced. "What on earth are you doing here? You've got some nerve. Haven't you caused enough trouble already?"

Determination faltering, he struggled to breathe. "I'm sorry, ma'am...but I need to talk to you about Annabel."

"You had better stay the hell away from her."

"Ma'am, I think she's upset. She's—"

"Of course she is, you idiot."

"No, I mean *really* upset, ma'am. Like...wanting to hurt herself. Or even...or even kill herself."

Louise removed her sunglasses, eyes flashing with recharged anger. "What did she tell you? Tell me everything right this minute!"

He haltingly explained how depressed and hopeless Annabel had become. The mindless cruelty of her classmates. How relentlessly she put herself down. How she blamed herself for her father's suicide.

Louise listened, increasingly pained.

"I had hoped she was getting better," she murmured. "I really did, but we both seem to be trapped. Always feeling angry or guilty or both. And we take it out on each other. I guess the truth is...no matter how hard we try, neither of us can get past his death. And now this..."

She slid her sunglasses back on, all business again, as if she'd revealed more than she'd intended.

"Okay, message received. Don't contact *any* of us again. Just leave our family alone."

—

He sought refuge in the library, wrestling for hours with textbooks and class notes. On breaks, he wandered the long rows of shelved books, past quiet carrels where other students sat hunched. He envied their single-minded worries about upcoming finals.

Once again, he felt like a rudderless ship atop the heaving swells of a violent sea.

It was past ten when he stepped into his room.

"Where the heck have you been?" Adam asked.

"Studying. Why, what's wrong?"

"Your mom called about five times."

"When?"

"A couple of hours ago. She's driving down."

"Here? What for?"

"I don't know. But man, she seemed freaked."

He rushed downstairs and paced the lobby's worn carpet. In the adjacent lounge, *Hawaii Five-O* was on TV, the sound blasting.

What could be important enough for Mom to drive down?

At last, her car pulled into the lot. They stood in muggy heat, under the harsh glare of a lamppost.

Why had she come? What was going on?

Two Navy officers had paid her a visit that afternoon.

They had news about Frank.

CHAPTER THIRTY-EIGHT

Carol's face was pallid, her hair unkempt. She wore faded jeans and a ragged denim shirt normally reserved for gardening.

"The North Vietnamese sent a new list of POWs with their status to the Swedish embassy," she said. "Your father's name was on that list." Her quaking voice went hoarse. "All it said was *Died in captivity*. That's it. Nothing else."

For a moment her words refused to register, floating in the air like the moths fluttering around the lamppost.

"Died in captivity? Mom, what the hell does that mean?"

"We don't know. The State Department's trying to confirm it."

"That's it? That's all? Some bullshit list the commies gave somebody?" His fist banged on the trunk of her car. She flinched. "When? When was he supposed to have died?"

"No one knows. But one of the POWs released last month...you know, from that list in the paper. Turns out he knew things about your father. How he'd crushed his shoulder and broken his left knee when he ejected. Those injuries never healed; he was apparently still in terrible shape, in constant pain."

"But Dad was alive, right?"

"Yes, but very weak and depressed. The casualty people think he'd spent the past year in solitary confinement. And about a month ago, he started refusing to eat."

"Not eat? Starve himself on purpose? That's crazy! Why would he do that?"

His mother shook her head. "No one really knows."

"But we got a letter from him! He said he was fine!"

"Sweetheart, that was written last June. The Navy isn't sure how or when he died."

"I don't believe it. Not Dad!"

"I don't want to believe it either. But—"

"Mom, how do we know *anything*?" He began pacing. "Where's the proof? Where's the evidence? Don't you see? It's a bunch of lies! The commies are lying! The government's lying! The Navy's lying! Everybody. Is. Fucking. Lying!"

She reached for him, but he twisted away.

"You don't truly believe this crap, do you?"

Her eyes held his for a long moment before looking off.

"Wait a minute. Maybe you *do*," Reed said.

"What do you mean?"

"I don't know, but maybe this makes it easier—you know, easier for you and Sam."

After an instant of stunned silence, she sprang at him and slapped his face, hard enough to knock him backward. Harder than even Dad would have done. "I don't have to take that from you! Not from anyone!"

Paralyzed, he could only watch her jump into the car and slam the door.

"Mom! Wait! Wait a minute!"

She'd already jammed the car into gear. It lurched forward, and Reed sprinted after it. He almost caught up when she slowed to pull onto the street, but she sped onto University Avenue. Dashing after her, he dodged pedestrians, struggling to keep the Ford's taillights in view for several blocks until it disappeared in heavy traffic.

Veering back toward campus, he kept running. Block after block. Inexorably pushing his legs forward because he could find no other way to fight the shame washing over him. Sweat streamed into his eyes; his chest heaved in the sultry heat. He ran until he couldn't any longer, then shuffled back to the dorm.

Staggered upstairs.

Shoved open the door of his room.

His mother was sitting at his desk, crumpled tissue in hand, gazing at the photograph of the family gathered at the officers' ball years ago. An image, Reed now understood, that hid so much more than it revealed.

"Your roommate let me in. Such a nice young man."

She'd apparently boxed up the anger she'd unleashed on him fifteen minutes ago. "Mom, I'm so sorry."

She leaned closer to the photograph as if drawing comfort from it. "You should know, it's not just you. I miss him too. Terribly. Every single day."

"Mom, I didn't mean what I said before."

"No, you've got a right to be hurt. To feel betrayed. No need to be ashamed of that." Her eyes drifted from the photo to his. "You may not understand this right now, and I don't blame you, but you should know that I'll always love your father. No matter what happens, that will never change."

Reed strained to process everything she'd said.

She picked up her purse and stepped toward the door. "It's late. Can you walk me out?"

Suddenly he didn't want her to leave. "Wait, do you want to stay over? There's probably room at the Lodge."

"Thanks, but no, I can't. Sandy's train gets in early tomorrow morning."

He followed her outside. She paused next to her car, lost in thought.

"You know…I can't stop wondering whether your father might have stopped eating because it was the only way he knew to keep resisting. To keep fighting the enemy."

"By starving himself to death? Mom, that just doesn't make any sense."

Yet he remembered the encoded words in the only letter they'd received: *unity over self.* Had Dad been willing to die rather than surrender his principles?

"It's possible that he couldn't hold on any longer…after enduring so much," she said.

Reed wiped sweat from his brow. "No way Dad would ever give up. I can't believe it."

"We'll never know. I sometimes think your father—just like his father before him—woke up every day looking for the next battle to fight. Not only in war but at home too."

She reached for her keys but made no move to leave. "You should also know that Sam and I have taken a break—for now." When he didn't respond, she continued, "I realize I haven't been much of a mother, especially these past three years. Let's face it, I've been AWOL."

"That's not true, Mom. I'm the one who's been a jerk."

"Nonsense. You always put so much pressure on yourself. To be the man of the house, to measure up to impossible standards."

Embarrassed, he looked away.

"I never said this when you were growing up, but I should have." She stepped closer and stroked his cheek as he closed his eyes. "You have *nothing* to prove to me. You already more than measure up. And you always have. You are my perfect son, who's now a perfect man."

Reed didn't believe a word of it. He was a dumbass shithead, through and through, but tears sprang anyway.

"As for our family, it's been broken for a long time. Now we need to pick up the pieces and start over."

She drew him into a hug. Reed surrendered and clung to her.

—

He finally fell asleep and awoke starving Wednesday morning. After devouring eggs, bacon, cheese grits, and biscuits, he sat alone in his usual corner next to the cafeteria window, avoiding conversation.

With finals nearly over, kids outside were tossing Frisbees, sunbathing on the grass, splashing in the pool. For them, back to business as usual. For him, a new, alien world.

How exactly did *anyone* die by not eating? What happened? You got so weak you fell down and couldn't get up? The whole thing was nuts. Dad was alive! Why believe anything the lying atheist commies said about him?

If the U.S. couldn't hold off the commies, they'd invade the South and slaughter everybody. After they'd promised to reunify the North and South, hadn't they attacked the city of Huê during the Tet Offensive and executed and murdered thousands of their own people?

At the gym, he pounded the crap out of the heavy bag, picturing it as a prison guard grinning diabolically as he tortured Dad. Reed bashed the guard's face into a pile of bloody goo.

That night, he called in sick for his shift. Meg instructed him sweetly to "get right to bed, drink tea with lemon and honey, and take two aspirin."

Right. Tea and aspirin. That would fix everything.

—

When his clock buzzed at five thirty Thursday morning, he knocked it off the shelf, yanked the pillow over his head, and groaned.

At breakfast, after an awkward silence, Adam pushed his plate aside. "Enough already. Come on, talk to me, man."

Reed conceded and told Adam what the Navy claimed, followed by all the reasons he was convinced it was bullshit.

"Damn. I'm sorry. Anything I can do?"

"Not really. But thanks. I kinda need to be alone for a while."

Reed spent the day sunk in listless indifference, blanketed by the darkness so many Lifelines callers had described. He slouched into his final classes, apathetic and unapologetic.

At the library, he reread the same words in his Thermodynamics book. *Incomprehensible.* Wrote an essay for Naval Engineering. *Incoherent.* Took his Differential Equations final. *Lucky to get a C.*

Crossing the dorm lobby on his way to dinner, he was surprised to find Sandy inside—fair hair gathered into a careless ponytail, eyes red-rimmed and puffy.

"Hey. What are you doing here?" She collapsed against him and began to sob. After a long moment, Reed disengaged gently. "I'm sorry, did I miss your call?"

She dabbed her eyes with the hem of her T-shirt. "You weren't around. So I just drove down."

"Okay. Are you hungry?"

"My stomach's tied up in knots. Haven't eaten all day."

Reed drove to Mother Earth, knowing Sandy was "leaning vegetarian." She ordered brown rice and beans with steamed vegetables.

On the wall behind them, the owners had already framed the May 4 newspaper with its Kent State headline and the photo of the girl kneeling over Jeffrey Miller's body.

"So," he said. "Do you believe what the commies said about Dad?"

She straightened the salt and pepper shakers. "I don't want to, but I guess I do."

His heart sank. She too had swallowed their lies. Feeling alone and betrayed, he tried to control the anger in his voice.

"What do you think is going to happen now?"

"What do you mean?"

"With his body. Where is it?" He spit out the words, machinelike. "What have the commies done with it? Huh? When do we get it back?"

Sandy winced; the hand on her glass of iced tea shook. "What do you mean? They have to let the Navy bring Dad home. They *have* to release him. How could they not?"

"Why? Why do they have to? What if they don't? What if we never get him back?"

"Why are you talking like this? It's so cruel." Fresh tears appeared, and she escaped into the ladies' room.

For years, Reed had seen the body bags on TV, respectfully laid out on airport tarmacs ready for loading onto C-141 cargo planes. America was committed to bringing home her fallen soldiers, but what happened to POWs who died in captivity?

He tried to push away the morbid images. Dad's corpse rotting in a cell. Or dumped into a mass grave. Or shoved into a crematorium and burned to ashes. Like millions of Nazi death camp victims, including Adam's family. Like all the soldiers in all the wars, lying namelessly beneath battlefields—leaving families to mourn without a body, a coffin, or a decent burial.

They walked around campus after dinner, the evening sun sinking behind the palms and oaks. Sidestepping their father's fate, they talked about routine stuff. Sandy starting law school in the fall. Reed's

ROTC training cruise in July. Although he was tempted to bring up their mother and Sam, a deep exhaustion enveloped him.

"Are you sure you're okay?" Sandy asked, standing beside her car.

"Yeah," he lied. "Thanks for coming down. I'm sorry I got so pissed at you."

"It's okay. I just keep thinking back to the last time Dad and I were together. The week before he headed back to Nam. Told him how much I loved him…I just wanted him to know…I'm glad I had the chance."

He felt gut punched. Before he could manage to speak, she gathered him into a hug and squeezed hard.

—

Determined to snap out of his lethargy, he crawled out of bed before dawn on Friday. Pushed himself to run five miles at his usual pace—no matter how humid it got, how much sweat marred his vision, or how badly his legs ached.

It didn't work.

He showered and dressed in his uniform, which was wrinkled. He ran fingers through his hair, which fell longer than regulation. *Who cares?*

Outside ROTC, he stopped as other cadets filed into the building. He was in no mood for more crap about the U.S. Navy—projecting sea power worldwide, ensuring freedom of the seas, defending America from its enemies. *Blah, blah, blah.*

Besides, what had the Navy done for his father? Screw it. He blew off the class. As if in punishment for such heresy, the clear sky turned leaden and rain descended in torrents. Wind whipped through palms and ripped moss from branches. He chose the longest route back to the dorm to ensure he'd arrive drenched.

Meg called him after dinner. "How are you coping? Adam told me about your dad."

Couldn't his freaking roommate keep his trap shut for once? "I'm okay, thanks."

"Good. Because we're short two volunteers for tomorrow night.

Could you possibly come at eight instead of ten? Only if you're feeling better, of course."

"Yeah, eight's fine."

"Great. That would be a *huge* help. See you tomorrow."

That night, he tossed and turned until he sank into a fitful sleep.

Still in his soggy ROTC uniform, he finds himself in the Mustang, driving along a narrow ribbon of highway toward a distant bank of fog.

The road is hemmed in by thick pine forest.

Enveloped by the fog, he slows, and the pavement gives way to gravel, dirt, and then mud.

The wheels slip, the car loses traction as the mud grows deeper…

The Mustang stalls, rear wheels spinning uselessly.

Above him, the sky grows black, releasing a deluge.

He stumbles out to find some help, shoes disappearing into the muck.

Trying to take a step, he realizes in horror that he's mired in quicksand.

The harder he strains to free himself, the deeper he sinks.

Until mud rises over his chin, mouth, and face…

Until he can hold his breath no longer—

Reed screamed as he woke up, soaked in sweat.

CHAPTER THIRTY-NINE

SATURDAY, MAY 16, 1970

"Can you believe this?" Adam shoved the newspaper toward Reed. "These neo-Nazi fascists are going apeshit."

Reed hadn't eaten breakfast and had arrived too late for lunch at the dining hall. Irritable, he drank a Coke and scanned the article. The previous day, police had shot and killed two students and wounded twelve at a Black college, Jackson State in Mississippi.

"Just what this country needs," Reed muttered. "Another total clusterfuck. See you later."

That afternoon, Adam caught up with Reed in the dorm parking lot. "Meg and I are grabbing some pizza in a while. Wanna come?"

"Not tonight." Reed stepped past him, but Adam followed.

"Look, last night you were screaming in your sleep again. I don't know…with your dad and all, I don't want to tell you what to do, but I think you need some company right now." Adam touched Reed's shoulder. "I'm really worried about you, man."

"Listen up. My dad's alive, and he's coming home! I don't give a flying fuck what the commies say. So go worry about somebody else for a change!"

—

Still not hungry, Reed skipped dinner and drove downtown to the Rathskeller. They were advertising LSD—Large Size Drafts—for only twenty-five cents. *Clever.* But hey, for a buck, he'd get good and ripped.

Drinking alone in a dark corner, he regretted how rude he'd been to Adam. At some point soon, he'd need to apologize.

It was well past nine o'clock by the time he stumbled out of the bar. The smell of stale beer and cigarettes and the pounding of the Rolling Stones' "Midnight Rambler" bled into the warm night.

He checked his watch. *Shit.* He'd completely forgotten his promise to arrive two hours early, at eight p.m. instead of ten.

Ten minutes later the Mustang rumbled to the curb at Lifelines. As he climbed out of the car, waves of nausea washed over him. Should've eaten something to soak up the beer.

Meg was on duty. Her eyes widened in shock at his drunken, disheveled appearance.

Reed collapsed into the empty chair and mumbled, "Sorry I'm late."

"Called your dorm earlier. You just missed Annabel."

His stomach knotted with dread. "What did she want?"

"I tried to find out, but she would only talk to you. Seemed super freaked out. After she split, I called her mom. Turns out Annabel left the house after lunch and hasn't been back since. Also, her mom found joints and Quaaludes in her room. Sorry…I begged her to stick around."

"Not your fault. Any coffee left?"

"Got a fresh pot brewing."

Just then, Jordan walked in. "Hi," she said to him.

Not *hi* as in *Nice to see you.* Not *hi* as in *What are you doing here, dickhead?* Just a flat, noncommittal *hi.*

Reed gaped at her appearance. She could have modeled for a western-wear catalog. Makeup immaculately applied and brushed hair for once. A Navajo necklace matching her bracelet. A blue denim dress that hugged her curves. And suede cowboy boots to top it off.

He pretended to read the call log. "What's with the cowgirl getup? Some rodeo in town?" He couldn't suppress his volcanic anger—vicious enough to punish the world for collapsing around him.

Jordan looked wounded. "Uh…my dad's jet is stopping here on the way to New York. He wants to talk."

"Meg said you weren't coming in tonight."

"Left my psych book here." Her voice softened. "Are you okay? You look like hell."

"Just tired."

"Uh-huh…well, I'm sorry. You should go home."

"By the way, Annabel's run away again."

"Not good. Listen, I've gotta split, but maybe we can talk later. Okay?"

Those penetrating gray-blue eyes were now filled with concern. Why? Hadn't she told him to get lost for good just last week?

In the kitchen, every cup was coffee stained. Reed scrubbed and filled one. He listened to the murmur of conversation from the quiet room. He was way too wiped to deal with anything tonight. Not Annabel, not a tidal wave of callers.

Stepping back into the hotline room, he asked, "Sure she said nothing else?"

"Well, I followed her outside to stall her. But she was in a big hurry. Said something about the river."

"The river? That's it?" Reed slammed the coffee mug on the desk, scalding his wrist with the overflow, and raced outside.

—

Moments later the Mustang roared to life, and Reed barreled onto Broad Street, weaving through stop-and-go traffic. When he hit a red light, his left hand trembled on the steering wheel as his right massaged the gearshift.

Fragments of conversations with Annabel rushed back.

When I die, I don't want to be buried.

No one cares anything about me.

How far is it to the other side of the river?

And fragments of her poems: *I am a ghost hiding in the shadows… surrendering to the darkness closing in…why not let it blanket me forever?*

More sober now, he smacked the steering wheel. Should have seen it coming. The signs were all there, clear as day. When she'd most needed a friend, he'd let her down, pushed her away to drown in his own despair. No matter what she'd said about him, though, no matter how messed up their relationship had gotten, he prayed that somehow the power of their connection would prevent her from doing something stupid.

It *had* to.

The light was taking forever to change. Screw it. Reed stomped on the gas and roared through the intersection. Horns blared. Oncoming traffic skidded to avoid a collision. He blew through two more red lights heading out of town.

At the Black River, he pulled up next to the green Chevy that belonged to Annabel's mom, then jumped out and ran to the shore. He recognized her jeans and sandals lying on the sand.

"Annabel!"

He scanned the fast-moving current, illuminated only by pale flecks of moonlight slicing through heavy cloud cover.

"Annabel!"

A cacophony of tree frogs and crickets answered him. What if she already lay at the bottom or had drifted downstream? Heart pounding, he spotted a glimmer of movement in the middle of the river. Annabel? Driftwood? Or just a ripple on the surface?

Ripping off his sneakers, he waded into the inky water, the muddy bottom sucking at his feet. Still shaky, he labored with clumsy strokes to the middle before pausing to tread water.

"Annabel!"

A crane screeched. A stiff breeze quickened the current. Reed imagined water moccasins stirring beneath him, gators paddling in from the riverbank.

"Annabel!"

But nothing was visible. A breeze swept across the water; his breathing grew panicked. He was certain that gators must be closing in on him.

He twisted to face the opposite shore a hundred yards away. Had she tried to make it all the way across? Kicking hard, he started swimming, but he could barely keep his head above water. The current tugged at his legs.

He turned back, but the memory of almost drowning as a kid

strangled his brain. He opened his mouth for air, but water gushed in instead, rank and sour. Disoriented, he gagged, flailed, and slipped under.

Which way was up?

For a long moment, everything went black—like the dark pit in which he'd always imagined his father was trapped.

Then he kicked as hard as he could, burst to the surface, swallowed more water, gagged again—

Until a slender but strong arm encircled his neck.

CHAPTER FORTY

"Quit moving, I've got you," a voice called.

Annabel.

Hyperventilating, Reed flailed.

Her arm tightened around him. "Stop fighting, or you're gonna drag us both under!"

Eventually, he calmed down enough to tread water. "I'm okay."

When she let go, he paddled alongside her to the shore.

Annabel clambered out of the river, her T-shirt dripping, moonlight painting her skin ivory.

Minutes later they stood together—Annabel in dry clothes, Reed soaked and trembling despite wrapping himself in a dusty blanket she'd found in the trunk of her mother's car.

"You didn't need to rescue me. But thanks for trying."

"I'm sorry I wasn't at Lifelines. Sorry I let you down."

"You didn't." Then she recounted her chaotic week. Violent arguments with her mother about the pregnancy. Ross blaming Annabel for poisoning his relationship with Louise.

"I couldn't take it anymore and had to split. I felt so alone and needed a friend. You're the only one I got right now."

Reed shivered and pulled the blanket tighter. "I get how rough things are. But about tonight...were you coming here to...you know, try to kill yourself?"

She didn't answer right away and seemed different—calmer, more mature, determined. "I don't know. Maybe. I was going to swim halfway across, tread water until I got totally wiped. Then just let myself go under. Or just walk in wearing a coat with rocks in it, like that Virginia Woolf lady we read about. But a part of me figured, how stupid is that? Why not just swallow a bottle of ludes, lay down in bed, and be done with it, you know?"

"You think you might try again?"

"Not sure. I guess I trust myself a little bit more. But I still don't know what I'm feeling half the time. So it's still possible. Besides, I got the craziness from Dad. It's in our blood."

Reed shook his head. "No way. You're your own person. You're *not* your father."

She ran both hands through sodden hair. "Anyway... Mom used to read me this nursery rhyme. Never actually understood it. For some reason it popped into my head today, and I can't stop thinking about it:

"*Yesterday, upon the stair / I met a man who wasn't there / He wasn't there again today / I wish, how I wish, he'd go away.*"

At first, the words didn't make any sense to Reed. "What do you think it means?"

"It's like his ghost, or spirit, or soul—whatever you want to call it—is still around. Like he's in purgatory. But I know he's dead...and never coming back.

"I love him, but I'm also pissed at him. And that makes me feel guilty. The thing is, he abandoned me. He'll never see me graduate from school. Or walk me down the aisle. I know I need to let him go, but I'm not sure how..." She took a deep breath. "What I *do* know for sure is that I'm pregnant, and I gotta decide. No one can tell me what to do with my body."

They walked silently to her mother's car. His emotions were raw, exposed. He felt humiliated about the way he'd panicked in the river. It suddenly occurred to him—maybe Annabel had always been the stronger one. Maybe *he'd* been the one who needed help all along.

"There's one thing I need to ask," he said. "When you said I was the worst thing that ever happened to you—do you still think that?"

"I did at the time. Not now." She pulled car keys from her jeans. "Sorry, gotta get home. Been driving Mom crazy for a year, and she doesn't deserve it. I have to convince her I can't keep my own shit together, much less have a baby. Not to mention getting totally shamed by everybody for the next seven months, or being hidden away somewhere like I'm a leper."

They exchanged a look that summed up all they'd been through together.

She brightened. "Let's talk before you head home for the summer."

—

The liquor store cashier glanced up from his newspaper. "What's wrong, son?"

"Got any Wild Turkey?"

"Last aisle in the back."

Reed grabbed a bottle and fumbled for his wallet.

"Sure you're okay, son?"

No, he wasn't okay. Wasn't that fucking obvious? After Annabel had driven off, he'd gone back to the dorm to change into dry clothes. Fortunately, Adam wasn't around to interrogate him. Then he headed toward Lifelines, intending to finish his shift. But the idea of talking to hotline callers—or to anyone, for that matter—was intolerable. He'd called Meg and begged off.

"No problem," she'd said. "I'm just happy Annabel's okay."

From the liquor store, Reed drove into the countryside, sipping the cheap whiskey. Force of habit drew him back to English Church Road, with its mile-long tunnel of arching oak branches. He couldn't get Annabel's weird nursery rhyme out of his head.

I met a man who wasn't there. He wasn't there again today. I wish, how I wish, he'd go away.

He understood why it spoke to Annabel. She needed to get past her father's death. But why did the words bother him so much? After all, *his* father was alive. Dad was coming home, no matter what anybody said.

The white road markings blurred—something wrong with his eyes. He drove faster, more recklessly—crossing the centerline, swerving onto the shoulder—until he felt a familiar presence in the passenger seat.

Commander Frank Lawson, bone-thin, in filthy prison pajamas and decrepit rubber sandals. His impassive eyes were fixed on the road ahead.

"What the hell are you staring at?" Reed demanded. "Look at you. You're a wreck. Why'd you stop eating?" He punched the accelerator. The speedometer needle passed eighty. "How stupid is that? What kind of moron stops eating in a fucking prison camp?"

Frank's head slowly swiveled toward him, eyes flickering with compassion.

"What's wrong with you? How could you leave us like that? Why'd you get in that other guy's plane in the first place? Just what were you trying to prove? Huh?"

No response.

"Who the hell do you think you are, anyway? Why don't you say something? You dumbass shithead!"

Frank's eyes returned to the road, widened in alarm. His skeletal finger pointed to the sharp left curve looming ahead. To the massive oak crowding the right shoulder.

Reed slammed on the brakes. Too late. The Mustang fishtailed, skidded, and sideswiped the tree. His head knocked against the driver's side window as he fought to bring the car to a shuddering halt.

In shock, he gaped at the passenger seat. Empty. Then he groped for the door handle. Blood dripped into his left eye as he staggered around to the passenger side. The fender was bent back against the right front tire. Head throbbing, he knelt, grabbed hold, and pulled it hard enough to free the tire.

He wiped blood from his eyes, found a bandanna in the glove compartment, and tied it tightly around his forehead.

His fingers shook twisting the ignition switch. The engine roared to life, but his foot trembled and slipped on the clutch, so he just sat there. Overcome by emotion. The shock of knowing he could've died. The shame of lashing out at his father.

He managed to coax the car into gear and guide it onto the pavement. After driving several hundred yards, the damn tire scraped against the fender again, forcing him to pull over. Kneeling, he yanked the fender hard enough to free it, but the effort caused him to slip and scrape his knees on the gravel. *Son of a bitch!*

With the tire occasionally brushing against the fender, he drove slowly back to the city. He'd need to get patched up—at the hospital, the university clinic, or maybe Lifelines. But somehow he found himself in Jordan's neighborhood and realized that was exactly where he'd wanted to go from the moment he'd crashed into that tree.

CHAPTER FORTY-ONE

A dim light shone from Jordan's living room. After hesitating for a long moment, Reed knocked on her door. Once. Twice.

Head pounding, he checked his watch. Its face had cracked in the accident, hands frozen at 11:20. The Navy watch that had tethered him to his father, nine thousand miles away.

Finally, Jordan appeared. Still in the cowgirl dress, barefoot, holding a whiskey glass. Hair tangled, mascara smeared, like she'd been crying.

"It's about time you showed up," she said, wearing a thin smile until she noticed his blood-soaked bandanna. "What the heck happened to you?"

"I was driving along when a tree got in my way."

"How rude." She stepped aside. "Come on in."

In the kitchen, Reed had trouble holding the whiskey glass Jordan handed him.

"I talked to Meg. Did you find Annabel? Is she okay?"

"Yeah, she was down at the river. You know, where the water runs deep and fast?" Jordan nodded. "I was sure she'd drown herself, but she seems okay."

"Thank the Lord. That's a relief." She stepped closer, gingerly touching the bandanna. "I wanna hear more about what happened, but this looks like shit. Come on, follow me."

In the bathroom, he set the whiskey glass on the counter, eased onto the toilet seat, and watched her rummage beneath the sink. She removed some cotton balls and a bottle of Mercurochrome.

When she dabbed the wound, he flinched. "Ouch! Dammit!"

"Don't be such a baby." She leaned closer to inspect the cut. Reed inhaled her scent—a mix of bourbon and musk. "You need a few stitches. And you might have a concussion. Why don't I drive you to the hospital?"

"No, just leave it for now."

"Always the tough guy, huh?" She cut and folded a square of gauze. "So…you gonna tell me what happened to you tonight?"

What to say? Where to begin? "I'll try."

Jordan taped the gauze to his forehead and leaned back to examine her handiwork. "It's not too bad, but I'd avoid mirrors for a few days if I were you."

—

They sat side by side on the sofa, looking out the bay window. The streetlamp cast an eerie white halo onto the sidewalk. Reed talked about his father. How the commies had said he'd died in prison. How he'd supposedly stopped eating. And how his mom and sister figured his father had just given up.

"And, like an idiot, I drank too much and smashed up the Mustang."

He dared not mention his father's presence in the passenger seat. "I just can't believe he's dead. There's no real evidence."

She took his hand and squeezed. "Or maybe you don't *want* to believe it?"

What if she was right? What if he couldn't accept Dad's death? But why couldn't he? Because he needed him to come home. Needed him to become the kind of father Reed had always wanted, but only now realized he'd never had.

"All this time, I imagined what it would be like when Dad came home. I could stop marking time, move on, become an adult. Life would be okay again. Except I don't think it ever really was."

Jordan padded to the record player. Flipped through the albums and lowered the needle to a record, then came back and collapsed onto the sofa.

Reed draped his arm across her shoulders, relieved that she'd let him back into her life yet wondering why she'd apparently changed her mind about him. Her head nestled against his chest.

"Won't that music wake up Olivia?"

"She moved out yesterday. Went back up home to Boston."

He recalled Olivia had invited Jordan to spend the summer at the Boston Women's Health Collective to help finish the *Women and Their Bodies* book. "Thought you were going up there too."

"No, we split up. It was good for a while…until it wasn't. I felt safe with her, but our heads are in different places now. Besides, I was using her. And that wasn't right."

Suddenly nauseous, he struggled to his feet. "Sorry, think I'm gonna be sick."

"Just don't make a mess."

Reed stumbled into the bathroom, lifted the toilet seat, and vomited until the painful dry heaves subsided. He found some Listerine, rinsed his mouth, washed his face. Then, ignoring Jordan's advice, he looked into the mirror. A beat-up stranger peered back.

He spotted the whiskey glass he'd left on the counter and scrutinized the amber liquid. Even before Dad had gone missing, he'd sometimes drunk too much. Afterward, he'd drunk even more. He remembered what a kid at Lifelines had once admitted: "The reason I do drugs is simple, man. It's so I don't feel the fucking feelings I feel when I *don't* do drugs."

For Reed, the alcohol had sometimes tamped down the undertow of anxiety and baffling outbursts of anger. Yet it had only numbed the despair that made so many days feel oppressive. Maybe it was time to talk to someone—someone he trusted, like Dr. Carlson. To learn how to surrender directly to the flow of life, no matter how turbulent its currents.

He dumped the whiskey down the drain. The jagged terrain of his psyche was way too much to explore, at least tonight.

Judy Collins was singing "Bird on the Wire" when he walked back into the living room, lit now by several candles on the coffee table. Jordan was swaying to the rhythm.

He stepped closer. She reached for him, stiffened instinctively when he embraced her, then softened against him, and they began to slow dance.

"What happened with your dad tonight?" Reed asked.

"He listened to me for once. Then apologized for everything that happened—and practically begged me to forgive him." She stopped dancing. "He promised…promised me things would be different between us if I came back home."

"I'm sure he loves you."

"Yeah…" she whispered. "In his spare time, at least."

"He's not perfect. But he's your father…" The words choked in his throat. "Maybe you should give him a break."

He drew her closer and sensed her weighing a decision. A beam of light from a passing car flared in her eyes, moist now.

With her hand behind his neck, she pulled him close and found his lips.

—

The blinds splintered the early-morning sun as Reed stood at Jordan's bedroom window. Behind him, she slept soundly. A surprisingly feminine, flowery quilt was draped over the bed frame. In contrast, a Remington print hung above the headboard—a moody tableau of two exhausted cowboys astride horses in the snow.

He recalled their night together.

Although she'd been willing at first, she hadn't been ready. She'd pressed against him with desire but shrank from his touch. He comforted her, and they held each other and talked for hours.

Reed asked why, after all that had happened, she'd given him another chance.

"I called to check on Annabel a few days ago. Finally got her to open up. Turns out you weren't the only guy she screwed, but you were the only one who cared."

"Guess that's a relief. I thought I was an irredeemable asshole."

"Well, you're still an asshole, but no one's beyond redemption."

"Good to know, considering how you've been busting my ass since the day we met."

Much later and still awake, Jordan admitted she'd feared getting close to any guy since that night in the barn. "Things were okay for almost two years. Then one day, I'm standing outside the Rot-cee building. I'm minding my own business—a law-abiding war protester—when this Rot-cee dude gets up in my face. His eyes are so dark, I feel like I'm getting sucked into a cave. Lucky for me, the guy's a jerk, so I'm glad he disappears.

"But then, a week or so later, wouldn't you know it? He shows up at Lifelines, of all places. Pretends to be a gung ho volunteer, which I'm sure is nothing but horseshit. Turns out, though, he's willing to work his cute ass off. Like some Eagle Scout. So I have to shift into major bitch mode to push him away, to make him suffer. Obviously, my plan failed…so here we are."

Reed smiled. That explained a lot. "So you're still thinking of transferring to UT for engineering?"

"Yeah, got all the paperwork done."

"So what about this? What about us?"

s"Sure hope so. Besides, I gotta keep that Beetle of yours running."

"Okay. So how far is it from here to Austin?"

"About a thousand miles," he guessed.

"With that hot car of yours and a gallon of coffee, you could make it in one long day, right?"

"Definitely."

They talked about their parents—distant, brutal, but loving fathers and accommodating but resentful mothers. About politics—Nixon's conniving lies, and when the horrible war would finally end. About the environment—how humans were torturing the earth. Even the nature of reality—the vastness of the universe, Adam's theory of cosmic consciousness, and Annabel's "bits of stardust" miraculously assembled into exquisitely flawed humans.

The night wasn't all heavy. They laughed about stupid stuff. How he hated chunks of cooked tomatoes in his chili. How she despised brown gravy drowning her mashed potatoes. He confessed to a paralyzing fear of heights. She admitted to a morbid terror of rattlesnakes.

Close to dawn, desire rose again. Her unease melted as she molded her body to his. Afterward, they'd drifted off to sleep…

And now Jordan stirred behind him.

"Morning," Reed said.

Holding the sheet demurely above her bare breasts, she sat up and yawned.

He walked over and kissed her. "What's on tap for today, trail boss?"

Her eyebrows rose with her chin—the haughty heiress accustomed to issuing orders. "First thing, fetch me some coffee, orange juice, and toast."

Reed crisply saluted and headed for the kitchen. "Yes, ma'am. Coming right up, ma'am."

—

Years later, he would often think back to that spring of 1970. His father's horrific imprisonment. His mother's affair. His tortured road to friendship with Annabel. The torrent of humanity that engulfed him at Lifelines. Falling fiercely in love with Jordan.

And how desperately he'd clung to the belief—in a season of violence, paranoia, and fear—that America would be rescued by reasoning minds, stout hearts, and steady hands.

But right now, waiting for the coffee to brew, his thoughts returned inevitably to his father. Could he accept Dad's death? Or would he continue to deny the likely truth and live—for however long—beneath an awful burden of uncertainty?

Outside, the Mustang sat forlornly at the curb, dented and filthy, pleading for restoration. Of this, at least, Reed was certain—he would make the car new again. Contemplating this simple task eased his inner turmoil, although the respite would likely be fleeting—like an ocean surf retreating from a beach, only to pause before gathering to assault the shore once more.

The sun rising above the trees splashed shadows onto the pavement.

A strong breeze drove clumps of moss across the yard. It was another spring day, full of promise, bright and clear.

Reed glanced down at the cracked face of his treasured watch. On a whim, he tried winding it. To his surprise, the hands sprang to life, and began marching forward.

ACKNOWLEDGMENTS

I owe a huge debt of gratitude to an amazing community of talented, professional editors and readers who helped make sense of multiple drafts of this novel. This list (in no particular order) includes Julie Tibbott, Rachel Stout, Callum Jordan, Katherine Pickett, Jade Visos-Ely, Samantha Gove, Juliette Townsend, Jayme Bigger, Dana Alsamsam, Stephanie Cook, Stephanie Moyers, and Kathryn Johnson. Special thanks to Rachel Keith, who helped pull the manuscript over the finish line.

I was also greatly assisted by several retired veterans of the Vietnam War, including: Commander Charles E. Vasaly, USNR, JAG Corps; Lieutenant Colonel Lee Taylor, USAF; Captain Mike McGrath, USN, who endured six years as a POW; and Lieutenant Dennis Carroll, USN. Special thanks go to Captain Dave Dollarhide, USN, who generously spent a morning with me in Florida describing his experiences as an A-4 pilot in Vietnam.

For translating a vision of the cover art into reality, thanks to Vanessa Maynard and Rhett Stansbury.

Dozens of nonfiction books and memoirs—among the voluminous historical record of the Vietnam era and the feminist movement—provided inspiration and context for this novel. A few include: *Honor Bound: The History of American Prisoners of War in Southeast Asia, 1961–1973* by Stuart I. Rochester and Frederick Kiley; *In Love and War: The Story of a Family's Ordeal and Sacrifice During the Vietnam Years* by Jim and Sybil Stockdale; *Thoughts of a Philosophical Fighter Pilot* by Jim Stockdale; *The League of Wives* by Heath Hardage Lee; *Faith of My Fathers* by John McCain with Mark Salter; *When Hell Was in Session* by Admiral Jeremiah A. Denton Jr.; *Over the Beach: The Air War in Vietnam* by Zalin Grant; *Freedom for Women* by Carol Giardina; and *Our Bodies, Ourselves* by the Boston Women's Health Book Collective.

I am also tremendously grateful to those friends and family who offered wise input, including Doug Ginsburg, Jill Kamen, Suzanne Gesin, Sam Levin, Renee Levin, Elly Levin, and Eva Tibor.

Above all, thanks to my life partner and writer/editor, Marie Levin Tibor, without whose love, encouragement, and support this novel would still be languishing on my laptop.

ABOUT THE AUTHOR

A veteran writer and video producer, Thomas Tibor has helped develop training courses focusing on mental health topics. In an earlier life, he worked as a counselor in the psychiatric ward of two big-city hospitals. He grew up in Florida and now lives in Northern Virginia. *Fortunate Son* is his first novel.

Made in the USA
Middletown, DE
19 November 2022